I dedicate this book to my mother who was an avid reader.

# STALKING OF A MIDLIFE WITCH

J.C. YEAMANS

RSP

REED SHORE PRESS

Stalking of a Midlife Witch

Copyright © 2023 by J.C. Yeamans

All rights reserved. Except as permitted under the US Copyright Act, no part of this publication may be reproduced, distributed, or transmitted in any form or by any means, or stored in a database or retrieval system, without the prior written permission of the author and publisher.

Published by Reed Shore Press under the Imprint Broomstick & Lace.

Lewes, DE  19958

ISBN: 979-8-88652-008-8

If you're reading this book and did not purchase it, or it was not purchased for your use only, please delete it and purchase your own copy from an authorized retailer. Thank you for respecting the hours of labor and investment of this author.

This is a work of fiction. Names, characters, places, and incidents either are the product of the author's imagination or are used fictitiously, and any resemblance to actual persons, living or dead, business establishments, events, or locales is entirely coincidental. The publisher does not have any control over and does not assume any responsibility for the author or third-party websites, social media, or their content.

For content elements, visit the J.C. Yeamans website: https://jcyeamans.com/content-elements/Although my series contains dark themes, Book Three's content has some darker elements. Please visit the link above if you would like more information on the contents before reading this book. There are spoilers.

Cover: Charles W. Clark, Reed Shore Press.
The cover design uses Rosarivo font (designed by Pablo Ugerman) and Photoshop brushes by Brusheezy.com.

Content/Line Editor: Christopher Barnes, Cissell Ink

Proofreader: Reed Shore Press

# PRONUNCIATION GUIDE

Gwynedd: GWYN-eth
Cockburn: CO-burn
Gorawen: GOHR-a-when
Nain: NINE
Shailagh: SHAY-la
Aonghas: ANG-us
Tuatha Dé Danann: TOO-a-day-DAN-ann
Mam: MAHM
Tad: TAHD
Ioan: YOH-an
Gruffud: GRIF-fith
Angharad: ahng-HA-rahd
Owain: OH-wane
Eres: AIR-ess
Cwtch: KUTCH (like butch)
Bean Nighe: BIN NEE-ah
Cat sith: CAT shee
Crwth: KROOTH
Cranachan: KRAN-e-ken

**Welsh and Scottish Phrases:**

Croeso i Gymru: CROY-soh ee GUM-ree Translation: Welcome to Wales

Da iawn: DAH ee-OWN Translation: Very good

Fel rhech mewn pot jam: VEL HRAYK MEH-oon POTE JAM Translation: Like a fart in a jam jar, useless

I'll be there now in a minute. Meaning: I'm on my way./I'm about to leave./I'm doing it soon.

Why's that now then? Meaning: Why not? Why wouldn't it be?

Ya wee bawbag (scrotum). Meaning: A greeting for close friends or family members. Also used as an insult.

# CONTENTS

# CHAPTER ONE

# A CHERISHED FRIENDSHIP

NICK SLINKS TOWARD ME on the bed, sporting a sexy smile and alluring brown eyes. His slender muscles balloon into those of a superhero from his pectorals and biceps down to his—MY EYES SNAP OPEN. And my hands are radiating an amber glow! I sit up in bed with my heart pounding like the hefty strokes on a bass drum and shake the magic from my fingers. Sweat and other bodily fluids stick my satin nightie to my skin like it's been glued. And it occurs to me. This must be why older women die from heart attacks when waking.

"Something wrong, Gwyn?" Archie asks, rubbing his icy-blue eyes. "You're all sweaty. Night sweat? Or a nightmare?"

I peer at him out of the corner of my eye. "You can call it that." I mean, I'd describe the vision as a wet dream. But he doesn't need to know I'm dreaming about his colleague and my friend, Professor Nick Evans. "Don't worry about it." I tap my upper chest and lie down until the back of my head sinks into the satin pillow.

"You've been having these nightmares frequently as of late." He strokes my cheek, and strands of his ash-blond locks spill onto his forehead.

Archie would flip out if I told him Nick was in them. I know they mean nothing. We haven't had sex for weeks. I'm just horny. Dr. Leslie Hughes, the acting chair of the Celtic Studies department and the Bearsden Coven Elder, added a course to his semester load. He's passed out every night after grading. My menopausal hormones continue to bounce around, and the sex deprivation doesn't help the situation.

"Please, stop stressing over the threat of the Tuatha Dé Danann," he says. "You're still carrying my dirk with you?"

"Yeah, but it's so big." I pull the heirloom out from underneath my pillow, and my long chestnut hair falls to my side. "I know I need it with me at all times, but I have to lug an enormous hobo bag on my shoulder to hide the weapon."

"Please, humor me? That old hedge witch was right. The Tuatha Dé could have been sniffing you out since your magic emerged."

"Well, I wouldn't rely on Agnes Pritchard's opinion. We all know she practices witchcraft by the seat of her pants."

There's no way to know if my family's tale of the Tuatha Dé seeking vengeance for the accidental death of one of their children is true. That I'm the offspring promised as reparation. Better to be safe, I guess. I lean in and kiss him. How I miss the sex. "It's been so long since we've…"

Archie rolls on his back and sighs. "It hasn't been that long."

"It's been over a month, but who's counting?"

"Apparently, you are," he says in a thicker Scottish brogue. "I'm sorry. That Introduction to Celtic Studies course Leslie dumped on me soaked up the last of my energy this semester."

"Maybe you're tired of me. Itching for a younger woman."

"I promise you, Gwynedd. I'm not tired of you. Your hazel eyes bewitch me as much now as when I first met you." Archie kisses me and sits up. "I am a wee bit stressed over the trip to Wales and

Scotland. And I imagine your nightmares are related to that as well. You must be eager to see if your Great-Aunt Gorawen is still alive."

"True, but what are the odds she's living? She'd be in her 90s and probably has dementia. Why are you stressed about going? Aren't you excited about visiting your family for Yule?"

"Of course, I am. But they can be overwhelming."

"I guess I'm gonna find out." I kiss his arm and slide out of bed.

"Where are you going?"

"This is my Sunday morning breakfast with Nick. Remember?"

"I don't understand why you continue to meet with him." Archie shakes a finger at me. "You know he still has feelings for you."

"Leslie and Trinity can't find out he knows about the coven. If these breakfasts satisfy him enough to remain silent, I'm fine with a few Sundays at the Raven Pub. Besides, I enjoy our conversations about Wales. And you're wrong. He told me he's dating."

"Are you sleeping at Leslie's tonight? You've stayed here every night this week. Frankly, I don't understand why you won't move in here. The tension is so thick in that house when you're there, a machete couldn't cut through it. Have you even said two words to her since you read your mum's letter?"

"Only small talk. I wanted our emotions to settle down, but now we're both too obstinate to talk things out. I figure the ball is in her court. She has a lot to answer for."

"True, but how do you exist in that house when you're there? In utter silence?"

"Her busybody familiar, Mr. Yeats, can't keep his mouth shut. He pretends to be me, mimicking my speech, and turns in the opposite direction, spouting words in Leslie's voice. We don't need to converse. He does it for us."

Archie chuckles. "He probably hates the two of you ignoring each other."

"I better get in the shower. It's almost eight." I turn toward the bathroom door.

"Gwyn, let me get the grades entered for the Fall Semester. And I'll have more energy for extracurricular activities. Spring Semester will be much better with the visiting professor from Northern Ireland joining the department. I swear. Leslie knows every academic in the UK."

I glance back and smile coyly. "Something to look forward to."

After a quick shower, I throw on a pair of jeans and a long-sleeve tee. The rain adds an extra chill to the mid-40s temperature, and I shiver on the way to my Prius. On the drive to the Raven Pub, I pass the site of the new parking garage. The city council approved the construction of a four-story structure on the site of the former parking offices—minus Lindsey Hope's vote, of course.

The Bearsden Coven convinced Elijah Jackson to run for the open position, and he won, despite the deluge of corrupt money pouring into the candidate Mayor Manley and his cronies supported. Elijah snatched the empty council seat without influence from the coven, too. Why wouldn't he? He's a social worker and head of the Bearsden Shelter—a perfect candidate to represent the community on the city council.

I enter the restaurant, and Nick Evans waves to me from the rustic wooden booth seat in the back. The muscles in his arms bulge, and I'm reminded of my dream. Derek Young has done a great job helping the young professor get "swole," but Nick's physique in my dream was an exaggeration. My best friend Ronnie Baldwin is practically living with her boyfriend Derek now. He's at her home so much, he should move in.

"Hi, Nick," I say as I slide onto the bench seat. "I can only stay for a quick brunch. I need to arrive at Mystic Sage by noon to work."

"Then I'm glad you cared enough not to cancel our date," he says, flirting.

My brow crinkles. "You know this isn't a date, right?"

"People can have a date and it not be romantic," he chuckles. "I enjoy your company. That's all."

"OK." The waitress pours Nick's coffee, but I cover my cup with a hand. "I'll have tea, thanks."

The waitress nods and motions for us to go to the breakfast bar. We fill our plates full of eggs, pancakes, and fruit and return to our booth. While we stuff our mouths, patrons prattle on about the annoying construction and renovations on Main Street. These breakfasts are adding pounds to my hips, and I haven't had time to get to the fitness center to work off the extra calories.

"How many of the translations have you read in your mom's grimoire so far?" he asks.

"I've read most of them," I say. "I've skipped around a little, hoping to find a spell I desperately need."

"What spell is that?" He tilts his head and pushes his dark-brown hair off his forehead.

I stare at those inquisitive eyes for a moment. "Nothing you can help with."

"Remember, I translated the entire journal. Tell me what you're looking for, and I can probably point you in the right direction."

It's bad enough Nick knows what's in the family spell book. I'm not telling him we're looking for an incantation to close the portal mound in Mitchell Hall's Celestial Gardens. He already knows too much. Fortunately, he's not mentioned the Tuatha Dé Danann threat once since he read the translation of my mom's letter to me. He must think the entire tale is poppycock.

"When do you and Archie leave for Scotland and Wales?" he asks.

"At the end of the week." I take a sip of my Earl Grey tea as an anxious twitch develops in his eyes. "We'll only be gone for a few weeks. Archie hasn't seen his family for over a year, so we're using part of Winter Session to visit them."

Nick leans over the worn wooden table and grimaces. "Well, I'm jealous. You get to visit Wales."

"Yes, I do." I chuckle at his expression and finish my tea. "I'm really excited to see it, although I'm only going to the town where my mother grew up. I won't see much on this trip."

"Do you think you'll find your aunt? What was her name?"

"Gorawen Thomas. She is...or was the sister of my mom's mother. Never married. I only hope she's alive. And lucid."

Nick looks away as if he's contemplating something and returns his gaze to me. "What do you hope to find out? The letter was fairly clear."

"I don't know." Why is he asking me about the letter after all this time? "Like I said. She's probably dead or alive and senile."

Nick grasps my hand and stares into my eyes. "I hope you have a wonderful time. But come back. You have friends who care about you in Bearsden."

"I will. And I wish you a Merry Christmas and a Happy Yule season."

I pull my hand back and rub my temple as a sudden grogginess dulls my head—damn menopausal brain fog. Nick nods and drinks the last of his coffee while he gazes at me. Could Archie be right?

I have a few minutes before my shift at Mystic Sage begins, so I stop by Ronnie's restaurant, the Sunshine Garden Café, to chat. She had new hanging lights installed over the tables in the booths—dark-blue globes speckled with white stars. Rays of light shine through the stars in the glass, creating a cosmic ambiance. Ronnie notices me standing at the front and motions to join her at a booth. The streak of white hair at her hairline has grown about six inches and swirls through her ringlets of crimson hair.

"Hey! I didn't think I'd see you before the Yule celebration on Thursday. What's the tea?" she asks as she drops onto the booth seat.

"Oh, nothing." I set my purse on the bench. "I've got work at noon and thought I'd drop in for a minute. The new lights are beautiful. You're taking your cosmic witch concentration seriously."

"Yeah. I love it. I'm thinking of taking an astronomy class at DUB next semester. Learn more about the constellations."

"You should...if you can fit it in. How's Derek?"

"He's been so supportive, considering I lied to him about being a witch. But he's at my house today working on my magic room. This conversation has to be short." She points to the patrons waiting at the hostess stand. "The crowds will pick up soon. Are you excited about your trip to Wales?"

"He's building you a place to practice the craft? That's so sweet. I'm excited about the visit but nervous, too." I wring my hands and huff. "All I have is the address of a post office box in her name, and I doubt she has a cell phone. Aunt Gorawen is most likely dead and buried. Then I will have wasted my time and money tracking her down."

My friend growls at me. "Oh, come on. You've always wanted to visit Wales. If you don't find her, you get to visit your parents' home. That's exciting! And you'll meet Archie's family in Scotland. You must be so excited to meet them and visit Edinburgh. I'm jealous."

"I have mixed feelings about meeting his clan. What if they don't like me? What if his father thinks I'm too old for Archie?"

"Oh, for fuck's sake, Gwyn. Archie is a grown-ass man. And you're a lovely person. I'm sure they'll love you."

"We'll see." I twist an earring and hold my breath for a moment. "I have to tell you about the dreams I've been having."

"Oh? Scandalous?" she asks with wide, azure-blue eyes. "I'm all ears."

"A little. I've been having dreams about Nick Evans. Like...loaded with sexual content."

Ronnie cackles and slaps the table. "You talk like you're giving them a movie rating. Please, tell me they're X-rated."

"We're in bed and about to...you know, do it. And then I wake up. It's so disturbing. I hope I don't have underlying feelings for Nick."

"Oh, hell. It only means you need some lovin'. You said you were in a dry spell because Archie's exhausted from schoolwork. It's only your subconscious messing with you."

"But I had a couple of dreams in the past that turned out to be premonitions." I suck in the aroma of fresh-baked bread in the booth next to us and exhale. "You're right. It's probably junk in my head, and I've spent a lot of time with him recently. I have to make sure he doesn't tell the rest of the coven he knows about us. It makes perfect sense my addled brain would insert him into a manifestation of my sexual frustrations. But ever since I had those premonitions about Archie and the Sluagh, I can't trust that my dreams are just dreams anymore."

"Completely understandable. Of course. I'm relieved you're placating Nick. The minute you get to Wales, you'll see. Archie will pop right up...if you get what I mean."

I grab my purse and slide out of the booth, chuckling. "Your mind is always in the gutter."

"You know it." Ronnie cackles as she stands. "I've gotta get back to the kitchen. See you at the Yule Celebration."

"It should be fun." I wave goodbye as she returns through the double doors.

I shiver from the chill of the rainy day while I stroll across the street to work. The sun glitters off white snowflakes hanging from the lampposts, and the town's giant menorah and lighted fir tree glow in the distance. Come nightfall, blue, white, red, and green lights will sprinkle the night with the spirit of Yule. I'm looking forward to this year's Winter Solstice Celebration. Considering I spent the last one trying to kill an Unseelie Fairy, this one can hardly be worse.

When I enter Mystic Sage with a ding, the aroma of cinnamon attacks my nostrils. Jeff Williams is stocking the game section with new board games and wooden puzzles. His wavy brown hair has grown into an unruly mess since he lost his family on Mabon. Who can criticize him? The state of his hair has taken a back seat to his grief. It's not every day your hateful aunt kills the only person you cared about.

"Hi, Jeff." I set my gargantuan bag behind the counter. "Need any help?"

"Nah. I'm almost done," he says. "Thanks for coming in today. I have to submit my last project online by tomorrow, then I'll be finished for the semester."

"That must be a relief. You had a tough semester." I pat him on the shoulder as he stands.

"Gwyn, I can't thank you and Shane enough for all you've done for me." Jeff stares at the floor as his eyes tear up. "I try not to think about Audrey, but it's so hard."

I step forward and wrap my arms around him. "That's never going to work. You should remember her and all the good times you had together, and what she sacrificed for all of us."

Jeff pulls away and wipes his eyes. "Thanks for the advice. I miss her so much."

Shane Murphy, our hippie boss and devoted friend, walks into the front of the store. He's kept the wiry strands of his snow-white beard trimmed shorter since the attack by Jeff's Aunt Edith and Uncle Edmund Kenilworth. Their magic fireball singed his whiskers so badly they shriveled up.

"Hey, darling," Shane says. "Thank you a heap for coming in. I know this is a busy week for you."

"I have to go. Gotta get that project done." Jeff heads toward the door.

"Don't forget to attend the Yule Celebration on Thursday, son." A grin peeks through Shane's beard. "You know you're welcome."

"I'll think about it. Bye," Jeff says as he exits.

"How is he doing at home since he moved in with you?" I ask. "He seems to put up a facade when he's here."

"He's had some difficult moments. The questions from the authorities over the disappearance of his aunt, uncle, and cousin wear on him, but that will dissipate as time marches on. The family's lawyer is an agent with power of attorney, so he's handled all the legal and financial issues since they went missing. After five years, the lawyer can have them declared deceased officially."

"I'm so glad you could take him in. He needs support going forward. You're a good man, Shane."

"I don't mind," he says, his southern accent seeping through. "Judith and I never had children. I love having him around."

The door dings, and a mother and two young boys amble in, heading toward the board games and puzzles.

"I guess I better get to work. I'll handle the front while you do inventory."

"Thank you, Gwyn. If you need anything, holler, and I'll come running."

Shane returns to the small storage room in the back while I ring up purchases all afternoon. It's amazing the occult and witchy stuff people buy as Christmas gifts. Because nothing says Merry Christmas like a skull with flashing red eyeballs. I relish a break in the onslaught of holiday shoppers around eight. My boss shuffles back in, rubbing his back.

"Why don't you head on home, darling? I doubt we'll get many shoppers after eight on a Sunday."

"Thanks. I'm pooped. I've not been home for two days. Sleeping there tonight." I lift my tote and throw it over my shoulder.

Shane's bushy eyebrows fall. "I know you and Leslie aren't on good terms right now, and you have every right to remain angry with her. But if she makes even the slightest effort to make amends, I implore you to find a path for forgiveness. Even an old witch can reform...if given the chance."

"I appreciate the sentiment. See you on Wednesday," I say, opening the door.

Shane's emerald-green eyes twinkle under the lights. "Be careful walking home."

The rain has subsided, but the temperature has dropped to the mid-30s. So, I slip on my gloves for the walk home to Drummond Lane. Swirls of white slither into the air as I exhale. The clicking of my leather boot heels echoes off the red-brick Georgian buildings on the Green, and my quick pace rubs the back of my feet. I stop for a moment to give them relief, but the echo appears to end far past when it should. After a few more steps, I pause again. Footsteps stop abruptly. I snap my head around to discover a student running out of the door of Menzies Hall, the pitter-patter of his feet dissipating into the darkness.

I scuttle in my boots across the maze of paver walkways while the footsteps continue behind me. My pace hastens along with my heart rate, and I glance over my shoulder repeatedly as the clack of heels grows louder. And boom! I run into something and fall on my ass!

"Gwyn, are you OK?" a familiar male voice asks.

I raise my head to find Nick offering a hand to me. "Oh, yeah. Sorry. I should have been looking where I was going." I grasp his fingers, and he helps me to stand.

"Why are you apologizing? You're the one who got knocked on your butt." He chuckles and leans into me. "I didn't think I'd get to see you again before you left, so I'm not sorry. I'm walking home from my office. Would you like me to escort you home?"

"No, I don't have far to go. But thanks for the offer." I laugh and wipe my wet ass with a hand while he keeps a grip on the other.

Nick's brown eyes reflect a warm glow, lit by a nearby lamppost. "Enjoy your trip to Wales, and I hope you find the answers you're searching for."

"Thank you, Nick." I slip my gloved hand from his grasp.

# CHAPTER TWO

# MAKING AMENDS

THE WOODEN FLOOR OUTSIDE my bedroom door creaks, and the clanking of dishes travels down the hallway. I've avoided Leslie all week, but she must be cooking a late breakfast in the kitchen today. We have the Yule Celebration tonight. I imagine she's going to make something special. I've not spoken more than pleasantries to the Elder since I confronted her regarding the Tuatha Dé threat.

Mr. Yeats, her chimera cat familiar, paces back and forth outside my door, waiting to pounce on me the minute I go to the bathroom to pee. So, I remain warm in my flannel PJs under the blankets and bed quilt, calculating how long my menopausal bladder can hold back the flood waters. I squeeze my legs together. Oh, hell. I throw back the covers and grab my robe off the bed as I rush to relieve myself. When I fling open the door, the feline hisses at me.

"Oh, shoosh. Get out of my way." I dart to the bathroom in the nick of time. While I'm sitting on the porcelain throne, I contemplate Shane's fatherly advice. He's only ten years older but reminds me so much of my dad—without the Welsh accent. I've sulked about Leslie's betrayal of my mom and me for three months. To be fair, Leslie has done little to improve the situation. But how do I forgive her after exposing me and inviting danger to my door?

I splash cold water on my face and brush my teeth. When I return to my bedroom, Mr. Yeats is standing in human form with his arms crossed, wearing his usual dark-gray, three-piece suit. He taps his foot and adjusts his spectacles before he lectures me for the umpteenth time.

"You must make amends, Ms. Crowther. Dr. Hughes has permitted your residence to continue here despite your cold shoulder, and you have not attempted even a microscopic effort to resolve the issues between the two of you. At my counting, nearly three months have passed—more than enough time to reconsider your actions regarding the professor. May I offer a suggestion to—"

I hiss at the yellow and blue eyes of the familiar, hoping he'll take the hint.

He glares at me, turns up his narrow nose, and purses his lips. "Your relationship will never improve with that attitude."

"Stop sticking your nose into my business, you busybody. And get out of my room!"

Mr. Yeats sighs and transforms into his cat presentation as he scuttles out. I hate to admit he's accurate. Either I figure out a way forward with Leslie or move out. But to where? I'm not ready to move in with Archie, and I can't return to Tyler's apartment.

I make my bed, smooth out the quilt, and shuffle in my slippers to the tiny kitchen. Leslie sits at the oak table for two in her pink chenille robe, drinking her coffee and flipping through a holiday sales paper. Long, silver bangs hang over one of her copper-brown eyes, and she pushes the strands aside, exposing a placid demeanor.

"Good morning, Leslie," I say as I retrieve a mug from the pine cabinet.

"Good morning to you, Gwynedd." She lowers her eyes and takes a sip of her coffee.

I prepare my Earl Grey tea and sit down across from her, avoiding eye contact as I drop two scoops of stevia in.

"Are you looking forward to your trip to Wales?" she asks.

"Of course, I am. I hope to find my aunt." My voice has an edgy tone, and I regret letting the irritation filter through.

"You realize the odds of finding her alive are dismal."

"You could express a little optimism. But showing support would require you to change your manner, wouldn't it?" I apply a swirl of amber magic with a wave of my hand. The spoon enters the cup and spins, creating a tiny water spout.

Leslie glares at me with her cat-like eyes while she clinks her nails on the coffee cup. "Gwynedd, I never meant to put you in harm's way. All those years passed, and I was certain you were in no danger. The tale of the Tuatha Dé is only a story passed down for generations. But I regret not telling you, and I'm sorry."

I rub my ears. Did those words actually fall off her tongue? "I appreciate your apology...even if it took you three months."

She sets her cup on the saucer with a clink and sighs.

"But I have similar doubts, too. It's why I need to search for my Great-Aunt Gorawen. I haven't been able to connect with my mom since the day...you know."

She stands and glances at the doorway. "Please, come into the office with me. I want to give you something of importance."

I follow her down the narrow hallway into her office, wondering what could be so important as to interrupt my breakfast. Mr. Yeats purrs atop the metal filing cabinet with his tail swishing back and forth. Leslie yanks out a drawer, and her chimeric cat familiar leaps onto the floor. After flipping through a few files, she pulls out a frayed, discolored piece of paper and hands it to me. There's an address scrawled on it in faded-blue ink.

"What's this?" I ask. Upon closer examination, I read Wales, UK.

Leslie lowers her eyes. "That's the address of the home where I visited your Aunt Gorawen."

"What? You spoke to her? And you're only telling me now?" I'm boiling inside, and beads of sweat erupt on my face and neck.

"No. I did not." The coven Elder peers at me through guilt-ridden eyes. "I should have told you about our encounter and the warning of your family's tale. During these past months, I've recounted the errors I've made in my life. I have many regrets. Losing your mother's friendship and trust is at the top of a very long list."

"I'm confused. You met my aunt but didn't talk to her?"

"Gorawen Thomas would not let me into her home. When I told her I'd been a good friend of your mother's, she yelled from behind the door, saying she had no niece named Lowri Crowther. The conversation ended, and I returned to Cardiff, where I was completing research."

My mouth falls open. "When was this?"

"A little over seven years ago." She slams the metal drawer shut with a bang.

"After my parents died." A light bulb illuminates my brain. "And you asked Archie to come to DUB?"

"Yes. I visited London on the same trip."

"You were making plans to recruit me that quickly after they passed away. How conniving." I shake my head. "But why speak with my aunt?"

"I wanted to discover how reliable this story was. No one I had spoken with in academic circles had ever heard of such a tale. When Gorawen Thomas said she didn't have a niece, I concluded I had the wrong woman. Thomas is one of the most common names in Wales."

"Why hold on to the address all this time?"

Folds form in Leslie's brow. "After viewing the state of my office when we first met, you need to ask?"

"Oh, right." I chuckle while I scan the office, recalling the piles of books and clutter that once existed here.

Leslie lays her cold, knobby fingers on mine. "Gwynedd, visit this woman and tell her who you are. She may not have wanted to speak with a stranger from America."

"But I am a stranger from America."

"Yes, but you are family. If this woman is truly your great-aunt, she'll be overjoyed to meet you."

"I accept your apology, but I hope you understand it will take a long time for me to trust you again. If ever." I squint at her and press my lips together.

"Indeed. I aim to earn that trust with the time I have left on this earth."

"I need to drink my tea, eat a quick breakfast, and get dressed. I want to pack my travel bags and take them to Archie's, so I don't have to come back to the house tonight. We have to drive to JFK tomorrow to catch a 6:15 p.m. flight."

As I amble toward the door, I pass a glass object on her desk. I pick up the heavy item and examine it. It's cut like a crystal and has a tiny black cauldron inside.

"What's this?" I ask.

"A Yule gift from Dr. Evans. He gave one to Archie as well. It's a paperweight. I have so many in my office at DUB already, so I brought the present to this office. It's odd he gave me one with a cauldron inside. I imagine he was making a joke, because we're pagans. He probably bought them around Halloween."

"Yeah, he's a funny guy." I avert my eyes and continue out of the office.

"I'll see you later at the Yule Celebration, then?"

"Yes. I'm excited to celebrate this year without needing to banish an evil fairy." At least, not tonight.

## CHAPTER THREE

# SEEING IS BELIEVING

I STAND IN FRONT of Archie's fireplace, snapping a photo of the painting of my mother. My aunt knew the storm was coming, but when? I summon my witch energy and face my palm toward the image of my mom, focusing an intention on her face and pleading for her to communicate with me. But only the annoying ticking of the clock resounds.

My hand drops to my side as Archie's footsteps approach behind me. A smile curls my mouth when his arms wrap around my upper body, and he places a kiss on my cheek with warm lips.

"Knew you were here when the door creaked open and the racket from your luggage rolled across the floor," he says in a soft Scottish brogue. "What are you doing?"

Air escapes my lips. "I tried to connect with my mother again. What am I doing wrong? Why won't she talk to me? I've tried for three months to conference with her through divination. If I don't find Aunt Gorawen, I'll need Mom's advice."

"Do you remember how much focus you needed? You've had quite a lot on your plate with classes, work, and living in a tense situation at Leslie's. I wish you had moved in here."

"We've already talked about this a gazillion times. I love you, but I need to stand on my own two feet for a while." I kiss him. "Besides, the conditions have changed since yesterday. Don't faint when I tell you, but Leslie apologized to me this morning."

Archie cocks his head. "Naw. Do you believe she means it?"

"Wait here." I rush to the foyer to grab my gargantuan purse and return to the living room, snatching the address from the bag. "Leslie gave me this."

"A Welsh address? For what?"

"Not for what, for whom. Leslie visited the old woman living at this address. She wouldn't speak with her, though. Said she didn't have a niece named Lowri, so Leslie  left and went to see you in London."

His eyebrows jump. "When she asked me to come to DUB and join the Bearsden Coven. Interesting." He reads the address. "Says B-W-C-L-E, UK. Oh, Buckley in Flintshire."

"That's where you found the painting."

"Aye," he says, glancing at the mantel. "In a small thrift shop. We'll knock on her door and hope she invites you in."

"We have to start there, anyway. If it's not her, or if the woman is gone..." I stare at my mom in the picture. "We'll be back where we started. By the way, I saw the funny gift Nick gave you and Leslie. The glass paperweight with a cauldron inside."

"Aye. I thought it odd he gave us gifts for Yule. He was trolling me most likely, but Leslie? I hope the present didn't prompt any suspicion."

"Nah. She suspected he gave her a cauldron, because she's a pagan." I lift my purse off the floor and remove the dirk. "Here. I almost forgot to remove this. I'm sure TSA won't let me through carrying a small sword in my bag."

Archie chuckles. "Naw. I'll lock this in the glass case, and we can walk to the Pumpkin House to help the others set up for the festivities tonight."

On the trek across campus to Victorian Row, my purse dangles easily without the bulkiness of the weapon. But apprehension grips my gut without the dirk in my possession.

The Pumpkin House sticks out with its orange siding and peachy gingerbread trim. When we enter, my fellow witch friends are setting up refreshment tables with drinks and the typical holiday sweets in the dining room to the left. I wave to my son Tyler, who is hanging with Zoe and the other Zillennial witches. Ronnie and Shane have set up a few chairs in the parlor where a large, potted spruce tree sets the tone for the Yule Celebration. The young witches will plant the baby tree in the local woods when the holidays are over—a new tradition they pushed for this year.

Trinity Johnson, the Bearsden Coven leader and Director of the Family for All LGBTQ organization, is chatting with Leslie and Agnes Pritchard, my mentor—and Leslie's former lover. I'm happy Agnes remained in the coven, but I wish they could work things out. The two curmudgeons deserve each other. Being the one to come between them by blurting out Leslie's deception leaves a bitter taste in my mouth. Archie joins the three of them while I amble over to Ronnie and Shane.

"Hi, Boss. Hi, Ronnie," I say, removing my gloves and fleece jacket. "Is Derek coming?"

"Yeah," Ronnie replies. "When the celebration opens for guests. We have to have our short meeting first."

"I wonder what our leaders have to share with us," Shane says. "Serious expressions on those faces."

My crimson-haired friend presses her lips together. "We'll find out soon. Gwyn, you leave tomorrow night on a red-eye flight. Are you ready?"

"Not really," I say. "I have enough trouble sleeping without sharing my slumber with 200 strangers. But I'll deal with it."

Elijah Jackson, the Black witch with electric-brown eyes, enters the foyer wearing a white puffer jacket. The door slams behind him, and everyone bursts into thunderous applause, whistling and shouting his name. Being a humble man, he lowers his head, smiling, and rubs the nape of his neck. "Thank you, everyone. I appreciate the support."

"We're all elated you won the special election to serve on the city council," Tanner Jones says as he pats him on the back. "With you on the council, they might actually get some things done this year."

Spence Huxley, Tanner's boyfriend and my old study partner, gives Elijah a big squeeze. "You had the election in the bag. The entire town knows what a great person you are."

"Thank you much," Elijah says in his cavernous bass voice. "I hope I live up to your praise."

Trinity interjects. "Of course, you will. You're the heart of this community." She's dressed to the nines as she always is, wearing a flowing dress to match her burgundy-colored tresses. As usual, her makeup compliments her velvety dark skin.

"I am certain Elijah will represent the town well. And the Fellowship." Leslie clears her throat. "I would like to say a few words before the Unremarkables arrive. Our non-witch friends and guests who aren't *in the knowing* must not hear what Trinity and I have to share. As part of the renovations, the city is considering the removal of the fairy mound."

"Oh, my gods." Skye McGowen, another past study partner and good Zillennial friend, twists her fire-red hair. "Wouldn't that be a major problem?"

"You fucking think?" Agnes Pritchard guffaws, and her salt-and-pepper hair falls onto her face. "When that mound formed, it was by sheer accident. And we've not found a spell to remove it. Who knows what will happen when the city digs into the ground?"

Archie has remained quiet until now. "When I was growing up in Scotland, we were told to be wary of the mounds. Leave them be, because they provided direct passage to the Otherworld. Certainly, don't plow them over."

Trinity nods. "We may have to influence the outcome...if you get my drift."

"What?" I ask. "I told you I wasn't OK with doing that again. It's not ethical. And with Elijah on the council, is it even necessary?"

Skye's light-blue eyes grow big. "Hey. Why don't we plan protests? I'm sure Spence, Zoe, and I could get other students on campus involved."

"Absofuckinglutely," Spence says. "I mean, to the Unremarkables, the fairy mound was only a make-believe section of Rose and Alistair Mitchell's Celestial Gardens, but it's an established marking. If they're going to build a playground for kids in there, it makes sense to preserve it."

Tyler raises his hand. "Not to be a downer, but if we lobby to preserve the mound, what happens when we find the spell and close the portal?"

"They'll believe there was vandalism," Archie says. "We'll have to deal with the situation when the time comes. Perhaps we could sneak in some dirt to replace what was there, but hauling in a massive quantity of soil would be a challenge."

Agnes throws her hands into the air. "Who the fuck knows when we'll find a spell to collapse the mound, anyway? We can't let a bulldozer get anywhere near it."

"We also need to discuss the obvious issue of the Seelie Fae children," Trinity says. "Workers came into the building this morning, and a can of paint poured onto their heads when they entered through the back door. Any guesses who the pranksters were?"

I clench my teeth. "They're only children. I'll talk to them again tonight before I leave."

"You better." Trinity rolls her jade-green eyes. "Anyone have anything to add for the good of the coven?"

Ronnie points a finger into the air. "I'd like to enter a request for a change in our rules."

The members get quiet as mice, and I stare at her with wide eyes, realizing what she's going to request.

"I want to present the idea of coming out to more Unremarkables," she says. "Vetted, of course. And after we can trust the person. Many of us are dating Unremarkables who know, anyway. After what happened at the conference last fall."

The young witches comment, "yaaas," and the older witches nod. Leslie pinches her lips together as she scans the tight circle. She knows she can't table this. We all have an equal say now. She doesn't respond, but our coven leader addresses Ronnie's request.

"Our guests will be here soon," Trinity says. "I have an opinion on this matter as my wife is an Unremarkable. But I promise you, we will visit your request in the new year."

Soon after, guests arrive for the Yule Celebration. Open houses show the community we aren't as *strange* as they imagine. Some locals have even brought their children, and the DUB students play Celtic games with them like Blind Man's Bluff.

We meet Elijah's new girlfriend, Jasmine Moore, who is a lovely petite Unremarkable woman with warm bronze skin and rich brown eyes. She has a feisty demeanor, not unlike another young woman I know. I can't wait to hear Trinity's take on allowing Unremarkable close friends or partners to discover the truth about us and the supernatural world. After all, her wife Charlie has known about the Fellowship's secret for years.

When the evening has wound down, the Fellowship cleans up and says their goodbyes on the porch in the chilly air. Agnes walks over to where Tyler, Zoe, Archie, and I are chatting.

"Gwyn, don't fret over the mound while you're gone." She tightens her fingers around my hand. "I have an entire room of spell books we can sift through when you come back. Meanwhile, I hope you find your aunt and some answers."

I give her a hug. "Thanks, Agnes. You should know Leslie gave me an address for Aunt Gorawen. At least, she thinks she's my aunt."

"No fucking way." Agnes peers at Leslie and smiles. "There may be hope for the woman yet."

I laugh. "And the two of you?"

"You're fucking trouble. You know that?" she asks.

"We do." Archie winks at me.

Not amused, I scowl at him and slap his arm.

Agnes laughs in her gravelly voice and heads toward the steps. "Happy Yule, friends."

"Happy Yule, Agnes," we all say.

"I'm sorry we won't get to spend the rest of Yule with you two," I say to Tyler and Zoe.

She lays her head on Tyler's arm. "I hope you find your aunt."

"Me, too, Zoe," I say, hugging them tightly. "I'll see you when we return. I love you both."

"Love you, Mom. Take care of her, Archie."

Archie wraps an arm around my son. "I will do my best, but she has a mind of her own."

Zoe and Tyler chuckle as they take off toward his sedan. When Archie and I step down from the porch, I turn toward Mitchell Hall. He follows me, but I stop.

"You don't need to go. I'll chat with them and be home before you have time to miss me."

"Gwyn, please don't argue with me. You don't have the dirk with you."

"I understand that, but Shailagh and Aonghas are a mess. If I go alone, they're more likely to listen to me." I kiss him. "I promise I'll make it quick. And I'll call if a big, wicked fairy shows up."

He frowns as he scratches his goatee. "Fine. But I'll wait for you in bed with your Yule present." He kisses me and offers his titillating tongue.

"Oh. I'll be fast as a road runner then."

I head toward Main Street, and Archie ambles toward the Green. I'm distracted on my short stroll to Mitchell Hall, knowing Archie will be lying in bed at the house—hopefully, buck naked under the covers with a spring in his you-know-what.

As I approach the mansion, a familiar sense of dread returns to the pit of my stomach. It's been a few weeks since I checked on the Seelie Fae, and the apprehension has built up, I suppose. I hesitate but push past the uneasiness, attributing the trepidation to last year's celebration in the gardens—when I attacked the Sluagh to save Ronnie.

The lock on the fencing opens with a wave of my amber glow, and I dash into the Celestial Gardens. I can't wait to gaze upon the Seelie Fae's golden-blond hair and mint-green eyes again. "Shailagh! Aonghas!"

The mound appears frozen in the dark under the gray, billowy clouds hovering above. A break in the puffs of gloom allows a beam of light to shine through, lighting up the far-right corner of the backyard. The gardening crew planted a new young hawthorn tree in the barren spot where the former one exploded a year ago. I recall the banishment of the Sluagh with Archie's ancestral dirk and tremble. Planting the favored host tree invites more evil fairies, but what do Unremarkables know?

Suddenly, I sense a presence behind me, and a foreboding engulfs my body. But I chuckle when I surmise the children must be playing a prank. As I turn around, I plan to admonish the Seelie Fae for trying to scare me.

My breath stagnates, and I can't move. A male fairy with long platinum blond hair and large, rounded shoulders and biceps stands in my path, ripples of muscle protruding from his abdomen. Rays of white emanate from his body, and expansive black and pale-gray wings expand outward. But the fairy has no face—only bright green eyes! I scream and run toward the gate, tripping over the shovels left by the gardeners. I brace my fall with my gloved hands. When I glance back, the masculine fairy is gone.

"Aunt Gwyn!" Shailagh and Aonghas shout as they dash to me. "Why are you on the ground?"

"Where did he go?" I ask, my heart pounding under my ribcage. A hot flash has soaked my shirt, and I unzip my fleece jacket.

"Who?" they ask. "No one is here but you."

I scan the gardens for any evidence of the monstrous creature. "You didn't see the fairy with the big wings?"

Shailagh and Aonghas giggle. "No, Aunt Gwyn. That's silly."

"It sure is. But is it?" I didn't imagine him. I brush off my clothes as I stand. "Listen, I know you're only playing, but you have to stop leaving funny things set up in the house. The can with the blue liquid you propped up? It's called paint. Not only did the prank make a mess, it could have hurt the workers. I'm going away for a while. Promise me you'll only play in the gardens from now on?"

The two pranksters giggle. "OK, Aunt Gwyn."

"I'll visit when I get back." They run off toward the hawthorn tree as I wave goodbye.

I'm exhausted and sweaty when I arrive at the house, but I know Archie waits impatiently for me in bed. I flip off my shoes and run upstairs to the bedroom, hoping I have a trace of libido left. He's fast asleep in his boxer briefs. Just as well. I'm not in the mood now. After stripping down to my panties and crawling underneath the sheets, I realize I need sleep, too. But the vision of the fairy haunts me, flashing like a strobe light behind my eye sockets.

He's searching for me.

# CHAPTER FOUR

# FINDING MY ROOTS

THE RED-EYE FLIGHT TO Manchester, UK, proves to be the worst way to get a quality night's rest. The low-pitched hum of the engines whirs inside my head all night, and when I nod off, a baby behind me emits a piercing wail. Once I slide back into slumber, I'm in a mist of white. I stab the Sluagh host tree, and the shrieking of the evil fairy wakes me with a start. I massage my thumping heart and swallow, trying to catch my breath.

Archie clasps my hand and whispers, "Did you have a nightmare about the vision you saw in the gardens last night?"

"No," I mutter. "I dreamed about inserting the dirk into the Host of the Unforgiven Dead. I'm gonna have to do it again, aren't I?"

"Let's not get ahead of ourselves. This is your first vision. And you said it only lasted for a couple of seconds. We hope to find a portal-closing spell long before he discovers your whereabouts. I'm glad you told me this morning, but I wish you had woken me when you got to the house."

"At first, I figured the daily worry had triggered a hallucination, and that could still be the case. But the apprehension that seized my body right before is what frightened me the most."

Archie kisses the back of my hand. "Try to sleep, my love. At least we're away from Bearsden for a while. The travel should throw your magic scent off."

I smile at his gorgeous, chiseled face and close my eyes, slipping into slumber to the image of his clear-blue irises.

When we arrive at the massive airport, it's 6:00 a.m., and I'm eager to deboard. Even the exhaustion can't quell my churning stomach. We're only one hour's drive from Buckley.

"What's taking so long?" I ask, rubbing my face. "I want to visit this address today."

Archie caresses my hand. "Gwyn, we have to get through customs, get our luggage, and rent a car yet. I doubt we'll have time to visit her today."

"Well, that blows."

I stare at the baby from hell behind me. He's cooing and smiling. Figures.

"I know you're fit to burst. But you want to be well-rested before you go."

"You're right," I say, tugging at my turtleneck and jeans. "I need to remove these constrictive clothes and send Tyler a message to let him know we arrived."

Archie always appears so comfortable in his long-sleeved Henley and jeans. I'd rather be wearing a T-shirt and yoga pants.

The pilot gives us the go-ahead to deboard, and we spend the next hour trudging through customs. The weather is like home—in the mid-40s and rainy. By the time we get the rental car, I've lost my second wind and reach for the door handle on the right side of the four-door sedan.

He chuckles. "You're going to drive, are you?"

"Whoops." I laugh and meander around. "This is my first time in a car with the driver's seat on the wrong side."

"For us in the UK, this is the right side." He winks at me.

"You think you're funny."

Once we're on the M56, I become sleepy and figure I won't miss much scenery. There is so much roadwork cluttering the North Cheshire roadway. A bump in the road wakes me just in time to pass a sign written in two languages—Croeso i Gymru and Welcome to Wales. A warm aura spreads through me. Or is it my magic searching for my roots?

"Ah, you're awake," Archie says, smiling. "I'm glad you didn't miss the welcome sign. I didn't want to wake you."

"It's so cool to see both languages, and I'm relieved. I can't pronounce Welsh at all. The words are like a cryptic puzzle."

"Aye. Gaelic is not much better to read," he says, using a thicker Scottish brogue. "Ah, we're here."

We pass the town sign. It reads BUCKLEY, Historic Brick-making Town—underneath the English, BWCLE in Welsh. But the other letters resemble misspelled words thrown on the sign at random. Where is Nick when I need him?

According to what I researched, Buckley has over 20,000 residents, including the surrounding area, not as many as Bearsden, if you count the students on campus. In the 1800s, the town had more than a dozen pottery makers and several brickworks manufacturers. A large cement manufacturer remains, but the kiln is a bit of an eyesore. The downtown shopping area has several brick buildings of an orangey-red color, and a few storefronts appear empty. It's not as attractive as Bearsden, but the city exhibits a small-town charm. My mom must have hated to leave.

Archie parks in front of a quaint brick home, a bed-and-breakfast he booked online. When I try to get out of the passenger seat, I rub my lower back. All the sitting has deposited a kink in my lumbar, and I moan, getting out of the compact sedan.

"I feel like shit. My back hurts, and I'm jet lagged." Archie lifts my suitcase out of the trunk, and I grab the handle. "Thanks, honey. I need a nap and a shower. My breath probably reeks, too."

Archie kisses me, and a wrinkle forms between his eyes. "A good assessment."

"You're not smelling like roses either." I frown and stagger toward the front door of the B and B where a Christmas wreath made of pine twigs and red bows welcomes us.

"Let me get the door, Gwyn."

We enter the foyer and find a small table to sign in and register our stay. As Archie writes our names into the ledger, an older woman with short, curly gray hair who's dressed in a sweater and wool pants enters from the back of the house.

"Croeso," she says in a soft-spoken voice. "May I help you?"

"Aye. Dr. Archibald Cockburn. I booked a room for two," he replies.

A grin spreads the woman's mouth. "Oh, a Scot. Are you from Scotland as well?"

"No," I reply. "I'm from the US. A town called Bearsden. It's in the state of Delaware. But my parents were from Wales. Hello, I'm Gwynedd Crowther."

"A Yank. Well, I'm happy to have you both," she says. "My name is Mary Griffiths. Please, call me Mary."

We both thank Mary for her hospitality, and we follow her upstairs to a bedroom at the end of a long hallway. She unlocks the door, and we follow her into an adorable room. The bedroom is quaint, with an antique brass bed covered in blue and white striped sheets. A folded thick quilt rests near the footboard. The rickety metal will make a shitload of noise if we have sex, and I'm counting on some serious frolicking now that we're on vacation. Or as Archie says—on holiday.

Mary hands me the key. "I'll trust you with this, Ms. Crowther. Being of Welsh descent and all. No offense, Dr. Cockburn."

I chuckle under my breath.

"None taken." He lifts a corner of his mouth and winks at me. "Thank you for showing us to our room."

Mary ambles toward the door. "I serve breakfast at 8:30 a.m., and I make a cracking bubble and squeak cake. Your man here wrote in an email you don't eat meat. These will fill you up."

"Thanks so much for accommodating me," I say. "Mary, we came here hoping to find my great-aunt. Is it possible you know of her? If she's still alive, of course. I never met her. Her name is Gorawen Thomas."

Mary stops and her blue-gray eyes widen. "Gorawen Thomas is your aunt?"

"Well, I'm not sure," I say, folding my hands. "I have an address for her, but I don't know if she's my aunt."

"The old woman I know is well into her 90s, but she's as smart as a whip. I don't believe she has any family. A local woman takes her meals occasionally, I've heard. If you need anything, ring the bell. Please, enjoy your stay."

Mary exits as I fall back on the brass bed, unzipping my ankle boots and dropping them to the floor. "I think I'm gonna catch a few winks as soon as I message Tyler." The internet signal is weak, but the DM goes through.

"I believe I'll join you." Archie plops onto the mattress next to me, and the bed moves up and down, squeaking. "I'm sorry. Should I have booked an American hotel off the expressway? Mary's B & B is close to downtown, though."

"Nooo. It's romantic being here in an old Welsh home."

"Let's nap now. The travel has caught up with me."

"Me, too." I roll over and cup his crotch. "I want to be rested for later."

After a couple of hours of shut-eye, we shower and get dressed in casual winter clothes for dinner. Several pub choices abound, but Archie remembers a great place on Mold Road. I break down and order fish and chips, because a vegetarian pub is too much to ask for, especially in a small Welsh town in the north. We both enjoy our typical British meal but finish up quickly once the karaoke begins. I don't need bad singing to trigger a menopausal migraine. It's dark when we exit, and the wet road shines under the streetlights with streaks of white and yellow.

"Why don't we take a walk to the center of town and work off the calories," Archie says, rubbing his stomach. "The rain has stopped."

I hold my palm up, testing his observation. "Sure. That sounds great. I'd like to visit the heart of Buckley."

We stroll to the town center where the narrow one-way road is blocked off for pedestrian traffic. Multi-colored lights hang across the paved walkway and reflect off the drenched surface. The primary shopping center has some restaurants and a supermarket, but many of the storefronts are empty. Buckley could benefit from revitalization.

Archie motions toward the entrance of the shopping mall. "I want to pick up some wine before the grocery store closes."

"Why don't you pick out something?" I ask. "I'll be nearby window shopping."

"Please, don't stray too far. It's dark."

"We've been so worried about some ancient, evil fairy god coming after me, and all it's done is stress me out. I understand your concern after I had that vision, but we're over 5,000 miles away from Delaware. Go get the wine and let me browse." I glance up and down the short street. "How far can I go?"

Archie chuckles. "All right. But don't make me search for you."

I point toward the mall entrance and wave my hand, motioning him to leave. Once he disappears through the doors, I stroll past a few shops and stop at a tattoo parlor with a skull on the sign above the door. Why does every tattoo studio have bones on its sign? Or an artist rendering of their tattoo gun with a needle? Do they expect an overt display of pain to entice people in?

When I peek into the studio through the glass at the sample artwork, the image of a man reflects off the surface. He has an oblong face and long, black hair tied behind his head. Our eyes lock, and every muscle contracts as my heart beats heavily in my chest. I flip my head around, but he's gone. A group of drunk locals passes by me, laughing and belching as they cross the street. When they reach the other side, I recognize the stranger who was spying on me. He's wearing a black trench coat and leaning on a cane. I swear he's staring directly at me.

"Gwyn? Where are you?" Archie yells from behind.

I turn my head to find him strolling toward me, holding a paper bag.

"There you are. What's the matter? You're as pale as a ghost."

"A man with long, black hair was staring at me." I twist my head around toward the stranger who was leering at me. But he's vanished.

"I don't see anyone, Gwynedd. Are you sure he was staring at you?"

"Yes. I'm sure." I glance up and down the street.

Archie raises a corner of his mouth. "You are an attractive woman, my love."

"Well, it's misogynistic and creepy." I scowl and inspect the crevices between the buildings.

"I didn't say it was appropriate. Only that he might have been admiring your beauty."

"Oh, screw that. Ewww. Now I feel icky," I say, grimacing.

He kisses me on the cheek. "Can we go back to our lodging? Where I can ogle you in the privacy of our room?"

"Now that, I'll allow."

I grin and grasp his hand, dragging him toward our B and B. When we enter our room, there is a chill in the air.

"Archie, can you check the radiator? I'm cold."

"Aye, but you're always cold. I saw bathrobes in the loo."

I saunter over to him and caress his chest. "I don't plan on wearing a robe. So, if you want to see me naked, you'll check the radiator."

He slides a hand over a butt cheek. "I'll get to it, then."

"I'm going to put on a sexy teddy. Warm the room up, lover." I kiss him lightly on the lips and head into the bathroom with my barely there clump of teal lace.

Goosebumps form on my arms and legs as I strip down to my bare skin, shaking uncontrollably. I squeeze my body into the lingerie meant for pre-menopausal women. Even though I'm petite, fat has shifted to my hips in menopause. On the bright side, the floral lace covers the cellulite on my ass—winning. The ceramic tile floor is like a slab of ice, and my feet turn a mottled shade of purple. I put my ankle socks back on and throw on the plush white robe hanging on the hook.

I jump out of the bathroom and stick out my leg seductively. "Ta-da!"

"You're all covered up," Archie says, lying on the bed in a black t-shirt and boxer briefs. "You understand visual stimulation entices men, don't you? Dare I say the socks aren't helping either."

I chuckle and jump onto the bouncy bed. "Of course I do, but I'm freezing. You know I can't get in the mood if I'm cold. If you want sex tonight, you'll deal with my socks. Is the radiator broken?"

"Naw. It's working but probably can't keep up with the draftiness of the windows." With a sexy smile gracing his face, he pulls back the sheets and pats the mattress.

I throw off my robe and climb underneath, pulling the quilt up to my neck. "OK. I'm ready."

Archie bursts out laughing and slides close to me. "I only got a glimpse of your seductive lingerie. Can I see more?"

"Sure." I push up the layers of bed linens for a few seconds and snatch them back.

"How am I supposed to make love to you if I can't see your naked body?"

I slide a hand down to his growing bulge and stroke him through his boxer briefs. "I think you'll manage."

He becomes rigid to my touch and kisses me deeply. Oh, how much I've missed this intimacy. The passion building from the heavy necking sends a tingling sensation down my torso. His woodsy cologne arouses me further as I slide my hand under his shirt to fondle his nipples. I want him so badly after a month without sex, but he takes his time. He's so gentle as he strokes my breasts through the lace. How lucky I am to have stumbled into this world of covens and supernatural beings that brought him to me.

"You're shaking. Are you still cold?" He raises a hand to summon his witch energy, but I pull it down.

"Not between my legs," I say, panting. "It's been so long, but I want you to make love to me without magic."

Archie grabs my bottom and grinds his manhood against me. My entire body heats up and suddenly, I'm not so chilly anymore. I pull his face to mine and kiss him as I run my fingertips through his blond waves. He presses harder against me, and I can't wait any longer.

"That's it," I say.

I grab the elastic of his underwear, tugging at them until they're off. With one pull, I unsnap the crotch of my teddy and wrap my hand around his hardness.

He chuckles. "Patience, my love."

"Not a chance." I pull him on top of me and guide his erection toward me. "I want you now."

When he enters me, I wrap my legs around him like a vise grip and dig my fingernails into his back, urging him to move faster.

"Oh, Gwyn, why did I let schoolwork overwhelm me? I'd forgotten how good it feels to be inside you."

"Then don't hold back," I say, sliding a hand to his tattooed butt.

Archie takes my cue and with every thrust, the bed squeaks louder, and the brass headboard clanks against the plaster wall.

"Maybe we should stop. Our recreational activities must be entertaining Mary." He laughs as he continues to *entertain* our host.

I chuckle and squeeze his butt cheeks. "I've waited over a month for this. Don't you dare stop."

The grating squeaks increase in tempo, matching the rhythm of our bodies, until they transform into a repetitious, high-pitched squeal. I bite my lip as a hot flash overcomes me, trying to hold back my yelp of pleasure, but I shriek like I'm in severe pain. Archie grunts and moans with his last vigorous thrust, and the bed frame collapses to the floor near the footboard.

"Shit!" I burst out laughing as we slide toward the bottom of the mattress. "Did we break the frame?"

Archie laughs and grabs hold of the mattress above. "It's made of brass, Gwyn. I doubt our lovemaking broke a metal bed. The bolts must have loosened from the movement."

"What are we gonna do?" I ask, catching my breath.

"Right now, I'm enjoying the last few moments of being one with you." He bends his head down and kisses me. "I love you, Gwynedd."

"I love you, Archie. Never let anyone or anything come between us."

"I won't, my love. But I better fix the bed."

We slide off the mattress, landing on the chilly wooden floor. I slip on my robe and run to the bathroom to freshen up while Archie assesses the damage. When I return, he has attached the metal frame to the brass footboard and is standing to inspect his repair. This man still takes my breath away. Striking as the first day I met him, I admire the toned muscles on his chest, torso, and arms—and his physique below.

I rush to him and wrap my arms around his midsection. "That was fun. Let's do it again."

"As enticing as the proposal sounds, perhaps we should count our blessings and get some sleep." He examines the footboard again. "I need tools to tighten the bolts properly. I'll check with Mary in the morning. She must have a toolbox."

I wipe my face and snicker. "How will we face her?"

"You think we're the first couple to have vigorous sex in that bed? I think not."

"I know, but it made a tremendous racket. You'd think she would have knocked on the door by now to check on us."

"I imagine she knows what happened and didn't want to embarrass us."

"Well, breakfast will be interesting. If we're finished with our horseplay, I'm gonna throw on my long-sleeved PJs. I'm freezing again. My hormones need to have a meeting and stick to an agenda."

Once I've changed into my pajamas and Archie has put on a t-shirt and lounge pants, we cuddle in the afterglow of our night's frolicking under the cozy blankets and heavy quilt. A beam from a streetlight illuminates his gorgeous face, and a slight smile rests on his mouth. I wish I could surrender to slumber as easily. I roll onto my back and bend my knees to avoid a sore lower back in the morning, and the reflection of the man with long, black hair returns to me. Why are some men so creepy?

# Chapter Five

# THE HOMECOMING

TINY SWIRLS OF STEAM rise as Mary pours boiling water into our teacups, and a hint of a smile forms on her face. "I trust the two of you slept well."

I stare at Archie and fiddle with an earring. "We did. Thank you for asking."

He clears his throat. "Mary, the bolts on the bed are a wee bit loose. Do you have a toolbox? I'd be happy to tighten them."

"Yes. I have some spanners in a drawer. I heard an unusual bang last night. Neither of you was hurt by the...incident?" Mary asks, attempting to squash a laugh.

"No. We're fine. Archie put the frame back together."

We all have a little chuckle, and Mary goes into the kitchen, carrying the teapot.

"Please, tighten the bolts," I say. "I don't want to embarrass the poor woman again."

Archie laughs as he sweetens his tea. "I think Mary quite enjoyed the comedy in the situation."

"Well, I'd like to not repeat it."

After breakfast, we drive to the outskirts of town to the address Leslie gave me. I sit in the passenger seat, tapping my polished fingernails on the armrest.

"What if the old woman isn't my aunt?"

"What are you waiting for, then?" Archie asks. "If it's not her, then you'll know. Are you scared to meet her?"

"Yes, I am. I'm afraid of what she'll tell me. Part of me would rather remain oblivious."

"So, we came all this way for what? Gwyn, you won't be prepared for what may come if you bury your head in a mountain of I-don't-want-to-know."

I gaze into his clear-blue eyes and open the car door. "Wish me luck."

"When will you realize it's not luck, Gwyn." He grins and winks at me. "It's magic."

I get out of the compact sedan and inspect the home as I pull up the zipper on my fleece jacket. The large two-story farmhouse has a stone exterior and multiple fireplace flues. I bet the home dates to the late 1600s. Sitting on a handful of acres, the property includes multiple outbuildings with sheep running about the lush, wet grass. A stone fence surrounds the structures.

My leather ankle boots sink into the earth as I tiptoe toward the house. A small, enclosed A-frame entryway juts out from the front. My chest tightens, and I suck in the cool, damp air. I tap on the substantial wooden door, and in a few seconds, it creaks open. A woman with short, frizzy gray hair who appears to be in her 60s pokes her head in the opening.

"May I help you?" the woman asks in a British accent. Or is it a Welsh dialect?

"Yes. I hope so," I say as my mouth twitches. "My name is Gwynedd Crowther, and I'm looking for a woman named Gorawen Thomas. Does she live here?"

"That depends. You're an American. Tell me now, why would a Yank be asking questions about the woman who lives here?"

"It's quite a long story, but I'll tell you the short version. I believe Gorawen Thomas is my great-aunt. Her mother and my grandmother, my nain, were sisters."

The woman inspects me up and down. "Wait here." She leaves the door ajar, and a faint discussion reverberates through the hallway before she returns. "I'm sorry. Ms. Thomas says she doesn't have a niece. I wish you well on your journey to find your great-aunt."

She shuts the door and crushes all my hopes. I trudge back to the sedan without watching my steps, and my boot squishes into something soft and slippery. In one fell swoop, I find myself in sheep shit. Ugh. I stand and examine the back of my jeans. Good thing there is a washer at the B and B.

Archie gets out of the car. "What happened?"

"I stepped in manure. You'd think they'd put up a sign at least...warn you about it."

He points to a rectangular section of wood attached to a post near the entrance of the stone fence. "There is a sign."

"Beware of the sheep fouling. Nothing on there says anything about poop."

Archie chuckles at me. "Gwyn, Brits use the word fouling instead of manure. Forget about the shit. What did the woman say to you?"

"Great. I'm reading English, and I still can't understand the British. She said Ms. Thomas doesn't have a niece. I guess we're done here. Let's go to...wait." I open the car door and retrieve my mom's family grimoire from my hobo bag.

"What are you doing?" Archie asks, arching his eyebrows.

"Betting on the magic."

I turn around and march toward the house with the spell book in my hand and shit on my pants. I knock one more time.

The gray-haired woman opens the door, squinting at me. "I already told you. You're at the wrong house."

"That may be. Please, give this journal to Ms. Thomas. If she really is my aunt, she'll recognize it. And you'll be coming back to invite me in. If she doesn't…" I hesitate and swallow. "Return the journal to me, and I'll be on my way."

She takes my family's grimoire and walks away. I wait there for several minutes, thinking I've taken a risk sharing the spell book with strangers. But I need confirmation.

The door opens wide, and she motions me in. "Please, come in. My name is Ellie Jones. I've been helping Ms. Thomas with meals and cleaning a few times a week. She said she would speak with you."

"Thank you so much." I grin and follow her into the house.

The historic home has stone floors and exposed wood beams on the walls and ceilings. We enter directly into a living room area where a wide stone fireplace takes up an entire wall. Holly and mistletoe decorate the immense mantle above the burning fire. Unexpected sunlight shines through a window, spotlighting the decorations. A Yule pine tree stands majestically in a corner, its aroma permeating the room, along with a hint of cinnamon.

An old woman with pale skin, white hair, and a withered body sits hunched over in an overstuffed brown chair, clutching the family spell book. Wearing an outdated, shapeless dress and slippers, she nearly disappears into her surroundings. She raises her head and stares at me for a long minute, and I recognize her hazel eyes—mine, my mom's, and Tyler's. A warm sensation overwhelms me, and I tear up. I stand there like a specimen under a magnifying glass and get a whiff of the sheep poop on my pants.

"Well…come close where I can get a look at you," Ms. Thomas says in a strained voice. "Ellie, would you mind fetching us some tea? I need a few minutes alone with Ms. Crowther."

I move closer, worried about the stench of the sheep *fouling*.

"You have an older face, but I recognize Lowri's image in yours. Is your mother well?"

My heart pumps with joy when she says my mom's name, but I hesitate to give her the sad news. "No. I'm sorry. Both of my parents passed away several years ago in a car accident."

Aunt Gorawen lowers her head, pressing her lips together until they disappear, and her eyes swell up with tears. "The letters stopped coming, so I expected as much." She removes a handkerchief from a purse next to her chair and wipes her wet, wrinkled face. "She wrote me letters every year, and I never wrote back. Too angry over her escaping to America and leaving me here alone. After all these years, all I have left is this broken body and a heaping pile of regrets."

"I don't know what to say, Aunt Gorawen. Is it OK if I call you that?"

Her mouth spreads into a cheerful grin. "It fills my heart to hear those words. Please, would you mind giving your long-lost aunt a hug?"

I walk over to her and bend down to wrap my arms around her aging body. Another whiff of manure enters my nose, and I pray the odor of her arthritis ointment covers the stink. When I stand up, she gestures to another chair near the fireplace.

"Sit down, niece. Why have you come here now to find me? Quickly. Ellie will be here shortly with the tea."

"I shouldn't sit on your furniture. I slipped on sheep manure in your yard."

Aunt Gorawen chuckles. "I thought maybe you farted."

"Oh, no," I snicker. "I hope my farts don't smell that bad."

Ellie enters the room with a rolling tray, holding a tea set, finger sandwiches, and scones. "Is there anything else I can do for you before I leave?"

"Hand my niece that tea towel," my aunt says. "Gwynedd, you can cover the cushion with it."

"It was a pleasure meeting you, Ms. Crowther," Ellie says, but doesn't seem to mean it. "Ms. Thomas, I'll call you tomorrow and see what you need from the grocery store."

Aunt Gorawen nods. "Thank you, Ellie. You are so good to me."

My aunt's neighborly caretaker turns to leave, and I dash to her. "My boyfriend has been sitting in the car all this time. He must be curious and cold. Could you tell him to come in?"

Ellie nods but glares at me, exiting through the front door without a reply.

"You have a man with you? Not your husband. I hope you will spend the afternoon telling me all about your life. And now that Ellie has left, you may speak freely about our family secrets." My aunt lifts her eyebrows toward the ceiling.

"I would love to. If you can stand the stench." I laugh out loud as the creaking of the front door echoes in the foyer.

Archie enters with his hands in his pockets. "Is everything all right?"

"Come here. I want to introduce you to my Great-Aunt Gorawen Thomas. Aunt, this is Dr. Archie Cockburn. He's an ancestral witch from Edinburgh."

His face lights up as he shakes hands with her. "So very honored to meet you. And relieved."

"Your man is quite handsome, Gwynedd," she says, giving him a once-over. "And a Scot. How did you ever meet him?"

"That is quite a tale to tell," Archie says, grinning.

Aunt Gorawen pours tea into her cup and waves her hand in slow motion as a faint amber glow appears. A spoon rises and scoops sugar into the cup while the milk spills out of a creamer holder. "Please, pull up a chair and have some tea and sandwiches."

We spend the afternoon laughing and sometimes shedding a few tears, talking about my upbringing and the events of the past year. I tell Aunt Gorawen about Tyler and how I hope she gets to meet him someday. She has us in stitches sharing memories of my mother as a child since she raised her after my grandparents died during an influenza outbreak. The discussion finally lands on the creation of the mound in the Celestial Gardens, the Seelie Fae children, and the family tale of the Tuatha Dé Danann. But I wait to tell her about my recent vision. Her demeanor becomes serious.

"Of course, that's why you're here." Aunt Gorawen sips her tea. "I was so angry with Lowri when she told me she and Rhys were going to attend graduate school in the US. We had a terrible argument. She had kept their plan a secret until right before they left. Your parents had only been married months before. Mind you, now, it was against my better wishes. Your mum stormed out of this house with Rhys close behind, and that was the last time I spoke with her."

"Her letter to me explained how scared she was. She must have believed it was the safest path for her." I recall the conversation with my mom when she popped out of the painting on Archie's fireplace mantel and bring up the photo on my cell phone to show her. "Do you recognize this painting?"

She gets choked up and clears her throat. "I wanted Lowri to stay here where I could help fight the Tuatha Dé fairy should it ever appear. My ancestral magic skills were powerful in my younger days. In the last few years, they have diminished. I can't practice the craft as I used to, especially with an *unknowing* caretaker. But in those days, I could have protected her. So, I did the next best thing I could. I want to show you something."

Aunt Gorawen grabs her cane and tries to stand. Archie rushes over and helps her out of the chair. We follow her down a hallway to a short door. She shoves a key into the lock and turns the knob.

"Since I practice the craft in here, I keep the room locked from Ellie's curiosity," she says.

As we enter, Archie ducks his head to avoid the header of the doorway. We gasp and gape at the sight. There are piles of paintings against the walls, all in various stages of completion. But they have one thing in common. They display the same figure of my mom standing in a field of wildflowers, and she's reaching toward a gloomy sky with an impending storm.

"I painted as many as I could and cast a spell on them to recruit protectors for your mum and her future daughter. I spread them as far as I could over many years. Eventually, arthritis stopped my work, and my magic became too weak for effective casting." My aunt chuckles. "I'm chuffed to bits one of them snagged an ancestral witch."

Archie and I lock eyes, and a part of me questions his devotion again. "I can't rely on others to protect me. Aunt Gorawen, please tell me everything you know concerning the Tuatha Dé and how I can prepare for his coming. I've completed some ancestral witch training with Archie, but I've only had minor success contacting my mom. I spoke to her briefly through the painting you created, but she didn't share much."

"Gwyn hasn't had quality focus with all the stress this has caused." Archie wraps an arm around me. "But she has labored for months, attempting to form a better connection."

"I was going to wait to tell you, but I think you should know," I say. "I had a vision of a male fairy in the gardens before I left. If the occurrence isn't due to stress, he's discovered my scent."

Aunt Gorawen stands as straight as she can, leaning on her cane. "That is disconcerting. You must practice divination here with me. Together, we will contact your mam...and your tad. We'll start in the morning at first light. We don't have much time."

"I would love that." I glance at my cell. It's almost dinnertime. "We should go, but I'll come tomorrow. What about Ellie?"

"I'll tell her to delay bringing groceries this week. Dr. Cockburn, would you mind running those errands while Gwyn and I practice?"

"Of course," he says. "I'd be happy to."

We amble to the front door, and I bend down to hug my aunt. It's obvious her life hangs on by the wisp of a thread, or by a strand of magic, and I'm sad I never tried to find her before now. She raises a hand, and streaks of amber glow flow from her fingertips into the air. The knob clicks, and the door creaks open.

"Magic comes in handy when your hands are mangled with arthritis. I'll see you early at the cock's crow. And I will share the warnings of the Tuatha Dé Danann."

# CHAPTER SIX

# FOCUS CAN BE DANGEROUS

JET LAG HAS FINALLY caught up with me, and I snatch my phone off the end table when the obnoxious alarm sounds. A sliver of light peeks through the window, sneaking into the room to wake me. How does a woman in her late 90s wake up this early? Oh, yeah. She's a seasoned witch. Well, I'm not. I roll over to face Archie, pulling the quilt against my neck, and find him staring at me in the morning twilight.

"Good morning, my love. What's going on in that head of yours?" he asks, smoothing out my hair. "Anxious about today?"

I caress his chest through his t-shirt. "Not about the divination. I'm eager to learn whatever she can teach me to contact my parents. But I'm on pins and needles about what she'll tell me about my unknown foe. Mom didn't seem to know much."

"At least we worked off some of your stress last night. You were more voracious than the night before."

"Well, I'm making up for missed opportunities. And it's exercise."

"You better get moving," he says, patting my bottom. "You don't want to keep your aunt waiting."

After a quick shower, Archie and I go to the dining area. Mary serves us another fabulous breakfast, this time without the embarrassment of breaking her bed. I message Tyler about the good news of finding Aunt Gorawen, and he texts back using a smiley emoji. We make the short drive to my aunt's home, passing a few residents on a morning stroll. When we arrive, Ellie is exiting the house—a rather early visit. I wave to her as I exit the car.

She marches over to me with a scowl wrinkling her face. "My husband, Owen, and I have been tending to Gorawen and her farm for many years now and never took a quid from her. We knew she had no family to help, so we were happy to do it. And we grew to love her. You show up, claiming to be her niece, and now she wants to change everything in less than twenty-four hours since your visit yesterday. We were supposed to inherit this estate when she died." She points an accusatory finger at me. "Tell me now, why are you really here?"

My jaw drops, and I stare at her, dumbfounded. I certainly can't tell her the truth...that I'm here so my aunt can help me prepare to fight off an evil fairy.

Archie gets out of the sedan and walks around to me. "Something wrong?"

"Ellie seems to think I'm here to claim my aunt's estate," I say. "I assure you that's not why I've come. I'm here to deal with a very personal matter—family history."

She purses her lips. "Well, she's asked me to ring her lawyer. And she's canceled Christmas dinner with us."

"Gwyn knows nothing about Ms. Thomas's wishes or plans," Archie says.

"I can speak for myself," I say. "Aunt Gorawen mentioned nothing about leaving the property to me. I promise you."

She huffs and walks off, heading toward the town center. Great. Another enemy to deal with. At least she doesn't have enormous wings and a family vendetta.

"Merry Christmas Eve to you, too," I shout in her direction.

"I'm sorry, Gwyn. It was presumptuous to speak for you."

"Oh, it's OK. I'll deal with her later. I better get in there. I'll text you a grocery list."

He caresses my upper arm. "May the spirits be open to you in your divination, my love."

"Thank you so much for coming with me. I love you."

"Of course, you do," he says, smiling arrogantly.

I shove him playfully. "Make yourself useful and go to the grocery store."

He chuckles as he kisses me goodbye, and I dash to the front door, skipping over the *fouling*. When I knock, the door creeps open, and I enter.

"Aunt Gorawen?" I yell as I enter the foyer.

When I peek into the living room, a floating, shimmering hand appears and invites me with a hooked finger to follow it down the hallway. I grin in awe at the magic, recognizing the charmed appendage from when I broke the spell on my mom's steamer trunk. When I arrive at the room where the unfinished paintings of my mom are collecting dust, the magical butler motions me in.

"Gwynedd? Is that you out there?" Aunt Gorawen asks. "I'm in the conservatory."

There are double glass doors on the left wall, and I walk through the open one into a sanctuary of greenery housing tropical plants and herbs. The shimmering hand whizzes past me with a whoosh and points to a seat next to my aunt, where she's potting some seedlings.

"Can I help you with the plants?" I ask.

"I would gladly accept your assistance." She communicates something in Welsh, and the magical butler whizzes off. "My extra hand doesn't need to spy on us while we're working."

I pick up an extra pair of gloves and slip them on. Aunt Gorawen passes the pot to me, and I squish the roots of the baby plant down into the dirt using two fingers.

"No, no, no, dear niece. You must be gentle. They are breathing, living things. Treat them as you would want to be treated. With care and respect."

"Let me try again."

With the next one, I place the seedling into the pot and fill in the potting soil around the roots, patting the soil down once I'm finished.

"Da iawn, Gwynedd," she says, patting my hand. "Let's move into the house, and we'll practice divination."

I grin and move next to her. "Grab my arm, and I'll help you inside."

"Sweet like your mother, you are. Take me to the altar against the wall. I've set up a cloth and set crystals on it."

The rustic pine table shows years of wear. Burn marks from prior spell castings and remnants of melted candles spot the wooden surface. She has placed our family grimoire near the divination cloth with black obsidian, citrine, and quartz crystals. Incense oil sticks are ready to burn.

"What are we burning? When I practiced with Archie, he used mugwort to help me focus."

Aunt Gorawen shakes her head. "Hmph. The Scots always take risks. Yes. Mugwort helps with divination, but it also attracts the fae if you plant it in your garden. I prefer using star anise. It will enhance your psychic ability and ward off evil and negativity—a much better choice."

I chuckle. "OK. I'll make sure to tell Archie."

"Oh, you needn't tell him. You don't have to share everything with your man. A woman should always have a few secrets—to keep him wanting for more." She squints at me, forming a lopsided grin.

"Why do I get the impression you were a vixen as a younger woman?"

"Ah. Those days are long buried beneath the earth. But I have colorful memories."

"Were you ever married? You still use the name Thomas."

"I was engaged to be married to a wonderful man named Ioan. He died of influenza about the same time as your grandparents."

"Oh, Aunt Gorawen. How awful. Mom never told me." I lay my hand on her shoulder.

"Lowri was young when they passed, and I took her in." She turns toward the table and lights the incense. "Raising her gave me a purpose to move on."

Then my mom left her here alone. Suddenly, knots twist tightly inside. "I'm sorry, Aunt Gorawen. She must have been terrified."

"Let's not dwell on what has passed. We must move forward to what is yet to come. Now, what can you show me?"

"Oh, I don't think I can show you anything. I've not been able to focus enough to connect with my mom. Using a divination cloth or through the painting. I have none of her personal belongings with me, like her photo or jewelry she wore."

"You have everything you need right here, dear niece." She lays her hand on the spell book. "I am so pleased you thought to bring it. I never trusted outsiders who came searching for me, claiming to know Lowri. The Tuatha Dé are extremely cunning beings."

Aunt Gorawen continues. "Take heed. They can shift into any form. Even glamour you, although the magical effect may only last for a short time on ancestral witches. A consistent clouding of your brain would require a charmed object, and he wouldn't use such an item on you. Because he has to win your true love. I imagine he would attempt to meet with you regularly to influence you. But he can't take over your mind completely—only steer you in the right direction. Or he may become impatient—snatch you and take you with him to the Otherworld without warning."

My mouth falls open as the once hypothetical becomes as clear as a sunny day. This explains why she sent Leslie away when the Elder came knocking on her door.

"That's terrifying, and the vision proves he's actually coming after me. It's not just a tale." .

"Undoubtedly, Gwynedd. And we have no time to waste," she says, squinting. "If you have no focus, we must begin there. We won't try to contact Lowri today. You must develop a deeper concentration, and you missed out on the daily divination during your younger years. It's much harder to learn the older you get." She slides the incense toward us. "I want you to breathe in the star anise deeply. Hold the essence in your lungs until you want to burst and expel it slowly."

I position my head over the incense and inhale until I can't stuff one more puff of air, holding the smoke in until I hack and cough violently. Aunt Gorawen pats me on the back and chuckles.

"Have you never inhaled incense before?"

"No," I say, wheezing. "I have terrible allergies."

"Your mam had the same sinus trouble. This could be more difficult than I imagined." Her eyes wander over the items on the table, landing on a crystal ball near the back. She pulls it to us. "Grab those obsidian crystals and squeeze them in your hands while you focus on the ball."

I do as she asks and stare into the magical globe. This is silly. I imagine I'm one of those fake psychics who offers readings in their homes, and a laugh breaks free. Aunt Gorawen isn't amused and scowls at me.

"Just like Lowri. She believed I was outdated and eccentric for wanting her to learn divination using a crystal ball. Refused to practice. And then she raised you without magic. Made you useless. Fel rhech mewn pot jam."

Her tone sounded condescending, and I grimace. "What does that mean?"

"Like a fart in a jam jar." She huffs and knocks her cane against the table. "Do you want to gain the skills to defend yourself?"

The Welsh people certainly know how to throw an insult. I'll give them that.

"Of course, I do. It's just that, I stare at the globe, and the phrase..." I lower my voice. "*Look into my crystal ball* keeps jumping into my head. From old black and white B movies." I chuckle, but she isn't having it.

"Gwynedd, the world has ridiculed witches for centuries. Tortured, burned, and murdered. And those were by the *unknowing*. We have another secret list of the same committed by supernatural beings. You cannot profess to be a witch and mock witchcraft in the same breath."

"You're right. I'm sorry. This time, I'll concentrate...without the mockery."

I cup the obsidian crystals in the palms of my hands and focus my intention on the crystal globe as the aroma of the incense penetrates my nostrils. My temples throb, and my eyesight becomes irregular, a kaleidoscope of colors flickering. Fantastic—a menopausal migraine now? I can't stop. A vision is forming inside the globe. My mom may be attempting to conference with me.

"Wonderful, Gwynedd," Aunt Gorawen whispers in a soft, strained voice.

The throbbing pounds relentlessly as my focus intensifies, but I push forward. A low-pitched, guttural voice attempts to speak. Maybe my dad is contacting me for the first time! My heart fills with joy, and I strengthen my concentration. I behold the vision—a faceless, muscular fairy with black and pale-gray wings.

He extends his hands toward me, and speaks, "I know where you are, Gwynedd Crowther, and I'm coming for you."

I scream and jump back like a rabbit, dropping the obsidian crystals to the ground. My hands tremble as I pant. I peer down at my aunt, and she grasps my hand.

"What did you see, niece? You must tell me. Don't hold back."

My vocal cords barely respond as the words sputter out. "He...spoke...to me. But...it wasn't my dad."

"Why's that now then? If not Rhys, then who?"

My head quivers no, and I swallow the lump in my throat. "The same Tuatha Dé male threatened me. He said he knows where I am. And he's coming."

Aunt Gorawen straightens her crooked back as much as she can. "We can't be sure this enemy has actual knowledge of your whereabouts. He has appeared to you in two regions of the world, following your scent, but he's only sniffing you out for now. He will lie and conspire to find you, though, and search for as long as it takes. Tell me about the first incident again."

"The same vision appeared near the portal mound in the gardens at Mitchell Hall—the mansion I told you about. I'd been so stressed about work, school, and other things. I ran and tripped. When I looked back, the image had disappeared. But the fairy had the same physique and wings but no face—only bright green eyes."

The door opens, and Archie walks into the room with my aunt's magical butler in tow. The shimmering hand darts past us and parks on the worktable. Archie chuckles as he enters.

"A convenient helper you have there, Ms. Thomas. I put the perishables in the fridge, but where should I put the..." He views the expressions on our faces. "What has happened?"

"Your aunt seems to believe your foe has discovered your magic scent but is only in the discovery stage," Archie says, sliding into bed. "I know the second vision frightened you, but we're still way ahead of him."

"I'm happy you're so confident, but you didn't hear him threaten you. This will affect my sleep again, and I was already having..."

"Nightmares?" he asks, stroking my cheek.

"Yeah." I can't tell him those were sex dreams. It will only make him feel bad about the dry spell. "Let's not talk about this anymore tonight. I've got to get some sleep. How? I have no idea, but I have to be at my best for tomorrow."

"Don't worry. You'll do well with your aunt's guidance. Learning from blood relatives will improve your divination success, and crystal balls aren't my thing."

"Well, after the encounter with that fairy, I'm not eager to use that globe again, either. I hope Aunt Gorawen has another option."

Archie pulls my chin toward his face. "I love you, Gwyn." He places a soft kiss on my lips, and his goatee tickles my skin.

"I love you, my protector," I say, smiling coyly.

He chuckles. "Let's not give too much credit to the charmed painting. You have no trouble defending yourself. Now get to sleep, stubborn woman."

Sleep? Not a chance.

# CHAPTER SEVEN

# FAMILY INTENTIONS

AUNT GORAWEN INVITES US to spend Christmas Day with her, Yule for us, but there are no restaurants open. So, we dress up a little and cook an eclectic meal for all of us, including some vegetarian dishes for me. My aunt brings out stacks of photo albums and introduces every relative I never met. There's not a chance in all the Otherworld I'll remember their names, but she prattles on and relishes in the sharing. My eyes become teary when she shares photos of my mom as a child.

We decide to leave magic and the threat of an evil fairy out of the equation for the day, which proves to be impossible with the magic butler flitting back and forth. The glittering hand brings us dessert and returns to collect the plates. But the day turns out pleasant and provides hours full of old family memories and new ones. I send Tyler a chat message, hoping he's enjoying Christmas with Zoe, although he's adopted our pagan Yule traditions this year.

The next day, we return our focus to ancestral divination. I lay out the cloth on the table and set the crystals on the material while my aunt's magical butler flies around my head, making me dizzy. My aunt drags a painted canvas to our work area.

"Where is your man while we practice?" Aunt Gorawen asks as she adjusts her long-sleeved cardigan over her loose skirt. "I'm sorry he can't stay, but we need to do this work using family bonds only."

"Archie's an ancestral witch and understands. Don't worry about him. He's antiquing. Loves the hunt for ancient Celtic artifacts." For an old house, it sure is warm in here. I unzip my fleece-lined DUB hoodie and loosen my jeans' button.

"The crystal ball created a path for the Tuatha Dé fairy to communicate with you. I had not planned on using one of the few finished paintings I have as a means of ancestral communication, but Lowri found a path through the one your man acquired. We will try as well."

"I'm so relieved. The idea of viewing my enemy through that glass ball scares the shit out of me."

My aunt leans against the worktable, and her face wrinkles like a prune.

"I'm sorry. My language can be...colorful."

She chuckles and taps my hand. "No worries, niece. I'm only two years shy of a hundred, so I've heard most swear words and in several languages."

"I imagine so," I chuckle. "Let's get started."

The shutting of the heavy front door echoes down the hallway, and I wonder if Archie forgot something.

"Ms. Thomas?" Ellie shouts in the distance. "Where are you? I've brought some sandwiches for lunch!"

Aunt Gorawen huffs. "I'll be there now in a minute! Gwynedd, put the painting of your mam on the table and lean it against the wall. And prepare the incense oil. This may take a while."

My aunt hobbles with her cane down the hallway to the entryway. I try not to eavesdrop, but the intense arguing rumbles throughout the house like an oncoming train. My ill-mannered behavior gains me nothing, because they're conversing in Welsh. As I place the canvas on the worktable, the entry door slams shut.

After ten minutes have passed, Aunt Gorawen shuffles back into the room.

"I shouldn't pry, but is something wrong?" I ask.

She throws a hand down and mumbles in Welsh. "I asked Ellie to give me the key to my house. She blew the lid off her teapot. It's for the best."

"Why would you ask for her key? You'll have to open the door for her every time she shops for you or brings food." I gesture to the shimmering hand assistant. "Your magical helper can't do it for you."

"No. But we can't have Ellie walking in on our practice, either. Our family has enough of a reputation for our witchery from years back."

"I wasn't going to mention this, but she was irate the other day. Screamed at me about coming here to earn your trust, so I could inherit your estate. She walked off in a huff."

"Ellie and Owen have helped me out for years, and I promised them the farm. But I didn't know I had a living niece." She clasps my hand and squeezes. "You are my blood. You should have my home, the farm, and all its contents."

My eyes tear up. "I appreciate your sentiment, but please, don't do that. At first, what Ellie said put me off. I mean, what rights do she and her husband have to the estate of an old woman who isn't related to them? But they've helped you out all these years with no expectations. Then along comes some middle-aged woman from the United States, claiming to be your niece. I'm sure the wheels of skepticism spun inside her head. And I couldn't tell her the real reason I'd come here."

"Quite right. But how can I leave our family's farm to them, knowing I have flesh and blood standing here before me now? You and your son are the last of our ancestral line."

I bend over to hug her and whisper in her ear, "Because they loved and cared for you when your only family abandoned you."

Aunt Gorawen sniffs as I pull away. "Will you desert me as well?"

"I won't forget about you," I say, wiping her face with a tissue. "I must go home. But I'll stay in touch...I promise. I am not my mother, and I'm not afraid. I will prepare for the coming of the Tuatha Dé and be ready to do what I must. With your tutelage, of course."

"Yes. We will make sure of it if it's the last meaningful task of my life I complete."

"Besides, could you see me on a sheep farm?"

She laughs and pats my hand. "Not likely. Well, let's practice. Time floats away like a feather in the wind."

For the next hour, we practice many avenues to foster successful connections. I focus my intentions using crystals, stones, and even the surface of the water while burning various incense oils and herbs to enhance my concentration. Aunt Gorawen's magical hand flits back and forth between the room and the conservatory, bringing us fresh herbs to grind and burn. Not too long ago, I would have freaked out at the sight.

I break out in a sweat, rip off my hoodie, and pull on the band of my turtleneck. You'd think hot flashes would be glorious in the winter, but they only make dressing complicated—freezing one minute and sweltering the next. My brain is about to burst when Aunt Gorawen suggests we take a break for lunch. We eat the sandwiches Ellie brought except I pick out the slices of lamb.

When we return to her magic room next to the conservatory, my aunt points to the canvas of my mom resting on the back of the worktable. "It's time."

"Time for what?"

"To meet your ancestors."

I gaze at the painting of my mother and grin from ear to ear. "Yes. Let's do it."

Aunt Gorawen removes excess items from the table—unused herbs, the crystal ball, tarot cards, and candles. I help her place them on a nearby shelf. I don't possess the apprehension I once had when practicing ancestral divination with Archie. My aunt's support provides the confidence I need to attack this head-on. She gestures for me to pick up the obsidian crystals while she sits in a rustic pine chair.

"Gaze upon your mam in the picture, but do not call on your parents. I want you to reach as far back as you can. Focus on your intention and invite our ancestors to visit you—for the first time."

I rub the palm of my hand and grind my teeth. "I wasn't scared until you said that."

"They are your ancestors, Gwynedd. They will welcome you with open arms and a warm heart."

"Then I'm ready to meet them. My entire life, I had no extended family. I wish my mom had been brave enough to return to Wales at least once...so I could have met you sooner."

Aunt Gorawen lowers her head. "I'm not sure I would have been receptive. But you, my niece, are procrastinating."

She chuckles and points at the painting. I cup the shiny, black crystals in my hands and send my laser-eye focus into the painting while anise oil incense permeates the air. As I inhale the aroma deep into my lungs, I appeal to my ancient ancestors using a strong intention of respect. The oil painting becomes fluid-like. Paint swirls on the canvas like a snake, as if a brush is guiding the way. The weathered face of an old man with long white hair and an epic beard protrudes from the painting.

"Who are you?" I ask in a breathy voice. "From what time do you visit me? I seek your guidance."

Excitement captures my sensibility, and I offer a hand to make contact. His face contorts into a hideous scowl, and his hand protrudes from the picture, shoving me away. My body flies back in slow motion as I struggle to grasp onto the air to stop my fall. And bam! My ass hits the stone floor of the magic room, and the crystals scatter.

"Ow! What the hell? Who was he?"

Aunt Gorawen chuckles. "That would be Gruffudd. He doesn't appreciate being bothered. Are you hurt?"

"No kidding," I say, rubbing my bruised ass. "I'm fine. I've injured my butt before. You said they'd want to meet me?"

"Well, not Gruffudd. I didn't expect you to reach so far into the abyss of our lineage. He's a thousand years back. But that's excellent, Gwynedd. Now, set your intention only a few hundred years ago."

I pick up my sore ass and head back to the table, snatching the chipped crystals on the way. Determined to connect with more distant relatives, I adjust my intention accordingly. I meet Angharad, a spinner of cloth, Owain, a warrior for the Welsh princes, Eres, a lady of the court, and so many more. After thirty minutes of introductions, I pull up a chair next to my aunt and collapse onto its hard surface, moaning.

"I need a break. My head is dizzy from the concentration."

"I imagine so," Aunt Gorawen says, tapping my leg. "Seeking conference with one's ancestors requires much energy. Take a moment to regenerate. Breathe. And then we'll seek a conference together—from your more recent past."

Regret wets my aunt's eyes, and I realize what she means. I guess she never tried to reach Mom through ancestral divination, because she believed my mom was still alive. Am I even ready for this confrontation? My stomach tightens.

"Are you sure you want to conference with her?"

She nods. "Yes. It's time I bury the pain."

"We'll seek a conference with her together, then."

I stand and help my aunt out of her seat, and we gaze at my mom's youthful face in the painting as we caress the crystals in our grasp.

"Shouldn't we have something personal of my mom's?" I ask.

Aunt Gorawen limps with her cane to the shelf and grabs the family grimoire, placing it on the table in front of the painting. She flips to a page with my mom's handwriting.

"We have all we need. Her entries are the last in the spell book. Let's lay a hand on the entry while we draw power from the crystal in the other."

After several attempts, she summons her witch energy, which sparks a glow from my hand. My mother's face morphs into a golden-yellow image projecting from the surface. She smiles when she recognizes me, but the expression fades when she sees our aunt.

"Oh, Aunt Gorawen." The vision of my mom floats in silence for a moment as she gazes at her aunt. She speaks in her familiar northern Welsh accent, "It has been so long. I hoped to visit you in Wales one day when I was sure Gwynedd was safe. That day never came to pass. I am so sorry."

Tears roll down Aunt Gorawen's face. "I spent many years wrought with worry over your welfare. But I am so overjoyed to talk to you. We don't have time to dwell on the past now. We must discuss Gwynedd's future. A Tuatha Dé male has appeared to Gwynedd twice by sensing her thoughts and her use of magic."

"Oh, Gwynedd, I failed you," Mom says.

"No. You didn't. If Leslie hadn't come after me, using my best friend to lure me into the coven, I would have continued on with my boring life devoid of magic. Both you and Dad did your best. My life is so much fuller. Richard turned out to be a disappointment, but I'm loved by a wonderful man. You have a smart and handsome grandson named Tyler, who also knows he's a witch. The Fellowship is full of caring and devoted witches who care for me like family. I have a magical existence now, and I embrace it."

Mom smiles and extends a hand with glimmering fingers of golden-yellow. My fingertips radiate with an amber glow as her energy connects with them, and Aunt Gorawen joins her knobby fingers to our witch energy. The intense bond overtakes my body, causing every muscle to contract. I break out in the hot flash of the century with sweat trickling down the sides of my face, but I don't care. I've never experienced such closeness with another being, not even Archie. Then Mom pulls her hand back.

"Lowri, I have told Gwynedd about the devious behavior of the Tuatha Dé Danann, and I'll share all that I know before she leaves—information you did not care to learn." My aunt presses her lips together into an expression of I-told-you-so. "But no matter, I will make sure she has the knowledge to detect and defeat this evil fairy who lays claim to her."

"Thank you, Aunt Gorawen. I should have trusted you, but I was young and scared. Although I brushed off the tale as hogwash for many years, Rhys and I decided we should withdraw from magic to keep her safe. Gwynedd, I hope to conference with my grandson one day. Your father is with me. He wants to speak with you."

Dad emerges, displaying a youthful, clean-shaven face, and my heart pounds with an overwhelming euphoria. "Dad? How I miss you. Your cheerful smile always gave me the will to face each day."

"Gwynedd, I'm elated to see you," he says in a soft Welsh accent. "You've done well to achieve this conference with your mother and me. I hope it's the first of many we will have."

"Aunt Gorawen helped me, but I plan to continue this work when I return home." I offer my hand, but Dad doesn't seem to notice.

"Take care, daughter. And protect yourself by any means. Your mother and I will be here whenever you need us."

Mom's and Dad's images fade, disappearing into tiny particles of golden-yellow.

"Aw, shit," I say, wiping the sweat from my face.

My aunt grins at me, exposing her crooked, yellowed teeth. "You did well, niece."

"But I wanted to talk more. I have a lot to share with them."

"You can only do so much in the couple of days you're here. I think you should rest now. And tomorrow, go with your handsome professor and explore some of the region. We have some beautiful parks."

"But I want to spend time with you, too. I only have two more days before we leave for Scotland to visit Archie's family."

Aunt Gorawen's mouth explodes into a brilliant grin. "If I die tonight in my sleep, I will die a contented old woman."

"I'm so glad, but please, don't die in your bed tonight. I mean, how would I explain all this to Ellie?" My brow crinkles.

She chuckles. "I've thought about that many times. What should I do about my magic room? When I pass, they will find everything."

"You know, we've been talking about this very thing in my coven recently. Maybe there are times we should come clean about our witchcraft and the supernatural. You should tell her."

"Pfft. She would think I've entered the land of dementia." She chuckles and taps her cane on the floor. "But I could introduce her to my magic butler. That would convince her."

"True. I suspect it would scare the shit out of her, too," I chuckle. "We'll talk about that later. You're not going anywhere yet."

There's a knock on the door, and I assume Archie has arrived to pick me up. Aunt Gorawen collects a few items on the worktable and hobbles toward a shelf.

"Let me help you put the divination tools away, and you could join us for dinner."

"No, Gwynedd. Enjoy the remainder of the afternoon with your man. I've nothing else to do, and I have plenty of leftovers from your wonderful meal yesterday."

"OK." I lean down to hug her. "Thank you for everything."

"My duty and pleasure."

"Conferencing with my ancestors and talking to my parents today was the best. Watching Aunt Gorawen seek peace with my mom filled my heart. This day couldn't be more perfect," I say as the unforeseen sun warms my face.

Archie squeezes my hand. "Aye. How lucky we are the clouds cleared. Fine weather for an afternoon hike. It's truly wonderful your ancestral divination was so successful. But you haven't forgotten there's a murderous fairy hunting you, have you?"

"You had to bring him up?"

"One of us has to be realistic, no?"

"Well, he hasn't found me yet."

I stop and glance up at the skull on the sign. An impulse to try something new and exciting overcomes me.

"Why are we stopping?" he asks, eyeing the tattoo studio.

I stare at him with a look of you-can't-stop-me. "I want a tattoo."

"Why would you want to subject yourself to all that pain? And where did this idea come from? Certainly not your aunt."

I laugh and cringe a little at the advertisement with the tattoo gun. "No. My idea. It can't hurt as much as giving birth."

"Doubtful, but how would I know? Are you sure? You'll be stamped forever." He sighs and motions toward the door. "After you, my love."

The artist has a clean set-up and explains the entire process to me. He says he uses fresh ink and sterile single-use needles as he works his artistry on my left breast. I grit my teeth as the artist completes his work for the next hour. While I grip Archie's hand, I squeeze with every prick of the needle.

"I didn't think it would hurt this much. Was the pain bad when you got the tattoo on your butt?"

He laughs. "I don't know, Gwyn. I told you. I was so drunk, I woke up with the tattoo. My arse burned like fire after, though."

"The arse is a painful area to get inked," the talented artist says. "And then you can't sit on your bum."

"As I remember, the next few days were miserable. Carried a pillow with me everywhere."

The artist lathers antibiotic ointment over my small but significant tattoo and places an adhesive bandage over it. "You're all done, miss. Come back tomorrow, and I'll check on it."

"Thank you," I say, beaming with pride.

Forever, I will gaze at the red dragon on my left breast and cherish the memories of my parents, Aunt Gorawen, and Wales. But will the symbol of my family's homeland provide protection against the fairy who seeks revenge?

# CHAPTER EIGHT

# HERE, KITTY-KITTY

A SPLASH OF LIGHT shines through the doorway, illuminating Nick's face as he caresses my cheek. He kisses my neck and brushes a hand across my nipple, prompting goosebumps on my skin and a warm sensation between my thighs. I run my hands over his toned muscles and down to his...

My eyelids flip open, and I discover my PJs are damp from night sweats...and the dream. When I roll over, Archie is resting his head on a bulging arm, staring at me with those magnetic blue eyes. The outline of his toned pecs protrudes through his black V-neck tee. He collects my chestnut strands, smooths them out, then slides a finger across my chin.

"How long have you been awake?" I ask, stretching.

"A wee bit. You were exhausted, both mentally and physically. I didn't want to wake you. But your body shuddered in your sleep just now. A nightmare?"

I stroke the soft whiskers of his goatee but ignore his question. "I'm sorry I fell asleep so quickly. It was such an emotional day. But productive."

If I'd stayed awake long enough for sex, maybe I wouldn't have dreamed about Nick. I should have slept with the young assistant professor when I had the chance, and my mind would have purged him from my subconscious longings.

"Are you in much pain?" he asks, motioning to my breast. "You can probably remove the bandage now."

"It's sore, but not too bad." I unbutton my flannel top and remove the gauze. The skin is pink around the inked area.

"I wasn't too excited about you getting the tattoo, but I admit the dragon looks damn sexy on your breast."

He places a soft kiss near the red dragon, and I moan as he takes my nipple into his mouth. When I search for him under the covers, I find he's as rigid as a piece of timber. No wonder they call it morning wood. My hormones won't settle down, and I'm still horny as a rabbit from my dream.

"We should probably shower," I say, panting. "We're gonna miss breakfast."

Archie's lust-filled gaze falls to my breast. "I have plenty to nibble on right here."

The temperature of the room remains chilly from the night, so he crawls underneath the covers. I chuckle as he removes my flannel bottoms and panties, shoving them toward me.

"I can't see what you're doing under there. Only a big lump."

"You don't need to watch," he says, muffled by the blankets.

And then his warm mouth finds me, already wet from the dream and the nipple play. I'd forgotten how adept he is at oral sex...how his touch raises desire in every inch of my skin. I wrap my legs around his head, whining in pleasure, and cover my mouth with a hand. He increases his nibbling and teasing, finds me again, and clamps his mouth on me until I'm almost there.

When he finds my hand, he intertwines his fingers with mine, summoning his witch energy to intensify my ecstasy. Not wanting to give Mary more to gossip about, I grab a pillow and press it hard against my face, just in time. I scream lustily into the sex-cry silencer.

Archie's voice sounds distant with the pillow in place. "Gwyn, you're suffocating me."

"I'm sorry. My body responds with a mind of its own when you add your magic to the mix."

I lift the bed sheets, peer at him under the covers, and snicker. He laughs as he crawls up my torso, placing kisses on my abdomen and breasts before reaching my face.

"You put a lot more faith in that pillow than it provided."

"Oh, my gods." I chuckle, imagining Mary's amusement at my rapture. "Your face is so red, like you've got a sunburn."

"Aye. Rather warm down there under the quilt, but I don't mind. I love pleasing you." He kisses me deeply. "We should shower and forage for whatever crumbs remain from breakfast."

"Don't you want to finish?" I ask as a whiff of my scent passes my nose.

"I'm a little exhausted after all that work. You can repay me later."

He chuckles and pats me on the butt as I jump out of bed, and I slip on my robe and head toward the shower.

"It's so cold out here. Join me?"

Archie lies back on the pillows and clasps his hands behind his head. "That shower is barely big enough for one person, Gwyn. You go ahead, and I'll be in after. I want to rest a moment."

"I wore you out? I'm supposed to be the older woman."

"Well, you wear me out, stubborn woman." He winks at me. "Get a move on, so we can eat."

After we shower and dress for the chilly temperatures, we head downstairs to beg for leftovers from breakfast. A basket sits on the entry table at the bottom of the stairs with slices of bread, packaged cold cereal, and some fruit. Mary walks in from the back.

"I see you've found the breakfast basket," she says. "The other lodgers finished, so I had to clean up, but I didn't want you to go without. I figured you would need the replenishment after sleeping in. You must have been exhausted."

Mary attempts to suppress a laugh, but a chuckle breaks free. Archie and I snicker and avert our eyes. She's being so polite about our libidinous behavior. I bet we disturbed all the lodgers if she heard our antics during our stay. Even if the walls are made of thick plaster.

"Thank you so much, Mary. We appreciate it," I say.

"Where are you off to today?" Mary asks. "Visiting your aunt again?"

Archie replies, "We're off to the old castle in the forest. The one built by the Kingdom of Gwynedd. A strange place for a castle. I supposed Gwyn would have fun visiting her namesake."

Mary nods. "No doubt. Have a wonderful afternoon. I believe the sun may visit us today. But I'd still wear your wellies."

"Excellent advice. We'll carry our boots with us," he says.

The fifteen-minute drive to the country park takes us past several farms full of dark-green pastures and winter crops—separated by ditches and overgrown hedges. A few have cattle in addition to sheep. When we get to the park, we change into our all-weather boots.

"I'm not sure if this is a brilliant idea or not," I say, slipping my hands into my gloves. "Taking a hike in the winter through a forest to see the ruins of a castle isn't my idea of enjoying the Yule season."

"Humor me. I've wanted to visit these ruins for years but never had the time. And look...the sun is shining for once."

"I'm getting out. I didn't say I wasn't excited about it...only wish the temperature was warmer."

The sun peeks through the leafless ancient woodlands of oak, ash, and birch, warming us as we make our way to the castle. We trudge on the muddy trail along the brook and pass a clump of waterfalls, stopping to snap some photos with our phones. No other hikers have ventured out on this winter day, which allows us to enjoy this cool yet romantic adventure alone. The forest rests in hibernation except for squirrels playing on the ground and birds calling through the treetops. After a few more minutes, Archie stops abruptly and runs a hand through his wavy hair.

"I have to go back to the parking lot."

"Why?" I ask. "We're almost there."

"I'm fairly certain I forgot to lock the car, and I don't want to test the insurance coverage. Go ahead. I'll walk quickly."

"Ok. Don't take long." I kiss him and pat his butt.

He disappears at the bend in the trail where multiple tree limbs extend, inviting lone travelers. I plod through the dense woods and view an opening up ahead. When I step through, I behold the small-scale castle built by the Kingdom of Gwynedd. But the ruins still impress me. The structure has the shape of a D and a tower built of sandstone, which has weathered into a dingy gray over the centuries.

When I arrive at a set of steep stairs, I trek up in my boots, hoping I don't slip. When I reach the top of the battlements, I grab onto the metal guards and take in the 360-degree view. What an amazing sight. Archie will love this. Movement behind the castle near the trees catches my interest, and a bright light flashes through the branches.

I journey down the steps as quickly as I can. Considering the stone has worn so badly and ruts have formed, they are hardly up to code. I rush to the rear of the castle and venture toward the edge of the woods. The area has no evidence of fellow hikers, but I discover an enormous bump of earth between a set of trees. As I approach the compact hill, I examine an opening on one side, flanked by vast slabs of stone with a cap.

Suddenly, a bright yellow glow emerges, spilling out into the forest. I inch toward the aperture to inspect the wondrous element more closely—mesmerized by the radiance. A high-pitched vibration pierces my ears, and I press my fingertips against them. But it does nothing to stop the grating noise. When I've nearly arrived at the entrance, a low voice rumbles. "Come to me…"

A large cat-like creature appears except the feline is the size of a Dobermann and has a splash of white on its chest. The animal stands on its hind legs, roars like a panther, and leaps at me, knocking me to the ground.

"Aghhh!" I scream at the top of my lungs.

My shrieks reverberate throughout the empty forest as I shove at the gigantic feline. The unique cat lands on its paws, runs past me, and disappears into the woods. I sit up and gather my senses.

Archie yells in the distance. "Gwyn!"

I stare at the entrance to the hill and contemplate what transpired. What was the light that shone through the crevice of the grassy knoll? Was the odd animal a cat or another type of creature?

Archie arrives, panting, and checks my body for injuries. "Are you all right? What happened? Did you slip?"

"I'm OK. Only a little muddy." I inspect my clothes as I stand and scan the woods. "Didn't you see that big cat?"

"No. What cat?" He raises his eyebrows and surveys the forest.

"It's gone now, but I swear a giant cat as big as a Dobermann, or maybe even a small bear, pounced on me. And I fell. But something else happened, Archie. A flash of light grabbed my attention from the top of the castle battlements, and I ran down here to investigate. A yellow glow emanated from that hill over there, and I became transfixed by it. And a deep voice called for me."

"From where?" he asks as his brow furrows.

I turn and point at the large knoll between the trees, and Archie goggles at the grassy hump.

"It may have been a dog, but we need to get out of here, Gwyn. Now."

He grabs me by the hand, and we run in our boots, sinking into the mushy trail.

"I don't understand. What's wrong? Why are we rushing out of here? You didn't even climb the steps of the castle."

His mouth twitches, and his breathing becomes labored. "That wasn't a hill, my love. That was a mound...with a portal."

"Oh, fuck."

"Are you sure that was a large mound?" I ask Archie as Aunt Gorawen hands me the family grimoire.

"Aye," he says. "You've only seen the minuscule mound in the gardens at Mitchell Hall. And I had no idea it was there, or we wouldn't have visited the castle."

"What do we do? I was supposed to practice more ancestral divination tomorrow with Aunt Gorawen."

My aunt clasps my chilly hand. "I don't remember a mound on the grounds of the castle, but I've not been for years. Tell me about this small one in your town?"

"Many years ago, when my mom and two other local witches tried to cast a fertility spell, the mound formed instead. I've searched the family grimoire for a spell to eliminate the portal but didn't find one. An assistant professor at Delaware University at Bearsden knows Welsh and translated the incantations for me."

"You take risks like Lowri. Gwynedd, your safety matters more than anything to me. We'll save the practice for another visit once the danger has passed. And when you return to Bearsden, concentrate on closing the portal."

"Listen to your aunt," Archie says. "There's no more time. I'm sorry. We must pack and leave. I'm thinking we should even change our flights and return home now."

"We can't do that. You haven't seen your family in over a year. Are there any big mounds near Edinburgh?" I ask.

"No, but I worry about remaining here. We don't have my family's dirk with us."

Aunt Gorawen's worried eyes flip back and forth between Archie and me. As she gazes at me with the deepest love and affection, she addresses Archie.

"Once you've left the area, I believe Gwynedd will be safe...for a time. You should go now to Edinburgh and visit your family, Dr. Cockburn. You don't want to experience regret when you're my age. Go visit your family while you're able."

He smiles at her. "Thank you for your prudent advice, Ms. Thomas. You're a wise woman."

"But before you take leave of me, I must share more of what I know concerning the fairy who hunts for you—warnings passed down by our ancestors." Aunt Gorawen clasps my hand. "I already shared with you how crafty this race of beings can be. You could prepare yourself...question everything around you. Even so, he may find you. But there are clues to beware of. If he presents himself in human form, he may attempt to win you over. Even try to win your love."

"Well, there's no chance of that," I say.

"I see that," my aunt says. "But he may not come after you for years. He's seeking you out through the mounds. That's for certain. But he has to find you first. As much as you love this man, you may not be together when the Tuatha Dé discovers your whereabouts."

Part of me knows she's accurate, but I can't imagine not being with Archie. He's devoted to me, and I love him with all my heart.

"What should I watch out for? How will I recognize him when he finds me?"

"It's difficult to pinpoint," Aunt Gorawen says as her head tremors. "The warnings aren't clear. The best translation says to seek your innermost feelings. Use your intuition. If you sense discomfort, stop what you're doing and flee. I'm sorry I can't tell you more, niece."

I caress her arm. "You have done so much for me. I wish there were a way to repay you somehow."

"Having you here is more than I could have hoped for. I want to give you something...two things." She pulls out a choker made with black crystal pieces. "I made this necklace of tourmaline, which is enriched with manganese and iron. The crystals will cause discomfort in your enemy. Wear it always for protection."

"And the second item?" I ask.

My aunt shifts close and wraps her arms around me, embracing me in a hug, but I sense more in the embrace.

"I'm giving you a cwtch. It's more than a hug or a cuddle. There is no English translation for the word. A cwtch embodies the family—a safe place." She steps back. "So, when you think of me, dear niece, remember the way you felt when I gave you this cwtch, and you will be in your safe place."

While I hug her one last time, I tear up. "I will remember." I realize this may be the last time I ever see her, and my insides ache.

"We better get going," Archie says. "We have to pack and check out of the lodging. Ms. Thomas, I can't thank you enough for all your help."

"Croeso, Dr. Cockburn," she says. "May your journey be uneventful."

"Aunt Gorawen..." The words refuse to fall from my tongue.

"No goodbyes, Gwynedd. We will speak again. In this world or the next." She grins and gestures to her magic butler to open the door. "May the gods be with you."

"I will keep in touch. I promise you."

"Go now! And be safe."

She waves goodbye and shuts the door behind us while an emptiness takes hold inside. Ellie is walking up the street as we're preparing to depart. She stops by the car.

"Are you leaving?" she asks, tugging at her gloves.

I'm not sure how to answer. "Yes. We had a…"

"Family emergency," Archie says. "We have to leave for Scotland."

"Oh, I'm very sorry to hear that." Although her face relays a contrary feeling.

"Ellie, I want you to know I spoke with my aunt about the will. She's not changing anything. What would I do with a sheep farm? And this isn't my home." My eyes roam across the front of the stone house. "I told her you and your husband earned this. But I am going to ask you for a favor."

A tentative smile curls her mouth. "Thank you, Ms. Crowther. What sort of favor?"

"I'd like to chat with Aunt Gorawen once in a while. Could you buy her a laptop computer or a data phone…or both? Set things up so we can chat online? I want to keep in touch with her."

Ellie grins widely as she nods. "Of course. I can arrange for her to talk with you…anytime you want. We care for her very much, Ms. Crowther, and want the best for her in her final years."

"Thank you." I hand her my contact information and drop into the car seat.

As we drive off, Ellie waves goodbye, smiling. I crack up at the sight behind her—Aunt Gorawen smiling through the front window and her magical butler floating above her head, waving goodbye.

# CHAPTER NINE

# THE COCKBURNS OF EDINBURGH

THE JOURNEY TO SCOTLAND seems to drag on like a never-ending trip into a dark abyss. We catch the M6, and except for a stop for dinner in Preston, Archie drives with determination to get us as far from Buckley as possible. The travel through miles of farmland with only the light from other vehicles has a numbing effect as I stare out the window of the car. The road changes to the A74 and soon after, a blue and white sign reads: Welcome to Scotland.

"Why don't you try to nap, Gwyn," Archie says. "We have a couple more hours before we arrive in Edinburgh."

"I'm too wound up to nap. As you would say, I'm gutted about leaving Aunt Gorawen in such a rush. Besides, it would mess with my sleep. As if I could sleep now."

He rubs my hand. "Your aunt could very well be right. The Tuatha Dé male may not find you for years. You'll have to live your life aware of the threat."

"Oh, joy. How am I supposed to do that? I either pretend there's no threat and leave myself open to capture, or I stress about it day after day until I stroke out."

I spread my fingers in the air and growl like a bear. Archie laughs at me and puts his hand back on the steering wheel.

"Well, I sincerely doubt the fairy would want you if you stroked out, but it's a solid strategy."

"You think you're funny. My blood pressure is probably sky high. And I can sense a hot flash coming on." I strip off my sweater, throw it into the backseat, and turn on the AC.

"Bloody hell, Gwyn. It's January in Scotland."

He turns all the vents toward me, and the icy air blows my long hair and a wisp of bangs off my face. In about five minutes, I'll likely grab my sweater again.

"Ahhh. I'll turn the AC off in a minute. I only need a *wee* bit of chill."

"And when we get to the hotel, you'll be complaining the temperature isn't warm enough."

"You wanted this old witchy woman. I come with raging hormones, heat fluctuations, night sweats, and a bitchy, stubborn demeanor. Wanna trade me in for a new model?"

"Not for all the magic in the world," he says, kneading my hand.

I caress his warm skin. "I love you, Dr. Cockburn. Thank you for putting up with me and all my troubles."

"Nonsense. My life was meaningless before you fell into it...literally. Several times."

"Yes. I remember. I was a bit of a klutz then."

A smile sneaks onto my face as I recall the first time he ignited my magic at the end of class, making me so dizzy, I had to clutch the edge of the table. Falling at the Old Men oak trees and tripping on the woodpile at his house followed soon after. It seems like a decade ago. And now I'm a skilled ancestral witch, with a vengeful fairy stalking me.

"Did you send a message to Tyler about the encounters you had here?" he asks.

"No. He'll only worry about me until I get home. I'm safe for now."

"Probably best. I should warn you about my family. They can be overwhelming to outsiders. They're typical Scots...welcoming to foreigners. Friendly and extremely caring for those in need. Loyal as an old dog. But...they can be judgmental and opinionated."

I chuckle. "We should get along very well, then?"

Archie's eyebrows fall into his eyes. "We shall see."

As we drive close to Old Town, Edinburgh, I'm taken aback by the castle atop the hill. Bright lights shine on the magnificent building, irradiating the walls in an orangey-yellow glow. The city has less traffic since it's close to midnight, but the streets bustle with the energy of the holiday season and the regular nightlife of pubs. I'm ready to collapse into a firm bed when we arrive at our American hotel, but I wait in the car while Archie checks us in. I peer at him through droopy eyes as he gets in the driver's seat.

"Please, tell me we have a top floor with a fabulous view of the castle. It's enchanting."

"No," he says, scowling. "We have no room."

"What? But you booked one, didn't you? I heard you make the reservation on the phone."

"Aye. I did." He brushes a hand through his ash-blond locks and exhales. A text notification sounds on his cell phone, and he rubs his goatee as he reads it. "My brother Quinn called and canceled the reservation."

"Why would he do that? Where will we stay now?"

"He wants us to stay with him at the family home."

"Oh. That doesn't sound awful. I figured you booked a hotel, because they didn't have room for us. You said he has a lot of kids, and your dad lives with them. Do they have room for us?"

"Aye. There's room. I only thought we'd have more privacy staying at a hotel." He stares out the car window, folds of wrinkles clutching his face. "They've gone to bed, so no introductions tonight."

I rub his shoulder. "It's only for a few days. They're family. And you haven't seen them for a long time. Of course, they want you to stay. Can we go now? I'm gonna pass out."

Archie pulls out of the parking lot. We drive away from Edinburgh Castle through an area called the West End, which has gorgeous Georgian townhomes built with sandstone. I can only guess how much they're worth. He pulls off the road and parks the car in front of one.

"Why are you stopping here?" I ask. "Did you leave something at the hotel desk?"

He scratches his goatee as he stares at me. "We're here."

"No way." I gaze up at the impressive four-story home, and it dawns on me. "Your family has money?"

"Aye. I didn't know how to tell you as I'm a wee embarrassed by the wealth. I prefer to live a simple life."

"And you believed you could hide this from me somehow? I don't care. Well, I care if there's a nice, firm bed for me to crash in. I assume they have an extra room, then."

"Aye. My bedroom. Quinn took over the home when he got married but kept my room intact."

What a stupid question that was. The house has enough rooms to host a weekend party—a fancy one paying a pianist to perform during the cocktail hour.

"Fantastic. Let's go in, or I'll collapse right here in this seat."

When I get out of the car, I marvel at the magnificent home. I follow Archie up the steps to a wooden door supporting a sunburst window above, and he turns the key. We enter the ground level into a foyer with stone tile and thick white molding around the ceiling. Ornate plaster detail decorates the high ceiling above. A huge wreath made from pine sprigs and pine cones hangs over a white fireplace on the left wall. A pine garland adorns the arched doorway into the hallway.

I peek into the kitchen and figure the ground floor must have sixteen-foot high ceilings, and the cornices are nearly two feet wide. The headers above the doors are at least a foot. Painting this house must take weeks, but I doubt they do it themselves. The walls are painted a neutral color, and the cabinets and furniture are modern in style, which is surprising for such an old home. Ten chairs sit around a long industrial wood and metal dining table. I can't imagine how big the formal dining room table must be.

"Damn, Archie," I say. "It's like a museum in here."

"Aye. I didn't care for the house much growing up. And the atmosphere became more sterile after Quinn took over and completed the renovations. The home lost its original character. I preferred the historical furniture my mum and dad had furnished the home with. The stairway is in the back."

He points to a turned wood and iron stairway at the end of the hallway. As we drag our luggage up the steps, I examine the stairs leading to the lower level below, which is exposed to the outside by a dugout around the outside of the house. The second floor has its own living area, but the other doors probably lead to bedrooms. We reach the top floor, which has a large open area with a couple of oversized chairs, a desk, and an entire wall of antiquarian books. The ceiling heights are more modest. There are three doors leading to more bedrooms, I assume.

"My room is through there," Archie says, gesturing toward the last door.

A dark-wood canopy bed rests against a wide wall, flanked by nightstands on either side. The chest of drawers sits centered on another between two massive windows, and a long sofa watches over a stone fireplace stained with years of soot. A built-in wall-length wardrobe takes the place of a closet, and there's a connecting bathroom through a door on the right.

I chuckle. "So, were you like Cinderella? Did they banish you to the attic?"

"Nah. I asked to sleep up here for the view."

He motions me to come to the window. I face the glass, and he wraps his comforting arms around me. In the distance, Edinburgh Castle is radiating its orangey glow and lighting up the sky.

"Wow. No wonder. It's a view to spark dreams of enchantment."

"Aye, and it did. Every time I gazed out this window at the castle, I would plot my escape from this household."

I glance over my shoulder at him and grimace. "I wouldn't exactly call this house a prison. Your childhood couldn't have been so bad."

"You're right. Why would I ever want to leave a home like this?" He raises his eyebrows. "Let's get changed and get to sleep. Tomorrow will be a challenging day."

We get dressed, brush our teeth, and climb into the antique bed. Archie kisses me goodnight and rolls over, surrendering to sleep in minutes. Yet I lie on my back with my knees bent, staring at the canopy above me. As exhausted as I am, the voice of the Tuatha Dé fairy rings in my head, and I can't push the memory of the dog-sized black cat out of my brain.

*"I know where you are, Gwynedd Crowther. And I'm coming for you."* The guttural voice of my foe wakes me from a deep slumber.

I sit up with my chest exploding from tachycardia and grab my flannel top to discover the material is damp—another night sweat. The sun barely peeks through the window shutters, but I'm too strung out to go back to sleep. Archie hasn't moved all night, and his chest rises and falls like the ebb and flow of slow-moving tides. I'd kill to snooze like him. I run to the bathroom to pee and snatch the plush white robe hanging on a hook. As I make my way down to the ground floor, the morning noises of a rising family fill the hallways—running water of showers, flushing of toilets, and slamming of doors.

I go downstairs and enter the spacious kitchen. A woman with wavy ginger hair who appears to be in her late 40s putters around the stove in a robe and apron, preparing to cook breakfast. When she turns around to grab a carton of eggs from the immense island, she notices me and grins. She wipes her hands on a kitchen towel and walks over to me. Her handshake is warm and welcoming.

"Ah, you must be Archie's lady friend," she says in a light Scottish accent. "My name is Margaret, but everyone calls me Maggie." She has a fair complexion and friendly blue eyes the color of sparkling sapphires.

"Mine is Gwynedd Crowther, but most people call me Gwyn. So nice to meet you. Archie is dead to the world. I've had trouble sleeping recently, and jet lag didn't help. Menopause adds fuel to the mix. Can I help with breakfast?"

"You're our guest. Find yourself a seat and relax." She breaks eggs in a pan and throws sausages into another. "Night sweats?"

"Yeah. The hot flashes come and go, but the night sweats have taken up permanent residence."

"Aye. They are the worst. In the winter, I freeze and wear a flannel nightgown to bed. By the morning, I'm stripped down to my knickers. But Quinn usually doesn't mind."

She snickers, flips an egg, and turns on the burner under a teakettle. A tall, stocky man in his early 50s shuffles into the kitchen in gray pajamas, a red plaid robe, and slippers. His thick brown hair has gray at the temples, and his blue eyes resemble a shade of steel.

"You must be Gwynedd," he says, in a thick Scottish brogue. "Archie has spoken about you many times in our online chats. I'm his brother Quinn. It's wonderful to meet you finally." He extends his hand, grinning.

"I'm excited to be here," I say as he wraps his fingers around mine. "Thank you for putting us up."

"Nonsense. I don't know why Archie insisted on booking a hotel. He knows I'd cancel the reservation, anyway." He laughs and pulls out a few teacups from a cabinet. "Och, Maggie! Did you not offer the woman a cuppa?"

"I would have gotten around to it. Do I look like I'm not busy, Mr. Cockburn?"

"I'm messing with you, love. I'll prepare some tea."

Quinn kisses Maggie on the cheek and pats her on the back. He pours steaming hot water into three cups over tea bags and brings two of them to the long table where I'm sitting.

"Thank you. It smells wonderful." I sweeten my tea and take a sip.

An older man in his late 70s with thick gray hair and the same steel-blue eyes ambles in, clopping like a horse in his slippers. His navy-blue PJs and robe blend into the perfect ensemble. When he speaks, I can barely understand what he's saying because of his heavier Scottish brogue.

"Och, Maggie. Those sausage links traveled up the stairs and handed me a personal invitation to breakfast." He cocks his head and squints at me. "Is someone going to introduce me to this strange woman sitting at our kitchen table?"

"I'm Gwynedd Crowther," I say, offering my hand. "You must be Archie's dad. Harris, right? It's a pleasure to meet you."

Harris wraps his burly fingers around mine and moves his arm slowly. "Aye. You're different from the other women Archie has brought here to the house. You're a Yank—and old."

I'm taken aback by his comments, and I'm sure my wandering eyes give me away. Archie rushes into the kitchen, panting, as if he ran down from the top floor. He recognizes my expression.

"I see you've met everyone, Gwyn. What are we talking about?"

I force myself to smile and talk through clenched teeth. "About my age, apparently."

"Gwyn is a brilliant woman, Dad. And a skilled ancestral witch. I'm a lucky man." He winks at me, and I blush.

"Och. We shall see about that." Harris turns to address his son. "You haven't visited for over a year, and I don't deserve a proper greeting?"

Archie approaches his father and gives him an awkward hug. "It's good to see you, Dad. You haven't changed. You're looking fit as ever."

"Come over here and give me one, too, ya wee bawbag," Quinn says.

Archie chuckles and hugs his brother, patting him on the back. "I missed you as well. And you, too, Maggie." He wraps an arm around her.

"Chuffed to have you here, Archie. And there's nothing wrong with being middle-aged, Harris." She stares him down, pointing with a spatula.

"What other discussions have I missed?" Archie asks as he kisses me on my temple.

"Och, nothing," Quinn says as he sets plates on the table. "We didn't have time to embarrass you with childhood stories yet." He snickers and walks back to the counter.

Archie peers at me and takes a breath. "That's a relief. Isn't Isla home from college? She must have graduated?"

"Aye. She's still in bed," Harris says. "Graduated at the top of her class, but she needs to hunt for employment. These young people think the job will drop in their laps."

Maggie places large serving platters on the table holding eggs, sausage, bacon, beans, and mushrooms. She retrieves a bowl of fruit from the fridge and adds it to the buffet of food.

"Isla is our youngest," she says. "Finished college early only a few days ago. Our other four offspring you'll meet tonight at dinner. Serve yourself, men. I'm not your maid."

"Oh, you have five children?" I ask, filling my plate with eggs and beans.

Harris pats Quinn on the back. "Aye. He's done a fine job replenishing the ancestral witch line. At least one of my sons has fulfilled his duties."

Archie lowers his eyes while he fills his plate with eggs and sausage. "Aye, Dad. We all know how well Quinn has procreated."

"A set of fraternal twins helped," Maggie says. "They were quite unexpected."

"I only have one son named Tyler. His last name is Wolfe, after his father. My husband, Richard, didn't want more children." I cringe, mentioning my dead, cheating husband, but it's not like I can pretend he didn't exist.

"You'll have to show me pictures later, Gwynedd," Maggie says, joining us at the table.

The sound of slippers on the tile echoes in the hallway, and a young woman with wild ginger hair like her mother's shuffles in glued to her cell phone. She's wearing hot pink flannel pajamas and gigantic bunny slippers with floppy ears. When she lifts her eyes from her phone and notices Archie sitting at the kitchen table, she screams and runs to him.

"Uncle Aaarchie!" She wraps her arms around him, sees me across the table from him, and squints. "Is this your new girlfriend?"

"Aye. This is Gwynedd Crowther," he says, a proud smile brightening his face. "Gwyn, meet Isla, my favorite niece."

"I'm your only niece, you arse," she says.

"Nice to meet you." I grin widely, causing my laugh lines to fan out.

She goggles at me. "You're fawking old."

# CHAPTER TEN

# FAMILY DINNERS ARE FUN, RIGHT?

To give me a break from the family judicial committee, Archie suggests we do some sightseeing in the afternoon. The temperature hangs in the upper 30s, but at least it's not raining. I'm ecstatic to get out of the house. The Cockburns are lovely, exuberant people who are extremely opinionated, and I have a difficult time biting my tongue around them. It's the holidays and Archie hasn't seen them for so long. No reason to rock the boat on this trip. I want them to like me.

"I apologize for my father and Isla's insulting remarks," Archie says, grasping my gloved hand. "I don't believe they were upset about your age—only shocked. The women I brought to the house a few years ago were..."

"Extremely young?" I ask in a snarky tone of voice. "Yes. We all know your dating leaned toward younger women."

"There was a reason for that, Gwyn. All my life, my father pounded into our heads the need to carry on the ancestral line, so I dated witches who could provide the option. I cared deeply for many of the women but never developed a love for them. I felt trapped in a predetermined existence as a child, and the situation worsened when I became of age."

"So, you escaped to London to earn your doctorate? Were you hoping to dodge the bullets completely by moving to the States?"

"Aye. I imagine. But the words of my father followed me there and to Delaware. Then I met you that day in the classroom when I subbed for Leslie. It was my job to recruit you, but it never occurred to me you'd capture my heart."

"This visit has helped me understand who you are a little more. Despite your family's behavior, I'm so glad we came here."

"Aye. I'm chuffed for you to meet them." He kisses me, and his lips warm my chilly face. "I only hope you can survive the next few days before we leave."

I chuckle and nudge him. "I can always hide in the attic."

We take a walk in Old Town on the Royal Mile, a cobbled street that connects Edinburgh Castle on one end to the Palace of Holyroodhouse at the other. A mix of shops, restaurants, muse-ums, churches, and pubs, of course, line the street along with the unusual modern Scottish Parliament near the palace. Constructed of stone, many of the buildings have five or six stories, and some date back to the medieval period. I snap a few pictures and send them to Tyler and Ronnie. When we retrace our steps to the castle, I recognize a name on a street sign to the right—Cockburn. And I point.

Archie arches his eyebrows. "A different faction of Cockburns. But there are many unique shops. The street curves like a snake. Why don't we save it for another day? We should tour the castle before we miss the last entry time at four."

"I'm so excited. I've never toured a castle before. Old Town was so impressive. More Americans should visit the UK. The history is amazing. I understand why my parents never returned to Wales, but a part of me feels cheated out of my heritage and visiting cities like this...you know?"

"I have to admit I missed walking in Old Town. Edinburgh is one of the oldest cities in Europe. But areas of the United States have their charm, too."

We enter the grounds of Edinburgh Castle and show the tickets Archie purchased online, the last two available. The massive structure sits atop a hill, and the view of the city is magnificent, even on this wintry day. When we move to the Great Hall, I gasp at the dark wood beams above. The walls have ornate wood wainscoting on the bottom and red paint above. Swords and Lochaber axes line the walls and decorate the area above an enormous carved stone fireplace with knights' armor guarding on each side. I wish all these tourists weren't blocking my view, though. The room is so packed I can barely catch a glimpse of the weaponry.

"The tea we drank is going right through me," I say, shaking my leg. "I've got to find the bathrooms."

Archie chuckles. "I'm shocked, I tell you. Shocked."

"Oh, fuck you," I whisper, smirking.

A cocky smile erupts on his face. "I certainly hope so."

I smack Archie playfully and exit the Great Hall, searching for the *loo* all the way back to the ticket area. Once I've relieved myself, I meander through the castle grounds to meet him at the Crown Square. As I shove through the hordes of tourists, I recognize a face in the distance—a man with an oblong face and long black hair. I freeze as adrenalin pumps through my veins, sending my heart into overdrive. My head turns for a split second to search for the stranger while the invading tourists obscure my view. He's disappeared.

I push through the crowd to get a better view of him, but when I get to where he was standing, he's gone. I puff white mist into the air while I examine the area. He's not anywhere. A migraine stabs my brain like an icepick, so I rub my temples and continue back to meet Archie.

"Ugh. I swear he was the same creep who stared at me in the Buckley town center. Or he was someone who resembled him. I'm so tired, I don't know how I'll make it through dinner."

Archie rubs my back through my coat. "Interesting. We need to get back, anyway. Maggie will serve dinner soon enough."

As we exit the castle grounds, I sift through the multitude of faces and sigh. The fatigue is affecting me so badly, now I'm imagining things. Damn these migraines.

My head pounds as if a Welsh brownie hammers behind my eyes, trying to burst every capillary. We've gathered at the formal dining table to celebrate the family's Yule dinner. Quinn and Maggie's adult children are friendly and personable, but they talk in two volumes—loud and ear-splitting. The eldest, called Quinny after his dad, is thirty years old. Fraternal twins Finlay and Fergus are twenty-eight. Harris, named after his grandfather, turned twenty-five a month ago. And Isla turned twenty-two the month before. All of them have the coloring of Quinn except Isla, who takes after Maggie. Excluding Archie's ginger-haired niece, they've brought significant others with them—all of them witches.

With my brain exploding, I have difficulty following any one conversation as the family and guests babble on about politics in the local coven, new magic spells, and Hogmanay, the Scottish celebration on New Year's Eve. It's utter chaos. A bottle of Scotch whisky hovers and meanders around us, filling glasses. I put my hand over mine. My migraine doesn't need fuel. Each of them uses magic to retrieve their food, except Archie, and my head spins as bread rolls fly in various directions over the table to their plates. Maggie sends a bulbous stuffed mystery meal flying in my direction, and I watch the ball of sustenance land on my dish.

I lean over to Archie, whispering, "What is this?"

"It's haggis, a Scottish dish. But you don't have to eat it."

"What's in it? Is it dead at least?"

He chuckles. "Yes. It contains sheep's pluck. The inner organs like the heart and liver. I forgot to mention you're a vegetarian. I'm sorry. There are vegetables. Pass on the haggis and enjoy the rest of the meal."

"I can't do that. It would be rude."

I stare down at the round ball full of sheep innards, and nausea settles in my stomach. After loading my plate with mashed potatoes and turnips, I force myself to insert a small portion of the animal's insides. And I swallow. My face flushes as the words ring in my head. *Please, don't vomit.*

About twenty minutes have passed, and Harris throws up a firecracker of magic into the air, illuminating the dining room with a splatter of color. The prattle dissipates. "Since Archie is here, why don't we reminisce?"

"Here we go," Archie mutters. He puts a piece of haggis in his mouth and chews deliberately.


"What do you mean?" I ask under my breath.

"I remember when Archie was a young teen, pudgy as a piggy he was then, and visited the loch down in the park. He came back and told us he saw a Bean Nighe. Said he was so scared, he fell into the loch." Harris bursts out laughing. "Came home soaked from his head to his shoes."

Quinn chimes in, pointing with a knife. "Och. That's what he said. But I'd always bet a few quid he pissed himself."

The laughter at the table increases, and Archie turns beat red in the face. I'm barely holding down the haggis, and drips of sweat sprout on my upper lip while my head continues to throb.

"Is that true, Uncle Archie?" Isla asks. "Were you afraid of a Bean Nighe?"

Archie doesn't answer her, choosing to stuff his mouth with turnips instead.

Harris continues with his tales of "Let's embarrass Archie." "But he worked off that fat and grew into a strapping man. What I can't figure out is why you're forty-five years old and still not got a wife. The gods know you brought home many witches who were fine candidates for continuing the line."

Archie glares at his father as his icy blues flare but remains silent. As I shove mashed potatoes into my mouth, an aura burns its way up through my chest, recognizing I'm not one of those "fine candidates." I fan my face, flapping a hand.

"Och, Dad," Quinn says, setting his whisky glass on the table. "Let it be."

Harris sends a bolt of magic at the ceiling, which breaks a bulb in a pocket light, and everyone gasps at the falling glass. The family and guests pick the shards off their plates as he continues to rant.

"No, I will not. He still has the viability and virility to produce heirs, yet he brings home this old woman who provides what? Certainly, no opportunities for children."

My eyebrows leap toward the ceiling as I turn toward Archie. He's grinding his teeth back and forth, but says nothing. While his chest rises and falls in erratic intervals, he huffs like a bull ready to charge. The family and guests shovel food in their mouths, sip Scotch whisky, and stare at their dinner plates, occasionally peeking at the head of the table.

"She barely says a word other than boring pleasantries," Harris says, glaring at me with his steely eyes. "A typical old Yank woman. And she cowers like the *unknowing*, hiding her magic among us. She's the reason you've not visited in over a year. She's probably..."

I sit up straight in my chair and pinch my lips together, holding back the dam of WTFs from spewing out.

"Enough, Harris!" Archie shouts as he jumps up from his chair. "How dare you insult my guest? Gwynedd is the one…"

"Stop!" I shoot a ray of witch energy at another ceiling pocket light, shattering it into tiny pieces, and stand. "Shut the fuck up, both of you. I can speak for myself, Archie. Why hasn't your son visited you? I've had a couple of rough years. I lost my husband, although he was a cheating bastard, found out I was an ancestral witch and my parents had kept it a secret, had to fight off a Sluagh fairy trying to kill me, and then defend our coven against an attack by a wicked ancestral witch family in a closed practice. Archie supported the coven and me through it all. So, you see, Harris. Your son was a *wee* fucking busy."

Archie sits down, chuckling, while his family and the guests snicker under their hands. Harris sits speechless with his head cocked and his lips parted. A steaming hot flash erupts, soaking my clothes and hair as if someone turned a hose on me. Globules of sweat drip onto my haggis.

"I've been called a lot of things in my life, but never boring. And I was trying to be nice by keeping my opinions to myself, because I wanted to make a good impression." I gaze at Archie. "I love your son. He's not perfect, but he does his best. And if that's not enough, he tries harder. I said goodbye to a great-aunt I only met a few days ago, and I may never see her again. And you have this gigantic family you don't fucking seem to appreciate. No, I can't have children. But I'd hoped to be accepted into your…colorful brood. Let's be truthful here. Quinn and Maggie seemed to have popped out enough babies for the entire clan."

As I make eye contact with Archie's brother and sister-in-law, I wipe the sweat off my face and neck. "I'm sorry I ruined your special Yule dinner. I'll take what's left of my dignity and go upstairs." When I've walked a few steps, I stop and turn around. "I changed my mind. I'm not sorry."

As I leave the dining room and head toward the stairs, laughter erupts, and Maggie's voice rings in the hallway. "Quinny, go grab two light bulbs. Your grandfather has done it again."

When I get to the bedroom, I change into my PJs and collapse onto the sofa, sighing. Soon after, Archie ambles in with a red and white parfait in a small glass with a spoon protruding from the top.

"Maggie didn't want you to miss dessert."

"She's a sweet woman. What is it?" I ask.

"It's called cranachan. Has whipped cream, honey, raspberries, oats, and a wee bit of whisky." He winks at me.

"Sounds fattening. Give it to me, and I'll eat my embarrassment away." I spoon a portion into my mouth. "Mmm...this is really yummy. Are you mad?"

He sits down, pulls my feet onto his lap, and gives me a foot massage. "Naw. Harris asked for the word bomb. I can't remember a time when he clamped his mouth shut for so long. I told them we're leaving tomorrow."

"Your dad won't be happy. I'll apologize to everyone in the morning. At least to those who are still here." I squish my eyes shut. "What must they think of me? Some menopausal, moody, mouthy woman."

"That would be accurate." He raises a corner of his mouth and winks again.

"Fuck you." A naughty smile sprouts on my mouth.

"I'd be happy to...right here on this velvet sofa."

He removes my feet from his lap and crawls over me. After placing the last of the whipped cream on his tongue, he kisses me, the bulge in his pants pressing against me.

"Mmm," he moans. "I want more."

I set the empty dessert glass onto the floor, and Archie unbuttons my flannel top, exposing my dragon tattoo. He plants soft kisses on my souvenir of Wales and works his way down and sucks on my nipple.

"Aren't you worried your family will hear us?" I ask, running my fingers through his locks.

"I don't fawking care." He summons his witch energy and lays his palm against mine, triggering an amber glow. "Let their ears burn with our passion."

"Yes," I say, panting. *Burn, baby, burn.*

Despite the fervent magical sex, I wake in the middle of the night. My tossing and turning may wake Archie, so I slip out of the canopy bed and sneak down to the living room on the floor below. I haven't seen it yet, so why not get a peek before we leave in the morning? When I open the creaky door, a table lamp is on, and Quinn is occupying the oversized chair beside it. I push the door shut.

"Trouble sleeping?" he asks with a raise of his thick eyebrows.

"Yes. Too wound up from everything that's happened, I guess."

"I imagine so. Archie told us about the Tuatha Dé fairy who is searching for you and the recent incidents. A scary situation."

"It is, but I'm trying to cope with the threat the best I can."

I sit in a chair across from him next to the baby grand piano nestled in the corner. Quinn pours some Scotch whisky into a glass and passes it to me.

"Share a dram with me. I believe you could use a wee bit."

"Thank you. I'd love some." I take a sip and tap my nails on the glass. "You're probably right. I'm sorry about my outburst at dinner. Everyone must think I'm dreadful."

He chuckles. "If you think you're the first person to have a row at the dinner table here, you'd be mistaken. We're Scots."

"But your dad must hate me," I say, grimacing.

"He said, 'She swears like a sailor, bitches like a dog in heat, and has a temper like a volcano.' His exact words."

My jaw drops, and I glance around the room.

"Then he growled and said, 'I LIKE her.'" Quinn snickers and sips his whisky.

"What?" I laugh, covering my mouth when I realize I'm too loud.

"Maggie had to do the same thing when we moved into the house. Had to claim her territory. Harris respected her for standing up to him."

"Did Archie hear him say those things about me? Because he didn't mention anything to me."

"Harris waited until Archie had left the room. Would never want to admit he was wrong in his presence." Quinn shakes a finger at me. "Don't tell him I told you, because he'd deny the words ever left his tongue."

The portrait of a striking woman with long, wavy blond hair and icy-blue eyes hangs over the black marble fireplace.

"Your mother, I assume. She's exquisite. Archie has the same sculpted face."

"Aye. But she was a feisty woman. I was nine when she passed. For a long time, I hated Archie. Blamed him for taking my mum away. I was only a kid. Later, he became my best friend, in addition to being my brother."

"Harris blames him, too...still." I admire the beauty of their mom again. "He must see her face every time he gazes upon his son."

"Aye. And Archie acknowledges his plight." Quinn leans forward in his chair. "He said you were leaving in the morning. You have good reason to return home with the threat against you, but could I beg you to reconsider? Convince Archie to stay at least through Hogmanay? The gesture would warm Harris's heart."

"I think I can convince him to stay," I say.

"I'm sure you can." He finishes his whisky and stands. "We better crawl back to bed."

"You never said why you're awake?" I ask, pushing out of my chair.

Quinn points toward the ceiling and snickers. "Our bedroom is directly under Archie's, and they share the same register vents."

"Oh, shit." I chuckle as my face flushes with embarrassment.

"No worries," he says through a muffled laugh. "Maggie sleeps with earplugs, because I snore. Or so she claims."

On the way out, I pick up a ceramic figurine from the table—a black cat on its hind legs with a white patch on its chest. "What is this animal called?"

"Oh, that's a cat-sith. Some say they're fairies who wander as cats and steal the souls of the dead. Others say they're witches who can turn into a cat. And once they change nine times, they're stuck as felines forever. Why do you ask?"

"I think one of those knocked me over near the mound at the castle outside Buckley." I place the knick-knack back on the end table. "Archie figured I imagined it, because I was in such a daze."

He tilts his head. "Who knows? Supernatural beings present themselves in their own time. Not ours. Goodnight, Gwyn. And welcome to the family."

My eyes become wet. "Thank you, Quinn. And goodnight to you."

I climb the stairs and sneak back into bed to find Archie in a post-sex coma. I lie in bed wide awake thanks to menopausal insomnia, recalling the actions of the cat-sith. Did the peculiar feline stop me from wandering into the mound?

# CHAPTER ELEVEN

# FAMILY OBLIGATIONS

THE NEXT FEW DAYS at the Cockburns take a wild turn for the better, playing magic games like amber ball bowling and floating cards of poker—their ancestral witch traditions. We use crystals as tokens, and Isla wins most of them. It's quite a leap from our checker matches on the steam trunk at home. I grow accustomed to the boisterous cross-streams of conversation, reveling in the family takedowns and self-deprecating humor. A few times, Harris raises a corner of his mouth and winks at me. And I recognize Archie in his father.

On New Year's Eve, we all make the short walk to the Hogmanay torchlight procession. Contagious energy fills the air with thousands of burning torches and the reverberating sound of bagpipes and drums ahead of us. We finish our night out by huddling together to enjoy the fireworks display over Edinburgh Castle. By the time we return to the house, my fingers and toes are numb. I change into my PJs but leave my socks on and jump into bed. Notifications display on my cell phone, so I check my chat messages.

Tyler: *Happy New Year, Mom. Hope you had fun. Only 8:30 here.*

Me: *Hogmanay was amazeballs, as you would say. Wish you were here.*

I want to tell him about the fairy incidents but decide it's better to wait until I return home.

Tyler: *Have you checked your email? Everyone in the coven has been trying to contact you and Archie.*

Me: *Why? Did something happen?*

Tyler: *Check your email, Mom.*

Archie slides into bed beside me and cuddles. "Put your fawking phone away. It's pushing 2:00 a.m."

"Tyler said I need to check my email. Something happened." When I open my mail app, I discover ten unread messages waiting in my inbox—six of them from Spence.

Archie props himself up on an elbow. "What do they say?"

"All of them are about the same thing. Mayor Manley is attempting to override the tie at the next council meeting so he can send a crew to poke at the mound. Make sure only dirt is underneath the grass."

"Bloody hell. He can't do that. He's attempting this now, because he knows he'll lose control once Elijah sits on the council. And there are fewer students on campus during Winter Session to stage a protest."

"What should I tell them? We're supposed to visit with your family for another two weeks."

He rubs his goatee. "Tell them we'll change our flights."

"Your dad won't be happy. He'll probably blame me again, and we're getting along so well now."

"Don't fret about him. If he carries on, I'll have Isla chip away at him." He caresses my arm. "We can't do anything from here, Gwyn. There are plenty of witches in the coven to hold off the Mayor until we return and meet to discuss how to proceed."

I set my phone on the nightstand and roll onto my side to face him. "Part of me hates to leave. Since we've been in Edinburgh, my brain fog has cleared and I've not had any contact with the Tuatha Dé, not even a nightmare." Or any sex dreams about Nick either, thanks to the fabulous naughty nights we've had in the UK. "I feel safe here."

"I'm chuffed to bits you like my family." He kisses me tenderly and laughs. "Because I barely tolerate them at times."

"You're too critical. Be grateful you have them, because one day, they may save your life. I admit I'm jealous of this big, outrageous clan of yours."

"Noted. We should sleep. I'm completely buggered. And Dad will undoubtedly blow his top when I tell him we're flying home sooner."

I kiss him and rub my nose on his. "I love you."

"I love you, Gwyn." He pats me on the butt. "Now go to sleep before I give you a reason to stay awake."

I chuckle and curl up next to him as he turns off the lamp, wishing I had more stamina.

Harris takes the news well, considering. He's disappointed but understands the situation. We pack our bags into the rental car and say the dreaded goodbyes. Quinn approaches and wraps his arms around Archie and squeezes tightly.

"Remember where you come from, brother."

"I will," Archie says. "You'll remind me, no doubt. Maggie, your hospitality was top-notch, as always."

"We miss you already. Please come again. And Gwynedd, you're welcome in our house whenever you need to get away." She lays her hand on my icy cheek.

"I appreciate the invitation," I say. "I had a wonderful time. Thank you all for the warm hospitality."

"You will let us know when you land in the States?" Harris asks in a demanding tone. "I want to know you've made the trip across the pond without issue."

"Of course, Dad. I always do."

Archie leans toward his father to give him a hug, and Harris wraps his arms around him, pressing his hands into his son's back. But this embrace seems different from the first one I witnessed between them—more heartfelt, more loving.

"I will miss you, son."

"I'll miss you as well, Dad," Archie says as he rubs his father's arm.

Harris steps closer and takes my hand in his. "I expect you'll see to it Archie finds his way back home. And sooner than seventeen months after this visit."

"I'll make certain of it." I squeeze his hand.

"You're not so bad, Gwynedd Crowther. Take care of my Archie. He doesn't always make the wisest choices. But you? You're one of the better ones." He hugs me and kisses the top of my head. "But you are fawking short."

"I am," I chuckle. "I'll work on that."

"We have to get on our way," Archie says. "The flight leaves Manchester a wee past the noon hour."

We get in the car and drive off, waving goodbye. On the trip to the airport, my heart aches at leaving my newfound family behind in the UK. I check the calendar for the next break in the semester and lay my head back against the headrest. Archie breaks the silence after ten minutes have passed.

"What are you thinking?"

"That we live too far from our relatives."

"Those exact words trickle out of my mouth every time I leave after a visit." He lays a hand on mine. "But we have family back in Bearsden as well. Tyler and the coven. I came to the States, hoping to put space between my family obligations and my desire to live life on my own terms, never expecting to form the bonds I have. And I never thought I'd find an ancestral witch to spend my life with. Even if she's as obstinate as a mule."

"I've gotten better. I wouldn't be me if I completely rolled over and became submissive." I bat my eyes at him.

He laughs uncontrollably. "No bloody chance of that happening."

I scowl and blink twice.

The mantle clock reads 8:30 p.m., but it's already the middle of the night in the UK. All I've done is sleep since we left Edinburgh—in the car, on the plane, on the shuttle to pick up his Tesla. Nevertheless, all I want to do is crawl into Archie's Victorian bed and shut my eyes. I send Tyler, Ronnie, and Trinity a group text, saying we're back. I retrieve my PJs and toiletries out of my suitcase in the living room.

Pausing for a moment, I stare at my aunt's painting resting on the fireplace mantle. A lot of love went into the strokes on those canvases, and I wasn't even born yet. My eyes swell up with tears, knowing I may never be in the same room with Aunt Gorawen again. Archie sets his luggage down next to the stairs, ambles over to me, and wraps an arm around my shoulders.

"You will see her again, Gwyn. We'll plan another visit...maybe during spring break. For sure, the summer, and we can stay longer."

"But she's so old," I say as my lip quivers. "The odds are against her living much longer. She has so much more to teach me before she..."

He caresses my shoulder. "Aye. But she has a reason to go on. I saw a sparkle in her eyes when we left she didn't have when we first met her—the day you slipped on the sheep fouling."

"True." I chuckle and gaze at my mom. "I have to connect with my parents again as soon as possible. I want to make sure I've not lost the skills Aunt Gorawen taught me. It's important to keep connections to your family, even if they're somewhere in the Otherworld."

"Or across the pond and here. Thank you, Gwynedd Crowther, for showing me the importance of family. Before this trip, they were an obligation strangling me like a noose. Now I can return home and enjoy the visit." He cups my face and kisses me tenderly.

"Let's go to bed. Or I won't make it upstairs."

Archie swoops me up in his arms. "I'll make sure you do."

# Chapter Twelve

# RETURNING TO REALITY

WHEN MY EYELIDS LIFT, moonbeams cast light upon Archie's family dirk, reflecting off the aqua gemstone on its handle. The empty spot next to me is cool. After slipping on my glasses and a visit to the potty, I make my way to the kitchen. My Scottish protector is sitting at the table for two, sipping tea.

"Good morning," I say, rubbing my face. "Have you been awake long?"

"About an hour. Our sleep will be a mess for a week. Come here." He sets his teacup on the saucer and hugs me. "Why won't you move in with me?"

"Oh, Archie. We've been through this before. I need my independence. And I only live two minutes away."

"Stubborn woman," he growls. "After the two incidents in the UK, I want to keep watch over you."

"And how are you going to do that exactly? Starting in February, you'll be teaching again, and I have to work. I set up my desk at Leslie's to log hours for the insurance company, and I have shifts at Mystic Sage. You can't be with me twenty-four-seven, so what's the point? And you've more than once said I can take care of myself."

He stares at me with those magnetic blue eyes and sucks in a pocket of air. "Will you promise me to carry the dirk on you at all times? Be vigilant?"

"I was carrying the damn thing with me everywhere before. Since we returned, the threat doesn't seem so impending now. Aunt Gorawen said the fairy might not find me for years. I can't live my life fearing he's around every corner. You saw how stressed out I was at your family's home when we arrived. I blew a gasket."

"No dreams of your nemesis last night?"

"Nope. I slept like a rock. Didn't even get up to pee," I chuckle.

"You'll tell me if there are any more incidents? Even if he presents himself during your dreams?"

"I promise. Now that I realize the vision is more than junk in my subconscious, I'll tell you. Have you heard from Trinity or Leslie yet? Are we meeting?"

I break away from his embrace and shuffle to the stove to turn on the kettle. He finishes his tea and goes to the fridge to pull out food for breakfast.

"Not yet. I imagine we'll meet tomorrow night."

"OK. I'm going to take my suitcase to Leslie's and fill her in on Aunt Gorawen. I'm also meeting Ronnie for lunch. How about you?"

"As much as I want to avoid school, I've got to make plans for a faculty mixer. The visiting professor arrives next week. I'd like you to come. We're allowed to bring our significant others."

"So, I'm significant?" I ask, batting my eyelashes.

He lays a hand on my cheek. "More than you'll ever know."

After breakfast and a long, hot shower, I stroll home, lugging the dirk in my hobo bag. I nudge the red side door and enter through the mudroom and hang my winter coat. Leslie is sitting at the kitchen table, drinking coffee, in a black suit. She's still the Acting Chair of the Celtic Studies department and must have office hours during Winter Session.

"Good morning, Leslie," I say as I roll my luggage through.

"Welcome back, Gwynedd. I trust your trip was successful?" Her eyes convey a sense of genuine concern.

"Yes. The woman living in Buckley is my aunt. I had to have her caretaker show her the family grimoire, and she let me in."

I hesitate to share what she told me regarding the Tuatha Dé, considering her past secrecy. Building trust isn't her forte, but I continue.

"We shed many tears. She helped me connect with my parents, and she shared information on how to protect myself. Thank you for giving me the address."

Leslie stands and stares directly into my eyes for a moment. "I meant what I said before you left for Britain. I'll be forthcoming from here on. Agnes and I spoke while you were gone. Finding an incantation to remove the portal mound will be our top priority. Meanwhile, we need to keep the city council from disturbing its soil."

"We received the emails. I assume we're meeting tomorrow evening?"

"Yes. Trinity will send a text this evening to remind everyone. I must get to the office, but I will talk to you later. You can share your impression of Wales...and Scotland."

"Sure. But mostly it was cold and rainy."

"Enjoy your day, Gwynedd." She moves toward the door.

"Wait, Dr. Hughes. I'll share the details tomorrow night with the entire coven, but I'll tell you first. I've had visions and contact with a male fairy. He's tracking me down."

"Indeed," she says, crinkling her brow. "I am truly sorry, Gwynedd. I wish I had chosen a different path than what I did. But you've changed us for the betterment of the community. And for that, I have no regrets."

"Well, it's water under the bridge now. Or should I say magic under the bridge?"

She chuckles, which probably only happens twice a semester. "Indeed. We'll chat more after the meeting."

She exits the house. After rolling my suitcase into the bedroom, Mr. Yeats paces back and forth in my doorway like a panther eyeing its prey.

"Oh, for the love of the gods, you can come in," I say.

He transforms from his chimera cat presentation into his human form. "Ms. Crowther, I am so pleased you are on better speaking terms with Dr. Hughes. She has been singing and humming when she practices the craft. I want to thank you profusely."

I scan the room. "Are you talking to me?"

"Of course I am." Mr. Yeats presses his lips together. "Are you being sarcastic?"

"Nah," I say, in a snarky tone. "Mr. Yeats, I need to work on my ancestral divination to connect with my parents and could use some assistance. Would you be interested?" I bite my lip, thinking this could be a huge mistake.

He clutches his suit vest. "Oh, Ms. Crowther, I would be honored."

"Great. I'll let you know when I'm ready. But now I have to unpack, so shoo."

I wave my hand and open my suitcase on the bed. He grasps the lapels on his suit coat and raises his head with a look of pride in his yellow and blue eyes.

"If you need my help, I'm only a few steps away."

As he leaves my room, he changes back into a chimera cat, and I recall the strange feline who pounced on me near the castle.

When I arrive at the Sunshine Garden Café, Ronnie is waiting for me at the door. She gestures toward the exit, frowning.

"Turn around, Gwyn. We've gotta march down the street to the Mitchell's mansion."

"I don't understand. Why?" I ask, arching my eyebrows.

A text notification buzzes my cell phone. It must be the same group text she received before I arrived.

Trinity: *For the love of all the gods, what are these kids doing? If you're available, get to Mitchell Hall.*

We run in our winter coats and boots in the frigid air until we reach a crowd gathering near the mansion that's spilling out into Main Street. Ronnie and I are both too short to see what's happening, so we push through the throng of people toward an opening. And there they are. The young witches from our coven, along with other students from campus, have formed a human chain across the entrance to the property. Tyler stands with them. Mayor Manley and a few police units huddle together, discussing what to do, I suspect.

"Oh, my gods," Ronnie says. "What the fuck is going on?"

"I don't know, but I'm gonna find out."

Trinity stands off to the side with her arms crossed, wearing a parka, and she's chatting with Elijah. He resembles a snowman in his white puffer jacket and DUB beanie. We rush over to them.

"Hey, Gwynn. Ronnie," she says, pointing. "What a whale of a mess they've gotten themselves into. Elijah got wind of a crew going in there to dig up the mound, and he told the young ones." She glares at him.

"Now, Trinity, I thought it was the best solution, considering all the options we didn't have. We only needed to delay them until I'm sworn in next week."

"They're gonna arrest them all," I say. "How will that affect their student status and their scholarships? Tanner and Tyler could lose their jobs."

I catch Tyler's gaze and send him a what-the-hell-are-you-doing frown, and he shrugs. Officers Wilson and O'Connor walk over to the students to chat with them. And so do I.

"Miss, you can't be here," Office O'Connor says in her high-pitched voice. "This is police business."

"Well, one of them is my son," I say. "So, I'm making it my business."

Officer Wilson comments in a deep voice to his partner. "Maybe we should let her talk some sense into them. Can't hurt."

"Thank you, officer."

I rush over to our young coven members, who are standing hand in hand, and scan their defiant faces.

"What's the matter with all of you? You're gonna get arrested. We can't stop this. Tyler, why would you go along with them? You could get fired."

Spence grimaces at me as he dances in place to get warm, his jet-black hair bouncing from side to side. "What the hell are you talking about? Forming a human chain of protest was Tyler's idea."

"Spence," Tanner says, nudging his partner. "I'm not sure Tyler wanted her to know that."

"Ooops." Spence rolls his lips inward.

"Gwynn, we had to do it, because...you know," Skye says, directing her eyes toward the garden gate.

"I tried to talk him out of protesting," Zoe says. "I mean, it's like an Antarctic freezer out here. My toes have turned into ice cubes."

"Are you going to say anything?" I ask my son.

I glare at Tyler as I shake in the frigid air. His nose and cheeks have a pink hue as white mist seeps from his mouth.

"You would have encouraged me to corral everyone and come here, anyway. I didn't have a choice, Mom."

I exhale into the icy air, understanding his predicament, but don't know what to say. Mayor Manley walks toward us, and the students stiffen their postures.

"You young people should go home now. You've made your point," the mayor says. "Leave before this protest gets out of hand, and you have regrets."

"Will you send the landscaping crew away?" Spence asks, dancing foot to foot. "If not, we're staying put."

"Well then, you give me no choice. Officers, you may proceed." Mayor Manley gestures to the Bearsden Police officers.

"Wait!" Elijah shouts as he approaches. "If you arrest them, you'll have to take me in as well." He steps between Zoe and Spence, joining hands.

"What do you want us to do, Mayor?" Officer Wilson asks.

Mayor Manley rubs his bald spot and flings a hand into the air. "Arrest him, too."

Officer O'Connor raises her head to the mayor's ear. "Sir, maybe it's not a good idea to arrest the incoming council member the week before he's sworn in?"

"Hmph. Fine. Let them freeze their butts off out here, then."

The mayor stamps off and talks to the landscaping crew, and they pack up and get into their trucks. The young people hoot and holler, smacking gloved high-fives all around. Ronnie and Trinity join us.

"I'm not saying I'm OK with these shenanigans," the coven leader says. "But I'm relieved the protest worked."

"Oh, admit it," Spence says, shaking. "You're proud of us."

Trinity grimaces. "Don't be so sure of that."

"Spence, are you cold?" Ronnie asks. "You've been jumping up and down the whole time."

Tanner laughs, and his brown hair falls onto his forehead. "Of course, he's cold. He has no fat on him."

"I told him he should wear two pairs of pants," Skye says. "But he wouldn't listen to me."

"I didn't think we'd be out here as long as we were. I'll know better next time."

Spence shudders, and Tanner rubs his arms through his jacket. Trinity glares at Tyler and Zoe with laser jade-green eyes.

"And what about you two? Cat got your tongue?"

"I only wanted to help," Zoe says while rubbing her hands together.

"I'm sorry, Trinity." Tyler lowers his eyes. "I'll check with you first next time."

"Damn straight, you will. I'll see you tomorrow at the Fellowship meeting. Get the hell home or back to work."

"I'll talk to you this weekend, Mom," Tyler says. "And you can tell me all about Aunt Gorawen and your trip."

I plead with Zoe. "Please help him stay out of trouble."

"I'll try, Gwyn, but he's your son," she says, wrinkling her nose. "He's just a teensy stubborn."

"You really went there?" I ask, blinking.

Zoe splays a wide-toothed grin, and I chuckle. As the young witches disperse, the rest of us huddle together out of earshot from the crowd and Mayor Manley.

"Good thing you were here, Elijah," Ronnie says. "Manley would have put them all in jail."

"I hoped my presence might change his mind. He better get used to it with me on the council." Elijah checks the time on his phone. "I need to return to the shelter. They've been serving lunch without me. I'm sure they're swamped. We'll talk more tomorrow night."

"I've got to get to work, too," Trinity says as she strolls away.

Ronnie and I chat on our brisk walk to the café. I didn't expect my first day back to start with such a bang.

My friend comments, "Well, the protest was exciting."

"Sure, but I bet it raised my blood pressure," I say, pulling my hood up.

"I can't wait to hear about your trip." Ronnie punches me playfully. "Did you get some, if you know what I mean?"

"For fuck's sake, Ronnie. Is that all you ever think about?"

"If I remember correctly, sex was the center of your dreams and our conversations before you left for Britain." She wiggles her eyebrows.

"Yes, we had a great time. Except for the incidents when the Tuatha Dé fairy contacted me."

Ronnie stops on the paver walkway. "Are you fucking kidding me?"

"No. I'll tell you everything that happened at lunch. But my visit with Great-Aunt Gorawen was wonderful." I grin, thinking about Edinburgh. "And we had a fabulous visit with Archie's family. It was different. Oh, I got a dragon tattoo on my left breast, too."

"Wow. Aren't you getting wild? I can't wait to see it."

We arrive at the Sunshine Garden Café, and Ronnie selects a booth for us before checking in with the kitchen. I receive a text notification.

Nick: *Hey, friend. Are you back? I think I saw you in the crowds near Mitchell Hall. I'd love to meet for coffee or lunch to talk about your trip. Let me know when.*

Part of me wants to ignore him, but I can't. I've got to keep him happy.

# CHAPTER THIRTEEN

# SAVING THE MOUND

ON THE WALK TO the Raven Pub, my teeth chatter in the icy temperature. The skies threaten to dump snow with billowy, gray clouds, but I'm ready for spring. Screw snow. I choose to trek through the Green and only pass a handful of students. When I reach the Old Men oak trees, I receive a text.

Archie: *Good morning. I miss you.*

Me: *LOL. You saw me yesterday and spent almost two weeks with me twenty-four-seven.*

Archie: *I must have withdrawal. Do you have the dirk with you?*

Me: **sigh* Yes. I have the family heirloom.*

*Archie: Thank you for humoring me.*

Me: *I resemble a bag lady carrying this gigantic purse.*

Archie: *You do not. Ha.*

Me: *I'll chat with you tonight at the meeting. Love you.*

Archie: *Love you, too, Gwyn.*

The Raven isn't too busy for a Thursday. Fewer students during Winter Session translates to lighter crowds. I didn't tell Archie I was eating a quick lunch with Nick. He doesn't have to know my every movement, and he's getting a little possessive. I survey the booths in the back room, and Nick motions to me. He smiles and stands to give me a hug.

"So, Tyler and other coven members rounded up students on campus to stage a protest?" he asks. "That was ballsy."

I sit down in the booth seat across from him. "Yeah. I wasn't too happy about their desire to protest, but he is my son."

He laughs as he picks up his menu. "What are they trying to do?"

"Stop the mayor and the city council from tinkering too much with the mound. We don't want them to discover its true existence."

"That fairies come through there?"

I stare at him but refuse to answer. Of course, he knows fairies can enter our world through the portal. He read my mom's letter.

"Well, I'm so happy you came back. I worried you might stay in Wales. It's an enchanting country."

"It was tempting, but something happened and we had to leave my aunt's early. Archie had a family emergency in Edinburgh."

I don't want to tell him about the fairy incidents. Why worry him? A little white lie never hurts, does it?

He averts his eyes. "So, you found her?"

"Yeah. At first, she wouldn't let me in. I mean, how was she supposed to know she had a niece? After I gave the caretaker the family grimoire to show my aunt, she knew I was telling the truth. I visited with her for a few days, and then we had to leave abruptly."

That's all I'm telling him. He knows too much about the coven and my witchy past as it is. Being *in the knowing* puts him in danger.

"Did she tell you anything about the...what is it called?"

"A Tuatha Dé Danann fairy...or a god, depending on who you ask or what folklore you believe." I shouldn't share anymore, so I change the subject. "But Great-Aunt Gorawen was a pleasant surprise. My mom always said she was eccentric. She has her quirks, but I liked her a lot. I was sad to leave."

Nick reaches across the table, lays his hand on mine, and tilts his head to lock eyes with me. But I pull my hand from his and pick up my menu.

"I wish you would confide in me," he says. "I want to help."

"I appreciate your concern, but you can't help. The less you know, the better."

He exhales his frustration. "Maybe someday you'll understand how much I care about you."

"I do, Nick. You're a good friend." I swallow and stare into his warm brown eyes. "If I need your support, I promise you I won't hesitate to come to you."

"That's what I want to hear," he says, grinning. "So, tell me about Wales."

Lunch passes by in a flash as I share my recollections of Buckley and the damp, chilly weather. Nick says he never visited the town but explored a castle in the area. I don't mention the one near Buckley because of the scary occurrence there. He probably has an immense knowledge of Celtic folklore but asking him specifics about anything would only prompt more questions.

I'm walking a tightrope between my *knowing* world and him being an Unremarkable...and how much to share with a loyal friend who cares for me—more than he should. For now, the few of us who are aware he's *in the knowing* must keep the fact from the coven. As we walk to our cars, I ask about his recent dates.

"I know you went out with some women last fall. Anything serious yet?"

Nick stares at me and frowns. "No. They were intelligent, attractive women, but they didn't interest me."

"Well, don't give up," I say, looking away. "There are plenty of women out there who will find you irresistible."

"But that's not the issue, is it? Meet for brunch on Sunday? Same time, same place?"

"I don't think so. But you'll be at the mixer next week for the visiting professor who's teaching Spring Semester, won't you?"

"Yeah. I'm the only professor in the department teaching Winter Session, but I'll make the time. I'll miss our brunch, though."

"Me, too," I say, but not really. "I hope your afternoon class goes well."

"Thanks. See you next week, Gwyn."

Nick gets in his car as I wave goodbye, acknowledging the emotions he's grappling with. I drive to the lot behind Mystic Sage and enjoy the heat of the car for ten minutes. Ronnie's right about the need to divulge our world to more Unremarkables. We have to push for transparency and vetting tonight. Once everyone learns about Nick, I can stop these brunches, and he can move on with his life without me cluttering his brain.

When I enter the store, Shane rushes to me from behind the counter, displaying a cheery grin, and embraces me. He's wearing his favorite hoodie with the moon phases, and his long white hair is hanging loose on his shoulders, blending in with his beard.

"Welcome back, darling. Ronnie stopped by earlier and filled me in on your trip. She told me about the contacts you had with the evil foe. I sure hope you're going to tell the coven tonight."

"Archie and I will share our experiences at the meeting. A vision appeared to me in the Mitchell's gardens before I left, too. My Great-Aunt Gorawen says this could be only the beginning. He could track me for years. But the sooner we close off the portal in the mound, the safer I'll be."

"I'm thrilled Tyler formed that human chain yesterday to stop the mayor from abusing his power. Although, I suspect you were none too happy with your son."

"No. I sure hope his employer doesn't find out. Or he'll be in deep shit." I drop my bag on the counter with a thud.

"What do you have in there? Not a gun, I hope?"

"No," I laugh. "Worse. It's Archie's dirk. He insists I carry the damn thing with me everywhere I go. Am I supposed to drag the weapon around with me for the next thirty years? Because the evil fairy may not find me until I'm old as dirt."

He bursts out laughing. "Let's hope so, Gwyn. That would be the best-case scenario."

"Is Jeff going to come later so we can attend the meeting?"

"No. He's not taking any classes this Winter Session. I told him he should take the time to return to New Jersey and go through his aunt and uncle's estate. I offered to go with him, but he didn't want me to close the store."

"I hope he's OK sifting through their stuff. But maybe the process will help him put the experience behind him—help him heal. So, you're short-handed. Would you like me to work extra hours? My classes don't start until Spring Semester."

"Thank you kindly, Gwyn. I was hoping you'd offer. Tonight, I'll close early. Not selling much after the holiday season, anyway."

I walk behind the counter to the cash register. "You know you can always count on me. I can tell you more on our stroll to the meeting."

Leslie, our coven Elder, brings the meeting to order with three taps of her staff. I share what happened in the Celestial Gardens and in Wales. Archie explains the dangers I encountered surrounding the incident at the mound near Buckley. Tyler's jaw drops, and his eyes narrow. I'll have to deal with his anger later. Chatter promptly ensues, and the young witches rehash their protest at Mitchell Hall, laughing and mocking Mayor Manley. But Trinity isn't amused.

"Go on. Laugh about your shenanigans now, but you all were in deep shit." She scowls at Tyler, squishing her face like a prune.

"If your mama and Elijah hadn't stepped in, the Bearsden Police would have hauled all your asses downtown to the city jail."

Agnes snickers and claps her hands. "Fucking fantastic. I've been in the Bearsden jail many times. No big deal. Grows stamina. Nothing but drunk students in there most of the time, anyway."

"I've been in there," Spence says, waving a hand in the air. "Nothing to brag about. It's not like you're thrown in with serial killers."

Tanner frowns at his partner. "Spence, you're not helping."

"But he's right, Tanner," Elijah says. "I actually slept in there one night, trying to convince a patron to go to rehab. Slept just fine."

"Well, if it's all the same to you, Agnes," I say, frowning. "I'd prefer Tyler to not have a police record."

"Come on, Gwyn. No one cares if you have a record for protesting. My list could fill the Regional Book of Shadows."

Archie chuckles. "I bet it would. A fine legacy."

I glare at him. "Please, don't encourage her."

Agnes cracks up, and everyone joins in except for Leslie and Trinity.

"Thank you, Ms. Pritchard. I mean, Agnes," Tyler says as his laughter fades. "Actually, I've been in there before. Don't worry, Mom. It was only a party raid. No biggy."

I cross my arms and glare at my son while my fellow witches chuckle. "We're definitely having a talk this weekend."

Zoe grabs Tyler's hand and peers up at him with her signature grin.

"Don't be too hard on him," Archie whispers in my ear. "You raised a responsible young man."

I grimace at Tyler as he pushes his tongue to the side of his mouth, failing to suppress a smile. Ronnie, Shane, and Skye chuckle at the situation but say nothing. Yes. We're a typical family who can laugh at ourselves, and I'm reminded our found family has roots as deep as our biological kin. Leslie takes over the meeting, a slight smile curving her mouth.

"Our coven leader speaks correctly to our state of affairs. I admire you young people for putting yourselves in danger with law enforcement, and I am grateful you took the risk under the circumstances. But where would we be if the Bearsden Police had incarcerated you for an extended period? What if we had needed your participation in an emergency incantation?"

"Aw, loosen up, Dr. Hughes," Spence says. "Mayor Manley was all talk."

Zoe throws her hands up. "It's not like they could put us in the city jail. It's tiny, and there were a lot of us."

"Oh, for fuck's sake, Leslie," Agnes chides. "They shouldn't have to consult the coven for everything."

Skye shakes her head. "Dr. Hughes is right, guys. We need to consult Trinity next time. If there is a next time."

"Lucky for us, Elijah gets sworn in next week," Ronnie says.

"Damn straight," Trinity says. "Elijah, do you have any suggestions for the meeting? Should we prepare a statement?"

Elijah nods. "I would. Maybe two or three students could suggest preserving the fairy mound as a tribute to Alistair and Rose Mitchell. It might help delay the demolition, at least until we've found an incantation to close the portal."

"That's an excellent idea," Archie says. "Meanwhile, we can all do our due diligence and search for a spell. I know the young witches don't have many resources, but the experienced witches in the coven should scour through their references."

The older witches spend the remainder of the meeting discussing the spell books they own and identifying key phrases to search for. Some words can have hidden meanings.

Trinity stands. "Before we leave, who will speak at the council meeting next week?"

Zoe shoots her hand straight up. "Please, I'd love to speak. I really miss the Mitchells, and I can get all weepy and everything. Play on their emotions."

"You know, I always like to talk," Spence says with his palms up.

"We know." Trinity throws him a wide-eyed stare. "But can you sit this one out? We need different voices. Tanner, would you present? I think it would be advantageous to have a graduate speak—a townie. Plus, you're a respected financial advisor."

"Sure. I'd love to advocate for the fairy mound," he replies.

Spence mocks his partner, mumbling to himself, and Tanner kisses the side of his face and chuckles.

"Are there any other items anyone wishes to discuss?" Trinity asks.

Ronnie raises her hand. "I'd like to reiterate my stance at the last meeting. I want us to discuss changes to our policies on Unremarkables. If more of them were aware of us, we wouldn't have to hide so much. I mean, I told Derek about us at the Delaware Conference, and he was extremely put off I'd lied to him. But he's OK with my witch status now. No one seemed fazed about it at all."

Oh, my gods, Ronnie, you are lying through your teeth. Archie, Tyler, and I know Derek discovered we were witches when he and Nick walked in on us at your house. His being at the conference was an immense help when the shit went down. But I'm happy she's pursuing this change. Archie and Tyler make eye contact with me, and I sink into my seat.

"I agree, but it's different for our loved ones than others in the town," Trinity says as she glances at our coven Elder. "Leslie, Agnes, and I discussed the vetting process over the Yule holidays. We'll discuss this more at our next meeting."

Leslie stands. "Before we dismiss, I want to say something. Elijah, I am so proud you will represent our community. I expect wonderful improvements to our town with you on the council."

The Fellowship erupts with hoots and hollers, and Elijah stands to speak with his thumbs hooked in the belt loops of his jeans.

"Thank you all. I admit I'm a little nervous, but I won't let you down. I'll represent us with the ethics we are striving to live by." He peers at me and nods.

"With that grand statement," Leslie says, tapping her staff three times. "You are dismissed."

We stack the chairs, and everyone gets wintered up in their coats, hats, and gloves. Tyler and Zoe wave goodbye to me, and I motion for Ronnie to join Archie and me. I swing my awkward tote over my shoulder. My best friend walks over, sporting a sly smirk.

"I'm glad you brought that up again," I say. "Trinity and Agnes seemed to have convinced Leslie to consider this major change without putting up much of a fight."

Ronnie shrugs. "Maybe she really is loosening up. We'll have to come up with a reasonable list to vet Unremarkables, though."

"I agree," Archie says. "And soon, hopefully. It's quite awkward working with a colleague who knows our secret and works under our coven Elder in the department."

"For sure. I'm gonna head out. Derek is supposed to be putting the finishing touches on my very own magic room. See ya, fam." Her curly crimson hair bounces on her shoulders as she shimmies away.

"Goodnight, Ronnie," we say as we slip on our gloves.

Agnes and Leslie approach us, a look of we-have-a-plan stamped on their faces. Agnes speaks first.

"Gwyn, Leslie and I spoke about the need to sort through those grimoires I've collected over the years. She would like you to join us at my house and begin the...how did you refer to it?"

"The laborious search through the references," Leslie says. "If those terms are acceptable to you."

Archie and I lock eyes, and I take a moment to process the offer. She certainly can't help if I disagree, but I don't trust her yet. What a conundrum.

"I would love your help," I say, grinding my teeth.

Leslie lifts her chin and smiles. "Splendid. I will speak to you later at the house about specific times. Agnes, I'll call you. Goodnight, everyone."

"Goodnight, Leslie," Agnes says.

The hedge witch has a longing in her pale-gray eyes as Leslie exits through the front door. She waits until her estranged lover is out of earshot.

"Don't worry, Gwyn. I'll keep a witch's eye on her the whole time. But I'm fucking excited. I've not flipped through the pages of those spell books for years. Goodnight to you both."

"Goodnight, Agnes," we say.

Archie and I exit the Pumpkin House to find Shane waiting for me. My boss checks his watch.

"Are you ready to walk back?" he asks. "I'm itching to get into my bedclothes and hunker down for the night."

Archie cocks his head. "Shane is walking you home?"

"No," I say, fiddling with my gloves. "I came from work with Shane after stopping for a slice of pizza. My Prius is in the parking lot behind Mystic Sage."

"I still don't understand." Wrinkles form between Archie's eyes. "Why did you drive?"

"Well, I was coming from the Raven Pub, so..." I freeze, realizing I've slipped up. "I met Nick for a quick lunch. It was last minute."

"I see." Archie runs a hand through his wavy hair.

Shane has been standing like an eavesdropper on a private conversation, stroking his white beard. "We should get on our way, Gwyn."

"Yeah, we should." I kiss Archie goodbye. "Goodnight, honey."

"Goodnight, Gwyn." He sighs as he walks toward the Green.

On the way back to the parking lot, the conversation freezes like the frosty January temperature. When we arrive at our destination, Shane breaks the ice.

"Well, that was one of the most uncomfortable moments I've ever experienced."

"I'm sorry, Shane." I unlock my Prius with a beep-beep. "I wasn't going to tell Archie, because he thinks Nick still has feelings for me. He may be a little miffed I didn't tell him right away, but I would have told him, eventually." *But would I have?*

Shane gestures toward Mystic Sage. "I left a box in the store when we took off for dinner. I'll say goodnight. Have a restful slumber."

"Thanks, boss," I say, grinning.

I reach for my car door as Shane enters the back door of the building, and a text notification vibrates my phone.

Tyler: *Why didn't you tell me about the fairy episodes? That's not OK, Mom.*

Me: *I didn't want you to worry. You've done enough fretting over me.*

Tyler: *We're gonna talk about this more at dinner on Saturday. Don't forget to invite Archie.*

A clamor of people laughing attracts my attention. When I raise my head to investigate, I swear the flash of a face appears under the buzzing, interment glow of a pole light—a man with an oblong face and long black hair. My heart takes off like a rocket as I fumble to open my car door. The light flickers, and the face disappears. I inspect every corner of the parking lot, but only a few drunk students stagger through. Stress has chipped away at my brain, but I'm certain the man from Britain was spying on me in the Bearsden city parking lot. I call Archie.

"Hello, my love. Are you worried I'm upset? Because I'm not. You have every right to make plans without consulting me."

"That's not why I called, but thank you for understanding. I'm behind Shane's store in my car. I saw that man from Buckley under the pole light on the other side of the parking lot—only for a few seconds. But I'm sure it was him."

"I don't doubt you, but it's quite strange you would see him here."

"Exactly. Who do you think this man is? Could he be the fairy who's after me?"

"No idea, Gwyn. But let me know if he crosses your path again. I think we should confront him. If you need me, please call, and I'll be there in a jiff. For now, go home and get some sleep. Put the dirk under your pillow."

"I will. Goodnight, Archie."

"Goodnight, my love."

I stare at the hazy glow of the pole light. Has my foe found me?

# Chapter Fourteen

# SPELL SEARCH

Mr. Yeats roams back and forth on this sunny Saturday morning, purring against Leslie's pants leg as she collects her leather satchel. He's acting more clingy than usual. I'm expecting him to present in his human form at any moment, and he doesn't disappoint.

"Where are you going, Dr. Hughes?" he asks while adjusting his spectacles. "Are you leaving with her, Ms. Crowther?"

"We are spending the day with Agnes Pritchard at her farmhouse, Mr. Yeats. I am certain you will find enough work to occupy your time." She buttons her cardigan over her blouse and collects her keys. "Gwynedd, shall we go?"

Leslie's chimera cat familiar fluffs his bowtie. "Thank you for the suggestion, Dr. Hughes. I will start in the magic room."

He transforms into his cat form and scuttles down the hallway. I adjust my long-sleeved tee over my jeans and put on my fleece jacket. Leslie slips on her wool winter coat.

"Why don't I drive us to the farm?" I ask. "I'm parked behind your car, anyway."

"Wonderful. I much prefer not driving."

"Great," I say as we exit the house.

I want to drive, because I have trepidation about riding with a woman in her late 70s who rarely removes her car from the garage. I shouldn't stereotype, but in her case, the lack of practice doesn't instill confidence. Leslie has difficulty lowering herself into the passenger seat of my Prius, and I worry she'll have trouble getting out when we arrive at Agnes's house. Too late now.

As we approach the Maryland border, we pass a few farms and a property housing horses. The fields are barren with the corn husks plowed under, but only a few months ago, the stalks were so high they hid the houses behind them from the road. On the way, I become intrusive, because why not?

"Have you visited Agnes's farm much recently? I mean, other than meeting to discuss coven issues."

Leslie stares out the window. "No. We have focused on the mound and the fairy who seeks to kidnap you."

"My Aunt Gorawen alluded to the fact this enemy of my family may not find me for years, even decades. I don't think we should fixate on the threat. I was so angry when I found out you hid the secret of the Tuatha Dé Danann from me. I've worried myself into a tizzy but..." I recall the face under the pole light in the Mystic Sage parking lot but decide to wait and tell her and Agnes together when we arrive.

"I am sad I caused you to live like this. If I could go back and approach the situation with more care, I would. Do you not want to pursue a solution? Live as if there is no threat? In my opinion, that's not realistic. Besides, we have to eliminate the mound before the city demolishes it, anyway."

"No. I'm not saying we shouldn't search diligently for an incantation or remain aware of the supernatural world around us. I agree we must shut it down. I only suggest we create a weekly plan to investigate the grimoires that won't burn us out, in case the shit hits the fan and we need our energy to fight. But we should live our fucking lives, too."

Leslie turns her head toward me and scowls. "Your speech has become more colorful since you trained with Agnes. But I understand what you're proposing. Can you really put the threat of this enemy behind you while we research?"

"If I don't, I might as well roll over and submit to him now."

"Indeed. We will start by searching for an incantation. When we discover a workable spell, the coven will cast it."

I turn onto the gravel road and park in front of Agnes's dreary farmhouse. It's in need of renovations, but she has no money for them. I grab my hobo bag and move to the passenger side, helping Leslie to pull herself out of my low-lying Prius. Maybe driving my car wasn't the best decision. We climb the steps of the front porch, and I knock on the door, but Leslie marches in.

"We're here, Agnes. Where shall we start?" Leslie peeks into the kitchen.

Agnes yells from the magic room, "I'm back here, hon. Getting organized!"

She's calling Leslie hon? That's a good sign. When we enter, Agnes is flipping through an old spell book next to several piles of antiquarian books and journals. She's wearing a loose-fitting black top over frayed jeans. I bet she's had that outfit since the '60s. Her salt and pepper hair hangs across her face, and she bats at her bangs between page turns. Spell jars, mortars and pestles, crystals, herb jars, wooden bowls, and baskets clutter the shelves—just as I remember. Several weeks of dust cover the items.

"Why did you pull them off the shelves?" I ask. "You've made a mess. Please, tell me you have a system for your piles."

"Not here five fucking minutes, and you're criticizing," she snickers. "We're doing this for you, remember?"

"I know. But I like to watch the steam exit your ears." I laugh and pick up a dusty grimoire.

Agnes chuckles. "You're a fucking mess, Gwyn. Why the fuck do I put up with you?"

"'Cause you love me, Agnes," I say in a low voice.

The coven Elder stands idle listening to our banter like she doesn't belong. I grab a pile of spell books and carry them to the wooden table in the center of the room.

"Leslie, why don't you sit here and examine the contents of these books? When you're done, I can bring more over. Agnes, why don't you set up there, too? Neither of you needs to be bending over all day."

Who am I kidding? My lower back hurts like a bitch every other day. But I'd love to watch them work together—for better or worse.

"A wonderful suggestion, Gwynedd. Agnes and I are more likely to recognize a useful spell, anyway."

"Well, that we can all agree on," I say.

Agnes sits down on a stool next to her on-again-off-again lover, and I fill them in on the sinister guy who stared at me in Buckley, Edinburgh, and now in Bearsden.

"At Edinburgh Castle, I only got a glimpse of his face, and he disappeared in a millisecond. I figured I saw a man who resembled him, but the same guy was staring at me in the Mystic Sage parking lot Thursday night."

"I assume you've told Archie," Leslie says. "We must investigate this man should he appear to you again. Discover his motivation."

Agnes grimaces. "What a slimy lech. Keep an eye out for him."

"I will," I say. "It's why I'm wearing this crystal necklace Aunt Gorawen gave to me."

"Ah. Tourmaline, right?" she asks. "It won't repel the bastard fairy, but the crystals will make him uncomfortable."

Leslie lifts her chin. "That was an excellent recommendation."

"Well, let's get started," I say, sitting on a pile of books. "I have no idea what I'm looking for."

Agnes opens a spell book fraying at the spine. "Do your best, Gwyn. Despite your inexperience, you'll know when you spot something. We can examine the spell for its effectiveness."

After only fifteen minutes, Leslie shouts, excited by her discovery. "Yes! I believe I've found a possibility." She runs a knobby finger down the page, and her face turns grim. "No, no, no. I was mistaken. We can't use this incantation."

"Why not, hon," Agnes says, leaning over the book to read. "This will work, Leslie. What's the problem?"

Leslie purses her lips. "Agnes, my dear. This spell requires a human sacrifice."

"So what?" She flings a hand in the air.

"Surely, you're not suggesting we actually commit murder?"

I drop a heavy book on the floor with a thud. "Agnes, you want us to kill somebody to perform a spell?"

"Well, I know a couple of people no one would ever miss, and they sit on the Bearsden City Council."

"My dear, we will hurt no one in order to cast a spell," Leslie says, clapping the book shut. "Gwynedd's new ethics requirement forbids the act, anyway."

Agnes snickers and turns a page in her spell book. "I was kidding, ladies. But it's a nice thought."

"You know this would be a helluva lot easier to search for a spell if they were in an online database," I say as I flip through another moldy, crumbly grimoire. "If we needed an incantation to revive a dead plant or a healing incantation for a severe wound, we could search on our data phones in seconds."

They gape at me as if someone told them they've lost their Medicare, and I blink several times.

"What? It was only a suggestion. The young witches would love it. Why can't we join the technology age?"

"Gwyn, sometimes you have ridiculous ideas," Agnes says while Leslie shakes her head.

By lunchtime, we've sorted through about thirty-some gri-moires and have found no incantation other than the one requir-ing murder, so we stop for lunch. We chat about various issues going on in the town, and the conversation meanders around to the creation of the fairy mound.

"So, do you know what went wrong to cause the spell to screw up in the first place?" I ask. "We should probably avoid making similar mistakes. Mom never mentioned anything. Do either of you have an explanation for why the mound formed?"

Agnes stares at Leslie. "Do you wanna tell her, or will I?"

"I was a neophyte in those days," Leslie says. "I'd only begun to explore my magic skills. Admittedly, there were areas in which I needed much more focus."

"For fuck's sake, I'll give her the short version." Agnes lifts her head, and her bangs fall back to expose her face. "While we cast the spell, a storm raged overhead, and she let her mind flit away into a world of academic bliss."

"What does that mean?" I ask. "Academic bliss?"

"I had researched an article on the folklore of the Seelie Fae, and while we were casting, the memory of them wandered in." Leslie takes a breath. "I'd forgotten any transient thought can be misconstrued as an intention."

I can't suppress my laughter. "You fucked up."

"Yes," Leslie says, frowning. "I'd committed a monumental er-ror, which has followed me all my days."

Agnes slaps the kitchen table and bursts out laughing. "My gods, woman, how it turns me on to hear you admit you've made a mistake."

Leslie glares at her with those cat eyes, and Agnes pushes her arm playfully. My heart warms as these two find their way back to each other, and I hope the relationship sticks this time. After lunch, we spend another two hours flipping page after page but find no incantations related to closing a portal, and there are no spell books left. I rub my temples, expecting a migraine from the eyestrain.

"We've gone through all your books, Agnes. Where else can we look?" I ask.

"Oh, we're not done," she says. "We have the books upstairs to go through, too. Let me show you."

The three of us climb the steep wooden stairs and enter a bedroom where she stores her extra books. I enter and gasp. The room resembles a section of a library with shelves along every wall. Tall books. Thick books. Tiny books. Journals with paper edges protruding in random directions. Stacked in piles and aligned vertically in a haphazard fashion, some books cling to the others on the dusty wooden edges, as if their existence relies on them.

"And I thought Leslie was a book hoarder," I say, scanning the references and novels. "Your office was a disaster, if you remember."

Leslie glares at me but remains silent.

"Yeah. People as old as us have a hard time purging," Agnes says. "I collected these over the years, thinking I might try spells with different chants and ingredients. I was always working. Being a waitress on my feet for hours a day wore me out, and I never found the energy to follow through. So, here they are."

"There must be hundreds of books in this room—maybe a thousand," I say as my stomach twists into knots. "It will take months or years to sort through them all."

Leslie pats my arm and exhales. "Indeed."

Tyler collects our empty plates and walks toward the kitchen, frowning. "You should have told me about the fairy trying to contact you, Mom. Stop keeping scary stuff to yourself. I'm a witch now."

"I thought she should tell you, Tyler," Archie says. "Let me help you."

"Sure," I say. "Gang up on me. Zoe, you need to come to my rescue."

She points a finger at her chest. "Me? I think they're right, Gwyn. You should've told him. How are we supposed to help if you don't tell us everything?"

Archie collects the remaining dirty dishes and follows Tyler into the kitchen, chuckling. With the collection of fairy incidents piling up, we refrain from telling Tyler about the creepy guy from Buckley. There's not much to share yet, and it would only worry him. I sip a little of my white wine and place the glass on the table.

"This is so not fair," I yell to them. "I'm the mom."

When Tyler and Archie return, they suggest we move to the living room. Archie and I sit down on the sofa, and I relax against his shoulder. Tyler drops into the oversized upholstered chair, and Zoe plops onto his lap. I'm so happy my son found her, even if the association triggered his ancestral magic. But I imagine his witch energy would have sprouted, eventually. Destiny seems to be on the winning team.

"So, you liked Great-Aunt Gorawen?" Tyler asks. "She wasn't as weird as you imagined she would be?"

I chuckle. "That depends on what qualifies as weird. She's almost a hundred years old and has a caretaker and a helper. The caretaker is a caring woman named Ellie, but the helper is...a magic hand."

"Ooo," Zoe says, sitting up. "Tell me about the hand." She spreads her fingers, facing her palm toward us.

"Aunt Gorawen calls him her magic butler. He's opaque, shimmering in a golden glow, and whizzes around the house following her wherever she goes, unless she doesn't need him. And then he flits off somewhere. A similar magic was used to lock the family steam trunk. I meant to ask her for the spell, but we had to rush out of there. Ellie is going to set her up with a laptop and internet, so we can chat. I want her to meet you, Tyler. She's really old and has a lot of regrets regarding your grandmother. Archie, tell him about the unfinished canvases."

He rubs his goatee. "There were several piles leaning against the walls. They were variations on the one that rests on my fireplace mantle—the one your mum used to speak with your grandmother."

"No shit," Tyler says. "Did she send them all over the place?"

"Apparently, yes. To attract witches and influence them to protect your mum." Archie clasps my hand.

"That's so romantic," Zoe says, hugging Tyler. "You came here to the US to search for her."

"Not exactly. The painting lured me here to protect her, but there was no love spell attached to the picture." Archie gazes into my eyes. "Gwyn cast that spell herself."

"And how did I manage that when I didn't even know I was a witch?" I ask.

"I'm still trying to figure out your secret." He chuckles and kisses me on the forehead.

Zoe laughs. "You guys need to get a room."

"She's right, Archie." As I stand up, I rub my lower back. "I'm so tired and achy after flipping through all those books today. And before you all ask, no. We found nothing."

"That's disappointing. I've found nothing in the few I own either." Archie stands and shoves his hands in his pockets.

"But we aren't finished," I say. "She has an entire bedroom upstairs with hundreds of books and journals. How did Agnes collect so many?"

Tyler finishes his beer and sets the bottle on the floor. "She's ancient, Mom. You had a lifetime of stuff to purge when we sold the house. Imagine if you had stayed there another thirty years? Ms. Pritchard has lived on the farm for forty, I bet."

"True, but I was a little overwhelmed. I don't want this fairy threat to define my life. I'm on edge all the time, and the stress could affect my sleep. Do you remember what I was like after your father died?"

Tyler and Zoe get out of the chair, and my son wraps his arms around my shoulders. "I love you, Mom. Don't fall into that rabbit hole again."

"Me, too, Gwyn," Zoe says, joining us.

"I love you, too, guys."

I break their embrace and slip my arms into my fleece jacket while Archie puts on his leather coat.

"We better get going," Archie says. "We'll see you both at the city council meeting. Prepare a magnificent speech, Zoe."

She grins, her teeth shining. "I'll be amazing."

Archie unlocks the back door, and I run into the mudroom to remove my jacket and boots. He's right behind me and hangs his leather coat on a hook next to mine. I shudder as I enter the kitchen, blowing on my chilly hands. We amble into the living room, and I collapse onto the loveseat. My sexy Scottish professor sinks into a cushion, pulls my feet into his lap, and rubs the soles with his thumbs.

"Dinner was cracking. I'm glad we spent time with Tyler. He's accepted his witch status so much better than I expected."

"Yes. I'm proud of him. He seems content with the changes, although I'm sure Zoe has helped him a lot. And he likes the young witches in the coven." I moan as he hits the right spots. "Mmm.

Your foot massages are the best, but my feet are so frozen, they're numb."

He chuckles. "Aye. The chill of your skin seeps right through your socks."

"What can I do about them? Damn menopause turns my hands and feet into ice cubes. It's why I wore socks during sex in Britain. I can't get in the mood if they're this chilly."

"Perhaps I can remedy the situation."

Archie continues to knead circles across the bottom of my feet while lustful yearnings flicker in his clear-blue eyes. An amber glow radiates in his hands, and I close my eyes, enjoying the fiery touch of his magic through my socks.

"Don't fall asleep on me," he says in his warm baritone voice. "I've longed for this night since we returned."

I lift my eyelids and shift my feet forward and back, fondling his groin with my heels. "Not if you keep making love to my feet."

A naughty grin emerges as he increases the intensity of his witch energy. I squirm, rubbing my thighs together as the arousal slinks up between my legs. He could keep this up for hours, and I'd be a happy girlfriend. But I want him inside of me. He unzips his pants, allowing his bulge much-needed relief, and I smile coyly at him. Accepting my invitation, he tugs at my pant legs, and I unfasten my jeans. He reaches for the waistband and pulls them down.

"Oh, it's chilly," I say, wiggling on the cushion. "Should we go upstairs?"

He says in a breathy voice, "I'll warm you up, my love."

Archie removes his jeans and boxer briefs and climbs on top of me, sprinkling kisses on my skin as he crawls up my body. He presses his lips on mine, offering his tongue, and I grasp his manhood and guide him in. I moan when he enters me and grab the butt cheek with the Horned God tattoo, encouraging him to go deeper. I raise my hand, summoning my witch energy, and he removes his mouth from mine.

"No, Gwyn. Let's finish without the magic, as we used to before all the witchery entered your life—when you were an Unremarkable." He gazes into my eyes as he makes love to me. "This is enough."

Archie kisses me again and quickens his stride, increasing his depth with each thrust. My heartbeat increases and pounds heavily in my chest as I wrap my legs around him. I clutch his back, wishing this would go on forever as the pleasure nears its peak. I yelp in ecstasy, and my scream urges him to join me. He grunts as he catches his breath and lays his head on my shoulder, panting.

"I love you, Gwyn," he says as his chest deflates.

I stroke his hair. "I love you, Archie."

We lie there, relishing in our afterglow for several minutes, as his heart beats slowly against my chest. My legs relax, and I caress his back through his long-sleeved Henley shirt. The weight of his body crushes me, and I wrestle to take in a full breath. But I want him to be close to me. His fingers weave through mine.

"Gwyn, why didn't you tell me you were eating lunch with Nick?"

I hesitate to answer. "I'm not sure. Maybe I don't think you need to know my every movement, every minute of the day."

Archie lifts his head and stares into my eyes. "I only want you to be safe, because I can't imagine my life without you now."

"I understand," I say, stroking his goatee. "I'll try not to forget the next time."

"Nick is taking advantage of you. You realize that, don't you?"

He sits up on the sofa, gesturing for me to join him. I curl my body next to his, and he kisses the top of my head. I try to calm his fears.

"We only need to humor him for a couple more months until we officially change the rules in the coven. And then we won't have to worry about him telling the rest of them, especially Leslie and Trinity. Trust me. I can handle him."

"I'm not so sure. He seems to have you on a short rope."

I clasp his hand. "Let's go to bed. And remember, tomorrow we can sleep in. No brunch."

After I wash up, I climb into Archie's magnificent walnut Victorian bed and pull the flannel sheets and blanket to my chest. While Archie finishes brushing his teeth, I receive a text notification. I grin widely, thinking it's Tyler, but it's not.

Nick: *Just wanted to say hi. I'll miss our brunch tomorrow. Is next Sunday OK?*

I exhale as my head hits the pillow and lay my cell phone on the nightstand. Maybe Archie's right?

# CHAPTER FIFTEEN

# OH, BLARNEY

By Monday evening, a polar vortex has dipped down into the Mid-Atlantic states, bringing bitter winds. But the council chamber of Bearsden City Hall is toasty from the throng of townies. The gentle giant social worker stands with his hand on a hardback of the Delaware Constitution, because a Christian Bible wouldn't mean much to him as a pagan.

"I, Elijah Jackson, do solemnly swear and affirm that I will support the constitution of the United States and the State of Delaware Constitution, and the charter of the town of Bearsden, and I will faithfully discharge the duties of the office of council member of the town of Bearsden, Delaware."

Members of the Fellowship and other townies clap and cheer as Elijah takes his seat on the city council. Everyone is here to support him except Shane, Ronnie, and Skye, who have to work. Mayor Manley, with his bad comb-over, sits slumped over at the center of the table, most likely realizing he's lost most of his power. The microphone squeals with feedback as he speaks.

"I want to welcome Elijah Jackson to the city council," the mayor says. "What a coincidence to have two Jacksons serve in our chambers."

Is he implying someone rigged the election? I'm fairly certain he and Jeremiah aren't even related. Jackson is a common name in Delaware.

Jessica Devine, the council member who ran against the mayor in the last election, shakes hands with Elijah. "You've been a reliable member of the community for years, and I'm elated to have you serve next to me."

Elijah puts a buffer between her and the mayor. Win, win.

Mayor Manley continues. "We will begin by reading the summary of the prior meeting minutes."

The agenda drags on for two hours until we get to the public comment section. I yawn several times, wishing the jet lag would resolve already. Tanner prepares his brief speech as Spence points to his cell phone—making suggestions, I assume. I'm always impressed with how well Tanner dresses, but tonight he appears especially handsome in a dark-blue dress shirt, tie, and black slacks. Even though he isn't speaking tonight, Spence has upped his usual game by wearing a turtleneck sweater and dark jeans.

Zoe and Tyler sit in the row in front of us. Her legs are shaking, and she's rocking in her seat. How will she handle addressing the Mayor and the council? Maybe Spence should have spoken. At least he's entertaining.

"And now we have come to the public comments," the mayor announces. "Remember, you have three minutes."

Spence pats Tanner's back as his partner stands and walks to the podium. "Mayor Manley and esteemed council members. My name is Tanner Jones. I was one of the community members who formed a human chain last week to block the partial destruction of the fairy mound in the Celestial Gardens at Mitchell Hall. Digging up the mound may seem trivial to you, but to those of us who knew Alistair and Rose Mitchell, it's as if you're tampering with their graves."

He shares stories of the Mitchells and the open houses they used to host and how children would dance around the gardens. When he finishes, the townies clap enthusiastically. Tyler hugs Zoe, and she rushes to the podium, pulling down the microphone to her petite frame.

"Hello, Mayor and council members of Bearsden. I'm Zoe Wu. I was a shy, lonely freshman when I first met the Mitchells." She sniffs and wipes her nose. "I could barely form a complete sentence at social events. One night I was sitting on the bench under the hawthorn tree...you know, the one we blew up at the Winter Solstice Celebration."

Oh, my gods, Zoe. This is not helping the situation to bring up the damage we caused to the gardens.

She continues. "Anyway, Mrs. Mitchell took my hand and led me to the fairy mound. I know you all believe it's only a make-believe pile of dirt..."

The Fellowship members gasp under their breath as we brace for her next words to spew out of her mouth. Leslie and Agnes appear one breath short of the ICU, and the others cover their mouths in disbelief. Trinity slaps her cheeks. But Tyler is grinning from ear to ear. Oh, Zoe. What are you up to?

"But the fairy mound is more than just soil. Mrs. Mitchell told me a story about two fairies who came to her in her dreams. They filled her heart with immense joy and gave her the will to move on with her life when she learned she couldn't have children." Tears stream down Zoe's round face, and she blots them with another tissue. "She told me to close my eyes and imagine whatever I wanted to be. I stood there, holding her hand, and dreamed of a life in which I could be myself and become an outgoing person."

The council members dab drops of empathy from the corners of their eyes while Mayor Manley rests his head on a fist, scowling. Elijah places a hand over his heart. Zoe has always had a special spot in there. She blows her nose like a trumpet into her tissues and finishes.

"And now look at me. I'm a completely different person. You say you want to build a children's playground in its place. I say it's already a playground that sparked the imagination of children whenever they played in the gardens full of fairy statues and fountains. Please, keep the mound as a memorial to the Mitchells."

As she takes her seat, the community members applaud. We are so proud of Zoe. Archie smiles with such admiration for her. He has seen so much improvement in this young lady since she became a witch and joined the coven. I'm overjoyed she and Tyler found each other.

Jessica Devine raises her hand to speak, and Mayor Manley motions to her. "Tanner Jones and Zoe Wu, thank you for your heartfelt stories. We truly appreciate your input. Going forward, the council will take your suggestions into consideration, but..."

No. Buts are never good. I squeeze Archie's hand.

"There is limited space in the Celestial Gardens," Jessica says. "If we are going to make improvements to the property to transform the space into a more accommodating area to all the community, the mound may have to go."

Elijah waves a hand. "May I have a word? This is my first night, but may I recommend postponing any work until winter has passed? It's been an extremely wet couple of months. Trying to implement changes now would only create a muddy mess. Meanwhile, we can request an artist's rendition of what the future space would include. What do you all think?"

The Fellowship and the other townies praise the idea with a round of applause, and the council members appear to agree.

"Fine," Mayor Manley says, throwing a hand up.

The city council votes to postpone work on the fairy mound until a later unspecified date, and the mayor adjourns the meeting. Outside, we sing our yahoos for Tanner and Zoe's presentations, but the old women in the coven aren't holding back as we huddle in the freezing weather.

"Zoe, you nearly ended my life tonight," Agnes says. "I saw flashes of the Otherworld pass by like a silent motion picture."

"Oh, Agnes, don't be overly dramatic." Leslie slips on her gloves.

Trinity shakes her head. "Don't ever spring a surprise on us without warning. Us old folk aren't as resilient as you young people. Our hearts can't rebound like yours."

"I'm sorry," Zoe says. "I hoped you would love what I said."

"You did great. Even the mayor seemed sad." Tyler hugs her.

"I wouldn't go that far," Spence says. "I think he was falling asleep. He knows he lost control tonight."

Elijah approaches with his girlfriend Jasmine, and we curb our Otherworld talk.

Tanner slaps a high five to Elijah. "Good luck, man. We're so happy you're on the council. Congrats, big dude."

"Thank you. I hope I don't disappoint any of you." Elijah pulls on his DUB beanie and clasps Jasmine's hand.

"I'm so excited for you," Jasmine says. "It warmed my heart to see you sitting up there."

Elijah bends down to kiss his girlfriend. "Thanks, sweetheart. I'm exhausted. It was a long day. Goodnight, all." They head toward the municipal parking lot behind Mystic Sage.

"I second that. It's a wee nippy," Archie says in a thicker Scottish brogue. "Shall we say goodnight, everyone?"

"Yes. I can't feel my toes already." I stamp my feet and dance around.

"We'll establish some parameters at our next Fellowship meeting on how to proceed with the council," Trinity says. "Take care, everyone."

Archie and I wave goodbye and make our way back to his house through the desolate Green. A never-ending threat looms in the frigid air, and for now, the mound is secure. But for how long?

On this snowy Wednesday morning, Mr. Yeats scurries from the magic room to the mudroom as I put on my fleece jacket. He snaps into his human form only inches away.

"Aghhh," I say, my ticker spiking under my ribcage. "Please, stop popping out so close to me. I don't need to test the strength of my heart daily."

He brushes the lint off his suit jacket. "I apologize. I wanted to make sure you remembered to schedule a time for the ancestral divination you wanted assistance with. You've forgotten to follow up."

"I'll let you know. I'm behind on a lot of things. Let's say sometime this week. I'm sure you'll remind me."

"Wonderful," he says. "Where are you off to this afternoon?"

I open the door, pulling hard. He is so intrusive, but maybe he'll let up if I throw him a scrap once in a while.

"There is a reception for the new visiting professor from Northern Ireland. But you must know already. Dr. Hughes is the acting chair for her department."

"I didn't expect you to attend a faculty reception," he says. "Are you the guest of Dr. Cockburn?"

"Yes. He asked me to attend as his significant other. I've got to get going. Don't wanna be late."

"Enjoy your walk to campus, Ms. Crowther." Mr. Yeats scuttles out in his ginger and black fur with his tail wagging.

I pull my hood on as I exit the house carrying my tote and stuff my hands in the pockets of my fuchsia puffer jacket. A blanket of gray hangs over Bearsden, and snow flurries sprinkle the skies as the bitter air cuts across my face. My nose will be as red as a cherry by the time I arrive at Stewart Hall.

Archie never tells me what to wear, so I sure hope I dressed well enough for a faculty social. Frankly, he'd prefer I wear nothing at all. But I wish he had offered a suggestion. I have on black, skinny knit pants and a long sweater covering my butt. Of course, I'm wearing the tourmaline necklace under my top. The high-heeled black boots make my legs appear longer, but they aren't practical for snow. What was I thinking?

When I enter Stewart Hall, I'm blasted with the heat of the building and immediately tear off my coat. I should have layered. Despite the winter weather, I'm likely to battle a hot flash or two in this sweater. Menopause sucks.

As I approach Archie's office, Nick Evans stands at the end of the hallway where a bend takes you to his office, the last door on the left. And behold who's talking with him—Laura Lovelace. Holy crystals. Is she going after Nick now? Poor guy. I should warn him about her, but I sort of like the idea of her stealing his interest from me. She is close to his age.

Archie's door opens, and he walks into the hallway. "What are you looking at?"

"Them," I say, pointing at Nick and Laura.

"Aye. Laura is finally finishing her dissertation and needs three advisors on her review team."

"So, she's asking Nick to be on the team?" I spy on their interaction.

"Aye. Along with Leslie...and me."

"What?!" A W-T-F scowl seizes my face. "How can you work with her after what she did at the pagan conference last fall?"

He speaks using a thicker Scottish brogue, "Gwyn, we have a small department. I have little choice in the matter."

I throw Laura a hex-filled glare. "I don't trust her for a witch's second."

"Aye. I have my doubts as well, but I'll push through the dissertation duties and be done with her. I promise."

"You're handsome in your blue dress shirt," I say, fiddling with his tie. "You wore this the first night you kissed me on the cheek under the Kissing Arch. I remember how the color matched the blue of your eyes under the moonlight."

"It was a romantic moment when I ignited your witch magic." He brushes a finger under my chin and chuckles. "And then you broke the heel on your sandal and had to walk to your Prius in your bare feet."

"Well, you know I'm a klutz."

"I'm well aware. Let's make our way to the lobby. The reception has started by now."

As we leave, I spy on Nick and Laura again. He's saying goodbye while he locks his office door. We walk upstairs to the octagonal atrium, which has had a recent facelift. The walls are bright yellow with crisp white molding around the eight archways. The terrazzo floor has white, dark gray, and black geometric shapes with a compass design in the center, marking north, south, east, and west.

Refreshment tables are set up on two sides of the space, blocking two of the archways. I can barely see what's on them because of the number of attendees. There must be more than the faculty and staff of the Celtic Studies department here, and their chatter reverberates in the boomy, two-story space. A few students wearing DUB polo shirts roam throughout, filling food trays and ice buckets. Unfamiliar faculty mingle while they drink soda from cheap plastic cups. The mixture of bad aftershave and cheap perfume makes me gag.

"How come so many people are here?" I ask, fanning myself. "The lobby is packed like sardines."

"We couldn't have a reception and not invite the English department. They occupy the upper two floors. Would have been bad manners." Archie pours himself a soda.

As I tug at my top, I wish I'd chosen layered comfort over a fancy sweater. I grab one of those adorable baby water bottles and drink half the contents.

"I didn't expect it to be so hot in here. You'd think they would turn the thermostat down with this many people."

"They're set for the drafts from the entry doors, I'm sure. I see the visiting professor speaking with Dr. Hughes. I can't wait for you to meet him. He seems a nice enough fellow. I'll return in a jiffy, my love." He squeezes my hand and rushes through the crowd of academics.

I finish my water and walk to the recycling bin to drop in my plastic bottle. When I turn around, I jump at Nick's presence, clutching my chest.

"You scared me. Well, scared is too strong a term, I guess. I wasn't expecting you to be standing here."

"Remember, I work in this building?" he asks, smiling. "I'm so glad you came. It makes up for the missed brunch."

"I needed the time to adjust my body clock. The jet lag hit me hard. Or it's my brain fog returning."

He stares into my eyes, almost attempting to reach past the surface. "I hope you're back on our time now, so life can return to normal."

"Normal?" I chuckle. "I don't think my life will ever be ordinary again, as you're aware."

"I understand why you feel that way, but maybe you're meant to live a unique existence. Something more extraordinary and beyond this world."

"Please...I barely function in this one." I laugh and pull at my sweater, which is getting snagged on my necklace underneath. "Is it me, or is it hot as a brick oven in here?"

He takes a drink of his soda and looks away, holding his stomach as if he's nauseous. "Too many people. There are a lot of English faculty and their spouses here today. Funny thing is, most of them aren't even teaching Winter Session—only came for the party."

"I saw you with Laura Lovelace earlier. Archie says you're on her dissertation committee."

"Yeah. There are only four of us in our department, and one is an adjunct. The visiting professor can't sit on the team, of course. How do you know Laura?"

I pause and scour my menopausal brain for a response. He can't know she's a witch, so I trip over my tongue.

"Uh...it's sort of awkward. She used to date Archie."

"Interesting." Nick's eyes twitch. "You probably aren't too happy about him being on her dissertation committee then."

Why is he poking the bear? "Well, he's with me. You know, after she defends her dissertation, you should ask her out. She's around your age."

"Is that right?" He peers past me and raises a hand to wave. "Archie's coming with the new guy."

"Gwyn, I'd like to introduce you to Dr. Seamus Duffy," Archie says, tapping me on the shoulder.

I turn around and my jaw drops as a pair of sea-green eyes stare down at me. "You! You're the creep from Buckley!"

A few heads turn toward us, and the nearby chatter fades. The visiting professor stands at almost six feet and looks to be in his 50s. His long black hair has gray at the temples and is tied behind his head. He's leaning on a black cane with an antique brass cat head. Dressed in a black suit and tie, he isn't taken aback much by my reaction as his oblong face with an upturned nose remains unchanged.

"Gwyn," Archie mumbles in my ear. "What are you doing? This is the new professor I told you about."

When I survey the guests, I find the fiery eyes of academics glaring at me. Leslie raises her head and sends a how-dare-you scowl in my direction. Did I make a mistake? Nick crosses his arms and observes the drama. I peer up at the creepy dude one more time and glimpse those sea-green eyes again. No, I'm certain he's the same guy.

"I should explain myself," he says in a singsongy Irish brogue. "I saw you in Buckley and thought I recognized you. Such a beautiful, memorable face you have. Exquisite hazel eyes, flawless skin, and a straight, defined nose. I was certain you must be the woman I remembered. But when I observed your reflection in the store window, I deduced I must have been mistaken. I offer my sincere apologies for causing you discomfort."

Archie addresses Dr. Duffy while his eyes flicker with skepticism. "It's quite a coincidence you were in Buckley when we were there. What brought you to Wales during the holidays?"

"I was visiting an old friend," he says. "I visit her in Buckley several times a year."

"Really?" I squint at him. "Do you ever visit Edinburgh, Scotland, perchance?"

Dr. Duffy cocks his head. "Yes. Occasionally. Again, I apologize Ms. Crowther."

He offers me his hand and a friendly smile. I accept his warm handshake, thinking what a blunder I've made.

"You can call me Gwyn," I say, glancing at the terrazzo floor.

"Please, call me Seamus. It's a pleasure to meet you. Archie has said wonderful things about you."

"Well, that was not how I wanted your reception to go, Seamus," Archie says. "I hope you won't hold the unusual introduction against us. We are very excited to have you here. Right, Nick?"

"Oh, absolutely," Nick says, shaking Seamus's hand. "We can't wait for you to lighten our load."

Seamus nods. "I'm eager to settle in. This was a dream of mine to come here and teach, even if the opportunity is temporary. Thank you all for your warm welcome."

The visiting professor peers in my direction, and suddenly, I want to crawl into Archie's office and shut the door.

"Gwyn, Seamus has done extensive research into Irish folklore," Archie says. "Especially the lore of the Tuatha Dé Danann."

"I've read some stories about them." I catch Nick staring at me in my peripheral vision. He knows why I'm interested.

"Maybe Seamus can set up a time to share his knowledge with you, Gwyn?" Archie asks. "Once he's settled into his office, of course."

"I would be more than happy to speak with you about Irish folklore. I never tire of discussing the history of the Tuatha Dé."

Seamus locks his eyes on me, and my heart rate increases with the intensity of his stare. Nick glimpses my frozen demeanor.

"I would love to meet with you when you have that conversation," Nick says. "I've always wanted to learn more about Irish folklore. If you don't mind me sitting in, of course."

"I'm sure we can arrange something once Spring Semester starts," Archie says. "But let's give Seamus time to get acclimated."

Archie and Nick introduce Seamus to a few more professors in the English department while I grovel under an archway and nibble on carrots. What an epic gaffe, and it proves I'm still struggling to handle the stress of the fairy vendetta.

Later at Archie's, I lie in bed, tapping my fingers together like a nervous Nellie as Archie gets dressed for bed. I check for the dirk under my pillow and receive a text notification.

Nick: *I completely forgot to confirm if we're on for Sunday brunch at the Raven.*

Oh, for fuck's sake. I throw my phone down. But I pick it up and text back.

Me: *Sure. We can chat about the visiting professor.*

Archie slides into bed and kisses me tenderly. "Sleep well, my love."

"You, too, honey."

He rolls over onto his side. No sex tonight, I guess. I ogle his muscular back through his t-shirt and deliberate over what to do about Laura Lovelace. She better keep her hands off him. I bet Agnes has a ton of hexes in her library full of spell books.

# Chapter Sixteen

# Meeting an Old Friend

In the hazy darkness of his bedroom, Nick stares into my eyes as he fondles my breast. "I love you so much, Gwyn."

I wake to sunrays burning my eyelids. If only the temperature outside matched the heat of the rays. Why am I dreaming about Nick again? Oh, yeah. The text to him was my last cognitive exercise before I fell asleep. Archie and I have to get our love life back in sync, like on the UK trip. I'm tired of Nick's unwanted excursions into my dreams. At some point, I'll cut off these brunches and convince him to move on, anyway. Patience, Gwyn.

When I enter the kitchen, Archie is already up and dressed, drinking his tea. I lean down and kiss him on the cheek.

"Good morning, honey. Have you been down here for a while? I didn't even feel the bed move when you got up."

"Good morning, my love," he says. "I woke about an hour ago. You were dead as a corpse, so I let you sleep. The water in the teakettle should still be hot."

"I'm not drinking tea before I leave. Ronnie expects me for breakfast. I forgot to tell you."

He stands and sets his cup in the dishwasher. "No matter. I told Leslie I would meet with Seamus Duffy today and show him around campus."

"I know you think I overreacted yesterday, but it was mega weird he was in Buckley at the same time as us. It's still a little creepy. Staring at my reflection in the store window was spooky as hell." I shudder and grimace.

He chuckles. "I'll admit he's a wee bit of an odd soul, but he's one of the top academics in his area of research. We're so thankful Leslie convinced him to teach this semester. He's an expert on the Tuatha Dé Danann. Please, set up a meeting with him. If you're not comfortable, Nick or I can sit in with you."

"OK. But he's an Unremarkable. He won't be able to discern what's real in the folklore. Because it's all nonsense to him."

"No. Separating what's authentic from the lore will be up to us. Have a wonderful day, my love. I'll chat with you later."

"OK. Enjoy your day, too."

He kisses me goodbye, and on the way out the back, he turns around and shouts from the mudroom. "Don't forget to put the dirk back in your bag. Menopause makes you a wee forgetful." He shuts the door with a whump.

How do I reduce the stress of the fairy threat when I'm carrying a sharp weapon in my hobo bag? I wash up and head over to Ronnie's house to eat breakfast with her and Derek. He cooks a scrumptious meal, knowing she has to run the café all day. It's so wonderful to hang with her as we used to. After she hooked up with Derek and I found Archie, we haven't spent enough girl-friend time together. I miss it.

Derek sets his coffee mug in the sink and comes to the kitchen table. "It was so great to talk to you, Gwyn. We need to do dinner now that you and Archie are back."

"I'll mention it to him. He would love to meet for dinner." I smile and drink my tea.

"I'm so excited for you to see my magic room," Ronnie says. "Derek did such a fabulous job. I'm lucky to have an Unremarkable boyfriend who supports my...hobby?"

"I would call your witchcraft more than a hobby," he says, grabbing his puffer jacket. "Have a great day, babe." He kisses her and heads to the fitness center.

"Bye, babe." Ronnie finishes the last drops of her syrupy coffee and eyes my necklace. "Did Archie give you that for Yule?"

"No. We didn't exchange gifts—too busy with school to squeeze in shopping. Aunt Gorawen gave this to me for protection, although the crystals would only cause discomfort to the fairy. Something is better than nothing, I guess. I started wearing it after an incident occurred behind Mystic Sage following the city council meeting."

I tell her about the disturbing man in Buckley and that he appeared in Edinburgh and under the light in the parking lot.

"That's messed up...and eerie as shit," she says.

"You don't know the half of it. Turns out the man is Dr. Seamus Duffy, the new visiting professor. I met him at the faculty mixer yesterday."

"No. Way. Did you confront him?"

"Yeah. Made a fool of myself by calling him a creep in the presence of all the faculty and their guests. He apologized and said I reminded him of someone. Said he was only trying to get a closer look at my face. Still freaked me out. He's a socially awkward academic, for sure." I stand and take the dishes to the sink. "Well, are you going to make me wait? I'm on pins and needles."

Ronnie jumps up and grabs her shin. "Shit. I always forget about my injury. And don't you dare frown. For the millionth time, the Sluagh attack was not your fault. The Kenilworths were behind everything. I'm sure glad they're gone."

"I'm happy about their demise, too, but I wish we could have figured out what they were doing to Audrey sooner. Maybe we could have saved her. Jeff has had a terrible time recovering from the entire mess."

I follow my best friend down the hallway to the spare bedroom, and she unlocks the door.

"Is Jeff back yet?" she asks.

"Shane said he'll return before the start of Spring Semester. He's sorting through stuff at his aunt and uncle's estate. I believe there's a butler who is *in the knowing* who can help him with packing all the magic stuff. Then he can hire some people to help assess the remaining contents of the house. The lawyer suggests he sell everything, and Jeff wants to purge stuff from his childhood there."

"Good thing he's an economics major. He's gonna be richer than the Mitchells were."

Ronnie pushes the door in, and I gape at the contents of her magic room. Derek installed built-ins on both sides of the center worktable. The standard magical items occupy the shelves, including wooden bowls, herb jars, crystal jars, a mortar and pestle, and various other items. She shows me around, and we end at the wall where my steamer trunk sits collecting dust.

"Wow," I say. "This room is fabulous. All you need now are herbs, some candles, and divination tools. You probably have the cleanest magic room of everyone."

"Give me time, friend. I'll destroy the table with the first spell. You know you can leave the trunk here for as long as you want. You don't have much room at Leslie's."

"No. I'll arrange for Tyler and Archie to move my ancestral stuff to Leslie's. You shouldn't have to practice around this heavy eyesore." I rub the wooden slats on the top. "I can squeeze the trunk into my room. Better I have access to my magic tools. I have to return to work at the insurance agency soon. Gotta figure out my schedule."

Ronnie stares at me and rubs her chin. "You appear distracted. Is everything OK with Archie?"

"Yeah. He went to sleep without even a hint of lust in his eyes. We're just out of sync again. Sex was great in Britain. And we had a moment the other night that was full of passion, but then he brought up that I'd not told him I was having lunch with Nick. One hundred percent my fault. Sometimes I don't feel like telling him what's on my daily schedule. He's becoming overly clingy."

She frowns and shakes her head. "Gwyn, you've gotta understand where he's coming from. He loves you. Probably worries about the fairy snatching you all the time. Cut him some slack."

"You're right, of course. And I'm dreaming about Nick again. Last night's vision wasn't very sexual, though. He said he loved me."

"Oh, my gods. You know, he probably does. We have to push this issue of exposing our true identities to Unremarkables. I'll bring it up again tonight at the meeting. It should be a short one now that the immediate threat to the mound has ended. The sooner you can cut Nick off, the sooner he's gone from your sleep."

"I'm with you there. He seems to pop into my subconscious whenever I'm having a dry spell with Archie. It's gotta be my menopausal hormones. I thought we were supposed to lose our libido, but I've been as randy as a bunny rabbit in recent months."

Ronnie cackles and punches my arm. "Join the club, friend."

"Holy crystals, Ronnie." I laugh as we amble back into the kitchen, and I collect my bag. "I'll text you when they can move the steamer trunk. See you later."

"Have an awesome afternoon and see ya at the meeting."

Mr. Yeats paces back and forth in his human form, making me fidgety. He shuffles to the table and pours a smidgeon of an herb into a small wooden bowl.

"You need to burn mugwort, Ms. Crowther. I understand your aunt told you to avoid its use, but the anise isn't working here. At least, try it one time."

"Aunt Gorawen warned against using mugwort, because it attracts fairies." I hate to admit he's right, but he is. "Oh, OK. But only what you put in there already."

He fluffs his bow tie and smiles. "Thank you, Ms. Crowther, for having confidence in me."

"Sure. But if that evil fairy contacts me, I'll banish you from my side forever."

He adjusts his spectacles and purses his lips. "That's harsh. But as you wish."

He grinds the mugwort in the mortar with the pestle and burns the herb, applying a lit match. I focus my intention on the picture of my mom, and her image morphs into a golden yellow surrounding her face.

"Yes! It's working!" I shout. "Come on, Mom and Dad. I'm here. Please, talk to me."

"Ms. Crowther," Mr. Yeats whispers next to my ear. "Calm down."

I glare at him. "Didn't Dr. Hughes ever tell you to never tell a woman to calm down? Times have changed since the turn of the century, dude."

He crosses his arms and scowls while I return my focus to my mom. I hold the obsidian crystals tightly in my fists and stare intensely at the photo. I summon my witch energy, and she materializes. The golden vision of my mother floats before me, shimmering like a pot of gold.

"Gwynedd, it's so good to see you again," she says. "Who is your friend? Can I trust him?"

I stare at Mr. Yeats and blink. "Most of the time. He's Dr. Hughes's familiar." I stand there rubbing the palm of my hand, wondering if this was a good idea after all.

"Dr. Leslie Hughes?" she asks. "You're summoning me inside her house?"

"Yeah. I wasn't thinking. I'm using her magic room, because I rent a room from her. But she isn't here. She's the acting chair of the Celtic Studies department, so she's on campus. But you should know she regrets everything now. It doesn't change what happened, but she's trying to make amends."

"I assure you, Mrs. Crowther," Mr. Yeats says. "Dr. Hughes has evaluated her past with the utmost scrutiny and has reformed her ways."

I grimace and send him a side-eye. And the door rolls open. Leslie freezes when she recognizes my mom's face—the best friend she betrayed so many years ago. All three of us remain silent for what seems like an eternity—one full of regrets. My mother's image fades a little, seeping back into the photo.

"Don't leave, Mom." I extend my hand and touch her shimmering face of gold.

Leslie moves forward. "Please, Lowri. I have so much I want to say to you."

Then something happens I couldn't have imagined in a gazillion years. Tears swell up in Leslie's copper eyes and roll down her pale, wrinkled face. Her lips quiver as she attempts to form her next words.

"I am sorry, Lowri, for all the transgressions against you and your daughter. I never believed my actions could ever have the negative effect on your lives as they did. But now the threat of the Tuatha Dé Danann has come to fruition. I cannot ask you for forgiveness, because I do not deserve it, but I promise you, as your devoted friend of yesteryear, I will do everything in my power to keep her safe."

The golden image of my mom shimmers in and out. "I never wanted to see you again, Leslie. You betrayed Rhys and me...and lied to the coven. Agnes didn't know the reason, but she knew enough to leave you, too. What heartache you caused for so many."

"Indeed. You are accurate in that assessment, and I have paid for it dearly with a lifetime of loneliness." Leslie never takes her eyes off my mom, facing her demons.

"Will you help Gwynedd find a spell to remove the portal in the Celestial Gardens? It must be done."

Leslie wipes her damp face with a handkerchief. "Of course, Lowri. We are already searching for an incantation and will continue until we find one. As long as it takes."

"Have you searched the family grimoire, Gwynedd? It may contain a spell." Mom morphs in and out.

"I did, but I found no incantation for closing a portal."

"But you can't read Welsh, dear. How was that possible?"

"A local college professor speaks Welsh. He translated the journal for me." I remember the last spell alerted Nick to my witch status.

"But what about the final entry?" Mom's face dissipates slowly, disappearing into the Otherworld.

Leslie wipes the rest of her tears while I scratch my chin. How do I explain my mom's last words without telling her Nick is aware of the coven's existence? I hope she missed them.

"What was Lowri referring to, Gwynedd?" she asks, clearing her throat. "What is significant about the last entry in the grimoire?"

My heart reaches a new level of tachycardia. "Uhhh...she wrote she wasn't going to make any more entries. That's all."

I'm not lying. I only left out the part about Mom mentioning my name and stopping her practice of witchcraft. So, now Nick knows everything about me. I walk over to Leslie and take her knobby fingers into my hands.

"Leslie, why don't we let Mr. Yeats clean up? I'll make us a quick dinner, and we can walk to the meeting together."

Leslie nods. "I appreciate your offer, Gwynedd."

While we're eating dinner, I text Archie and tell him we'll meet up at the Pumpkin House. He's eating dinner with Seamus Duffy, so he'll be near Victorian Row. On the brisk walk there, my hands are numb even with thick insulated gloves, and the icy cold air stings my face. I ask Leslie about the visiting professor.

"I meant to tell you I'm sorry I screamed at Dr. Duffy at the reception. It was such a shock to meet the man I saw in Buckley. Do you know him well?"

"Oh, yes," Leslie says in a raspy voice. "For a few years now. We met at an academic conference on Celtic Studies in Wales."

"So, he travels to Wales. He mentioned he was visiting an old friend in Buckley. What a coincidence he has a friend where Aunt Gorawen lives."

"He travels all over the UK when he's completing research. Not unlike myself. It's where the Celtic cultures are. So, I expect he has friends everywhere."

When we enter the Pumpkin House, the Fellowship has set out chairs in the parlor. Leslie taps her staff to start the meeting, and Trinity recounts what transpired at the council meeting for those who missed it. We vote to make a plan on how to proceed with the issues concerning the portal and the threat to my life.

Elijah stands to address us. "I've spoken with fellow council members who support the community. They're gonna need convincing why we should keep the mound. Right now, they're leaning toward replacing the site with a children's playground. Who knows what will happen if they dig into the area?"

My fellow witches groan and shake their heads. This is the worst news yet. If we can't convince the council members on our side, we're up shit's creek without a paddle.

As Elijah sits, Trinity stands and looks directly at me. "I understand we have new ethics rules, but we may have to suspend them in this situation. Gwyn, as long as that portal is open, it's like a satellite for a fairy to tap into. You realize the seriousness of this issue, don't you?"

"I do," I say. "But I don't support casting spells of influence. We should find another way. It's winter, and the Seelie Fae don't come through the portal much."

Tyler jumps up out of his chair. "Screw that, Mom? If a spell of influence guarantees the vote to keep the mound from being tampered with while we research a way to close the damn thing, then we should do it. And do it sooner than later."

He sits back down and crosses his arms. Spence, Skye, Zoe, and Tanner chuckle while I cringe in silence. My son has never spoken to me with such nastiness, and I can't respond. I lower my eyes to the floor.

"Tyler, I understand why you are so passionate about this," Archie says while he rubs my back. "You're worried about your mum."

Skye throws up a hand. "I'm with Tyler on this one, Gwyn. I think we all support him. We may have to change the rules for this. Your life is at stake."

The other young witches nod in agreement, and I sigh in frustration. The older witches chat among themselves. Even Ronnie shrugs. This is a fight I can't win.

"Gwyn, I applaud the ethics you want us to live by. You're a better woman than me," Agnes says. "In the end, I'll vote against you...for your own good." She blows me an air kiss.

Trinity stands, tapping her stiletto heel. "For now, we're fine. How is the search for a closing spell coming along? Have you found anything?"

"Well, yeah." Agnes frowns at the Elder. "But Leslie says we can't use it."

Leslie glowers at her. "The spell isn't usable. It requires human sacrifice."

"Like we haven't sacrificed others before?" Agnes asks. "Or don't you remember what we did to the Kenilworths?"

Shane shakes his head. "Now, Agnes, you know we were only defending ourselves. An entirely unique situation."

"Personally, I'm with Agnes," Spence says. "I can think of a few people who should volunteer."

Tanner's mouth falls open. "Do I actually live with you, dude? Where did that macabre idea come from?"

Spence chuckles and flings his palms up. "Whaaat? I'm only considering all the options."

"We will not commit human sacrifice, Spence." Trinity puts her hands on her hips and huffs.

The hedge witch bursts out laughing, and everyone joins in her amusement. Spence most likely is joking, but we never know with him.

"Gwyn, Agnes, and I will continue to sort through the spell books in her library," Leslie says. "But we could use some help."

Agnes glares at Leslie. "Fuck no. I don't think I'm OK with everyone invading my library."

"If you can ask me to suspend my ethics, you can allow others to peruse the grimoires in your collection," I say. "If you really wanna help me."

"Oh, for fuck's sake. But I'm not throwing a party." Agnes scowls and gives us the bird.

"I wouldn't mind helping," Archie says. "Or do you have suggestions?"

Agnes scans the circle. "Tyler. He has more skin in the game than the rest of us. The students...since they have the time. Spence, Skye, and Zoe, you're welcome to come."

"Well, is there anything else?" Trinity asks.

Ronnie speaks up. "With these issues upon us, I propose we continue the discussion of vetting a few Unremarkables at the next meeting. We may need to divulge our existence earlier than planned."

"We'll put your request on the agenda. Go in peace." Leslie taps her staff three times.

When Archie and I walk onto the porch, Tyler and Zoe are waiting for me. I throw him a mother's frown—as bitter as the night's air.

"I'm sorry, Mom," Tyler says. "But I think you've gotta be realistic about what's going down. We would all rest well if we secured the mound."

"Fine." I roll my eyes. "When the time comes...IF we have to, I'll agree to a spell of influence."

"See, I told ya," Zoe says. "Your mom is reasonable. Let's go. My butt's cold."

"Goodnight," Tyler says, hugging me. "We'll see you on Saturday."

Zoe waves. "Goodnight, everyone."

Archie and I wave goodbye to them as they take off toward the municipal parking lot, and Leslie says goodnight to Agnes. We walk back with the coven Elder to Drummond Lane, discussing the convenience of having an academic specializing in Irish folklore. How much more hounding can I take? I get it. Dr. Duffy is a resource I should tap. I wish he weren't so freaky. Leslie heads into the house, and I stay outside to share what happened that afternoon.

"I imagine she experienced a swath of emotions speaking with your mum after all these years," Archie says. "Your mum mustn't have been too happy with you, either."

"No. It was stupid to do divination there. But I hoped Mr. Yeats would stop bugging me so much if I let him help me. He is a good familiar but an annoying one, too. I think the confrontation resolved many years of anger and resentment. I've never seen Leslie cry, and I wasn't sure she was capable. I should stay here tonight. In case she wants to talk more."

"Naturally. How things change. Only a few months ago, you never wanted to speak with her again. I'm proud of you for giving her a chance to redeem herself."

"Well, she hasn't won full redemption yet. But she's on the right path."

"When will you sleep over again?" His alluring eyes tug at me.

"Probably Saturday night. I've got a busy day tomorrow."

Why stay at his house on Friday if all we're going to do is sleep? I can do that in my own comfy bed.

"Just as well," he says. "I have a dinner meeting with Laura Lovelace to discuss her dissertation. Don't be concerned. I'm insisting on meeting in public. Goodnight, my love."

He kisses me and strolls toward home. I hate the jealousy I have toward Laura. Archie is with me, not her, and I have confidence in his love for me. But I don't trust her. She's like the Wicked Witch of the East. I bet Skye would say, "Wouldn't it be amazeballs if a house fell on her?"

# Chapter Seventeen

# A First Time for Everything

The temperature has dipped into the teens, and I dread dressing for the day. Agnes will probably have the heat turned down, but Leslie has hers turned up. What the hell do I wear? I decide to layer my tops and stuff a sweatshirt into my hobo bag—company for the dirk. And I clasp the necklace of crystals around my neck. I'm lugging a weapon around, and now I'm choking myself daily with a ring of black crystals. What's next?

Leslie and I get an early start at Agnes's farm, but we aren't expecting Tyler, Zoe, Spence, and Skye until later. Zillennials don't work well until after ten, apparently. Archie had to get started on Laura's dissertation read-through, so I told him to stay home.

We labor for almost two hours and take a break for tea. I tell the older witches to rest at the kitchen table while I retrieve cups and saucers. But Agnes insists on micromanaging me the entire time.

"No, not that cabinet," Agnes says. "The one on the right. Not that door. One more over."

"Your organization makes no sense." I finally open the cabinet with the tea bags. "Oh, here they are."

When I pull down the plastic containers storing the tea bags, I discover painted black mason jars. I place one on the table and pop some bread slices into the toaster.

"So, you're hiding preserves from us?"

Agnes chuckles. "That's not jam, Gwyn."

"Oh, Agnes," Leslie says, rolling her eyes. "You shouldn't keep your herbs in a kitchen cabinet."

"What?" I ask. "What kind? You haven't marked the glass?"

The front door creaks open, and footsteps approach us. Tyler, Zoe, Spence, and Skye have arrived. Skye waves as she enters and sniffs.

"Good morning, fam. Mmm, I smell toast."

"I didn't know we were eating brunch." Zoe sits down at the table.

"Hi, Mom," Tyler says. "Sorry, we're so late. But it is Saturday."

Spence has been eyeing the black jar on the kitchen table. He picks it up, unscrews the top, and inhales a whiff of the contents.

"I thought you said you weren't throwing a party, Agnes." He wiggles his eyebrows and laughs.

"May the gods help me," she says. "I'm not. Put the top back on my pot before it loses its potency."

I frown at Agnes. "You're storing your marijuana in a kitchen cabinet? What happens if you get caught? They'll fine you."

"Oh, who's gonna come to my home, searching for pot," she says. "Unless a student tells on me. Even then, I'm in my 80s. No one would believe them."

Spence snickers. "Don't be so sure. You don't have the best reputation. The townies think you're weird as fuck."

"They have a valid point, Agnes." A faint smile emerges on Leslie's face.

"Let 'em talk," Agnes says. "We're losing precious time. Put my pot back. Finish your tea and toast so we can go upstairs. I hope you brought your own lunch, because I'm not a fucking restaurant."

We all crack up and head upstairs to tackle the piles of grimoires we've set aside. When we enter the library, the young witches gasp. Zoe runs around the room, surveying the books on the shelves. Tyler tries to keep up with her, but it's futile. Skye picks up a tome and immediately flips through the pages. Spence clutches his heart as he scans her personal library.

"I'm in paradise. There must be a spell for everything in this room. We have to discover a suitable incantation in one of these books."

"Yeah, but Mom may be dead by the time we find it," Tyler says with a snort.

I frown and blink at him. "Well, aren't you positive today?"

"He's being realistic, sis," Spence says. "There are a lot of grimoires in here."

Leslie nods. "It's an accurate assessment. We may need the entire coven to help sift through this plethora of books. And we need to prepare for the possibility a spell does not exist."

"That's not fucking true, and you know it," Agnes shouts. "We found an incantation. A teensy human sacrifice is a small price to pay to save Gwyn."

The young witches and I raise our heads toward the older women, waiting for Leslie to speak her mind. She pinches her lips together and glares back at Agnes while her face turns as red as an overripe tomato. The coven Elder doesn't disappoint when she delivers her final commentary on the matter.

"Shut the fuck up about a sacrifice, Agnes."

Is this the first time she's ever used the F word? She must be furious Agnes is harping on about this spell again. We gape at them but hold back our laughter, awaiting the rage to spew from Agnes's vile mouth. She squints at Leslie as she approaches her, and I worry

Agnes will become violent. When she raises her head to Leslie's face, I shift closer, preparing to stop a possible slapping frenzy. And she kisses Leslie hard on the mouth.

"My gods, I love you, woman." Agnes chuckles and strokes her lover's face.

We join them in their laughter. I bet this is the first time Leslie has allowed anyone to view her fervent relationship with Agnes in the open. It's a significant moment for her. The coven Elder clears her throat.

"We should get back to work. The sun pushes on in the sky, and we will lose daylight."

Spence sniffs and rubs his eyes. "That was the most beautiful expression of love I have ever seen."

"You're a sap, Spence," Agnes says as she rubs Leslie's shoulder.

Zoe hugs Tyler. "I think it was romantic."

"All this love admiration is wonderful, but Dr. Hughes is right," Skye says. "We need to get back to work. Someone has to remain clear-headed to keep us on track."

Taking Skye's lead, we work all day except for lunch. I spend the entire afternoon putting on my sweatshirt and taking it off—on and off. The heater works, but only sometimes. I survey the shelves and pick the promising tomes, stacking them in piles and carrying them to the library table for Skye to inspect. Overwhelmed by the overabundance of books, my brain revolts with a throbbing headache.

By the time we're finished, I'm exhausted from the hot flashes and the pounding in my head. All I want to do is crawl into bed, but it's only five o'clock. We gather at the front door and put on our coats. I thank all the Zillennial witches for giving up their Saturday, but Leslie is less impressed.

"I understand you value your Saturday mornings," she says. "However, beginning at eight would add two hours to your research. Do any of you disagree?"

The young Fellowship members stand in silence. If they've learned anything, they know you never give the Elder a rebuttal. A slight smile curls the corners of Leslie's mouth, and she raises her chin.

"Splendid. We will meet next Saturday at eight."

"Fine," Spence whines. "But I can't focus before ten. Everyone knows that."

"And you can concentrate after ten? Since when?" Skye snickers.

Spence crosses his arms. "My mind is a moving object."

"That's for sure," Zoe laughs. "Just kidding. We all appreciate how smart you are."

Tyler nods. "And talented. You've been an awesome teacher. I wouldn't have progressed so quickly in my magic skills without your training."

"Enough with all the sappy praise," Agnes says. "I'm hungry and need to make dinner."

The young witches say their goodbyes and leave. I lift my hobo bag, sensing the weight of the dirk inside in my exhausted state, and wait for the Elder.

"Leslie, where's your coat?" I ask.

"I've decided to stay at Agnes's tonight. She can make sure I arrive home tomorrow."

"OK," I say, grinning. "I'll see you at the house. Thank you both for devoting so much of your time to safeguard me."

"Yeah, yeah." Agnes smirks and waves me on. "Get the fuck out of here. I'm hungry."

"Enjoy your evening, ladies."

The drive home takes about fifteen minutes with traffic, and on the way, I remember I forgot to text Archie when I left. He wanted to start dinner. When I arrive, there's a car sitting in the driveway, so I park in front along the curb. I can't imagine who's visiting him. Maybe Dr. Duffy?

I push the door in. Laura Lovelace is standing in the hallway laughing as Archie finishes a story. What are they talking about? He clamps his mouth shut when he makes eye contact with me. Laura turns around and abruptly cuts her laughter. I glare at them, enraged.

"Laura was just leaving," he says, averting his eyes.

She smirks at me on the way out. "Archie, I'll see you at the Raven next week."

I slam the door behind her, hopefully hitting her ass as she exits. When I spin around, Archie shoves his hands in his pockets.

"She came uninvited, Gwyn. Just barged into the foyer when I turned the doorknob. She dropped off hard copies of changes in her dissertation for me to read."

I squint at him. "You appeared to be having a ball when I walked in. Hardly the appearance of someone perturbed. She broke the boundaries you laid out."

"I was quite angry and told her to leave." He runs his fingers through his wavy hair. "She handed me the paper and was on her way out when she remembered a story about another doctoral student. He had trouble finishing his paper after he deleted a portion inadvertently. I shared my experience of how I almost dumped a flash drive storing my dissertation changes into the River Thames, and we both laughed. You walked in. That's all."

"Her behavior worries me."

My shoulders fall as I sigh, exasperated at the situation. Archie shifts closer and strokes my chin, melting my vexed insides with his icy blues.

"Gwyn, do you trust me?"

"Yes. I do. But she's a deceitful witch and a liar. Please remember what she did at the Winter Solstice Celebration and the pagan conference. I don't think my threat scared her at all."

"I'm an ancestral witch, Gwyn. With powerful magic skills. She would have to receive help from another being stronger than I to transform my affections."

He cups my face with his warm hands and kisses me, and I wrap my arms around his middle.

"You're right. Personally, I hope she latches onto Nick. Would be terrible for him but great for us."

Archie chuckles. "That's an awful thing to wish for him, but it's an accurate assessment. I missed you all day. Can we eat dinner and go to bed early?"

A mischievous grin captures his mouth as I follow him into the kitchen.

"Sure. I'll help you cook."

"You never said how the research went at Agnes's," he says, opening the fridge.

"Found nothing." I laugh, recalling the emotional interaction between the coven Elder and my hedge witch mentor. "But I got to hear Leslie say fuck."

Archie stops with food in his hands and gapes at me. "What triggered her to swear?"

"Agnes brought up the portal-closing spell again—the one requiring a human sacrifice. I think she was yanking Leslie's chain, but the Elder had had enough. We thought Agnes was going to clobber her right there with all of us to witness it. Instead, she kissed her. It was such a touching moment."

"And probably the first time she's allowed Agnes to show affection to her in public. I have hope for them."

"She's staying the night there," I say while I cut the vegetables. "It's why I drove straight here instead of parking at her house."

He sets a pan on the stove. "It's wonderful to witness all these changes in Leslie. She appears to be much happier."

Once we've finished dinner, we clean up the kitchen and head upstairs. While Archie washes, I lie in bed in my satin chemise, rubbing my temples. He comes out of the bathroom and slides into bed, ready for action. Kissing me tenderly, he plants soft kisses on my neck as he works his way to my breasts. But my nipples don't respond to his touch. My body has nothing left from the day, and the headache still stabs like an icepick in my head.

"What's wrong, my love? You aren't in the mood?"

I acknowledge the yearning in his eyes and lay a hand on his cheek. "I want to. But I'm so exhausted, and this headache won't subside. I'm sorry."

"Don't ever apologize for feeling ill. I'm happy to have you by my side. Our bodies are a wee out of sync. It happens."

"Are you sure? You waited all week."

"And I'll wait as long as you need." He kisses me again and whispers, "Goodnight, my love."

"Night, honey."

His mouth warms that special spot between my legs, and I'm almost there. He's so adept at finding the exact way to touch me, and I can't hold back any longer. I shudder and quiver as I clutch the sheets. When I glance down at my lover, smiling coyly, he raises his head. And I see Nick. MY EYES FLIP OPEN.

Archie is staring at me, a question hanging on his brow. "Are you all right? You shook the bed."

I goggle at him. "Did I? I was dreaming."

"About what? You quivered like...did you have an orgasm in your sleep?"

My lips part, and I blink several times. "I'm not sure I remember."

"Well, at least you got to enjoy yourself with me in your dreams." He chuckles and kisses me. "Care to continue?"

"Sure." How do I have sex with him after dreaming about Nick? This is so wrong. My cell phone alarm goes off. "Oh, I can't. Sunday brunch."

"Another time, I guess. We need to push the issue of vetting Unremarkables. Once Leslie and Trinity are aware of Nick, you can drop these brunches for good. I was against the idea at first, but now I think it's our only option."

"Yes. We have to vote for it soon. I've got to shower and get out of here. I don't wanna be late."

After dressing, I clasp the tourmaline necklace under my shirt and head out the door. Breakfast with Nick at the Raven Pub is more awkward than ever before. Every time I look at him, I recall his face between my legs in the dream, so I lower my gaze to the waffles on my plate. Screw my hormones and the migraines. If I'd not had the headache, I could have had sex with the man I love, and this infatuated Unremarkable wouldn't invade my slumber.

"Gwyn?" Nick lays his hand on mine. "Gwynyedd Crowther?"

I stare into his eyes as my groggy head steals my focus. "What?"

"You're someplace else this morning. Didn't you sleep well?"

I stop chewing and swallow. "Not the best. No."

"Wanna share? You know I'm an outstanding listener."

He places a slice of pineapple slowly on his tongue, never taking his gaze off me, and I squirm in my seat. This has to end, but how? I lay my utensils on the plate and wipe my face with a napkin.

"Nothing to share. Only typical menopausal sleep disruptions. Nick, although I enjoy these brunches with you, I'm gonna have to cut back. Every Sunday has become too much. Once Spring Semester starts, I'm going to be swamped with classes, work, and studies. I'll be lucky to find time for Archie. You understand, don't you?"

He finishes his coffee, slams the mug on the wooden table, and rubs his stomach. "Sure. I assumed you enjoyed our friendship, but I guess not."

"You're taking this the wrong way. We'll still meet occasionally, but not every Sunday. And frankly, the calories from these brunches have taken up parking on my hips."

"You have a fine figure, Gwyn. I don't know why you insist on finding fault with it."

Nick penetrates me with his smoldering brown eyes, and I slip into a brief daze. He peers over my shoulder and shifts in his seat.

"I'm meeting someone now," he says. "I told her to come in a half hour, but she's early."

"Hey, Nick." Laura Lovelace leers down at me. "Gwyn."

"Hi, Laura. I wasn't expecting you for thirty minutes," Nick says.

"Oh, I pride myself on being early."

"I better go," I say.

I put money on the table to cover my brunch and slide out of the booth seat, grabbing my purse before I stand.

Laura snickers at me. "You look like a bag lady with that tote."

"Bye, Nick." I ignore Laura and turn to leave.

Nick raises his palm to me as Laura sits down. As I exit the Raven, speculation swims in my head. Why is she meeting with him? For dissertation help? Is it a date? And I realize. I don't give a shit.

Shane puts on his puffer jacket. "I'm going home now, Gwyn. Thank you for closing up."

"No problem," I say. "Sundays tend to be sparse. Not good for your profit margin, but great for my book reading time."

His grin breaks through his white beard. "Enjoy your evening and call if there are any problems. And Gwyn, be careful walking home."

Shane exits with a ding, and I settle in behind the cash register to read a book on practicing witchcraft in the modern age. When my butt goes numb, I close the book and grab the duster. I meander around the store, dusting the shelves and jars as customers enter to do nothing more than quell their curiosity about the occult.

Around 7:45 p.m., I return to the hard stool behind the counter and open my paperback. The door dings, and a customer enters. When I peek out over the top of my book, Seamus Duffy is browsing the puzzles. I don't say anything, because I'm hoping he doesn't recognize me. As he roams around the store inspecting the games, herbs, and other occult items, he favors one leg over the other. When I'm sure he's headed toward the exit, he limps toward me and places a jar of mugwort herb on the counter.

I close the book, set it on the chair, and ring him up. He cocks his head and stares at me as he did in Buckley. I don't care what Archie says. This man sends a chill up my spine.

"Gwynedd Crowther? Am I remembering your name correctly?" Dr. Duffy asks in his Irish accent.

"Yeah. That's my name," I say, placing the mugwort in a paper bag.

"Nice to meet you again. You're closing soon, aren't you?"

He picks up the bag, and I peer up at his eerie eyes.

"Yeah. I lock the doors at eight," I say.

"Leslie says you live with her. I'm renting a house in the area. Would you like an escort?"

I'm tongue-tied, because I have no desire to walk with this strange man. My stomach does somersaults while I tear the knot out of my tongue.

"Perhaps my offer was too forward? I'll be on my way."

He heads toward the exit, but I remember I have the dirk in my hobo bag. Maybe I should give him a chance?

"Dr. Duffy, an escort would be great."

"I'll wait for you outside, then." He limps out.

After turning out all but the security lights, I set the alarm and lock the front door. The visiting professor stands like a nightmarish image from a Halloween movie in a long, black winter coat as he leans against the lamppost. I have to stop stereotyping, but the apprehension gnaws at my gut.

"Shall we go?" he asks, motioning with a hand.

I stroll beside Dr. Duffy with my hands clinging to my hobo bag as we pass the parking garage undergoing construction. He limps a little and leans on his cane as he walks. I want to ask him what happened to his leg, but it would be rude. Our conversation includes small talk until we hit the opening for the Green and have to descend a flight of stairs. He takes his time, favoring his left leg, so I slow down, not wanting to bring attention to his old wound. The icy air cuts across my face as I wait.

"I'm sorry for holding you back," Dr. Duffy says.

"Never apologize for a disability." I hesitate, but curiosity has gotten the best of me. "Dr. Duffy, if it's not too intrusive, what happened to your leg?"

"Please, call me Seamus. I stepped into a private matter I shouldn't have. Came out with a permanent reminder of the intrusion."

"Does your leg hurt?"

"Only when the temperature drops drastically. As it has recently."

"I'm sorry you have to live with the pain."

His explanation didn't tell me much. I'm still wary of this man and clutch the dirk through the cloth material of my tote as we meander on the paver walkways through the Green.

"Once the semester begins, give me a ring. It would be wonderful to have a discussion with you regarding Irish folklore."

He stops for a minute, and his gaze hypnotizes me. I swallow as I fidget with an earring. Why does he affect me this way?

"My semester will be busy, but I'll contact you when I have a spare hour."

We've arrived at the alleyway between Campbell and Menzies Halls. I'm thinking I really don't want to die today, but I continue down the dark, barely lit shortcut to the east side of Bearsden with my heart leaping toward my ribcage. When we come to the intersection of Drummond Lane, we stop under a streetlight. The visiting professor's sea-green eyes shine like glass.

"Thank you for the escort, Seamus. I hope you enjoy the rest of your evening."

"You as well. And tell Dr. Hughes, I'll see her in the morning. Goodnight to you."

He hobbles toward Main Street while butterflies take flight in my stomach. Did he walk me all this way when he actually rents a place back there? Why would he do that?

# CHAPTER EIGHTEEN

# SPELL FATIGUE

FEBRUARY ARRIVES WITH A snowstorm as the deep freeze continues. Delaware winters are usually on the mild side, but every few years, we get blasted. From inside the toasty house, the rounded heaps of white resemble fluffy cotton balls. I can't stand this weather, but at least it keeps the Seelie Fae from crossing over. I guess they prefer warmer temperatures, too.

The coven voted to delay a decision on revealing our existence to any new Unremarkables, which sucks, but for now, it's OK. Nick hasn't contacted me in a month. The business of the start of Spring Semester has kept Archie and me apart, but what can we do? Sometimes daily life impedes one's love life. Despite the hectic schedule, I'm more clear-headed since I removed Nick from my calendar. I'm sleeping again, and he hasn't popped up in my dreams—and thankfully not between my legs.

The young witches join Leslie, Agnes, and me every Saturday to sort through the grimoires, but the time they're devoting to the search is wearing thin on them—and me.

"I found one! I found one!" Skye screams and runs over reading the incantation but stops as if she ran into a brick wall. "Never mind. Read it wrong. It's a spell to shut a door to your house."

"Why the hell would a witch create an incantation to shut a house door? Are they too lazy to get out of a fucking chair?" Spence snickers. "What a waste of good magic."

Agnes scowls at him. "Wait until you're so old it hurts your eyeballs just to lift your eyelids."

"Excuse me," he says. "I expected spells with more value and cool magic. So many of these are worthless as shit. Like this one. A spell for preventing dust accumulation." His eyes bounce around the room. "Clearly, it doesn't work."

Tyler, Zoe, and Skye chuckle while Leslie and I keep our composure.

"Give me that book." Agnes grimaces and snatches the tome out of Spence's hands. "Didn't you read the summary at the beginning? It's a collection of spells to rid your house of evil."

Skye cracks up. "Dust is evil? I'll have to remember this incantation the next time I want to skip cleaning."

Leslie chuckles under her breath, and Agnes throws her a side-eye.

"The idea is to create a fresh palate to aid in more important incantations, Mister Smart-Ass." Agnes slides the book back on a shelf.

"Now that makes sense," Tyler says. "So, the spell can be more successful. Can I borrow that book?"

"I am so impressed by how you pick up on the subtle things, Tyler," Leslie says. "Keep up your training, and you'll surpass your peers."

Leslie glances at Spence and smirks.

Zoe snickers. "Oh, bam. Did you feel that smackdown, Spence?"

"What?" Spence asks, gaping at his professor. "I don't think I can handle a saucy Dr. Hughes."

Everyone laughs, and a smile erupts on Leslie's face. Agnes kisses the Elder on the cheek.

"That's the Leslie I know."

"We've been at this for a month," I say, slamming a book shut. "Most of these spell books repeat each other with minor variations on ingredients and word usage. None of them come close to closing a portal mound. March is around the corner, and the fae children will emerge once the snow melts. At this rate, we'll not find a spell for years."

Leslie tilts her head. "What is the alternative, Gwynedd? Suspend our search? I promised Lowri I would not stop until we found an incantation to remove the portal. It's only been a month. We push on as planned."

"We have so many grimoires left, Mom," Tyler says. "There has to be a spell in one of them."

Zoe peers up at me with those loving brown eyes. "Don't worry, Gwyn. We'll come every week, even if it takes all year."

"I'm not capitulating," I say. "But while we spend every Saturday in this room searching for a solution that may not even exist, we're forfeiting a chunk of our lives. Except for Agnes, we all have jobs or go to school—or both. I don't think it's fair to ask Agnes to do it alone. She may be a retired hedge witch, but she only has so many days left on this earth."

"Order the coffin now!" Agnes shouts and drops a book on the table with a whump. "For the love of the gods, I'll decide what's fair to me. I'd been meaning to organize this library for years. Now that it's started, I might as well continue."

Spence talks with his hands moving in all directions. "What if we want to keep looking into infinity? Are you gonna stop us?"

"Yes. We should make that decision," Skye says.

The young witches huddle together, crossing their arms in consensus.

"You all are truly family," I say. "I'll never be able to repay you for your devotion to me."

Agnes snickers. "You think I'm not keeping an updated list? You still haven't painted my kitchen cabinets."

I frown at her and return the grimoire to the shelf. "Well, I'm pooped. Why don't we stop for today? If we don't manage our time well, we'll get burned out and won't have the stamina to continue."

"I agree," Leslie says. "I'm a little tired as well."

"Can we borrow a few books?" Spence asks. "I'd like to practice of few spell variations."

Skye raises two books, flipping her fire-red hair over her shoulder. "Me, too?"

"Me, three?" Zoe asks as she picks up a small pile.

"Oh, all right." Agnes waves a hand down. "Please, be careful with them. They're older than me."

"Why not do a session now?" Tyler asks. "Agnes, are you OK with us using your magic room?"

"Why the fuck not?" she says, exhaling. "Can I trust the four of you not to fuck things up?"

Spence points both index fingers at his chest. "Moi? Of course."

"We'll be careful," Skye says as she pulls her wavy hair into a ponytail.

Zoe grabs a book and runs to the door. "I've got the spell I want to cast!"

Tyler, Spence, and Skye follow her downstairs, and a door slams shut. Agnes and Leslie sit down in their chairs, and each of them picks up one more book to occupy themselves while the young witches practice in the magic room. I find a small one and do the same. Except for the sound of paper rustling, we relish the tranquility. We love them, but sometimes silence is golden—or at least a dull mustard.

"Now that Tyler is out of the room, I'm gonna speak my piece again." Agnes pats her salt and pepper bangs off her face. "I will never stop looking, even if it takes me until I'm a hundred years old. And I plan to make it to that milestone."

I laugh as my finger slides down the page. "I wouldn't attempt to give you orders, Agnes."

"Gwynedd, have you remembered anything unusual from your dreams? Remember, they can double as premonitions. Archie said you had visions of the Sluagh that ultimately came to fruition."

"Nothing like that. Only regular nightmares." I laugh out loud, and they stare at me, perplexed.

"Nightmares are comical?" Agnes asks.

Should I tell them? Why the hell not? They won't tell Archie. "Both. It's kind of personal. My hormones have been all over the place. When Archie and I have...dry spells, and I don't mean the magic kind, my subconscious takes over."

"How does dreaming about your man become a nightmare?" Leslie asks.

"Because it's not Archie." I lower my voice and cringe. "It's Dr. Evans."

Agnes guffaws and slaps a book on the table. "Fucking hysterical. I used to have dream porn about Leslie when I was with my old girlfriend."

"This isn't the same thing, but now you see why I call it a nightmare. I dated him for a while, but Archie and I got back together. Nick and I remained friends, so my mind must be messing with me."

"Indeed, it is." Leslie stares oddly at me for a moment and returns to her book.

Suddenly, screaming reverberates throughout the house, and we rush downstairs as fast as the old witches can muster. We fling open the magic room door, and the young witches yell, "Shut the door! He'll get out!"

A tiny man wearing a red pointed hat is running back and forth across the room, climbing the shelves and throwing items. He expels an evil laugh when glass crashes onto the wooden floor.

Everyone shouts, "Catch him!" We dart from corner to corner, trying to capture his little body, but he's too quick.

Agnes stops unexpectedly to catch her breath. "Leslie, we don't have the time or energy for this. Help me, please."

"My pleasure," Leslie says.

She moves next to Agnes, and they raise their hands to summon their witch energy, creating an amber magic bubble to trap the gnome. In a swift movement, they scoop up the tiny man and hold him captive as he screams. Then they melt him into a colorful blob topped in red.

"Eww. You killed the poor little man," Spence says. "That's gross."

"We're really sorry," Tyler, Zoe, and Skye say in unison as they gather around the remains.

"What the hell was that?" I ask. "He resembled a garden gnome."

"Your assessment is accurate, Gwynedd," Leslie says.

Agnes huffs as she shakes a finger at the young witches. "A spell to turn my garden statue into a live being required all of you, so don't try to wiggle out of this. Come on. Fess up. Who's idea was this?"

Tyler, Skye, and Spence lower their eyes to the floor, but Zoe peers up at us and shrugs. "Oops."

After class on Monday, I trudge through the snow to Stewart Hall to visit Archie. He's been so swamped with helping Dr. Duffy settle in on top of his own classes and critiquing Laura's dissertation, I haven't seen him for a few days. I turn the doorknob to his office, but it's locked. A buzzing sensation seizes my body, hinting a witch is behind me, and I grin. I spin on the heels of my boots but flinch when I discover Seamus Duffy standing inches away.

"I am deeply sorry," he says in his singsongy Irish brogue. "I should have warned I was behind you." His black hair is so thick and long.

"No. You're fine. I was expecting Archie. He must still be in class."

I'm so confused. Perhaps Leslie walked by? The visiting professor's eyes are glassy, almost glowing. Does he do drugs?

"I'm glad you happened by," he says. "We never scheduled our chat. What time is convenient for you? I may be free."

"Uh, sometime this week would work," I say, hugging my bag. "How about Wednesday? I have a break in the afternoon around three."

Seamus nods once. "Perfect. I look forward to our talk. Have a wonderful day, Gwynedd."

He continues on down the hallway, limping slightly. As he turns the corner, Nick Evans talks with him for a minute, and he limps on. Nick spies me from a distance, and a giant grin spreads his mouth. As he approaches, I force a smile.

"Hi, Gwyn. I'm so glad I ran into you. I was going to send you a text. There's a Welsh Early Music concert at the School of Music. I bought tickets for us!"

Holy shit. Why would he purchase them before asking me first? "When is the performance? I'm pretty busy, as I told you I would be."

"It's on Saturday. So, it won't interfere with studies during the week."

No, but how about my love life? It will be my first free Saturday in a month. "I don't think so. I appreciate the offer, but you should have checked with me first."

"Oh, come on, Gwyn." He pouts and bats his eyes comically. "A crwth player will perform at the concert. How cool is that?"

"OK. What time? I'll meet you there."

He was going to pressure me until I said yes, so why fight it? I mean, I'd love to hear a crwth in person. He smiles as if I'm agreeing to a first date.

"Awesome. Meet me there at 7:30 p.m., and we'll have time to find a good seat and catch up."

He walks down the hall with a skip in his step. Archie exits the classroom where I first met him and talks to a young woman from the class. When he nods and tries to break away, she keeps blathering. He notices me at his office door and points in my direction. The girl frowns and tramps up the stairs.

"What are you doing here?" he asks as he unlocks the doorknob. "A wonderful surprise."

An undergrad dashes by, yelling Archie's name as she passes. "Hi, Dr. Cock-burn!"

I chuckle, remembering the first time I mispronounced his name, but Archie isn't amused. He frowns and shakes his head as I follow him into his puny office.

"I'd like just one year, or even a semester, where every student learned how to pronounce my name correctly."

"You know that young woman was flirting with you, right?" I blink twice.

"Yes. Until I saw you and told her my girlfriend was waiting for me." He shuts the door and pushes me against the wall, kissing me hard. "We need to find a night you aren't busy or exhausted. They're turning blue, Gwyn."

I chuckle and lay my hand on his package. "If only there was something you could do alone to remedy the issue."

"Sometimes you can be quite the tease." He adjusts his bulge and removes books from a chair for me. "I'm going to sit behind my desk and cool down. I have another class and can't go in with this."

"I'm sorry." As I sit, a paperweight on the desk catches my attention—the one Nick gave him for Yule. "I agree. But carving out time in either of our schedules will be challenging. Me with work, school, and spending every Saturday at Agnes's, and you with your course load."

"Did you find a spell with any mention of closing a portal?"

"No. Everyone was so tired. The students have school. Leslie is Acting Chair. Most of the spell books contain the same damn incantations. We needed a break, so we stopped early. This could drag on for years, and nothing has happened since those initial contacts. We'll burn out like a short candle if we don't pace ourselves."

"Be sure to carry the dirk with you at all times."

"Aghhh. Yes. I told you I would," I say, pinching my lips.

"I have to check, because you're a very..."

"Stubborn woman. Yes. I admit I can be, but not on this. The family heirloom will travel with me wherever I go. I promise."

A seductive smile slinks onto his lips. "So, you should have plenty of energy on Saturday if you're pacing yourselves."

"Yeah, but..." I bite my lower lip. "I told Nick I'd go to a concert with him at DUB's School of Music. He bought tickets already. A collegium group will perform Welsh music—old stuff with a crwth player."

He brushes his hair with his fingers. "How long will the concert last?"

"It's about an hour." I glance at my cell phone. "I've gotta get home to log some work hours. Last I checked, I still have to pay tuition."

Archie stands and walks me to the door. "Will you be too tired after a long concert?"

"If I am, you have my permission to wake me up with that magical hand of yours." I kiss him and stroke his goatee. "Before I forget, I'm stopping by Wednesday afternoon for a meeting with Seamus Duffy when you're in class. I'll be fine by myself."

"I'm glad. He's highly researched on the Tuatha Dé. Before you leave, I wanted to mention something I've been researching. You're already aware of the possibilities of premonitions in your dreams. But I've never shared what other options exist for ancestral witches. Besides triggering your magic skills, I may be capable of communicating with you through my thoughts."

"Like telepathy?" I laugh. "That would be so cool. I wouldn't need a cell phone to chat with you."

He chuckles. "It's not quite the same, Gwyn. I would send an intention, and you could respond to it. Or not. I'm not exactly sure how the messaging works. I'm still researching with my dad. Tough to practice with him from the other side of the pond."

"He probably loves being consulted. Makes him feel valued."

"Aye. He was excited when I called. In any case, I should try it with you. Come for dinner on Saturday. We have to go through a wee ritual before you leave for the concert. And I'll attempt to send an intention to you. You can report back when you return."

I swing my huge purse on my shoulder and amble to the door. "Sounds like a plan. I received an email from Ellie. She finally set up the internet at Aunt Gorawen's house, and she bought a laptop for her to video chat. I can't wait for Tyler to meet her, even if it's through a video chat."

"That's wonderful news. We left in such a rush. You should pick her memory for more information. If you can think of anything."

When he opens the office door, Laura is waiting outside with a backpack on her shoulder and a smirk on her face.

"I'm here for our meeting."

Archie gestures for her to walk into his office and leans into my face. "Goodbye, my love." He kisses me deeply, then winks.

I glance at Laura, grinding my teeth. How do I learn to transmit intentions? I'd love to send her a hex—a painful one.

# CHAPTER NINETEEN
# THE LEERY PROFESSOR

Wednesday morning, I stop by Ronnie's, so she can show me how well her magic room is functioning. She invites me to create a fresh protection pouch to store in my purse. After she sets up the ingredients and witch tools on the table, she clips her crimson ringlets to the top of her head. While we're grinding the herbs, I tell her about Saturday's decision.

"I'm glad you're avoiding burnout." She brings the wooden bowl and places it near us. "You can't let that bastard fairy win."

"Of course not," I say with conviction. "But we have lives, too. I only pushed for a balance."

"Please, don't let your guard down. We should add St. John's wort and yarrow. Four-leafed clover would be better, but who the hell has time to crawl around the ground to find the elusive plant? Make sure you carry that dirk with you everywhere, too." She points at me with the pestle.

"Do you and Archie have a pact or something? I admit I've not been carrying a protection pouch in my purse since we returned from Britain. Not enough hours in the day to keep them fresh with school and work. I forgot about those herbs to help repel fairies. Good idea."

"Archie and I don't have a formal agreement," she says. "But we both love you. You better make time to make new pouches, too. Who knows how long the spell search will take?"

I pour my ground herbs into the wooden bowl. "After we told the young ones to stop for the day, they went downstairs to the magic room and brought a garden gnome to life who wrecked the place. Leslie and Agnes melted the tiny man into a rainbow blob."

Ronnie's cackles. "Oh, my gods. Agnes must have been so pissed."

"She made them clean everything up." I laugh, recalling the incident. "Probably the cleanest that floor has ever been."

"I'm sure. How are things with Archie? You said you've barely seen each other since the semester started."

"Exactly the reason I pushed for a balance. I will not allow an evil fairy to disrupt my life completely."

Ronnie adds her ingredients to mine, and I mix them all together with a wooden spoon, chanting softly.

"You know what?" she asks as she raises her hands above the bowl. "This is the first time we've produced a spell together. We weren't permitted during training."

I grin and face my palms over our concoction. "This protection spell will be the bomb."

We summon our witch energy and cook while we chant the incantation, being careful with the intensity of our amber glow. Once the magic mixture has cooled down, I pour it into a purple velveteen pouch and tighten the drawstring.

"Please be careful. The fairy could surface years from now or tomorrow. I don't want to lose you, friend."

I wrap my arms around her. "Don't worry. We'll all be fine. Archie and Tyler are coming to pick up my family's steamer trunk on Sunday. Thank you for hiding the bulky thing all this time."

"You're welcome. Part of me wishes you would leave the damn thing here so we could practice magic together."

I lift my oversized purse and toss in the protection pouch. "We can plan regular magic sessions with breaks for caffeine."

"Awesome. How about we eat dinner with the guys at the Raven Pub for a change? We don't always have to eat at my café."

"Sure. But we should arrive early on Friday. The undergrads flock there to drink." A bawdy smile sneaks into my mouth. "Saturday, we'll finally get a night together again. It's been weeks. But I have to meet Nick for a concert after dinner with Archie."

Ronnie grimaces. "Whyyy? How did you get stuck going anywhere with him? I thought you stopped spending time with the man."

"I ran into him at Stewart Hall when I went to visit Archie. He had bought the tickets and was so excited. The performance will only last about an hour."

"We have to push the vetting of Unremarkables again. Or just come out and tell Leslie, Trinity, and the other Fellowship members about Nick. What can they do? Expel us for committing a mistake? I don't think so. We didn't openly break the rules."

"I hope you're right," I say, hugging her goodbye.

On the drive back to the house to park and walk to campus, I mull over what Ronnie said. Could the repercussions be that bad?

Now that the temperature has risen above freezing, the piles of snow are melting, creating a slushy, soggy mess. I trudge across campus in my jeans, long-sleeved tee, and clunky snow boots. When I enter Stewart Hall, the rubber of my boots squeaks all the way down the stairs to the basement. Seamus Duffy's office is around the corner next to Nick's. I have some time to kill before

I meet with Seamus, so I stop in the main office and knock on Leslie's door.

When she opens the door, her eyebrows arch. "Gwynedd, what a pleasant surprise. Please, come in."

"I have a meeting with Dr. Duffy in ten minutes, but I thought I'd stop by and say hello."

I glance around the room that Archie once occupied, thinking of a subtle way to ask her about the visiting professor.

"How well do you know Seamus Duffy?" I ask.

"We're more acquaintances. I met him at a conference in London, and we've kept in touch over the years. Occasionally, we schedule lunch or afternoon tea when I'm in Britain. Why do you ask?"

"Oh, no reason, really. He acts a little odd, and sometimes I feel uncomfortable around him."

"Seamus Duffy has an impeccable academic curriculum vitae." Her cat-like eyes glint under the lights. "Researchers spend a great deal of time alone. They're introverted beings who don't necessarily enjoy the company of many people. Maybe you're sensing this personality trait."

"Maybe," I say, fiddling with an earring. "But why is he here teaching hundreds of students, then? That was rhetorical. Well, he's probably waiting for me now. Thank you for talking to me."

"See you at home."

I leave her office and make my way to the professor's office. Tension gathers in my chest as I stand at his office door, sensing a slight buzz throughout my body. I look over my shoulder, expecting to find Archie or Leslie nearby, but no one is there. When I throw my fist at the door, it flings open. Dr. Duffy is dressed in black pants, a burgundy dress shirt, and a tie.

"Gwynedd," Seamus says. "I was about to come looking for you...in case you had difficulty finding my office."

I stare into his eerie eyes. "You're right next to Nick's. There aren't any others. The English department has slowly confiscated them down here, too."

"Yes. Leslie says this department constantly fights to retain their space." He gestures with his hand. "Please, come in."

The door to Nick's office opens, and he darts to us. "I thought I heard your voice. You're meeting with Dr. Duffy, I assume."

"Yes," Seamus says. "We're going to have a chat about Irish folklore."

Nick rubs his hands together nervously. "Gwyn, maybe I should join you? I might add information to the discussion."

He knows I'm leery of the Irish professor, but I think Seamus would be suspicious if Nick crashed our meeting. I'm overreacting, anyway. Leslie's probably right. The visiting professor has limited social skills.

"That's not necessary," I say. "But thank you for offering."

Nick grins awkwardly at Seamus, returns to his office, and shuts the door.

"Shall we begin?" he asks.

I enter the visiting professor's office and inspect his desk, shelf, and walls. Diplomas hang on the wall to the right of his desk, and his shelves are full of references. He motions for me to sit in an upholstered chair across from his desk, and he limps without his cane to his chair.

"Dr. Cockburn says you have a particular interest in the Tuatha Dé Danann." Seamus leans back in his office chair. "Why the special interest in them?"

"My family. An old tale they handed down through the years—an innocuous story."

He cocks his head. "It's curious why a Welsh family would share an old tale about Irish gods."

"I was told they're both. Some people call the Tuatha Dé gods, but others refer to them as fairies. Which is correct?"

"It depends on who is asking the question." He folds his hands on his lap.

What an odd answer. I stare back at the professor and squint. "What does that mean...exactly."

"If you are a member of this supernatural race, you're more likely to reference yourself as a god. Considering the egotistical nature of gods."

I gawk at the professor for a stretched minute and chuckle. "Ah. You're making a joke."

"I am sorry." He laughs and adjusts his tie. "My delivery isn't always the best. Must be why I chose academics over being a stand-up comedian."

"No. The delivery was excellent. Not everyone will get the punchline, though."

"So, my students tell me." He smiles and passes a book to me. "This is one of my personal references. You're welcome to borrow the book for as long as you need."

"Thank you, Seamus." I flip through a few pages and land on a picture. "Who are they supposed to resemble? Hypothetically, of course."

"However, they want to present themselves. They're known as shifters. The name translates to 'the folk of the goddess Danu' or 'tribes of the gods' if using the shorter version of the name. They live in the Otherworld until they cross over into our existence through portals in the great mounds. Folklore depicts a time when they used to intermingle with humans but retreated into their world." He speaks about them as if he believes they actually exist.

"I'll definitely read this reference. Can you tell me any more about them? Do they have other powers besides shifting their appearance?"

Seamus leans forward on his desk. "The Tuatha Dé are a supernatural race who never age or become sickly. They have magical powers and can control the elements of the world."

"They sound unstoppable," I say as I wring my hands.

"Some would say they are unbeatable, yes." His sea-green eyes shine like glass under the ceiling light. "If they existed, of course."

"Well, that's why we call it folklore, right?" The time on my cell phone prompts me to end our conversation. "I have to go, but thank you very much for the information and the book." I stand and stroll to the door.

"Gwynedd, if you have any other questions, please don't hesitate to ask. I would love to chat again. If you're so inclined."

"I'll put a note in my phone."

I exit the office, reflecting on Dr. Duffy. I don't know what to make of him. His demeanor leaves me with an unsettled feeling, as if he's hiding something.

Tyler set up his laptop on the kitchen table, preparing for the video chat with Aunt Gorawen. I sure hope Ellie is tech-savvy, because for damn sure, my aunt isn't.

"Thank you for leaving work early," I say. "I really want you to meet her at least once. She's almost a hundred years old. And her magic skills are weaker, but still amazing. I hope we're as strong in our 90s."

"Good thing you have a few more years to find out." He gets the chat session ready through my social media account, and we wait for a ring.

"I can't wait for you to meet her magic butler. It's a hand helper that assists her with everything." I check the time on my phone. "Of course, Ellie doesn't know about the hand or that Aunt Gorawen is a witch."

The phone icon appears on the screen, ringing, and Tyler taps the green icon. Ellie's face appears, an enthusiastic grin brightening her face.

"Hello there. This is so exciting. I see you. Can you see me?" she asks.

"Yes," I say. "Thanks for setting up our chat."

Ellie motions for my aunt to sit in the chair facing the laptop. "Ms. Thomas, when you're finished, touch this to end the chat."

My aunt's wrinkled face lights up when she sees our faces on the screen. "This is so remarkable. Thank you for arranging this, Ellie. You may go now."

Her caretaker waves and exits the house. Aunt Gorawen examines the foyer to make certain she's left and returns her focus to the computer screen.

"It's so wonderful to gaze upon your face again, Gwynedd, and confirm you're well. So, this is Lowri's grandson, my nephew. I am so happy to meet you. Your mother spoke about you all the time during her visit."

"Hello, Aunt Gorawen," Tyler says. "It's so awesome to see you in person."

"Tell me about yourself, young man. Do you have a young woman to call your own?"

Of course, she would ask about a girlfriend, and Tyler tells her all about Zoe. He shares the details about his job, learning about his ancestral witch ancestry, and how we've searched for a spell to shut down the portal but have come up dry so far. I catch her up on the recent decisions by the city and the potential danger to the magical space. Aunt Gorawen taps her cane on the floor.

"But you're all right, Gwynedd? No more contacts from the wicked fairy?"

"No," I say confidently. "After we left Buckley, there were no more visions. But I carry around Archie's family dirk with me. It kills fairies...or at the least, injures them."

"And you should continue to do so, niece." My aunt presses her lips together and addresses Tyler. "Take care of your mother, nephew. Family always comes first."

"Don't worry," he says. "I will."

"There's a visiting professor here from Northern Ireland, and I saw him in Buckley when we were visiting you, too," I say. "I had a meeting with him, and he shared some information on the Tuatha Dé folklore. He also gave me a reference containing many stories about them."

My aunt nods. "Did you find anything in that academic book? Because they rarely have accurate information, being lore."

"The book listed four treasures of their race. The Spear of Lug. The Stone of Fal. The Sword of Light. The most cherished was Dagda's Cauldron, which never went empty and could feed an army of men. Dagda was a druid and a king and had the power to control the weather, time, and many other aspects of the world. Nuada was the first king. The book contains an overabundance of lore, but you provided me with more useful information."

"Not surprising. Academics don't know the true stories."

"I'm so glad my mom has you to advise her," Tyler says. "I have to run to the bathroom, but I'll be right back."

While my son takes care of his bodily functions, I pick her brain.

"While he's gone, I want to ask you a question. You said a Tuatha Dé fairy can shift its appearance. Could one mask itself as a witch?"

"I suppose anything is possible," she says. "Why do you ask?"

"I didn't tell you how I met the visiting professor. I was at the town center browsing and caught him staring at me in the reflection of the storefront glass. He quickly took off. When Archie and I were visiting Edinburgh Castle, I'm sure I saw him there, too. Don't you think that's strange?"

My aunt turns her head toward the foyer. "I have to go. Ellie is at the door. We'll talk again soon."

The connection ends as Tyler hurries back. "Did you lose her?"

"No. Ellie came back, and Aunt Gorawen ended the conversation."

And I didn't get my answer.

"I'm thrilled we could all do dinner finally," Ronnie says as she lifts her wine glass. "We haven't gotten together since the Yule Celebration before you guys left town."

Her azure-blue eyes sparkle as she gazes upon her boyfriend Derek, and ringlets of crimson hair cascade onto her shoulders from an updo. She's stunning in a fitted red dress. Derek seems like a completely different man in a dress shirt and jeans. Archie's wearing the blue shirt I love so much. I take a sip of wine but dribble a bit on my green skirt.

"Shit. You can't take me anywhere." I dab the spot with my napkin. "The past few months have been busy, for sure. Derek, I haven't had a chance to tell you what an awesome job you did building her magic room. Ronnie helped me make a protection pouch. We had so much fun."

"Thanks, Gwyn," he says, a modest smile curling his mouth. "I thought she should have her own space now that she's achieved a level three status."

Archie winks at Ronnie. "We're all proud of her. And I look forward to seeing your work when I pick up the trunk tomorrow, Derek. I admit I still have reservations about talking openly to an Unremarkable. I like to remain cautious. Don't take offense."

"None taken," he says, taking a drink of beer. "I'll be at the house to help you load the trunk into Gwyn's Prius. Not sure it will fit."

"If not, I'll leave the back open. I'm not driving that far. For sure, Archie can't use the Tesla to move the thing." I wrinkle my nose at him.

Ronnie snickers. "Like he would let you put that heavy heirloom in his Tesla."

"It's a sedan, Ronnie. Not practical." His mouth twitches.

"What's happening with the mound now?" Derek asks. "Is the removal on the back burner still?"

"Aye," Archie says. "Until March at least, but then we'll have to fight the council. Ronnie probably told you about our dilemma."

Derek nods. "She did. If the allies knew the true issue at stake, I bet they'd vote your way."

"Or flip out," Ronnie says. "Gwyn and I have pushed the Fellowship to vote on revealing ourselves to more Unremarkables. Vetted first, of course. But they postponed the decision for a while."

"It's either that or a spell of influence," I say.

I glance at Derek and wait for the questions to fall. A wrinkle forms between his dark-brown eyes.

"You have used magic to sway council votes on issues?" he asks.

"Yes. We have," I say, pressing my lips together.

In my peripheral vision, I catch Archie and Ronnie frowning at me, but Derek seems unfazed by my admission.

"Cool. So, you could change their vote if necessary?"

Ronnie glares at me. "Except Miss Goody-Two-Shoes insisted on adding an ethics clause to our coven rules. So, no. Technically, we can't."

"Gwyn has influenced many decisions since she came into our lives." Archie grasps my hands. "And for the better."

"Well, I recognize the conundrum of the situation," I say. "We have to wait and see."

We limit our conversation when the waiter approaches with the bill folder. He thanks us for our patronage and walks back to the kitchen as two familiar people walk through the doorway, following the hostess.

"Shit," I say, gesturing to the doorway. "Guess who walked in together?"

Archie glances at Nick Evans and Laura Lovelace. "They're probably meeting to talk about her dissertation."

"Whaaat?" Ronnie asks as she peeks at them over her shoulder. "They're both dressed to kill. If they're dating, he should stop bugging Gwyn as much. But what a horrible situation for the poor guy. Does he even know she's a witch?"

"How could he know?" I ask. "He only knows about our coven."

Nick catches me staring at him, and he grins. I snap my head back to the present company. I shouldn't have looked at him. It will only fuel his hopes for a change in my affections. They are dressed well, though. Maybe he's giving Laura a chance?

We all chip in to pay the bill and say our goodbyes in the Raven parking lot. Archie drives to Leslie's house and parks in the driveway.

"I wish you could stay with me tonight. We could get an early start on our extracurricular activities." Lust flares in his eyes.

"It gives you something to dream about." I smile coyly and kiss him. "I'm pooped, anyway. This was a long ass week."

"Since you started this semester, you never seem to have time for us. Are you tiring of me?"

"Nooo," I say, caressing his arm. "All this work to search for an incantation, my two part-time jobs, classes, and the threat of a vengeful fairy have tapped me out. I've not even had time to lift weights or do cardio. I'm getting flabby again. Starting tomorrow, I should feel more refreshed. But I have to reorganize and clean my bedroom to make room for the trunk after spending the morning in Agnes's library."

He strokes my chin. "I understand. I'll see you tomorrow for dinner, then. Sleep well, my love."

"You, too, honey."

I kiss him again and get out of his Tesla. As I walk into the house, I think back on dinner at the Raven. As much as I want Nick to develop affection for another woman, his falling for Laura could open a can of worms—the enormous, slimy kind you find in a B-movie horror film.

# CHAPTER TWENTY

# NO IS AN UNDERRATED WORD

As I move my furniture, I contemplate my insane schedule. It requires reorganization, too, or I'll never have time for Archie. I'm going to pay for all this furniture moving with a sore back and achy knees, and I won't have anyone to blame but myself. The pine shelf won't budge an inch. I grunt and groan as I press my hip against the wood.

"Would you like help, Ms. Crowther?" Mr. Yeats asks from the doorway. "I am an assistant, remember?"

I lean against the wall and puff at my wisp of bangs. "Sure. Be my guest."

He adjusts his spectacles and blows on his palms. "Where do you want the shelf? If you asked me, I'd center it on the opposite wall."

"I'm not asking. It only needs to move one foot. That's why I was trying to slide it."

"Not a problem." He rubs his hands together, touches the wood, and slides the shelf to the left with a splash of glittering magic. "Is that enough?"

"Yes." My lips part. "Why didn't you tell me you could perform magic on the fly?"

He straightens the vest of his gray three-piece suit. "I'm not a showoff."

"Really? Well, thank you, Mr. Yeats. That saved me a lot of time and wear on my back."

"My pleasure, Ms. Crowther. I'll leave you to the remainder of your work."

He shuffles out of my bedroom, transforming into his cat persona. Of course, he leaves when the cleaning begins. I shake my head and grab my duster. The wooden floor in the hallway creaks.

"May I help you, Gwynedd?" Leslie asks.

"Nah. You've spent the last five Saturdays helping me, including this morning. I can handle a bit of *evil* dust. Enjoy the rest of your day."

"Thank you," she says, chuckling. "May I ask a rather personal question while you clean?"

"Sure. Ask away."

"You've spent quite a lot of time with Dr. Evans. More so than I, it seems. What do you make of him? From a personal perspective." She pushes back her silver hair from her face, exposing her copper eyes.

"He's a likable man. He's funny and loves everything Welsh, and if I didn't love Archie, I might have considered his affection for me seriously. For a while, he dated other women, but still seemed unusually infatuated with me. Which makes no sense. He's fifteen years younger than me. But his mom is near your age. He hasn't spoken about any other family."

Leslie tilts her head, squinting. "Why didn't you cut him off? Say no."

"Uhh..." I pause. "Well, he said he wanted to remain friends because we share an interest in Welsh heritage and history. I stopped the Sunday brunches, but I'm attending a concert with him at the School of Music tonight. He bought tickets."

"The Celtic Early Music concert? The tickets to the Collegium performance sold out a month ago. You're lucky Dr. Evans bought those early."

"He implied he bought them recently." I bite my lip.

Leslie lifts her chin. "I must be mistaken. My head hasn't been too clear as of late. The amount of work I've had has affected my memory. I hope you have a wonderful time. The music should be lovely."

She ambles down the hallway to her office. As I finish cleaning, I ponder over the tickets. Nick must have planned to invite me all along.

I sit on the living room loveseat across from Archie as he attempts to *send* me an intention, and I peek out of one eye. He's holding an amethyst crystal in the palm of a hand and has his other raised, an amber glow radiating from his hand. I try to suppress my amused psyche, but the more I hold back, the fuller the bubble becomes. Finally, the dam breaks, spilling uncontrolled laughter.

"Gwyn, you aren't helping." He sighs and lowers his hands. "I watched my dad carefully in our video chat. I can't figure out what I'm doing wrong. My brain works like mush recently—clouded with work, I guess. I hoped the addition of another professor would help more."

"I'm sure Harris taught you well. My head probably needs to be more receptive, too—clear of all the shit that's going on." The mantel clock dings the first of seven. "I better get my coat and gloves on. Nick expects me to arrive for the concert by 7:30 p.m."

I scoot to the oak hall tree to put on my dress boots and black wool coat, lifting my purse off the floor when I'm done. Archie approaches, shoving his hands in his pockets, and frowns.

"It shouldn't bother me you're attending this concert with Nick, but it does. I want you here with me."

"Going to this performance should hold him for a while. By the time he bugs me again, the coven should know. And I can blow him off for good. If he's falling for Laura, the problem will become moot, anyway."

"Hurry back when the concert ends. I'll be waiting." He kisses me deeply.

"Hmm," I say, moaning. "I can't wait."

I have to trek to West Campus but decide to take a detour via Main Street. The city halted construction of the parking garage because of the snowstorm, but work has resumed. Very few people have ventured out on this Saturday night, but I pass a few drunk students on the way. The temperature has warmed to the 40s again, but I'm wearing a bulky sweater over my favorite pair of skinny jeans. I didn't want to dress too fancy or sexy. Nick doesn't need any encouragement.

As I approach the opening to the Green, a peculiar clicking on the paver sidewalk crops up behind me. I turn around and survey the area but see nothing I can attribute to such a noise. After a few more steps, the sound of wood striking the pavement increases. I stop and snap my head around. Another quick scan of the buildings and sidewalk provides no clue to the mystery, so I brush it off and quicken my already brisk pace. As I pass Mitchell Hall, I discover the construction fencing gate is ajar. I check for people nearby and tiptoe through the iron gate to the Celestial Gardens.

The ground squishes like one of those blue scrubbies I use to clean my pans, and the air has the odor of freshly melted snow—a pungent mixture of earthy mud and rotting wood. The opening to the mound is still under the faint light of the crescent moon. When I move closer, the aperture lights up, and the Seelie Fae children come running out.

"Aunt Gwyn! Aunt Gwyn!" Shailagh and Aonghas shout. "We haven't seen you for so long." They skip to me, hugging their tiny bodies. "We don't like to come out when the air makes us shake."

"I can't agree more." As I rub my gloved hands over their tiny fingers, I inspect the Celestial Gardens, wary of being in the portal's vicinity. "The weather will improve over the next month, and work will begin in the gardens. You may need to hide in your world more often. There is a possibility the city people will come and destroy the mound."

"No! Don't let them take it away!" they yell. "We don't want to stop visiting you."

I can't tell them we may close the portal, anyway...and why. "I have to go now, but promise me you'll stay in your world during the day when the workers are here."

Shailagh and Aonghas giggle and run toward the mound. "Bye, Aunt Gwyn."

They disappear through the entrance without a pledge. That's not reassuring. I tiptoe out through the construction fencing and jump when Seamus Duffy startles me. He's leaning against the lamppost near the Mitchell's mansion. The hazy glow of the light shines on his sea-green eyes and black hair. He resembles a panther stalking its prey.

"Dr. Duffy. How long have you been standing here?" I ask, clutching my purse to my chest.

"About five or ten minutes...fifteen at the most," he replies. "I observed you enter the gardens and thought I'd wait to say hello."

I stare at him and swallow. "Yeah, I was peeking at the improvements. I don't have time to chat, because I'm on the way to a concert at the School of Music."

"What a coincidence. I'm attending the performance as well. Would you like to walk together?"

My chest tenses up, but the path from here to the venue is well-lit. "Sure. Why not?"

As we make our way across University Avenue using the pedestrian crosswalk, we have to stop for cars with drivers who apparently flunked driver's education. They nearly run into the professor, and he falls to the pavement.

"Are you OK, Dr. Duffy?" I assess his injuries and help him stand.

"I'm fine, Gwynedd." He brushes off his long black coat. "Lost my balance when I feared the car might hit me. Please, call me Seamus."

I nod and give him his cane with the cat head handle. "OK, Seamus. Are you ready to walk?"

"Assuredly," he says, steadying himself on his cane.

We're only a block away, but I ask Seamus over and over if he needs to go to the emergency room. After a few chuckles and many "I'm fines," there is a break in our conversation. His cane clicks in a steady rhythm when the tip contacts the paver sidewalk, sounding eerily familiar. My heart pumps into overdrive.

"Seamus, I don't want to be rude, but Nick Evans is waiting for me inside. Is it OK if I run ahead?" I press my bag against my chest.

"Of course, Gwynedd. I hope you thoroughly enjoy the concert."

"You, too," I say as I rush into the building.

Nick is sitting on a bench outside the concert hall and grins when he sees me coming. "I thought you changed your mind." He stands to greet me.

"No." I catch my breath. "I ran into Seamus Duffy, and we walked here together. He's a little slow with his disability, so it took longer than I planned."

"We should go in. The concert will start soon. What a pretty necklace. You were wearing it the other day when you met with Seamus."

"Yes, my aunt gave it to me for Yule."

He gestures toward the right set of double doors, and we enter the music hall. There are a few seats in the back, one row with two at the end. Nick goes in first, and I take the aisle seat. When I scour the audience for Seamus, I don't find him anywhere. I squeeze my tote into my seat between Nick and me.

"I hoped you would arrive earlier, so we could sit closer, but this is fine," Nick says. "We can chat after."

I force a smile and think privately...*hell no*.

Nick grabs his stomach and sniffs. "Are you wearing perfume?"

My head quivers no. "I only use soap. I have severe allergies."

He grimaces. "Maybe someone near us is wearing perfume...or carrying potpourri."

Potpourri? He couldn't be smelling the herbs in the protection pouch, could he? The lights dim, and the first set of performers walks onto the stage, a Baroque flutist and a lute player. The third set includes a crwth player, and I shift in my seat, anticipating the music. It's so beautiful, and I recall the recording of the Welsh bard Leslie played in her Celtic Studies class last Fall Semester. When I glance at Nick, he's staring at me, a glimmer of hope shining in his eyes.

He places his warm hand on mine and whispers close to my face. "I love sharing this moment with you."

My heart flutters and a warm, tingling feeling sparks between my legs. Holy crystals. I'm not reacting to his touch, am I? I pull my hand from his, and the twitch turns to arousal. An aura burns and moves up my torso as I cross my legs, but I can't stop the sensation from intensifying.

I grab my purse and coat. "I need to go to the bathroom…right now."

"Don't you feel well?" Nick asks.

I don't have time to answer him, because I rush out of the concert hall, hunting for the bathrooms. The lobby is empty, but I find the public restrooms on the right. I storm into a stall and slam the door behind me. I shut my eyes, attempting to stop the inevitable, and a vision of icy-blue eyes appears. Damn you, Archie. I give way to the arousal, banging against the metal dividers repeatedly. Women's voices echo in the restroom when they enter. My lips roll inward to clamp down on my vocalizations, but it's futile. I scream in ecstasy as the intention reaches its peak.

When I get my breathing under control, I realize I'm wet—everywhere. My sweater is damp, my bangs are stringy, and my panties need changing. I'm going to murder you, Archie Cockburn. There is no way I can return to the concert hall looking like this, so I wad up some toilet paper and blot the sweat on my face and neck. I consider waiting, but he may send another intention. So, I brave the embarrassment and open the stall door. Two young women gape at me, but I'm not stopping to assess my appearance.

As I clear my throat, I avert my eyes, saying, "Hot flash."

I dart out of the building and cross the Green, running over the grass and paver walkways. A fresh wave of intention reaches me as I arrive at Archie's house, and I shove the front door in. He's in the living room setting up wine glasses next to the fireplace, which has a fresh fire crackling. He ogles me and chuckles.

"What happened to you?"

"Oh, you know damn well what you did." I zip off my boots and rip off my sweater as I approach him. "Why did you embarrass me like that?"

"I didn't expect the intention to work, Gwyn. I'm telling you the truth. What did you experience?" A hint of satisfaction rests on his face.

I glare at him. "I had an orgasm in a fucking bathroom stall."

He laughs and wipes my damp hair aside. "I'm so sorry. It wasn't my intention."

"Really?" I pull off his Henley shirt and unbuckle the belt in his jeans. "Seems to me you got exactly what you intended."

A mischievous smile emerges as he unfastens my bra. "Truthfully, I only sent a sliver of intention. I never expected it to be so...successful."

He kisses me passionately and guides me to the plush carpet by the fireplace, and we tumble to the floor. I pull off my jeans and panties and tug at his pants, grabbing his boxer briefs as I yank them off. The warmth of the fire provides all the heat I need as I climb on top of him and moan in lustful bliss. He summons his witch energy, inviting me to do the same, and I touch his hand with my amber glow.

As our lovemaking intensifies, he rolls me over and enters me again. The pleasure reaches a fervor that surpasses all the rest. I press my fingers into his back, screaming so loud it may shatter the window glass. My shrieking must trigger him, because soon after, he yells my name with his release. He pants in my ear as his breathing calms.

"Archie, you're crushing me." I gasp for air until he slides off.

"I'm sorry, my love. I didn't want to leave you." He lays a hand on my abdomen and caresses the skin. "This reminds me of another amorous night. Do you remember?"

My heart still leaps toward my ribcage while I shudder next to him, and the musky scent of our lovemaking fills the air. "Of course. How could I ever forget the night I learned I was a witch? I was brimming with so many emotions that evening."

"Do you regret any of this?" He collects my hair and drapes the strands across my breasts. "You would be safe from this evil fairy if I hadn't sparked your witch energy. Despite how much I love you, I should have let you be."

I roll onto my side and fondle his pecs. "Oh, Archie. Yes, I had times where I wished I could go back to being an Unremarkable, but the truth is. I never was one to begin with, because my past was only hidden. Don't blame yourself. I can't imagine my life without you." I kiss him and nuzzle his face. "After I told the fae children workers may show up to remove the mound, they became distraught. I said they should remain in their world during daylight. I hope they listen, but they giggled as they ran off. When I came out, Seamus was waiting for me under a lamppost. I think he followed me there."

"What makes you believe such a thing? That's quite the accusation."

"I swear I heard the clack of his cane behind me on the way there. The same sound occurred when he walked me to the concert." A buzzing reverberates in the living room, and I remember I set my phone to vibrate during the concert. "Oh, shit."

I crawl over to my hobo bag and drag it to the carpet.

"You're not going to answer your phone, are you?"

"No, but I just realized I forgot to send Nick a text when I left. He must be worried out of his mind."

"You best check your messages, then."

He gets up and walks to the steamer trunk to retrieve a quilt while I check my notifications.

"Oh, my gods. He sent about twenty texts and left voice messages. I'll send him a quick one, so he knows I'm OK."

Me: *Nick, I am so sorry. Got really sick and had to leave. I was so overcome with illness, I forgot to text. Exhausted now. I'll contact you tomorrow. I promise.*

Nick: *That was rude. You should have sent me a message. I was worried beyond comprehension, but I'll talk to you tomorrow.*

I set my phone down. "He's angry. But I don't care. I'm done. There was a moment tonight when he placed his hand on mine, and I knew. He's still in love with me despite what he says. He's only dating Laura Lovelace to cover up his true feelings. I'm going to tell him to stop contacting me."

"What about Leslie and Trinity...and the others? He may tell them he's *in the knowing*." He pulls the quilt over me.

"Not if I tell them first."

After Archie and Tyler drop off my steamer trunk on Sunday, I thank them and head to work. Jeff is unpacking a box when I enter Mystic Sage.

"Hey, Gwyn," Jeff says. "How was your Saturday? Uneventful like mine?"

I snicker uncontrollably and realize he may ask for an explanation. He laughs as he pulls herbs out of the box.

"That good, huh?" he asks.

"Let's leave it at that." I calm my laughter as I drop my bulky bag behind the counter. "Is Shane here? I want to chat with him about something."

"Yeah. He's in the back. I think he's taking a break and checking his cell phone for messages."

"You seem in better spirits. Or are you putting up a front?"

"No, cleaning up the estate was cleansing," he says, exhaling. "Who knew throwing out shit was so cathartic?"

I pat his shoulder. "I'm glad, but I'm here if you ever need to talk."

"Thanks, Gwyn."

Jeff continues with his work, placing jars on the shelves. Routines help, too. I meander into the crystals room, and Shane sits as he reads an email on his phone—a look of concern wrinkling his face.

"Something wrong, boss?" I ask as I lay a hand on his shoulder. "Did you get bad news?"

"Nothing for you to add to your plate of worries, darling." He stuffs his phone into his pocket. "Received an email from a very old friend who wants to visit. I said I wasn't interested."

"Oh, in other words...it's none of my business. Shane, I have to tell you something. A confession of sorts."

He pulls on his beard. "Sounds serious. I'm always here for you, Gwyn. Tell me your darkest secret, and it's safe with me."

"You know Derek became aware of the coven at the pagan conference. But that's not when he actually learned about us and Ronnie being a witch. I was at her house showing Tyler Archie's dirk and the powers it yields. He walked in on us...and Dr. Nick Evans was with him." I clench my teeth.

Shane's emerald-green eyes bulge out. "Well, doesn't that take the rag off the bush? You've been hiding this information for quite some time. Why tell me now?"

"Because he's been holding it over my head. I promised him I'd owe him forever if he kept it to himself. Plus, I think he's in love with me despite Archie and me getting back together. I'm thinking of telling everyone at the next coven meeting. Come clean. Maybe everyone will stand with me. What do you think?"

"I can't imagine how they'll respond. But I bet we'll find out on Thursday."

His ruby-red lips stretch into a silly grin, and I laugh at him. A notification rings on my phone.

"I have to answer this text. It's from Nick. He wants to discuss why I ran out on him last night. Too long a story to explain."

"Good luck, darling. I know firsthand dealing with old flames isn't for the weak."

As I amble into the front of the store, I text the assistant professor.

Me: *I'm sorry I didn't text yet. I'm at work.*

Nick: *You were inconsiderate for leaving me there alone. And not telling me you left.*

Me: *I told you I was overcome with illness. And I said I was sorry.*

Nick: *Can we get together and discuss what happened?*

Me: *NO. I don't want to meet with you anymore. Please, understand.*

Nick: *What?! That's not fair to me. I want to see you.*

Me: *NO. NO. NO. And this is my final text.*

Nick: *You'll regret this, Gwyn.*

# Chapter Twenty-One

# WHAT'S THE BUZZ?

The next couple of weeks pass with no drama, and it's fabulous. My brain fog has diminished, and I'm able to concentrate more on what matters. I should have cut off Nick Evans long ago, although I worry about his last text to me. Ronnie believes I'm overthinking the meaning of his last words. We had become good friends, and I probably obliterated any chance of a reconciliation. But I don't regret it, so he's wrong.

The weekly coven meetings have been short except for planning the celebration of the spring equinox. I've created a schedule to balance my school and work commitments while continuing the Saturday grind to find a portal-closing spell—even carving out time to get to the fitness center. Archie and I are finally back in sync after the entire intention debacle, and he promises never to send that *thought* to me again. Next time, my reaction could be worse than an orgasmic hot flash.

By the middle of March, the threat of snow has passed, and sixty-degree temps hint at the coming of Ostara and new beginnings. Crocus and daffodils sprout, dotting the landscapes in indigo, lavender, yellow, and white. I worry less about the impending doom of a vengeful fairy—a peril that may never come to fruition. Construction on the new parking garage is in full swing, and the renovations at Mitchell Hall have resumed on the exterior of the house. It won't be long before they get to the gardens.

Archie and I attend the Monday council meeting with many of the older witches since the discussion of the fairy mound landed on the agenda. I despise these meetings. They always last over two hours, and of course, public comment is last on the agenda. Elijah has been a wonderful addition to the council, but he's the only member who currently supports the retention of the mound. Because he's a witch and *in the knowing*.

After the meeting starts, a few townies trickle into the town hall. When I turn my head, I discover Nick and Laura have entered. They find seats in the back row. I turn back around and sink into my seat, because I'm not ready to deal with him yet. I nudge Archie and point behind me. He peers over his shoulder and waves to Nick.

"Don't bring attention to us," I whisper. "I have no desire to talk to him."

"Gwyn, I work with Nick. I have to remain cordial."

"Well, I don't," I mutter. "He's here with Laura."

"Aye. They're together a lot recently. Must be getting hot and heavy between them."

"Good. She should leave you alone then."

I peek at them nonchalantly. But who am I kidding? Since when am I nonchalant?

Mayor Manley taps on the microphone. "We will now discuss the removal of the mound in the gardens at Mitchell Hall. We postponed this issue a month ago due to the weather, but a vote on the matter will take place at the next meeting. The council has discussed the issue at length in executive session and most of us agree the landscaping crew should level the corner. We appreciated the public comments made in favor of its retention as a memorial to the Mitchells, but we must also consider the best use of the space."

My shoulders fall. This is awful news, which means we'll have to use a spell of influence at the next city council meeting. Mayor Manley sits up there, sporting a smug expression, since this decision leans his way.

"Do any of the council members want to comment before we move on?" the mayor asks.

Elijah raises his arm, and his bass voice resonates in the room. "I support retention of the fairy mound. My grandmother ran the Mitchell's Art Foundation. I grew up visiting their charming mansion and beautiful gardens regularly. Those of us who have a more personal connection to them obviously have stronger convictions and reasons to retain the memorable icon. I question how many of you ever saw the Celestial Gardens at the height of its beauty." He rubs his jaw. "I would like to invite all of you to visit the gardens before you cast the final vote."

Jessica Devine lifts a hand. "I think we have a duty to entertain Mr. Jackson's request, so I commit to visiting the Mitchell's property at a mutually agreed upon time, preferably in the evening. I encourage others to attend as well."

Ronnie whispers in my ear, "What the hell is Elijah doing?"

"I have no idea," I whisper back. "They shouldn't be anywhere near the gardens at night."

A sneaky grin emerges on Archie's face. He must know. Nick and Laura exit early after the discussion of the fairy mound ends, and my chest relaxes. When the meeting adjourns, we huddle together on the sidewalk and wait for Elijah.

Leslie's eyebrows fall as she slips on her gloves. "I am concerned Elijah has invited the entire council to investigate the mound. I understand what he is attempting, but this will expose us to council members who will not be moved by a display...especially if the Seelie Fae should decide to join us."

"For fuck's sake, dear," Agnes scoffs. "You worry too damn much. Do you really think Manley and his cronies will bother? Not a chance in all the Otherworld."

"What happens if the children pop out to play?" I ask.

Shane chuckles. "We would have much to explain."

"May the gods help us if they do." Trinity crosses her arms and shakes her head. "Elijah has some explaining to do."

"I doubt that would happen," Archie says. "But we should have a plan."

"Damn straight," Trinity says.

Ronnie taps my shoulder. "You should talk with them, Gwyn. Make sure they know to stay hidden."

"That is a sound idea," Leslie says. "Gwynedd, speak to the children once we know the date and time."

Agnes snickers. "Because they have fucking watches? Their sense of time differs from ours, dear. Time progresses slowly in the Otherworld compared to here."

"I don't know about that, Agnes," Ronnie says. "Moves pretty damn slow here, too."

Elijah approaches, rubbing his hands together. "It's all set. They're meeting us Thursday night at seven. But only our allies. Mayor Manley and his *friends* declined."

"That doesn't give us time to meet, Elijah." Trinity scratches her head. "We'll have to gather at the Pumpkin House on Wednesday evening. I'll text the young witches about the change. It's late. Charlie wanted to watch a movie when I got back. Goodnight, all."

We say our goodbyes and disband for home. As Archie and I stroll through the Green in the cool night air, I admire the romantic haze of the lampposts.

"Where is your mind wandering to, my love?" he asks, grasping my hand.

"Oh, I'm contemplating my script for next Wednesday night. When I'll tell the coven about Nick Evans and push for revealing our coven to other Unremarkables like Ronnie has proposed."

"Having second thoughts? You don't have to follow through."

"No. It's the last thing I need to get off my chest, and I think I'll have support. Maybe not the entire coven, but most of them. I mean, you, Tyler, and Ronnie already know. Oh, and Shane. I told him, too."

Archie stops in his tracks. "When did you tell Shane?"

"Only recently. But Tyler has kept it from Zoe all this time. He's itching for me to divulge our *wee* secret. The young witches are more progressive, so I expect them to go along with Ronnie and me. Trinity? She could go either way. Elijah? I'm not sure if he's ready to tell Jasmine yet. Agnes, for sure, doesn't give a shit. She already hangs witch-for-hire on her door...along with selling *herbs*."

"Only Leslie remains a definitive no, then. She'll never agree, Gwyn. As the former coven leader, I have to say this decision must be unanimous. Revealing ourselves puts all of us at risk."

I sigh. "Shit. I'm still telling the coven. Everyone should know Nick's *in the knowing*. It's only fair."

"Agreed. Are you staying tonight? Not for sex. I'm exhausted. I've had difficulty focusing at work, so I should turn in early. Since Leslie went home with Agnes, you'd be alone in the house with Mr. Yeats."

"Shit. That's right. I guess you decided for me."

Tuesday night after dinner, I take a stroll to Mitchell Hall, hoping the construction fencing gate is unlocked again. But I discover the workers are being more careful since they're working on the exterior renovations. They can't have materials walking off the job, can they? I do a quick scan to my left, my right, and behind, and summon my witch energy to open the lock. I sneak in and dash to the rear of the Celestial Gardens.

"Shailagh? Aonghas?" I call out to them. "Are you here?"

There is no movement in or around the mound, so I meander across the gardens, stopping to admire the fairy sculptures and water fountains. A buzzing electrifies my body, and I spin around, examining the area under a sliver of moonlight. I clutch my hobo bag, slip my hand inside, and clasp the handle of the dirk as my heart skips a few beats. But nothing strange appears.

"Boo!" the fae children shout and giggle.

I shriek like a banshee and grab my chest. "Shailagh and Aonghas, don't ever scare me like that. You'll take a few years off my life I can't afford to lose."

"We're sorry, Aunt Gwyn," they say. "We thought you wanted to play."

"No. I came to warn you about some visitors who will be here on Thursday night. I don't know how to translate the time into your world. Make sure you peek before crossing over from now on. If I call your names, you'll know it's safe. I have to leave now, but I promise I'll make time to play when it's much warmer. Ostara is only around the corner."

"All right, Aunt Gwyn. We can't wait to play!" They run off toward the portal, crossing over with a flash of light.

I survey the area surrounding Mitchell Hall before tiptoeing out, and I close the lock, applying my amber glow. Buzzing overtakes my torso again, and I flip my head all around me, finding no one. Aunt Gorawen seemed to think the fairy could shift himself into anything...even a witch as cover. I search for Seamus Duffy under the spray of the streetlights and in far-off shadows. Where is he hiding? I walk expeditiously eastward on Main Street until I reach the campus and rush down the steps to the paver walkways.

The entire length of the Green has a foggy mist hanging over it from the unusually warm day, and the lamppost lanterns peek through, resembling tiny moons floating in the air. My new sneakers squeak as I walk on the damp walkway, and the roar of passing traffic increases as I approach University Avenue. Once I cross onto the lower section of Central Campus where classes occur, few students pass by. Except for the occasional undergrad dashing to the library, the Green has a tranquil ambiance.

As I stroll toward the Old Men oak trees, faint clacks echo against the Georgian, red-brick classroom buildings. I think nothing of the sounds at first, but the clicks occur in regular intervals—someone walking with a cane. I stop and survey the area behind me, but the low-lying fog blankets everything in gray fluff. My torso buzzes, and I glance at the library. Maybe I should run? NO. I slip my hand into my large purse and clasp Archie's family heirloom. And wait.

Out of the misty fog, Seamus Duffy appears. He grins at me, and I stomp to him, my fingers wrapped tightly on the dirk inside my bag.

"Are you following me?" I ask.

Seamus's smile fades, and his eyes narrow. "I assure you, Ms. Crowther, I am merely on the way to the library. Am I following you? If you were headed this way, then yes. I am."

I keep my grip on the weapon. "It appeared as if you were. Walking on the Green at night can be spooky, and I was attacked here once."

"That would make anyone wary, would it not? Would you like an escort home? I'd be chuffed to accompany you."

Those sea-green eyes captivate me, and I lose track of how long I've waited to reply.

"Gwynedd? Did you hear what I said?" he asks.

I shudder. "Yes. I heard you. No. I don't have very far to walk from here. You go ahead to the library. I'm sorry for the accusation." But I'm not really.

"No need to apologize."

Seamus touches my hand, and my body seizes as if I stuck my finger in an electric outlet. I yank it away and pull my bag to my chest. I struggle to control my breathing, and my heart rate rockets to the moon. He shoves his hand into one of the pockets of his long black coat and lowers his eyes to the ground.

"Goodnight, Seamus," I say as I inch back.

"A pleasant evening to you, Gwynedd."

Seamus limps toward the angled walkway leading to the library, and I run across the Green to the alleyway, not stopping until I arrive at Archie's house. I enter through the front, slamming the door behind me.

"Archie!" I flip off my sneakers. The basement door is open, so I dash downstairs, shouting his name repeatedly.

"I'm in the magic room, my love," he yells. He's practicing the craft at the table and flipping through the pages of a spell book. "Any problems with the Seelie Fae?"

"No. They were fine, but..."

I grab my chest and try to catch my breath. He turns around, discovers my state, and rushes to me, laying a hand on my cheek.

"You're all flushed. What's wrong?"

"I ran into Seamus on the Green," I say, panting. "He said he was on the way to the library, but I'm certain he was following me."

"Gwyn, you've felt this way before. What makes you so sure this time?"

"When he touched my hand, my entire body stiffened like he flipped a switch and turned on the electric panel."

A crinkle forms on his brow as his hand falls to my shoulder. "That is alarming."

"Yes. It is. He's been stalking me since Buckley. He's always around. Tries to be awkwardly cordial. Every single time, I have a sense of discomfort around him. *And* he's Irish. Do you think Leslie will believe me?"

Archie grasps my hands. "Avoid him at all costs. Meanwhile, I'll consult with the Elder. He's an old acquaintance, so it's a delicate matter. You had the dirk on you?"

"Yes," I say, expelling air in exasperation. "What do we do?"

"I'll speak with Leslie privately, and we'll bring this up at the next coven meeting." He embraces me tightly. "Don't panic. Your aunt says he'll try to win you over." He cups my cheeks and kisses me. "That will never happen."

I lay my head against his firm chest and listen to the steady beat of his heart. How can he remain so calm? I want to screech like a bean nighe.

# Chapter Twenty-Two

# SPILL THE TEA

Leslie calls the coven meeting to order with three taps of her staff. "By now, you all are aware of the presentation in the Celestial Gardens tomorrow evening. With the completion of the external renovations to Mitchell Hall, the city has removed the fencing. Trinity will explain further in a moment, but first, Archie would like to address another pressing issue."

"Thank you, Leslie." Archie stands, scratching his goatee. "Gwyn had an experience last evening that was concerning. Although she has had prior uncomfortable feelings when interacting with Dr. Seamus Duffy, last night was the most worrisome. His touch triggered a reaction in her like an electrical charge. We believe Seamus is the Tuatha Dé fairy who's been tracking her down. He's here in Bearsden, masquerading as a professor. Leslie and I discussed the issue, and she would like to speak about the incident as well."

The metal chairs creak as the coven members become restless in their seats. Elijah rubs his jaw, and Shane twists his beard. Ronnie flashes me an oh-no expression, and Tyler glares at me, scowling. The others lean forward in their seats and turn an ear toward the Elder.

"I have known Dr. Duffy for many years," she says. "Although I find it difficult to believe he's a threat, we cannot dismiss the signs. Gwynedd first encountered him in Buckley, and he has stalked her other times."

"I have a class with him," Spence says. "He acts a little weird, but outside of class, he doesn't talk much—always couped up in his office. What do you think, Skye?"

Skye shrugs. "He's always been friendly to me. Offers to meet with us anytime to discuss research. Gives knockout lectures. I never doze off."

"He sounds absolutely horrifying," Tanner says wryly.

Agnes interjects. "Trinity, Leslie, and I discussed the matter this morning after Archie alerted us. We can't ignore his behavior."

"No, we cannot," Trinity says. "We have to assume he has some sort of plan to win Gwyn over, so we all must help her by avoiding Dr. Duffy as much as possible. You students, go to your lectures. Do your work. But don't converse with him outside of class unless it's related to your academics."

"Why didn't you call me, Mom? That's not OK." Tyler frowns at me.

Zoe nudges him, mouthing, "Stop."

"Talk to him," Archie whispers. "He'll only worry if you don't."

"We decided Archie should talk with Dr. Hughes first. When Seamus laid his hand on mine, my entire body felt electrified. It scared the shit out of me, and I ran to Archie's. I wasn't sure the professor was the one until last night. I'm telling you now that we're sure."

The parlor rumbles with babble, and my son throws me a side-eye.

Leslie interjects. "I recommend we proceed with caution. As much as we can, we should limit our interaction with Dr. Duffy while we investigate him."

"Which will be burdensome for Leslie and me," Archie says. "He keeps to himself, so that will help."

Spence crosses his arms and makes a duckface. "Mood."

"Let me know if I can help in any way," Tanner says. "Research his background online and peek at his finances. Money can shed light on many things."

Trinity stands and addresses us. "Thank you, Tanner. In the meantime, tomorrow is our only opportunity to change the minds of our allies on the council without using magic." She stares at me and puts her hands on her hips. "But if this doesn't work, we'll have to vote to use a spell of influence. You understand the urgency, don't you?"

"Yes." I sigh and lean back in my seat.

"Good," Trinity says. "We need to come up with a plan, and fast. Suggestions?"

Skye shoots her hand in the air, beating Spence and Zoe by a nanosecond. "Gotta schedule another protest like in the winter."

"Absofuckinglutely," Spence says. "With the warmer weather and the Spring Semester timing, we can convince a ton more undergrads to take part, too."

"We could make signs saying, 'Save the fairy mound and you save the legacy of the Mitchells.'" Zoe shimmies in her seat.

Tyler catches my gaze, waiting for my approval, I assume. I mouth, "OK." He smiles at Zoe and squeezes her hand. Agnes and Leslie sit back and soak in the recommendations.

Trinity motions at Elijah. "You know your fellow council members better than any of us. Would you like to lead this?"

"Yeah, I don't mind," he says. "We need to make a huge impression. Take them on a small tour of the gardens, pointing out the significance of each sculpture and structure, including the fairy mound. Try to impress the importance of saving what was the soul of the Mitchells—their belief in fairies."

Ronnie waves her hand. "An organized protest would be great optics, especially with the council members coming to visit the gardens. Give them a tour...awesome. But do you know what would really impress them?" She wiggles her flaming eyebrows.

"Yaaas!" Spence shouts. "Let's do it!"

"Calm down, hon. You're making me nervous." Tanner rubs Spence's shoulder.

Skye chuckles. "It would certainly impress them."

"I'm so confused." Zoe's eyes hop around the circle.

"Are you suggesting what I think you're suggesting?" Shane asks.

Archie and I lock eyes. The young witches appear to support the idea, and a wicked grin erupts on Agnes's face. Leslie tilts her head back and forth as she deciphers the hidden meaning, and she taps her Elder staff loudly on the floor several times.

"Absolutely not. We have not had a vote on revealing our magic and the supernatural world to other Unremarkables. Significant others and family are already stretching the rules, and I acknowledge they are inevitable. But we cannot take the risk of exposing ourselves to others in the town."

"Oh, Leslie," Agnes says. "I've professed to be a witch for decades. No one pays me any mind."

Elijah wrings his hands. "But claiming we're witches is a far cry from showing people fairies exist, Agnes. You have to agree."

"Well, I don't, but I won't argue with you, Elijah." Agnes pats Leslie's hand.

"What if we already took a risk?" I glance at Archie and Ronnie as I suck in all the air I can...and blurt it out. "I already told an Unremarkable I'm a witch, and there's a coven. He also knows about the Tuatha Dé threat against me, the existence of the Seelie Fae, and the portal mound."

Leslie cocks her head, her visage transforming into a scowl to end all scowls. Shane, Tyler, Archie, and Ronnie shift in their seats, preparing for a cataclysmic response. The others flip their heads back and forth.

So, I tell them all. "Dr. Nick Evans knows about...everything."

"What the hell, Gwyn?" Trinity shouts. "What were you thinking? This breaks so many coven rules, lady."

Leslie gasps and struggles to take in air. "I can't breathe. I...I can't breathe."

"Oh, dear," Agnes says. "Inhale with me, sweetheart. Breathe in. Breathe out. Breathe in. Breathe out." As she breathes with Leslie, a few of us run over to them. "Get the fuck back. She's only having a panic attack."

I rub the palm of my hand. "I'm sorry. I shouldn't have spewed it out so bluntly."

"Oh, she'll be fine in a minute. Was the best way to tell her. Like ripping a bandage off a hairy arm." Agnes laughs and rubs Leslie's back. "You all right now, sweetheart?"

"How long has he known?" Leslie's mouth quivers while she taps her chest.

"You best start from the beginning," Trinity says. "And don't leave out any details."

Ronnie answers for me. "Since last fall. It was my fault. I forgot to lock the door at my house, and Nick walked in following Derek when Gwyn was showing the magic of Archie's family dirk."

"Wait," Spence says. "You mean he found out before the pagan conference? That's so funny. Does Dr. Evans know Skye, Zoe, and I are witches?" He turns his head right and left. "Oh, fuck."

The young witches chuckle, including Tyler. It's always funnier looking back on a mishap once the secret slips out.

Archie chimes in. "I have a confession as well. Ronnie and Gwyn told me about Nick, but we determined we should not tell you, Leslie. Nick has kept silent, so I don't think we need to worry about him."

"Gwyn told me, too," Shane says. "Since we're confessing our transgressions this evening."

"Personally, I'm offended, Gwyn," Spence says, crossing his arms. "You didn't tell me."

"So, how many knew?" Zoe counts on her fingers.

Skye snickers. "Five, if you're counting Derek."

"So, this begs the question," Elijah says as he rubs his neck. "If Dr. Evans knows, and he's respected our secrecy. Perhaps we can do the same with the allies on the council. I should probably confess, too. I've told Jasmine I'm a witch."

"This goes against all of our rules," Leslie says, trembling.

Agnes rubs her back. "Oh, fuck the rules, woman."

I push up from my seat. "I propose a vote, but Archie and I agreed the decision should be unanimous. We're all in, or we're all out. Stand with me if you believe we should introduce the Seelie Fae children to the council allies. Show them the real reason they can't level the mound. Plead with them to give us time to shut it down, and once the task is completed, they can do whatever they want."

Archie stands and clasps my hand. "I'm with Gwyn. This is more ethical than a magical influence."

Shane, Elijah, and Ronnie push up from their chairs. All the young witches jump up out of their seats and high-five each other. Agnes stands, shaking a fist, which leaves our leader and the coven Elder.

"Leslie," Trinity says. "I've agreed with you all these years. Unremarkables are safer not *knowing* about the supernatural. Casting spells of influence provided simple solutions to combat the corruption in the town. But this situation has nothing to do with Mayor Manley and his cronies. Without understanding the fairy mound's true meaning, the allies will vote to level it. I'm sorry, but I vote with Gwyn." She stands and folds her hands.

The coven Elder sits alone, her stern expression relaying the desire to hold on to her principles. If she stands with us, she is breaking every regulation in the Regional Book of Shadows she has supported for fifty-some years. We smile at Leslie, but we don't pressure her. She has to be comfortable with her decision. But we can't control her hedge witch lover.

"Oh, come on, Leslie," Agnes pleads. "Deep down, you know this is the best solution. Sure. It's a scary proposition to expose our true identities. We have no guarantee how the council members will react. But we'll figure out what to do together. I can't believe I'm saying this." She offers her hand. "Because we are stronger together than alone."

Leslie scans the circle, observing our smiling, supportive faces...and pushes out of her seat. Everyone hoots and hollers, and the coven Elder cracks a smile.

Agnes hugs her lover. "You won't regret this, sweetheart."

"I will remind you of this declaration when the council members scream and bolt out of the Celestial Gardens tomorrow evening." Leslie remains standing and waves her hand for us to quiet down. "This decision will change everything. So, prepare yourselves for the unexpected. Go in peace, my friends."

We stack the chairs and exit onto the porch into the cool, crisp air. The anticipation of a new dawn blows on the horizon. My fellow witches gossip over the impending "big reveal," and their chatter dissipates as they descend the porch steps. Tyler sends me a thumbs up as he and Zoe depart. Archie and I wave goodbye and head toward the Green.

"By this time tomorrow, a few more Unremarkables will be *in the knowing* and have the information to distribute to the world." Archie caresses my fingers. "Are you prepared for the possibility?"

"Yes," I say, sighing. "Because the alternative was unethical."

He kisses the back of my hand. "I'm so proud of you."

"Thank you, honey. I have work tomorrow afternoon at Mystic Sage. Do you want to meet for dinner before the *reveal*?"

He grimaces. "Naw. I'm booked. As much as I loathe the idea, I'm meeting Laura at the Raven for dinner to review more of her dissertation. I've not had the focus to advise her well. I'm tired of working with this overload. It's muddled my brain."

"I can't wait for this semester to end, so you don't have to advise her anymore."

"Well, if Nick and Laura's relationship progresses, we'll not have to spend much time with either of them."

I'm glad he's hopeful, but my optimism took a flying leap when Seamus Duffy zapped me with his fairy buzz.

# Chapter Twenty-Three

# What Fairies?

Thursday afternoon, Mystic Sage has a steady stream of customers. Even with all three of us working, I barely have time to take a break to pee, which stresses my menopausal bladder. Shane advertised a sale to celebrate Ostara. Who knew the students would rush to buy spring equinox apparel?

I guess it's easy to understand where the enthusiasm comes from. We grew sick of the snowy winter months, and now we're excited for spring to hop on in. I'm eager to wear short-sleeved shirts, jeans, and hoodies—one step closer to summer. Pastel hues of yellow, blue, pink, and lavender decorate the store, bringing a cheerful environment to the normal dark aesthetic of the occult wares.

T-shirts and hoodies covered in half-sun and half-moon designs sell first. Apparel stamped with Happy Ostara above a forest with bunnies and eggs comes in a close second. I'm thinking my boss should plan an Earth Day sale, too. The tourmaline necklace scratches my bare skin, so I store it in my tote while I work. I'm safe in the store.

I'm elated Shane will reap the benefits of this onslaught of customers, but even a ten-minute lull would make me happy. Jeff walks to the back to help Shane with the boxes being delivered while I hang at the register. In my haste to ring up a customer and bag their merchandise, I knock the skull mug holding pens onto the floor for the umpteenth time.

As I crouch behind the counter to collect the writing utensils, the door dings with another customer. When I stand to return the mug to its rightful place, Nick is leaning on the counter. I gape at him in a frozen stupor.

"Hi, Gwyn." Nick smiles as his warm brown eyes ooze with regret. "You wouldn't answer my texts or agree to see me, so I had to come here. And I promise I won't bother you at work again. I'm so sorry about my irate texts. I hate how things spiraled out of control the way they did. The night of the concert, I was out of my mind. When you disappeared and didn't answer my texts or voicemail, I worried someone abducted you." He bends over the counter and whispers, "By the you-know-what."

He gazes into my eyes, holding them captive. Suddenly, my stomach aches, and I reevaluate my behavior that night. Was I selfish? Absolutely. I totally was. This poor man has had to hunt me down and apologize for his justifiable concerns over my unexplained disappearance. I close my mouth and swallow.

"I suppose your reactions were valid, and I understand why you were upset. But your texts really bothered me."

"I've not slept at all since then, knowing how you might have perceived them. It's why I came by the store. I couldn't be sure you'd read an email from me or a text." He straightens his back and lowers his eyes to the floor. "Well, that's all I wanted to say. Take care, Gwyn."

He turns toward the door. The lull I wanted so desperately came at the wrong time, which gives me time to respond.

"Nick? I'm glad you came. I should have sent you a text right away. My illness is no excuse, but I hope you'll accept my apology for making you worry."

"Of course, I do." He moves back to the counter. "And if you ever need someone to talk to about anything, I'm still your friend."

He lays his warm hand on mine and stares into my eyes again. After a prolonged moment, he smiles and exits the store. How could I have screwed up so badly? Easy. Texts are a terrible way to communicate. He obviously still cares about me, but he's settling for friendship. I want to shrink behind the counter and hide.

Archie and Ronnie agree I should give Nick some slack. I didn't handle the situation the best. And to be fair, Archie's partially to blame. He hijacked my head using his lustful yearnings. How was I supposed to fight off the onslaught of *thought intentions* sent by my lover?

When I arrive at Mitchell Hall, I discover the young witches and fifty-some students have gathered to support the retention of the mound. They're lined up along the paver sidewalk near the freshly painted iron gate, holding signs bearing the phrases "save the fairy mound" and "honor the Mitchells." The street light casts a spotlight on the protestors as they chant, "Save the mound." I wave to Tyler and the others as I pass through and run into Ronnie and Derek outside the gate.

"Hi, Derek," I say. "Are you joining us?"

"Yeah. Ronnie had this foolish idea I should come." He leans into me. "In case the council members have trouble...adjusting."

"Remember how Derek and Nick reacted? And I don't sleep with our allies on the city council." She slaps Derek's arm and cackles, but he's not laughing.

"Well, I didn't sleep with Nick," I say. "He was pissed at me for a while. We should head in."

The older Fellowship members gather in the Celestial Gardens awaiting the council members and finalizing their plan. We've all worn comfortable clothing like jeans and sneakers since the ground hasn't dried out completely. A few of us have flashlights to highlight the fairy sculptures and garden beds. Under the sliver of moonlight, the gardens hardly inspire saving. Except for the new baby hawthorn tree in the corner, the landscaping desperately needs restoration.

When Trinity sees Derek approaching the mound with us, she scowls. "What in all the Otherworld? Why is he here?"

"Maybe I should go?" Derek asks.

Archie steps forward. "Naw. He should stay. The council members may need some convincing. Thank you for coming."

"It was my idea," Ronnie grins and pats herself on the back.

"Indeed." Leslie tilts her head. "The young witches will join us once our allies have arrived."

Trinity adds, "They will dismiss the Unremarkable students and hang out there until they've all left. We can't have witnesses to what we're doing. Elijah, what is your plan for introducing the pranksters?"

Elijah rubs his palms together. "I'll lead them around and describe the areas in need of improvement. The many rose bushes and hedges. I'll give them a background on the significance of the sculptures Rose Mitchell chose. We'll end at the fairy mound. At that time, I believe someone else should introduce our resident pranksters."

"Are you looking for volunteers?" Agnes asks. "I'm the oldest here. They're more likely to believe me."

Shane raises his eyebrows. "Or think you're senile."

"You don't have to fucking insult me," she says, frowning.

Archie suppresses a laugh. "He's being realistic, Agnes. You were quite the recluse for many years. An abundance of stories floats about the town regarding the self-professed witch on the farm."

Agnes rolls her head around. "You're right. Then who?"

Our eyes roam around the impromptu circle. I'm about to recommend Tanner, and I realize they're all staring at me. "I'll never convince them who we are. They don't know me from a hole in the wall."

Trinity chuckles. "You won't need to. We'll show them our magic after you invite the Seelie Fae to come out and play."

"The children trust you, Gwyn," Archie says as he rubs my back. "They won't come out and reveal themselves to our visitors without your reassurance."

I roll my eyes. "Oh, OK. But everyone needs to be ready to jump into the pit. In case they scream and try to run out of here before we can explain who we are and what the mound is."

"They are here, my friends," Shane says, pointing. "No turning back now."

Jessica Devine, Corey Jones, and Jeremiah Jackson walk through the gate, the young witches following them. We turn on our flashlights to light the way.

"Welcome Jeremiah, Corey, and Jessica," Elijah says. "Thank you for accepting the Fellowship's invitation on such short notice. We're all so busy and serving on the council snatches precious time from our loved ones. We greatly appreciate your sacrifice. If you have questions as we take you on a tour of the Celestial Gardens, please don't hesitate to ask."

Corey Jones responds. "Elijah, all three of us respect you, but we want you to understand we need to do what's best for the community."

"But we are keeping an open mind," Jessica says.

Jeremiah nods. "We owe you that."

What a perfect night for Elijah to lead the council members on a tour of the Mitchell's gardens. The temperature remains on the warm side, and the aroma of spring's first growth permeates the air. The newest council member gestures to the far side, and the other three members follow him around as he supplies details about the garden. Elijah must be sharing stories of his grandmother, because they laugh as he talks.

Leslie motions to the young witches. "Tanner, Skye, Tyler. Could you keep watch on the gate? Make certain no other Unre-markables enter. If anyone tries to come in, tell them we are having a meeting with the council members, and they aren't permitted on the grounds."

"Will do, Dr. Hughes." They rush toward the gate to stand guard.

"Spence and Zoe," Trinity says. "Be ready to...I can't say what. Because I have no idea how they're going to react. May the gods help us."

Archie gestures toward Elijah. "It appears they're moving to the fairy mound."

"Then what the fuck are we waiting for?" Agnes says. "Let's go."

Ronnie nudges me. "This is it, Gwyn. Good luck."

Archie squeezes my hand. We form a semi-circle to deter the council allies if any of them should try to dart. Jessica, Corey, and Jeremiah follow Elijah to the front of the mound, where the tiny opening invites questions. I move forward.

"Hello. My name is Gwynedd Crowther," I say. "If you go online and investigate larger mounds similar to Rose Mitchell's diminutive one, you'll discover openings in them, too."

Jessica shifts closer and points her flashlight at the aperture. "It's not big enough for more than a small child to squeeze through."

In my peripheral vision, my fellow witches nod, encouraging me to continue. Here goes nothing.

"Funny you should mention children, because that's why this fairy mound is here," I say. "Rose Mitchell wanted to have children and couldn't. A local Bearsden tale says a group of witches cast a spell to bring forth children for Rose, and it did. But they were fairy children."

"What an adorable story," Jeremiah says. "Rose had a creative imagination to create her gardens around the idea. I understand your sentiment, but again, we should consider the advantages of removing this pile of dirt. Let's be honest. That's all it is."

I fiddle with my earring. "Actually, the tale is real. Two fairy children cross over to our world through here. The opening is a portal to another dimension we call the Otherworld."

The council members gawk at me and chuckle. Jessica shakes her head. "Your group is entitled to its beliefs, but we can't vote according to your faith. The public would castigate us for such a decision."

"Believing in the existence of fairies is not part of our religious beliefs, Ms. Devine." Spence gestures toward the mound. "We don't worship them or anything. They're just mischievous pranksters called Seelie Fae. Show them, Gwyn."

Corey Jones cocks his head. "Show us what?"

I step forward and call on the fae children. "Shailagh? Aonghas? It's Aunt Gwyn. Can you come out?"

We wait, but the children don't show their tiny faces. They must be too frightened. I scan the semi-circle of my fellow witches and shrug. Their sullen expressions convey consternation. We hadn't considered the children wouldn't respond to my call.

"We love what you're trying to do," Jessica says. "Yes. Children would create these fantasies when they played, but this plot of land would serve them better with a playground set. I think we're done. Thank you for..."

The portal lights up, and the council members gape as the Seelie Fae cross over into our world. Shailagh and Aonghas dash to me when they see all the people. They wrap their tiny arms around my legs as their golden-blond hair blows in the March wind. The young witches dance, and high-fives make the rounds, ending with fist bumps between Elijah and Derek. Agnes and Leslie smile at the children. Archie moves by my side.

Jeremiah laughs as he points at the mound. "That's amazing. I'll give you that much. There's an electrical line running to the inside. Genius."

"Why didn't you tell us?" Corey asks. "Not that it's gonna change my mind. It's dangerous. What if children enter and won't come out? Adults can't fit through there to retrieve their kids."

Shailagh's head pops up. "Yes, you can." She motions to Aonghas, and they rush to Corey and grab his hands, dragging him toward the fairy mound.

What are they doing? "Shailagh and Aonghas. Where are you taking him?"

Corey bursts out laughing. "They're taking me to their leader! Hey, your eyes are minty green. That's weird."

Shailagh and Aonghas giggle as they drag Corey closer and closer to the mound. Unexpectedly, they dart into the portal—and disappear! We gasp. Jessica Devine and Jeremiah Jackson stand frozen in a catatonic state like the fairy sculptures in the gardens.

Zoe's eyes widen. "Well, that was cool!"

"What the fuck?" Agnes yells. "Did anyone know about the capability of human transfer?"

Leslie hyperventilates and taps her chest. "This is terrible. We have to get Mr. Jones back. We need his vote."

I run to the mound and inspect the gap. "Shit, shit, shit. What do we do, Archie? I'm pretty sure the town will notice an entire person is missing. And there are witnesses."

"I'm stumped, Gwyn," he replies. "I never imagined this was possible. The aperture is so small."

Spence and Skye meander around Jessica and Jeremiah, who remain dazed and in shock. As they wave their hands at our allies' faces, they don't even blink. Their chests barely inflate. This is a dire state of affairs for the Bearsden Coven.

Skye pushes up on her toes to inspect Jessica's eyes. "Nobody's home."

"They're not responding," Spence says. "Should we shake them?"

"Dude, don't touch the council members. They could sue us." Tanner grabs Spence's hands and pulls them down.

Shane touches Jessica's hand. "Cold and white as a sheet. We may need to take them to the emergency room."

"Now you know that's not an option," Trinity says as she examines Jeremiah. "We have to handle this ourselves—use magic."

Tyler runs to me. "Mom, you have to do something. Call them back. You're the only one they listen to."

"You have to try, Gwyn," Archie says.

I move close to the opening and shout into the void. "Shailagh! Aonghas! You bring that man back here right now." I point down to the ground, but there's no movement in the portal. I grimace at my witch family. This can't be good for my blood pressure. I extend my hand into the aperture, triggering a white light. "Shailagh! Aonghas! Bring back Mr. Jones, or I'm coming in after you!"

Archie shakes his head. "Gwyn, don't!"

And in a flash, the children emerge through the passageway with Corey Jones in tow. They run off toward the hawthorn tree to play while he grabs at different sections of his body, checking for missing parts, I guess.

"What happened to me?" he asks, shaking like he's seen...another world.

"I believe you passed into the world of the Seelie Fae, Mr. Jones," Trinity says.

Leslie, Agnes, and Archie examine his body and determine he's fine as far as they can tell. Now, what to do about Jessica and Jeremiah? Corey approaches his fellow council members.

"What's the matter with them?"

"They're in shock or some kind of trance," Leslie replies. "They witnessed your abduction."

Agnes chuckles. "Abduction, my ass. He went willingly. He only thought he was heading into a pile of mud."

"How do we get them out of this stupor they're in?" I ask.

Archie stands before Jessica and Jeremiah and brings his hands together, clapping loudly. They blink but don't move otherwise. Elijah and Trinity join him, and they try one more time. The two allies breathe deeply and hyperventilate while they gape at us.

"They're real," Corey tells them. "I went through that hole with those golden-haired fairies and came back."

Jessica catches her breath. "But what about the rest of you? Are you fairies, too?"

Agnes laughs and slaps her leg. "Fuck no. We're witches."

"Don't blurt it out like that," Trinity says. "But what she said is true."

"What?" Jeremiah goggles at us. "So, the Fellowship is a..."

"Coven," Leslie says. "But we function as any other small group of individuals who support our community in any way we can."

Elijah addresses the council members. "Jessica, Jeremiah, Corey. This has been an enormous shock to you. We revealed ourselves and the true nature of the fairy mound to you because of the unknown repercussions of its destruction."

"We have been searching for a portal-closing spell," I say. "Not only for this problem. The Seelie Fae are mischievous but fairly benevolent. Unfortunately, there is an evil fairy in town who is after me to seek revenge on an act one of my ancestors committed hundreds of years ago."

Archie approaches them. "We desperately need your help. Can we count on your vote to save the mound? Until we discover a solution to close its portal. After that, you're welcome to level it."

The three council members huddle and chat among themselves while we wait, twiddling our thumbs and preparing for a negative response. When they're finished, Jessica raises her head to speak.

"We're uncertain what the right thing to do is." Her hands tremble. "It's not ethical for any kind of influence to affect our votes. But we understand why you were so adamant about its retention. We will vote to keep the fairy mound for now, but you must do what is necessary to get rid of those..."

"Fairies," Zoe says, sharing a wide-toothed grin.

Jessica huffs. "Yes. I haven't decided yet how I feel about a hidden coven in our town, either. Obviously, we won't tell anyone."

"Who would believe us?" Corey says.

"I don't know about you all, but I'm ready to go home," Jeremiah says. "And rethink our entire existence." The council members exit the garden, prattling among themselves.

Trinity waves her hands in the air. "I'm with Jeremiah Jackson. Let's go home. For optics, I suggest we not attend the next city council meeting. Elijah can report back to us."

"And Jessica Devine made it clear," Agnes says. "We must find an incantation to remove the portal mound. We continue our Saturday research until we find one."

"Indeed." A look of urgency contorts Leslie's face.

Tyler and the other young witches enter reminders into their phones for Saturday and Sunday. I puff at my wisp of bangs.

"We'll find a spell, Gwyn," Archie says, clasping my hand.

The fae children giggle and play, skipping around the garden beds. What will happen to Shailagh and Aonghas when we finally close the portal?

# CHAPTER TWENTY-FOUR

# LOST IN MISTRANSLATION

Friday after lunch, Mr. Yeats assists me in the magic room, grinding up mugwort to burn. Screw the star anise. I need to chat with Mom and Dad quickly, and my brain fog has been awful since my shift at Mystic Sage yesterday.

The familiar slides the mortar to me. "I added a little extra to rush the conference along."

"Thank you, Mr. Yeats," I say. "You've been a fabulous assistant."

While I pour the ground herbs into the wooden bowl, he straightens his vest and stands back.

"I don't want to distract you from your concentration." He picks up a poetry book and settles into the corner chair.

I raise my hand and summon my witch energy, burning the mugwort within seconds. As I focus on a new photo, one of both my parents, I splay my amber glow toward the picture. Mom's gold image appears first, and my dad emerges after hers.

"Gwyn," Dad says in his Welsh accent. "It's good to conference with you again."

Mom smiles. "What can we do for you, daughter?" she asks, inspecting my face. "You're upset, Gwynedd. What has happened?"

"A huge shit show." I cover my mouth. "I'm sorry. You never liked it when I used profanity. The city council was going to vote to level the fairy mound, and we don't know what will happen if they disturb the soil. So, the coven voted unanimously to reveal ourselves to three of the council allies and tell them about the Seelie Fae and the portal."

"And Leslie voted for this?" Mom's voice reverberates in the room. "I don't believe it."

Dad shakes his head. "Not possible. Leslie believed in total secrecy."

"Oh, she had some encouragement from Agnes," I say. "They're together again. Leslie is trying to adapt, but fifty years of obstinance bends at a slow pace."

"How did the Unremarkables respond to the reveal?" Dad's image fades in and out.

I roll my eyes. "Two of them went into a trance, and the Seelie Fae took one of them on a field trip through the portal."

"A human entered through the passageway?" Mom asks, gaping at me. "Oh, Gwynedd. That's concerning."

"Yeah, we didn't think he'd come back. But I chastised the children, and they brought him back through."

I focus my energy with more intensity, because my parents' shimmering images fade a little. Mom continues speaking in an elevated voice.

"I'm worried about your safety, Gwynedd, not the Unremarkable. If he passed through the portal, then so can you. My worst nightmare about the mound was the Tuatha Dé crossing over through it. Or coming here via another passageway and finding you to take you to the Otherworld."

"Oh, shit," I say, not having thought of the implications.

My parents flinch at my swearing, and I apologize again. I break the news to them about Dr. Seamus Duffy, sharing every detail.

"Oh, I'm so worried for you, daughter," Mom says. "What will you do?"

"Do you and the coven have a plan?" Dad asks.

"Leslie, Archie, and some others are going to investigate his background," I say. "Search for clues. Meanwhile, we have to find a spell, or he may try to take me to his world through the portal in the gardens."

"Yes. You do," Dad says. "Mum said you read through the entire family grimoire and found no spell to close a portal. Perhaps it's worth another look."

"Gwynedd, even though you didn't find an incantation in the spell book, try again and search for alternate words that may have a hidden meaning." Mom's face dissipates slowly.

"We're continuing the search on Saturday. I may not get back to you until after Ostara. We have a small celebration planned. I love you, Mom and Dad."

I grin at my parents as their images fade. Mr. Yeats closes the book and comes to the worktable.

"The conference went well, Ms. Crowther. I hope the interaction gave you the information you needed."

"Not as much as I wanted," I say. "Can you clean this up for me? I want to go through the family grimoire again."

"I would be happy to," he says. "Do you think it's worth the time?"

"It can't hurt to flip through the pages again. I'm reading the spell in the translated English, not Welsh, so another sift through shouldn't take long."

"You mentioned the visiting professor? A Dr. Duffy, I believe."

"Yes. Dr. Hughes and Dr. Cockburn are investigating his background and limiting their interactions with him at work as much as possible. I have no reason to run into him again. He'll never win me over, anyway."

The familiar motions toward the door. "Go on. You have more important matters to tend to."

"Thank you, Mr. Yeats." I hug the familiar and kiss him on the cheek.

He straightens his vest. "You're welcome, Ms. Crowther."

I dart to my room, unfasten the lock, and throw open the steamer trunk lid. The spell book and the hard copies of the English translations remain buried underneath the tray. I pull out the binder, hop on the bed, and fluff the pillow behind me. And I read through the pages one more time. Nick's translations are so detailed, excluding the many typos. I'm surprised he didn't figure out I was a witch sooner.

The afternoon gives way to the sun's shifting rays as I scour for a spell to shut down the portal, but I finish by five. I'm putting everything away when *Don't Stop Believin'* plays on my cell phone.

"Hi, Shane. What's up?"

"Hello, Gwyn," Shane says in an anxious tone. "Jeff called from the house. A water pipe burst in the bathroom. I've got to call a plumber and clean up the mess. He's been finishing a paper for the last two days. Has to turn it in before Spring Break. Could I bother you to come in?"

"No problem," I say, leaning on the trunk to get up. "I'm on my way out the door. See you in ten minutes."

"Thanks, darling. I owe you one."

"I'll add them to the rest and turn them in for a big IOU later. See ya soon."

It's kind of eerie at Mystic Sage on Friday evenings. Few customers ever drop in, so we usually get a good amount of inventory and restocking completed. But I'm alone in the store, which has the atmosphere of the local morgue. If I wasn't stuck at the cash register, I could restock the herbs. Instead, I read a few pages of the horror book Ronnie recommended to me but shove the gory story back into my hobo bag when the heebie-jeebies set in. I lack the concentration to follow the plot, anyway. What was I thinking? My cell phone vibrates in my jeans pocket, and I practically fall off the stool.

Nick: *Hope I'm not bothering you. Just wanted to make sure we're still OK?*

Me: *Yeah. I've been super busy. Sorry I haven't contacted you.*

Nick: *I watched the protest at Mitchell Hall last night. Anything I should know about?*

I pause. I can't tell him what really happened, so I improvise.

Me: *The Fellowship met with the council members to lobby for the fairy mound.*

Nick: *How did it go? Laura and I attended the last meeting.*

Me: *I saw you there. We're hoping they vote to save the mound.*

Nick: *Phew. That's good news. You all must be happy about that.*

The door dings, and Laura Lovelace strolls in. She glares at me as she ambles by. After inspecting the herb jars, she sets a couple in her basket and moves into the crystals room. I monitor her on the digital camera as she places a red candle next to the jars. She lifts her gaze toward the camera and smirks. When she sets her items on the counter, I try to converse in a pleasant tone of voice, which demands every ounce of patience I don't have.

"The new supplier Shane has is fantastic, don't you think?" I ask, smiling.

Laura raises her head. "They're adequate for my purposes. You don't work on Friday evenings. Where's Shane?"

"A water pipe burst in his house, so he asked me to come in tonight."

She only comes here on Fridays? Explains why I never see her shopping here. I ring up her goods—two jars of saffron and a red candle. Holy crystals. Has she been casting love spells on the assistant professor?

"So, Nick and you are dating? That's nice," I say, but not meaning it.

"We've been hanging together. He's one of my dissertation advisors. And we have some things in common."

Not much to base a relationship on, but whatever. I hand her the eco bag with her merchandise.

"Ingredients for a love spell," I say. "Wouldn't you be happier if you let the relationship grow naturally? Like after you complete your dissertation?"

"Mind your own business, witch." Laura leans over the counter and sneers. "I know what I want, and I'll have it. Karma is a bitch." She snatches her items and exits the store.

What the hell does that mean? She can have Nick, because I don't care. I rub my temples. Oh, she's just talking trash. If her coven knew she spoke to me in this manner, they'd expel her ass. I enter a reminder into my phone to never work Friday evenings again, because my menopausal brain won't remember. A text notification lights up my cell.

Nick: *Everything OK? You didn't reply?*

Me: *Sorry. Laura came into the store to buy a few items.*

Nick: *Are you there by yourself? I could run right over and keep you company.*

Me: *I am, but it's almost eight. I'll lock up soon. Thanks for checking on me.*

Nick: *Let me know if you change your mind.*

I spend the rest of the evening dusting and playing games on my phone. As I'm locking up the store, a transient thought passes through my mind. Is Laura trying to break up my relationship with Archie? I guess she doesn't realize her weak witch spell won't have any effect on an ancestral witch. A wicked smile creeps onto my lips.

While I make the trek to Archie's, lugging my purse with the dirk and the heavy book, the fatigue of the long day hits me like a semi-truck, and I call him.

"I'm on the way home, but I'm pooped. We can hang out over the weekend. If we have time after sorting through Agnes's library."

Archie groans into the phone. "Of course, I'm disappointed, but I'll live. I'm pure done in as well. I could barely string words together today to form complete sentences. The students had a chuckle or two over my garbled lecture. Avoiding Seamus Duffy has proven to be more difficult than expected. For a man who keeps to himself, he's been awful inquisitive this past week. He asked about you a lot. I'm glad you have little reason to run into him. How was work?"

"Me, too." Air passes through my lips. "Work was dead except for when Laura Lovelace stopped in. What a bitch she is."

"What happened? Did she talk to you?"

"Yeah. I think she's casting love spells on Nick. She bought ingredients. Should we tell him?" I tap nervously on the back of my phone.

He hums into the phone. "Do you have proof? If not, then we shouldn't. Let it go for now. Nick can take care of himself."

"But can he fight off magic? I don't think so. He texted me while I was working. Asked about the protest."

"Did you divulge what happened?" Archie asks, elevating his voice.

"Hell, no. It's bad enough he knows about the portal mound."

"Aye. Better he's in the dark." He pauses for a minute. "I hate to tell you this, but I have to cancel our dinner plans for Tuesday. I have to meet with Laura one last time about her dissertation. She couldn't meet with me any other night."

"Ugh. That was supposed to be our special Ostara dinner, since the coven is celebrating the spring equinox on Wednesday. She ruins everything. I hope she's not creating a love spell to cast on you."

"She can try all she wants. I've told you her magic will have no effect on me, because I'm an ancestral witch. After Tuesday, I can handle the final edits online, and we'll both be rid of her. But I'll be home by eight. Come by after work."

"Okaaay. I'm at the house now, so I'm gonna say goodnight. I love you, Archie."

"I love you. Sleep well, my love."

I nudge the door and enter the mudroom. My toes wiggle in delight when I remove my shoes. Mr. Yeats welcomes me home in his chimeric cat form, purring and rubbing against my jeans.

"Hello, Mr. Yeats," I say. "Where is Dr. Hughes?"

He meows and scuttles off, and I follow him into my room. Leslie is sitting on the floor in her nightgown and robe, flipping through the pages of my binder containing the spell book translations.

"What the fuck, Leslie? You have no right to go through my family's steamer trunk!" I drop my hobo bag on the bed. "This is not the way to build my trust in you."

The look of surprise on her face tells me she wasn't expecting me back so soon. Or she lost track of time. Or...

"Gwynedd, I'm sorry. I didn't mean to intrude. Your door was ajar, and I noticed the lid was open on your trunk. I shuffled in, intending to close the top. Since Yule, I haven't been as sharp as I usually am. My age has finally caught up with me, I suppose. I was intrigued by the binder with translations of your family's grimoire and the leather tome itself. I remember examining the Welsh words, hoping to gain the knowledge to read and speak the language one day. Curiosity captured my better judgment, and I compared Nick's translations to the original Welsh. It's rather excellent, barring a multitude of typos. He does impeccable work."

"That's no excuse. You violated my privacy." I pinch my lips and stare her down.

"Indeed, I did. But I'm ecstatic. Gwynedd, I believe I've found a spell to remove the passageway to the Otherworld." A jubilant grin lights up her face.

"What?" I ask, gaping at her. "No. That's impossible. I sifted through the grimoire twice—one time this afternoon before I went to work. I found nothing."

"True, but you read through the translations of your mom's spell book, not the original Welsh. There is an extremely old spell to close a passage to another world. I want to show the incantation to Agnes, Trinity, and Archie and get their opinion." She points to the details on the original page in the grimoire.

"I don't understand how I missed this. Are you saying the translation was wrong?"

Leslie lowers her eyes to the binder and turns a few pages. "Yes. Nick did not translate this particular incantation well. He only missed a couple of old Welsh words."

"Well, that sucks." I kneel next to her and lay my hand on her shoulder. "I'm sorry I yelled at you. If you hadn't peeked in my trunk, we'd still be flipping page after page in Agnes's library."

"It was unjustified, but yes. I'm glad I gave into my inquisitive inclinations." Leslie struggles to push up off the floor, and I help her stand.

"Don't feel bad about the poor cognition," I say. "I'm in my early 50s, and my brain fog has been horrible this year off and on—a part of aging we have to get accustomed to. I should probably tell Nick about the mistake. He'd want to know he screwed up."

Leslie grasps my hand with her knobby fingers. "Gwynedd, please don't tell him. He's a young academic, and you shouldn't embarrass him. It was his only mistranslation of the spell book. You will gain nothing by pointing the error out to him. I, on the other hand, will have a discussion with him about the error...very soon."

"OK. If you think so." I pull on my earring. "All that work at Agnes's, and we could have closed the portal by now."

The coven Elder raises her chin. "Indeed."

# CHAPTER TWENTY-FIVE

# SPELL PREP

I LAY THE FAMILY grimoire on Agnes's worktable and open to the page with the incantation to close a passageway. I hope this is the last Saturday I have to spend at her house regarding the damn portal closing. Leslie sets her English translation on the table next to the tome. I read through the chant, and the English words seem as cryptic as the Welsh. I'm basically useless. What do I know about ancient chants for spellcasting?

"You'll have to guide me through this," I say. "This is Greek to me."

Agnes cracks up. "No. It's fucking Welsh."

"You're not funny." I throw her a dirty look.

Archie chuckles at our banter. "Even translated into English, old chants can be difficult to decipher."

"It's amazing how much two words can fuck up the entire nature of a spell." Agnes frowns at Leslie. "You should ask this young professor how he fucked up so bad."

"I intend to," Leslie says, lifting her chin. "I have a meeting scheduled with him after we've closed the portal. We can discuss this more later once we've completed our task."

Trinity addresses Leslie and Archie. "Have either of you found anything in Seamus's background that's suspicious?"

"Nothing more than what we already knew about him," Archie says. "Leslie has known him for many years, and his CV checks out. But we can't rule out the possibility that the real Dr. Duffy is actually dead and replaced by a shifting Tuatha Dé."

"Scary...but makes sense. Leslie, there are holes in the recipe," Trinity asks. "Did you mean to leave these blank spaces?"

Leslie pushes her silver hair to the side of her face. "The blanks are intentional. I could not decipher some ingredients. You must understand witches during this time were being persecuted and burned at the stake. They had to write in rhymes and riddles to avoid detection. Many old grimoires use alternative names to represent the herbs to mask their spell recipes and chants. This incantation resembles a type of Hearth Magic similar to what Kitchen Witches practice today. Sorcerers who practiced this version of witchcraft considered their hearth the heart of their home. But I believe we can insert adequate substitutes."

"Eh...don't worry," Agnes says, retrieving a wooden bowl. "I've been substituting ingredients for years. Hedge witches are all about adding a pinch of this and a drop of that. It's why it's called witch...craft." Her wide grin spreads the wrinkles on her face.

Trinity shakes her head. "I don't know. Winging a special spell like this sounds risky to me. I wish you could discern what those missing pieces are."

"I bet Aunt Gorawen could help," I say.

Archie rubs my back. "Have you tried to contact Ellie again?"

"Yeah. No response yet. I guess she's busy running the property."

"Who is Ellie?" Trinity asks as she places herb jars on the worktable.

"She's my aunt's caretaker," I say. "Ellie and her husband run the farm for her, and Ellie brings her food a few times a week. But she's an Unremarkable. She doesn't know Aunt Gorawen is an ancestral witch."

Leslie places a mortar and pestle on the table. "Do you think Ellie is avoiding you? You said she was upset about you showing up."

"Nah. It's March, so they're in the middle of the planting season." I clip up my hair to keep it from falling into the bowl. "Ellie probably doesn't check email much, and Aunt Gorawen doesn't know how. My aunt and I only had one video chat. I introduced Tyler to her, so I don't believe she's ignoring me."

Archie adds, "It's true Ellie didn't trust Gwyn at first. How would you like an American woman showing up and claiming to be Aunt Gorawen's Grandniece? Especially when she owns such a large estate."

"How did you convince her?" Agnes asks. "Did you show her your birth certificate?"

My mouth falls open slowly. "I didn't think of taking my birth certificate with me. That would have been smart. But I had something better—the family grimoire."

"Fucking brilliant. More convincing than a birth certificate. Anyone can fake those." Agnes lights a blueberry candle.

Trinity reads the label on the candle jar. "Since when do we use scented candles to prepare spell ingredients?"

"I never heard of a scented candle having special properties." Archie rubs his goatee.

"It's not for the incantation," she says. "It fucking stinks in here. I need to clean."

We all crack up and gather around the table.

"Gwynedd, did you conference with your parents regarding the spell?" Leslie asks. "They may have offered some suggestions."

"I tried, but I couldn't focus well enough the last few days to get through to them. But I'll keep trying." I measure the mugwort and pour the herb into the bowl.

Archie measures out the next ingredient, and Trinity pours in the final herbs. All five of us huddle around the bowl and raise our hands with our palms facing the table. Agnes squeezes in the middle, shoving us to the left and right.

"There are too many fucking cooks in the kitchen," she whines.

The hedge witch raises her hand and calls on her witch energy. The amber glow melts the ingredients into an adequate concoction, but we have no way to test it.

"I believe we're ready to tell the others," Trinity says. "I hope to the depths of the Otherworld this incantation works."

Once the Fellowship receives confirmation from our city council allies regarding the special Ostara Celebration request, Trinity sends a group text to the coven for an emergency meeting. On Sunday, we gather at the Pumpkin House on a night with clear skies, and the stars twinkle above, offering us a sense of hope. When Leslie announces the discovery of a possible incantation to close the portal, my fellow witches shriek and laugh at the news. They're probably relieved they don't have to spend more days at Agnes's house.

The young witches ask in overlapping voices. "Where did you find the incantation?" "When are we going to cast the spell?" "Will it work?"

"We'll gather after dark on Ostara," Leslie says. "Elijah has already contacted our council allies. They approved our request. What other choice do they have?"

Trinity explains, "We don't know how long the casting will take, so dress warmly for the cool evening temperature."

"What about the Seelie Fae?" Zoe asks, pouting. "What will happen to them?"

My son wraps his arm around his love. "We can't worry about the children. Mom's life is in danger as long as the portal remains open."

Tanner, Spence, and Skye nod in agreement. Elijah fist-bumps Shane.

"Tyler understands what's at stake," Archie says, grasping my hand. "Plan for possible unexpected consequences. Agnes will explain the details."

The hedge witch pushes up from her chair, rubbing her back. "Like any spell we cast, repercussions can occur. Leslie and I will both lead the chant, because I can't fucking memorize the words like I used to. We're fairly certain the reference in the incantation refers to a portal. The language of the time can be difficult to interpret, and I'm relying on Leslie's translation. Be prepared for everything and anything."

"Get lots of rest, everyone," Trinity says. "You must be in top condition. Gwyn's life depends on it."

The coven Elder dismisses us, tapping her staff. Trinity, Agnes, Ronnie, Archie, and I join her on the porch.

Trinity taps the heel of her stiletto. "I sure hope this spell removes the mound. Would solve a mess of problems."

"Agnes, do you believe this incantation will work?" I rub my twitching eye.

"I can't guarantee a fucking thing, Gwyn," she says. "We can only try. It's all we've got." She grabs Leslie's hand. "Let's go, Leslie. I'm exhausted."

"We'll send out reminders on Tuesday to prepare. Goodnight, everyone." Leslie helps Agnes hobble down the steps.

"I kind of want Derek there," Ronnie says. "In case something happens."

Archie lays a hand on her arm. "I understand your concern, but I think Derek will need to sit this one out."

"Ronnie, if the spell should cause us harm in any way, Derek would only get hurt," I say.

"You're right." She hugs me. "See you both on Wednesday."

We descend the stairs to the paver walkway and wave goodbye to my best friend. She still has apprehension surrounding large spell castings, and the guilt pinches at my insides. At least this time, we don't have to agonize over the looming threat of an evil fairy trying to kill me. Oh, wait...

On Monday night, I attempt to conference with my parents one more time—after the prior eleven that failed miserably. The aroma of burned mugwort permeates the living room—a smell closely resembling marijuana. It's almost midnight when I throw my hands down in frustration. I gaze at the painting of my mom resting on Archie's fireplace mantel and fall onto the soft cushion of the loveseat. He sits down next to me and caresses my arm.

"You did your best, Gwyn. You've been at this for nearly four hours. Try again tomorrow night when you come here after work. If you're unsuccessful, try again after we've closed the portal on Wednesday. We all will have improved concentration once it's done. I, for one, can't wait. I'm tired of repeating myself during lectures, although the students enjoy my comical failings."

"Damn this menopausal brain. I hoped to reach one of them—Mom or Aunt Gorawen. Make sure we're interpreting the incantation correctly. Although I have more faith in my aunt than my mom."

"Still no reply from Ellie?" he asks as he cleans up the wooden bowl of burned mugwort.

I check the email on my cell again. "Nope. I hope she's not ignoring me. I'd hate to fly all the way to Wales only to find out her internet was down."

"Be patient. She'll contact you in due time. You certainly can't travel there until Spring Break, anyway."

I move toward the hall tree to put on my fleece-lined hoodie and my sneakers. Archie wraps his arms around my torso and smiles.

"I'm glad you're sleeping in your bed tonight. You should be well-rested tomorrow to attempt another divination conference. I also have other reasons for you to have plenty of energy."

The annoying mantel clock ticks, and then the first of twelve dings begins. I lift my tote and bend my head back to kiss him.

"I bet you do," I say, opening the door. "See you tomorrow night, honey."

"I look forward to it, my love."

# Chapter Twenty-Six

# UNEXPECTED CONSEQUENCES

Tuesday morning begins with brilliant rays of sunshine peeking through my curtains, but I've got butterflies in my stomach—the kind that can't seem to find a place to rest their wings. A busy day awaits me: classes, paperwork to complete for the insurance company, and hours at Mystic Sage. I may not have the energy left for divination and a night of passion with Archie when my shift ends. I always sleep the best in my own bed, because I can't keep my hands off my gorgeous man. At least, I'm starting the day well-rested. When I check my cell, a text notification from Archie lights up my screen.

Archie: *I hope you slept well. Everyone must be at full strength tonight.*

Me: *Yeah. Didn't even get up to pee.*

Archie: *LOL. It's a miracle.*

Me: *You're not funny. But I love you.*

Archie: *You have my heart, my love. See you tonight after eight.*

"I'm going to dinner now, my devoted employees." Shane checks his cargo pants pocket for his wallet. "Gwyn, I'll see you tomorrow evening after closing."

I force a smile. "Can't wait. Enjoy your evening."

"Will do," he says as he exits the store.

Jeff ambles behind the counter. "I'll work the cash register if you would prefer to stock the shelves."

"Yeah. I'd love to empty boxes tonight," I say, shuffling toward the board games and puzzles. "I've got nervous energy."

"How come? What's happening tomorrow night?"

"I guess I can tell you. But keep this under wraps. We're going to cast a spell to shut down the portal in the mound."

"Oooh. Shane didn't tell me you found one. That's awesome."

I pull out a few games from the large box and place price tags on them. "Well, we don't know if the incantation will work, but we have to try."

"I'm pulling for you all. You deserve to have something go right for once."

"Thanks, Jeff. I appreciate your support."

By 7:00 p.m., I finish with the board games and move into the crystals room. Customers come and go, knocking into me in the claustrophobic space. After twenty minutes have passed, my body tenses with a soft buzz, and I turn around in my squatting position to find Seamus Duffy staring down at me.

"Dr. Duffy. Why are you standing there?" I ask.

My heart beats like a hammer in my chest, and the desire to bolt out of the store overwhelms me. But the professor captivates me with those shining, sea-green eyes.

"I didn't want to interrupt you while you were working," he says. "I was waiting for you to finish."

"What can I do for you? Are you interested in a specific crystal?" I put the last of the loose crystals into a basket and stand.

"Oh, not at all." He locks his eyes on mine as he speaks. "I stopped in for some herbs. Shane Murphy keeps a well-stocked store with a unique supply one can't find anywhere else." He leans into me, and a smile cracks his placid face. "Certainly not the grocery store. When I saw you back here, I thought I'd stop and say hello. I haven't seen you since the stroll to the library."

The pounding beneath my ribs increases with every passing second, and I discover I'm holding my breath. I have to force the air out of my lungs to speak.

"Well, I hope you find what you came for. I have to get back to work." I move toward the doorway.

"Before you return to your duties, I wanted to invite you to dinner one night this week. Not as a date. I know you and Dr. Cockburn are a couple. I only want to show you a collection of Irish folklore books and paintings I brought with me from Northern Ireland. Some are limited edition prints of the Tuatha Dé fairies."

Light glimmers in Seamus's eyes, and he smiles awkwardly at me. Suddenly, a vision of the faceless fairy with immense black and pale-gray wings flashes in my head. The logical part of my brain urges me to scream, but I suppress it and come up with a quick plan.

"I'll get back to you," I say. "Jeff is waiting for me to take over the cash register."

He nods once. "I look forward to hearing from you."

I squeeze past him and rush into the front of the store, dashing behind the counter to pick up my hobo bag. In the rush, I knock it to the floor, and the contents fall out everywhere—everything but the dirk. While I shove my necklace, wallet, and the rest of my stuff back into my oversized purse, Jeff squats to help me.

"What's the matter with you?" he asks. "Your face is white as a ghost."

"I'm worried Seamus has been stalking me, and a vision appeared while he spoke to me. Can you close the shop tonight? I need to get out of here and tell Archie."

"Sure, Gwyn. Would you like me to delay him?"

"That would be fantastic, Jeff. Here are the keys to lock up. Don't forget to set the alarm."

Jeff walks over to assist Seamus, who has been examining the dried herbs. I pick up my purse and dart out of the store while I have the opportunity. As I run toward the opening in the Green, I grasp the dirk through the cloth of my purse. When I stop to catch my breath, I check for the protection pouch, but it's not in there. The special concoction I made at Ronnie's must have fallen out. Every part of my being shakes to the core as I run across the paver walkways to the shortcut to Archie's house. I enter, shut the door, and bolt the deadlock.

He's not in the living room or the kitchen, so I check the basement. But the light isn't on. A grin erupts on my face. He must be preparing for our special night upstairs. I'm not in the mood now, but I sneak upstairs to surprise him. The bedroom door is ajar, and the flicker of burning candles greets me. I tap my chest to calm my breathing and saunter through the doorway.

I can't believe the image before me—Laura and Archie lying naked in his bed. She can't be here. I blink several times while I pant. This is a nightmare. The floorboards creak when I move, and the sleazy witch stirs. She nudges Archie.

"Hey, lover. We have company." A sinister smile forms on her plump lips, and she snickers.

"What?" he says as he rubs his head. "What's happening?"

He squints at Laura and looks toward the doorway where I'm standing. I say nothing. What is there to say? He slept with Laura. I rush out of there and stagger down the stairs, knowing he's going to follow me and make up ludicrous excuses for his behavior. He drank too much. She seduced him or cast a love spell on him somehow. Archie shouts at Laura in the distance.

"Get the fawk out of here, witch!"

"You wanted this!" she yells. "You dragged me back here after dinner, saying you wished we had stayed together all this time."

"Get your clothes on and leave, or I'll throw you out!"

I wait at the front door as they argue, grinding my teeth to suppress the tears. Footsteps echo in the stairwell, and Archie approaches me in his robe and bare feet. He brushes his locks with his fingers.

"Gwynedd, I swear to you on my ancestors, I don't remember what happened. We finished reviewing the notes on her dissertation, and she offered to buy me a glass of Scotch, a small one. Not enough to give me more than a wee buzz."

I want to believe him. Laura is a conniving witch, and she bought those love spell ingredients at Mystic Sage. So, I give him the benefit of the doubt.

"The spell was for you then, not Nick. But you said she couldn't cast one on you."

"No, she couldn't. I'm perplexed over what transpired after dinner, Gwyn, but I will find out." He strokes my arm.

"Maybe she set you up? Like at the pagan conference? You didn't actually have sex with her." I pant and tremble while I anticipate his answer.

"Gwynedd." He lowers his eyes to his groin. "I won't lie to you. Evidence points to the contrary."

I squish my eyes closed, wishing I could awaken from this nightmare, and my head spins. He removes his hand from me, and I stare into his distraught eyes.

"You should have never trusted her." I turn around and open the door.

"Please, don't leave. I will sort this out, Gwyn. I promise you. We'll figure this out together."

"It's not my job to sort it out, Archie. It's yours."

I step onto the porch, hugging my bag, and stroll aimlessly in a daze, unaware of what direction I'm headed in. My speed increases to a steady jog until I'm running full throttle toward the Sunshine Garden Café. It takes me about ten minutes to reach Main Street, and I stop to catch my breath. I'm across from Roots of the Earth.

When I look up at the second floor, Nick is standing by the window of his apartment, lifting weights. He takes a break and stares out the window for a minute, surveying the street below. Instantly, I'm drawn to him, and my head becomes dizzy—my mind clouded in a smoky haze. I decide I shouldn't bother Ronnie at work, so I survey the area for Dr. Duffy and walk across the street using the pedestrian crossing.

As I knock on Nick's door, I contemplate what I'm going to say. I'd not treated him well recently and wasn't understanding of his affection for me. But now I'm hurting. All I want is for someone to hug me and make me feel wanted.

He answers the door shirtless, with the button on his jeans hanging open. I'm taken aback by his developed pectorals, arms, and abdominal muscles, glistening with sweat. Derek has trained him well. He cocks his head.

"Gwyn. Is everything OK?"

"No. Can I come in?" I ask.

"Of course." He gestures with his hand to enter. "Did something happen? You seem upset."

How do I tell him without sharing the facts about Laura? If he has any affection for her, this will wreck any chance they had. Oh, screw it. She doesn't deserve a man like him.

"I ran from Archie's. I walked in on him and Laura in bed...naked. Archie confirmed they had sex."

The tears won't flow, because I'm too confused—my heart full of anger and distrust. My mind floats as if I'm in another universe.

"Oh, Gwyn. I am so sorry," he says, moving closer.

Nick embraces me lovingly, and I lay my head against his chest, so warm and defined. His heart beats steadily in my ear while I surrender to the calm. I gaze at him and his smoldering eyes burn with desire. But he continues to hold me in his comforting embrace. Jitters rock my stomach, but I push through the discomfort. I inch my lips close to his, and he accepts the invitation, kissing me tenderly. When I pull back, a whiff of his musky sweat passes my nose.

"I so missed your lips, your enchanting hazel eyes, your beaming smile," he says, caressing the side of my face.

He clasps my hand and leads me into his bedroom. The room is dimly lit with one tiny lamp that has a thin scarf over its shade. There's a dresser on one wall, and nightstands on either side of the king-size bed.

"I hate to break this wonderful, sexy mood, but I was working out when you knocked. Give me a few minutes to wash up a little." He kisses me again. "You'll still be here when I'm done?"

I stare into his eyes full of unfulfilled yearning. "Yes. I'll wait for you."

After he dashes into the bathroom, I set my huge purse on the bed. I massage the family heirloom through the cloth and remember why I ran to Archie's in the first place. Dr. Duffy may be following me, so I move my bag to the nightstand and fidget with my crystal choker. I want to follow through with this. I deserve to experience pleasure from this man who loves me so deeply. My aching heart craves to feel whole again.

Nick comes out of the bathroom naked, and I gape at him. After extensive fitness training, he's a vision I never imagined existed underneath those nerdy professor clothes. Amorous desire emerges on his face as he approaches me, rubbing his defined abdomen.

"Can you take off your necklace?" he asks, licking his lower lip. "I want to kiss your neck."

I unclasp the choker and set it on the nightstand next to my bag. He slips off my blouse and unhooks my bra, slowly removing it. A soft gasp passes his lips when he sees the dragon tattoo on my left breast.

"Did you get the tat in Wales? So sexy." He grabs my thighs and lifts me to the mattress, kissing me fervently.

I become queasy again. Damn it. Stop being a nervous Nellie. You can do this. I unzip my jeans, and Nick pulls them off, chuckling. With a hook of his fingers on the elastic, he slips off my panties and drops them to the floor. He joins me on the bed and places soft kisses on my neck while he fondles my breasts. He explores my body, brushing his fingers across my ribs, and outlining my toned abdomen. As his hand slides lower, I grip his arm, recognizing the path he's on. My legs part, accepting his strokes, and I yelp in response.

"I want to you remember this forever," he says as he finds my sensitive spot.

Nick nuzzles my neck and plants soft kisses as he moves to my nipple, taking it into his mouth. I moan and writhe while his hands work their magic. He's patient and takes his time while I tremble. I can't discern how much time has passed when I let out a shriek the neighbors must hear. He continues caressing me as I quiver. I never imagined he could be so adept. He kisses me while he kneads a nipple, and I search for him, wrapping my hand around his manhood. He moans and lays a hand on my face.

"Do you want this, Gwyn? I must know you want to be with me."

"Yes. I want you to make love to me."

As he climbs on top, he whispers in a breathy voice, "I've wanted this for so long."

He presses hard on my lips as he enters me, and the jitters return like a peeping tom. I push through the knots tightening in my stomach, trying to enjoy the love this man is giving me. An unquenchable desire coaxes him to take his time, while I wait for him to reach his peak.

"Oh, Gwyn." He caresses my cheek and speaks in a guttural voice. "Making love to you is more fulfilling than I ever imagined. It can be like this forever." He grunts and shakes with his release, panting as he kisses my cheek.

I slide my hands off his back as I wrestle to take air into my lungs. "Nick, I can't breathe."

"I'm sorry. I wanted to feel every inch of your skin." He rolls over and lies on his side, placing his hand on my chest. "I'm so happy you came to me tonight."

As he caresses my skin, he never takes his eyes off mine. When an uncontrollable urge to vomit overwhelms me, I dash to the bathroom and throw up in the toilet. I shut the door and search for toothpaste to freshen my mouth. While I rinse with water from the spout, my mind becomes clear as a cloudless sky. This was a huge mistake to come here. And it wasn't fair to him.

Nick yells from the bedroom. "Are you OK, Gwyn?"

"Yeah," I say, lying through my teeth. "I'll be out in a minute."

I sit on the toilet and weigh my options. Who am I kidding? What options? What a gigantic error I've made. I exit the bathroom, collect my clothes, and rest on the edge of the bed.

"Nick, you're a wonderful man."

"Why do I sense a but coming next?"

"I acted irrationally, because I was out of my mind in emotional pain." When I lay my hand on his, regret takes hold. "I shouldn't have come here."

He strokes my face. "You're wrong. This was meant to be."

I'm not capable of speaking with reason in my emotional state, so I decide to crawl through the web of this mess later. "I should go home and sleep in my own bed."

"Please, don't go. Sleep beside me tonight. I understand you're a little upset. Rest and we can talk in the morning."

"No. I have to get a good night's sleep. My witch skills must be top-notch tomorrow." I put on my clothes in a flash like there's a fire in the building.

"What's happening tomorrow?"

I hesitate, because we're supposed to keep our clandestine plan hush-hush. But I have to tell him something, or he won't let me leave without drama.

"We found an incantation to remove the mound. Tomorrow is the Ostara Celebration, so we're shutting down the portal afterward. The Fellowship made arrangements with our allies on the city council."

His eyes widen. "Where did you find the spell?"

I swallow and bite my lip. "In my mom's grimoire. I told Leslie you know about the coven. She sifted through the translations you gave me and discovered you had mistranslated a few words. She found a bunch of typos, too. Don't feel bad. She said the old Welsh is difficult to translate easily. She scheduled a meeting with you to discuss it." I give him a peck on the cheek. "After Ostara, I'll text you, and we can talk."

I pick up my hobo bag from the floor, shove my choker in, and head toward the bedroom door.

"Gwyn, we belong together. You must sense that."

I smile at him but don't reply, exiting his apartment in silence. As I stroll home, the words pound away in my head like a jackhammer. WHAT A COLOSSAL MISTAKE.

# CHAPTER TWENTY-SEVEN

# ABOUT LAST NIGHT

I TOSS AND TURN all night, waking to night sweats and visions of a Tuatha Dé fairy haunting me—and Dr. Seamus Duffy. When the sun's rays cut through the curtain, they might as well be knives slicing my skin. How am I going to get through this day? I check my phone for the first time since I left Archie's house and discover several texts from him.

Archie: *Where are you? Please, text me, so I know you're all right.*

Archie: *I'm so worried about you. Text me, please.*

Archie: *I understand why you're angry and upset. Please, tell me you're safe.*

Archie: *I love you, Gwynedd. I'll figure this out.*

I drop the phone on the bed and wipe my face. At least he didn't send twenty-five of them. My phone reads 9:10 a.m. I slept nine hours, but my brain tells me I only got four. I pick up my cell and send him a text.

Me: *I'm just checking my phone. I'm OK.*

He replies immediately.

Archie: *I worried about you all night. Didn't sleep at all.*

Me: *Me neither.*

Archie: *Where did you go? I checked with Leslie and Ronnie.*

Remorse tugs at my heart. I fucked up so badly. I can't tell him the truth. Not until after the spell-casting tonight. Our minds must focus on the task at hand.

Me: *We'll talk tomorrow. I promise. Let's get through tonight.*

Archie: *I understand. No matter what happened, I love you, Gwyn.*

I don't reply. My actions last night taint anything I would say. I can't explain what came over me. My bladder is about to burst, so I run to the bathroom. While I sit on the toilet, I recall the incident when Seamus came to the store. I need to tell Archie, but I'll fill him in later after the casting. When I come out, Mr. Yeats is waiting for me. He eyes me over like the curious cat he is.

"You appear to have had a miserable night," he says, fidgeting with his tie. "You were supposed to spend the evening with Dr. Cockburn. I understand it's rude to pry, but did something untoward happen?"

My eyes drop to the floor. "You could say that, but I don't wanna talk about it."

"Understood. I am here should you have the desire to vent."

He transforms into a cat and scuttles into the office. I drag my lifeless body into the kitchen, rubbing my temples, and make some Earl Grey tea. I may need a double. Leslie has left for school, and I imagine Archie is in class. I text Shane, telling him I need to cash in on an IOU, so I can nap in the afternoon. I call Ronnie and beg her to come to Leslie's. The next ten minutes pass at the speed of a snail before she arrives. I meet her at the door.

"Good gods, Gwyn. You look like shit. What happened last night?"

I groan. "Oh, Ronnie. The evening was one of the worst nights of my life—only second to finding out Richard died."

"Damn. You better start from the beginning." She peers at the coffeemaker. "Fabulous. There's coffee left. I have a feeling I'm gonna need to fuel this conversation."

She heats a cup of leftover coffee in the microwave while I tell her about Dr. Duffy and the vision I had at Mystic Sage. I finish with the heartache of finding Archie in bed with that wicked witch from Hockessin. I take a sip of my tea and drop the cup onto the saucer with a clink.

"Did he explain himself?" she asks, setting her mug on the kitchen table. "Not that there was anything to discuss. Unless Laura made things appear as if they…you know…"

"He said there was evidence they had committed the deed, but he doesn't remember a damn thing."

"Do you believe him?" Her brow furrows.

"Yes, but he put himself in that position when he could have insisted on not working with her in person. He says he's gonna figure out what she did, but he told me she couldn't cast a spell on him without help."

My best friend rubs my arm. "You should give Archie a chance to prove himself, but I understand if this affects your relationship, especially with his past. You know you can depend on me. Why didn't you call or stop by the café?"

"I ran toward the Sunshine Garden Café. But when I got to Main Street, I stopped across from Roots of the Earth. Nick was staring out the window of his apartment." I swallow and blink several times.

Ronnie goggles at me. "No way. What happened?"

"You know Nick came by the store, and we talked. Things were better after I recognized how selfish I'd been the night of the concert. When I saw him standing there in the window, something came over me. The next thing I knew, I was knocking on the door to his apartment. When I told him about Laura and Archie, he hugged me. It was so comforting. When I lifted my head, he kissed me and..."

"Oh. My. Gods. I always said you should have jumped his bones, but I didn't expect you'd follow through with the suggestion."

"I got caught up in the moment, but the nervous knots in my stomach were so bad, I threw up after. Are you disappointed in me?"

"After all the men I slept with? Come on. You're not perfect, Gwyn. You were upset and wanted someone to console you. I assume you haven't told Archie yet."

"No...I will, but not tonight." I rest my arms on the table. "I called in sick, because I barely slept last night. And I've decided not to go to the Ostara Open House. Could you leave early and meet me here? So, I'm not walking to Mitchell Hall alone."

"Of course. I'll tell everyone you're under the weather and need to harness your energy for the spell casting." Ronnie bends over the table and takes my hands in hers. "Please, don't beat yourself up over this. Let's get through the incantation, and then you can figure out the drama. What about Nick?"

"He may have been dating Laura, but he loves me. I made his night." My head throbs, so I press my temples.

She snickers. "I bet you did. I'm sorry. You don't need my sarcasm. Did Nick say he loves you?"

"Not outright. He went on and on about us being meant for each other. It'll break his heart when I tell him I made a mistake."

"Worry about your love life tomorrow. We have to shove through today first." She pushes up from her chair. "I have to get to the café since I'm attending Ostara, but I'll come back at 7:30 p.m. We'll trek to Mitchell Hall together."

"Thank you. Normally, I'd go with Archie. Going with Tyler would require an explanation, and I don't have the wherewithal for that."

Ronnie turns the doorknob. "Get some rest and clear your head. You'll need your focus tonight. See ya later."

She exits with the slam of the door. What focus? I'm devoid of any. I shuffle through the kitchen doorway and run into Mr. Yeats.

"Were you eavesdropping?"

He straightens his vest and averts his eyes. "I may have heard a few things."

I roll my eyes. "Out with it. You're about to burst a bubble with some kind of information."

"Yes. First, I'm very sorry about your evening. You mentioned this Laura witch may have influenced Dr. Cockburn by casting a spell. Since the professor is an ancestral witch, she would have needed the help of a being with stronger magic."

I put my hands on my hips. "What are you saying?"

"Did the idea ever occur to you that the other magical being might have been the Tuatha Dé fairy who is hunting for you?"

"No. The idea hadn't occurred to me," I say in a sarcastic tone. "But thank you, Mr. Yeats...for your eavesdropping."

He straightens his vest and smiles. Then frowns.

The wind gusts every few minutes, so I pull up the hood on my fleece-lined sweatshirt, checking my neck for the tourmaline necklace. The temperature is mild, so I have on a T-shirt, jeans, and sneakers with the expectation the casting may take all night. Casting the spell shouldn't be difficult under the luminosity of the half-moon. As we approach Mitchell Hall, I prepare what I'm going to say to Archie.

When Ronnie and I stroll through the iron gate to the Celestial Gardens, the Fellowship stands near the mound. Agnes and Leslie are describing the process for the casting, I assume, as their hands move in the air, pointing to and fro. The young witches gather and gaze at the old witches.

Trinity, Shane, and Elijah prepare the area in front, clearing debris. They're all dressed in jeans and sweatshirts, comfortable clothing for possible nasty repercussions. As the mound formed and grew, Agnes said a storm raged for weeks, causing trees to fall over from root rot—not a pleasant outcome. Archie glimpses us coming through the gate and rushes over.

He locks eyes with me and speaks in a thicker brogue. "Are you all right?"

"Yes. I'm OK." But I'm not. I grimace and fidget with my hobo bag.

"I'm gonna leave you two alone. See you in the circle." Ronnie touches my arm and ambles toward the others.

"I'm determined to find out what Laura did to me during dinner, Gwyn. I promise."

"I need to tell you something, too, but we should wait until tomorrow. Let's keep our minds on the casting."

"Of course." He gestures to follow him. "Agnes and Leslie started a wee early. If you and Ronnie follow along, you'll be fine. The incantation is fairly simple, actually. But Agnes says a violent storm occurred when they created the mound. She said the fallout from closing a portal could be far worse than trying to open one."

Spence eyes me. "Hey, sis. I hope you're feeling better. We missed you at the celebration."

"Hey, Mom," Tyler says, hugging me. "Are you OK?"

"Yes, I'm fine. I didn't sleep well, so I took a long nap."

Agnes waves her hands in the air. "Enough with the fucking chit-chat. We need to get started. You young witches, find a place between two older witches, so we can more easily balance our power. This incantation isn't familiar to me at all, and we're relying on Leslie's translation. As competent as she is, if she misinterpreted one word, we're back to ground zero. If it works? Prepare for pelting rain and flying ice chips."

"Why do you think I wore my raincoat?" Trinity says. "I come prepared."

The others chuckle as we form our coven circle, arranging ourselves as Agnes requested. We're as close to the mound as possible, but are we close enough?

Leslie raises her chin, squinting. "As soon as everyone has adopted a more serious tone, we will begin."

"Sorry, Dr. Hughes," Zoe says. "I'm ready."

Skye grins. "Me, too. Let's get this done."

Leslie begins. "As I explained earlier, I will provide the wording for the chant. Repeat the words after me, and..."

She stops talking and directs her gaze toward the entrance to the gardens. Because of my petite stature, I can't see who or what has captured her attention. Ronnie's eyebrows jump, and she looks at me. She mouths the words, "It's Nick."

My heart palpitates, and I dash over to talk to him. He breaks through the circle before I can stop him.

"What are you doing here?" I whisper. "I said we'd talk tomorrow. Please, go."

"I had to come, Gwyn." A somber expression contorts his face.

I tilt my head, thinking I heard a faint Irish accent in his voice. How odd. "We don't have to talk tonight. I promise I'll call you tomorrow. You can't be here."

My fellow witches shift closer, trying to eavesdrop on our conversation. Archie moves next to me, and Leslie approaches. Agnes isn't far behind.

"Dr. Evans, you need to leave," Leslie says. "You're not permitted to be here during our spell casting, even if you're *in the knowing*."

Agnes is more direct. "Get the fuck out, Professor. We have work to do."

"Nick, why are you here?" Archie asks. "How did you even know we were gathering?"

"I told him, but I didn't think he come here." I shift even closer to Nick and whisper, "Don't do this now, please."

Archie glimpses the angst on my face and stares at me, perplexed. Nick surveys the expressions on my fellow witches' faces, full of bewilderment and what-the-fucks.

"After last night, I had no choice," he says. "I couldn't wait for you any longer. I came here because I can't allow you to close the portal."

My eyebrows arch. "Why are speaking with an Irish accent, Nick?"

"Because he's Irish." Fury builds in Archie's eyes.

An arrogant grin forms on Nick's face while he waits for the light bulb to click in my head. My lips part as my menopausal brain deciphers what Archie said.

I peer up at Nick. "Fuuuck."

I take a few steps back, and Archie follows me. All the signs were there. The queasiness the first time I tried to have sex with him. The nausea and vomiting last night. My intermittent brain fog. I didn't recognize the signals. He experienced discomfort the night of the concert when I had a protection pouch in my bag. MY HOBO BAG. I check for dirk through the cloth, but it's missing.

"Fuck, fuck, fuck," I mutter.

Archie whispers next to my ear. "Grasp the dirk, Gwyn. It's our only hope."

"It's not in there," I say, panicking.

"Where the fawk is it?" Agitation distorts his voice.

"I don't know." Where is his family heirloom? The lingering haze in my head clouds my thinking.

He glares at me. "Where were you last night?"

My eyes drift to Nick and back to Archie. The disappointment in Archie's eyes stakes me in my heart. My fellow witches yell, their voices shouting over each other. "What the fuck is going on?" "Why isn't he leaving?" "Why doesn't he want us to close the portal?" They huddle around us while Leslie speaks.

"Even with my incoherency of the last few months, I developed suspicions when I read your translations of Gwynedd's family spell book. It's why I scheduled a meeting with you for tomorrow. I wanted to be sure before I made accusations."

"Well, you can cancel the meeting. I won't be here," he smirks.

"Fuck you, asshole." Agnes gives him the bird.

Nick laughs and extends his hand. "Come with me now, Gwyn. This contract was written long before either of us was born, although I've been alive much longer."

I stomp close to him, gritting my teeth. "You can't force me to go. I don't care what your ancestors demanded. I do not love you, Nick. My body tried to warn me about your true identity the entire night, despite your glamouring. But no matter what you did, I didn't fall in love with you. So, you can't have me."

Spence goggles at me, pointing. "Did you sleep with Nick?"

Tanner frowns at his partner. "Dude, don't embarrass her."

"You can't take her, you bastard!" Tyler shouts as Shane and Elijah hold him back.

The other witches stare at each other in dismay. They must understand they can't battle Nick and win. My heart races with adrenalin as my anger intensifies. What are we going to do? We didn't plan for an incantation to repel a Tuatha Dé fairy. How do we fight him?

Nick's brown eyes turn bright green while shafts of light emanate from his body. His otherworldly voice resonates in the space.

"I searched for you for hundreds of years until I discovered your magic scent. When I confirmed you were the one, I set out to win your love as my ancestors prophesied, but as you all like to say, 'I'm out of fucks.' You're coming with me, Gwyn."

He reaches for me, and Archie tries to push him back with his witch energy. Nick swings his arm, knocking Archie several feet away to the ground. Elijah and Tanner run to him.

"Archie!" I shout. "Fuck you, Nick."

He smiles wickedly. "Yes. You did."

Without warning, the others push past me and attack Nick, throwing fireballs of magic, and I slip on the grass. Shane, Ronnie, and Elijah run at him while Archie, Tanner, and Spence jump him from behind. As Trinity, Agnes, and Leslie attack him from one side, Tyler, Skye, and Zoe leap at him from the other. He repels them with an easy swipe of his hand like he's swatting a fly.

"Tyler!" I scream.

My fuzzy brain fails at formulating any solution to my predicament, so I stand and summon my witch energy, directing my amber anger toward Nick. He blocks the magic rays with the palm of his hand.

"Gwyn, I can take you by force, but I'd rather you come with me freely. I don't want to hurt anyone."

Suddenly, my fellow witches chant and send a combined amber ball of fire at Nick. But he blocks the attack with his other hand, diverting the sphere of magic back to them. Their bodies fly like blowing debris, landing on the grass. While my hand continues to spar with his, I look back at my witch family and search for Tyler. He pushes himself up, and the others rise, too. Blood trickles down the sides of my son's face, and my witch friends have abrasions and contusions.

I glare at Nick, recognizing the futility of the fight, but I refuse to give in. Blood boils in my veins as I shove my amber glow at him. He casts his gaze upon my son and exhales.

"I can't go back empty-handed, Gwyn. If you don't go with me, I'll have to take Tyler. Your choice."

So, the family tale comes to fruition after all. I have no choice but to go with Nick or he'll kill my son in my place. Archie and

Tyler run to my side, with the others close behind. The amber glow dissipates as I lower my hand, and Nick withdraws his fairy magic.

"Don't attack Nick again," I say. "I'm going with him."

"No, Mom! You can't give up!" Tyler screams.

Archie pleads with me. "Gwyn, we'll fight him to the end, if necessary."

"He said if I don't agree to go, he'll take Tyler." My heart tears inside. "If he takes my son, I…"

Tyler weeps, and his hands dig into my arms while he embraces me. Archie lays a chilly hand on my face. The others yell. "We can fight him, Gwyn." "We'll send him back to the Otherworld." "Don't give up." But I can't allow them to sacrifice themselves for me. Nick is right. Destiny wins tonight.

I gaze into Archie's wet eyes. "I'm sorry."

"We need to go, Gwyn," Nick says, extending his arm.

I grasp his hand, and he marches toward the gate, tearing me away from my family. I look back one more time, and Tyler is crying on Archie's shoulder. The young witches run after me, but Trinity, Agnes, and Leslie stop them from their foolish endeavor. I follow Nick to his apartment, dreading what awaits me there. When we arrive, he unlocks the door with a slight wave, and we enter. He guides me into the bedroom and locks the doorknob with his supernatural power.

"You made the correct decision," he says, smiling warmly. "First, we have to perform a love ritual. It will be the most sensual and beautiful thing you'll ever experience. I've trained for this all my life. All that unnecessary fighting made me sweat. I really hate this human form. I'll take a quick shower. It shouldn't take more than ten minutes. I bought you a silky chemise for the occasion. It's on the bed."

Nick caresses my flushed cheek and kisses me. I shudder at his touch and clutch my necklace. When he ambles into the bathroom, I panic, pacing around the room. I have to figure out a way to stay alive. I strip down to my panties and slip on the chemise, dropping my clothes into a pile on the floor. But I keep on my socks. Fuck him if he thinks I'm gonna endure cold feet while he fulfills his ancestor's revenge.

Instantly, a buzzing enters my body, and my brain seizes. I grab the sides of my head and fight back against the intrusion but relax when I recognize the blue of Archie's eyes. Within seconds, my mind clears as if the sun has parted the clouds. An image appears—the dirk.

Why did he send me a thought intention of his family's heirloom? I don't know what happened to the damn thing. Instead, I inspect the drawers of Nick's dresser, foraging through his clothes for an object I could turn into a magic weapon. Nothing. I check the drawer of his nightstand, finding pictures of me taken from a distance—not stalky behavior at all. This is futile. I dash to the other nightstand, biting my thumbnail as I open the drawer.

The sparkle of the aqua gem breaks through a thin scrap of cloth. Last night's encounter replays in my head as I recall the hazy memory. I put my purse on the nightstand but found it on the floor when I returned after puking my guts out. Archie must have deduced Nick took it out last night when I was here. I pull the dirk out, shut the drawer, and devise a plan. After placing a king-sized pillow to the right of me, I remove the leather sheath and slip the weapon underneath. I wait for Nick on my knees. How can I do this? He was my friend. The door to the bathroom opens, and my back stiffens. He saunters toward me, naked, sporting a seductive smile and an egotistical air, and jumps onto the bed.

"I'm confused," I say, averting my eyes. "You translated my mom's letter revealing you would search for me. Why translate the words correctly? You could have invented a story, and I would never have known you were coming for me."

"I wanted to win you over, and you would have discovered the truth, eventually. You'd never believe I was the Tuatha Dé fairy if I was the one to warn you." His eyes glint under the lights while he strokes my arm. "And the deception worked."

"When did you know for sure I was the witch you'd been...seeking?" I almost say hunting or stalking, but I'm afraid it will trigger him. "When you walked in with Derek?"

"I suspected long before," he says, inching even closer. "Your scent brought me to Bearsden. But I never imagined you would stroll right into my office after I set up here. When you handed me your family's grimoire, I read through the pages in one sitting. I dragged out the translations to build our relationship. You disappointed me by not trusting me enough to tell me you were a witch. That's why I stopped seeing you for a while. And Archie ruined everything. But that's behind us now." He clutches his abdomen as if he's nauseous and eyes my neck. "You'll need to remove your necklace."

As I undo the clasp, I remember he asked me to remove the choker last night. My heart palpitates while I attempt to delay the inevitable, and a queasiness grips my stomach.

"So, what is this ritual, Nick? You make love to me and kill me after?"

"What?" He bursts out laughing. "No, Gwyn. That's something your ancestors made up along the way to frighten you and your family. Please, call me by my Tuatha Dé name—Nuada. I'm named after the first king."

"You aren't going to kill me?" I cock my head. "Then why am I here?"

He caresses my cheek. "You were promised to me, so we can procreate and replace the child who died generations ago."

"What?" I erupt in nervous laughter. "Nick. Nuada. You know I can't have children, right? I'm in menopause. That ship sailed a couple of years ago." My heart relaxes, and I sigh in relief. This is my out. He'll understand I'm useless and let me go.

"In this world. Once I make love to you in my fairy form, you'll become immortal and fertile again. If we're successful during the ritual, you'll conceive tonight. Then we'll travel to the Otherworld through the portal."

Have a baby in my 50s? Oh, hell no. "I'll never see my son again. Don't you want me to be happy?" If he really cares, he'll release me.

"Once you've transformed, you'll want to go, Gwyn. Your family here will mean nothing to you. You'll perceive them as mere humans." He guides me onto my back and kisses me. "Don't be afraid. I'm going to shift now."

When he sits up on his knees, his body morphs as his muscles balloon on his chest, arms, and abdomen. Large wings of black and pale-gray sprout from his back. A warm aura overwhelms me as I recall Nick in my dreams. He's exquisite—a vision of perfection. But now he's Nuada. His bright green eyes glimmer like shiny quartz crystals, and his long, platinum-blond hair flows onto his rounded shoulders. My eyes fall to his groin, and I gasp. OK. I'll admit. For a teeny-weeny, infinitesimal nanosecond, I imagine what it would be like to make love to this creature.

And I snap back to the morbid reality of the situation. *I have to kill Nick.* Or I'll never see Tyler, Archie, or my friends again. So, I slide my hand under the pillow and clasp the wooden handle.

"I wish I had made love to you the first time in my fairy form. I love you, Gwynedd."

The door creaks open, and a deep roar similar to a cat's meow resonates in the room. A Doberman-sized black cat with glowing green eyes pounces onto the wings of Nuada, drawing him back and exposing his torso. I won't have another opportunity. So, I shove the dirk into his abdomen with every ounce of strength I have, summoning my witch energy as the weapon slides in.

The enormous cat scuttles out of the room as Nuada yells in a deep, reverberating voice. "Gwynedd, what have you done?"

I cry out in a guttural voice as I release the ignited dirk from my hand. The amber magic spreads out from the wound, seeping into his body like slithering snakes. White light beams from his eyes and withered extremities while his cheeks sink into his jaw. His muscles contract as the skin turns corpse-gray, and his purple veins protrude, resembling spider-like webs. The rays emanating from his body dissipate as his carcass falls, and I leap from the bed.

Footsteps rumble through the apartment, and Tyler rushes into the room with Archie, Trinity, Elijah, and Ronnie following him. My witch energy still radiates from my hand.

"Did you see the cat run past you? The big ass cat?" I ask.

Tyler hugs me and rubs my back. "What cat? Are you OK, Mom?" Cuts and bruises cover his face.

"Yes. Nuada, that's his fairy name, wasn't going to kill me. Only take me to the Otherworld to be his mate. But I couldn't let him." I avoid making eye contact with Archie.

Trinity moans in pain as she hugs me tightly. "I thought we lost you, lady."

"He didn't hurt you?" Ronnie asks as she examines my body. With the bloody abrasions on her cheek and neck, maybe she should check herself?

"No," I reply. "He wanted to mate with me."

"Oh, my gods," she says, embracing me.

I glimpse the shriveled corpse in my peripheral vision where Archie and Elijah are inspecting Nuada's mummified body. Ronnie pulls a blanket off the bed and wraps it around my shoulders. After removing the dirk from the carcass, Archie shifts next to me.

"Will you go to my house? Tyler and Ronnie will take you."

I peer at his face and discover bloody contusions on his left cheek. "Do you want me to?"

"Aye. In case you have some kind of reaction to his powers. Tyler, when you get outside, tell Tanner and Spence we need their help to remove the remains. To where? I don't know yet."

Trinity places a kiss on my head. "Let's go, Gwyn."

I slip on my sneakers, and Ronnie collects my pile of clothes, along with my hobo bag and necklace. When we leave the apartment, the hallway is empty, and we continue down the stairs to the parking lot. The Bearsden Coven has been waiting, and they run over to me. Tyler delivers the message to Tanner and Spence, and they dart upstairs to the apartment.

Skye, Zoe, and Shane hug me and tell me how relieved they are I'm alive, but the realization of what I did and why doesn't erase the fact I killed Nick Evans.

"You did what you had to do, Gwyn," Agnes says, patting my hand. "He would have whisked you away to the Otherworld." A trickle of blood has hardened on her face.

Leslie pushes back her silver side bangs, exposing the abrasions on her skin. "Gwynedd, we all knew this would come to pass, and now it's done. I only wish I had met with Dr. Evans sooner, and I should have shared my doubts about him with you. I'm deeply sorry."

"We all fuck up, Leslie," Agnes says. "But I think the professor glamoured you, too."

"Yes. With the paperweights he gave you and Archie for Yule," I say. "Ronnie and Tyler, let's go."

As I stagger to my son's sedan, a tall man leans on a cane, standing in the shadows on the far side of the parking lot. I blink, and he's gone. And I question whether I saw him at all.

# Chapter Twenty-Eight

# THE ETHICS OF MURDER

Trinity comes along for the ride to Archie's house. We barely speak on the way. What is there to say? I murdered Nick Evans. When I stabbed the Sluagh to save Ronnie, the evil fairy presented as a disgusting tandem of ravens trying to kill me. My attempt was justified, and I'd only banished it back to the Otherworld. But in this reality, my foe wasn't actually seeking revenge. So, my principles grapple with the realization of my actions.

We enter the house and take off our shoes. Ronnie suggests I rest on the loveseat while she puts water on the stove for tea. A cup of chamomile will erase the fact I just killed someone?

Tyler sits on one side of me while Trinity finds a spot on the other. Stuck in the middle, I sense they're watching me as if they expect wings to burst out of my back at any moment. I tighten the blanket around my upper body. Nick's scent pervades the material.

"Stop gawking at me. I'm OK. He didn't change me into a fairy." I fold my hands confidently.

Their wary eyes convey they aren't convinced.

"Mom, a lot of shit went down tonight," Tyler says, frowning. "And you're acting like what happened isn't a big deal."

I glance at my son and swallow. "I did what I had to."

"Yes, you did, Gwyn," Trinity says, rubbing my back. "Don't ever think otherwise. But you have to admit, the circumstances must have affected you. You act as if you only had a bad day at work."

Ronnie ambles in with the chamomile tea and passes the cup to me. "Careful. The water boiled."

"Thanks, friend. I can always depend on you to prepare quality beverages."

Steam rises from the cup, and I blow on the hot liquid while my hands shake. Tyler rubs my shoulder to comfort me.

"You're still a good person, Mom," he says. "An admirable witch. What you did wasn't murder. He was a thing, not a human."

My eyebrows jump, and I spew my confession like I'm being interrogated by the Bearsden Police. "I found the dirk and hid it under a pillow. I created a plan of attack. And when I had the opportunity, I rammed the weapon into Nick's abdomen without a second thought." I blink several times. "I believe that's the definition of premeditation. So, yeah. I think the police would say I murdered Nick."

Ronnie crosses her arms and frowns. "For the love of all the gods, Gwyn. He was going to transform you into a fairy and drag you into the Otherworld. You had no choice. You better reconcile with that fact. If you don't, we're gonna have a serious girl talk."

She plops down on the steamer trunk facing the loveseat and squints at me. I chuckle under my breath, and she pats my leg.

"Accurate words from a good friend," Trinity says. "Listen to her."

"You're strong, Mom." Tyler smiles and punches my arm playfully. "More badass than I ever imagined you could be. I'm so proud of you. I'm glad you killed him. He was stalking you in Bearsden for months under the guise of being someone you could trust. If you didn't love Archie...Nick or Nuada, whatever the hell his name was, may have actually won you over, and you'd be gone."

I drink another sip of my tea, trembling. "Still, every fiber of my being says I murdered a good friend, even if I realize he wasn't. It's gonna take a looong time for me to reconcile how he duped me."

"Oh, for fuck's sake, Gwyn," Ronnie says. "Consider this. He hunted you for hundreds of years, finally discovered your magic scent, shifted into human form, and invented a false persona to come to Bearsden. When he confirmed you were the witch promised to him, he set out to win your love. But he failed and had to threaten to take your son to convince you to go with him to the Otherworld."

"Is this rehashing supposed to make me feel better?" I ask in a sarcastic tone. "Because it's not working."

Ronnie cackles. "You didn't let me finish. That supernatural being full of immeasurable powers should have won, but you're still here."

I smile at my crimson-haired friend and take a cleansing breath. "What about the portal mound? The city council expected us to shut it down."

"We'll have to reschedule," Trinity says. "Leslie, Agnes, Archie, and I will discuss viable options with our allies. When we've got a new date selected, I'll text everyone. Leslie believes the Tuatha Dé were probably expecting this Nuada to return with you. We have no way of knowing what he communicated to them. After the incident with Corey Jones, we know the size of the opening doesn't matter for the transmission from their world to ours. They could come sniffing around and cross over through there."

"But there's no guarantee the incantation will work," my son says. "Agnes said as much. What do we do if the spell can't close the portal?"

Trinity pats my hand. "One step at a time, Tyler. One gargantuan step at a time."

The front door opens, and Archie enters. He kicks off his shoes, hangs his jacket on a hall tree hook, and sets his family's dirk on the table. As he shuffles into the living room, my eyes fall to the floor, and I finish the chamomile tea. Trinity groans as she pushes off the loveseat.

"I'm getting too fucking old for this shit. Every muscle, tendon, and ligament hurts like a bitch. Tyler, will you drive me back to my car?"

"Sure," he replies. "If it's OK with you, Mom."

"Of course," I say. "Please tell everyone thank you for trying to defend me."

Ronnie stands. "You can tell them yourself at the spell-casting."

"I'll call in the morning, Mom," Tyler says as he pushes off the loveseat.

The three of them walk to the foyer to put on their shoes. They glance at me one more time and wave goodbye before exiting the house. The door shuts, and only the obnoxious ticking of the mantle clock interrupts the silence.

I adjust the blanket around my shoulders, and Archie sits on the steamer trunk in front of me, waiting for me to speak. But the words can't find a pathway out.

"Talk to me, Gwyn," he says in his warm baritone voice. "Did he harm you in any way? I understand if you're not ready to talk about what happened, but I need to know for your safety—and the coven's. Did Nuada carry out the ritual?"

"No. I killed him before we..."

"What a relief." Archie exhales and inspects my arms and legs. "Are you hurt?"

"No. Not physically. But I talked to Trinity, Ronnie, and Tyler, and it helped."

I still can't bring myself to look directly into his eyes. He takes my hand and caresses the skin with his thumb.

"I informed the Fellowship you found me in bed with Laura right after you left last night."

"They'll expel you for impropriety. Ronnie knew already, anyway. I told her this morning."

"Not likely. Leslie and Trinity demanded answers from the Hockessin Coven immediately after I told them. The Hockessin witches found Laura today and performed a verity incantation. Trinity received a text from their coven leader tonight after you left the gardens. Apparently, she and Nick were working together with mutual objectives. He increased her power enough to cast a short-lived spell on me to cause a rift between us. The charmed paperweights clouded our thinking—kept the Elder and me from picking up on clues. He must have tried to glamour you at every opportunity, hoping to win your love. Giving you a charm wouldn't have allowed for that."

"So, dating her was only a cover, and being on her dissertation committee was a convenient excuse to spend more time with her." I rub a fist into the palm of my hand.

"Leslie and Trinity will file a formal request, asking for Laura's expulsion. Every coven will bar her from becoming a member."

I close my eyes and take a purposeful breath as I stand. "I need to shower."

"A bath might relax you more. Should I fill up the tub?"

"No. I want to take a shower." And wash Nuada's faint scent from my body.

"Let me help you upstairs, then."

Archie follows me to the bedroom, grabbing the dirk on the way. When we enter, I drop the blanket on the floor and kick it into the hallway. He sets his family's heirloom on the dresser.

"I'll turn on the water...warm it up for you."

While he prepares my shower, I shake in the chemise alone with my bucket load of remorse. He motions for me to go in, so I slip off my socks and panties.

"I'll be resting on the bed if you need anything," he says, turning around.

"Please, stay." I stare down at the tile floor. "I'd rather not be in here alone."

He shuts the door to trap the heat in the bathroom. "I'll check my email while you shower, then."

I strip off the chemise, shoving the ritual clothing into the trash. The hot water soothes my body as it sprinkles down my back. As I scrub with the loofah, the scent of Nuada emanates from my skin, so I press hard, increasing the friction. The shower door opens, and Archie steps in fully dressed. He snatches the loofah from my hand.

"Stop, Gwyn. You're going to rub your skin raw."

"I have to...I can smell his stench on me," I say gruffly.

The water has soaked Archie's clothes, but he doesn't move. "Things will improve with time, and I'll be here to support you. I'm not going anywhere."

The guilt builds inside me like a volcano ready to erupt. "I know it's not my fault, but how can you even set eyes on me after I slept with that...thing."

Archie cups my face, forcing me to look at him. "Because I love you."

He kisses my forehead, and I lay my head on his soaked shirt. When I finish my shower, I towel off and put on cotton pajamas I stored in a dresser drawer. I climb into bed and wait for him to return from tossing his wet clothes into the dryer. I grab my cell phone. Unread messages from Nick Evans light up the screen, and I delete all of them, one after the other. My son sends me a text.

Tyler: *Just checking on you again. Are you OK?*

Me: *Yes. I'm lying in bed. Thank you, dear.*

Tyler: *I hope you and Archie can get through this.*
Me: *I'll chat with you tomorrow. I'm gonna try to sleep now.*
Tyler: *Goodnight, Mom. I love you.*
Me: *I love you, too, son.*

Archie enters the bedroom as I set my phone on the nightstand. He retrieves a key from behind the headboard, unlocks the glass case, and places the dirk on its holders. After setting the lock, he grabs his pillow.

"Why don't you use the bed, and I'll spend the night on the loveseat. Try to sleep."

"Wait," I say, sitting up. "You can sleep here."

His loving eyes comfort me as he shuffles to my side. "What you went through will require a great deal of healing, and I expected you would need some space for a while. I understand."

"I don't want to be alone, Archie." Tears swell up as I touch the empty spot beside me.

He returns to his side, slides into bed, and turns out the lamp. "Go to sleep, Gwyn."

As I lie in the darkness, I try to rid my mind of the day's events and focus on the future. Ronnie said, "You're still here." Hell, yeah. I am. I roll my head toward Archie. His chest rises and falls, instilling a calmness in me. Streams of light from the lamppost spill into the room, and he catches me staring at him. I slide my hand under the covers and touch my pinky against his. He turns on his side and intertwines his fingers with mine.

"We'll get through this, Gwyn. It won't be easy, but we will."

"I know he glamoured me sporadically, but I chose to stay even with the signals confronting me all night. I feel the need to say I'm sorry, but it doesn't seem enough."

"Then say more."

"I love you, Archie."

I squeeze his warm hand, and he lays the other on my cheek.

"And that's plenty."

# CHAPTER TWENTY-NINE

# SPELLS ARE HARD

THE CLINKING OF GLASSES rings through the stairwell as I make my way to the kitchen in my pajamas. Archie is dressed for school in a DUB polo shirt and chinos. An omelet sizzles in a pan while he loads the dishwasher, moving from one task to the other without stopping.

"Good morning. You appear rushed." I pull out a chair and sit. "I'm skipping classes today."

He runs his fingers through his locks. "Understandable. I have to arrive early and meet with Leslie. We anticipate a mob of students waiting at our doors, asking why Dr. Evans hasn't shown up for class."

"Oh, shit," I say, covering my mouth. "What will you tell them?"

"No fawking idea. We have to act surprised, of course. At some point, we'll report him as a missing person. Leslie, Seamus, and I will have to cover his classes and post his position, eventually. The remainder of the semester will be pure hell. As it turns out, your suspicions about Seamus were misplaced. I'm glad we never confronted him. Would have let the cat out of the bag prematurely."

"But he's the reason I left work early and came to your house. He came to the store, and when I was talking to him, a vision of Nuada flashed in my head. Why?"

"Who knows, Gwyn?" He sits at the table and shovels eggs into his mouth. "Nick could have sent the visions to frighten and confuse you. Laura could have been screwing with your head. Does it matter why you saw them? He's gone, and you're safe now."

Am I? We haven't closed the portal yet. "Do you remember me yelling about a big cat when you ran into Nick's bedroom?"

"Vaguely. But I figured you had imagined it in your state. None of us saw a cat, not one the size of a large dog, anyway."

I huff. "I know what I saw. The black feline reminded me of the cat near the mound at the castle in Buckley—the one that knocked me to the ground."

"I believe you, Gwyn, but I didn't see the animal either time. No one did." His brow crinkles as he sets his fork and plate in the sink. "I wish I could be here with you today. Text me if you need me."

"I'll be OK. I'm going to Ronnie's for lunch." I open my email, and my shoulders collapse. "Ellie finally got back to me. For some odd reason, she found my email in her spam folder. She wants to set up a time for me to video chat with Aunt Gorawen."

"Just as well. Now you have wonderful news for her." He leans down to hug me. "Get through this one day, and all the others will fall in line. I'll talk to you later, my love."

Archie kisses me goodbye and heads out the door. After eating a quick breakfast and dressing, I stop by home to change. I nudge the door in and enter the mudroom. As I remove my sneakers, Mr. Yeats scuttles into the kitchen and transforms into his human persona. He pounces on me, his embrace clinging to my torso.

"Oh, Ms. Crowther, Dr. Hughes told me about the close call last night. I am so relieved to find you unharmed."

"Thank you for your concern." I pat his back.

He releases me from his familiar paws. "Is there anything I can do to help you recover?"

"Yes, actually. Later, I'll need to have a conference with my parents. Could you assist me?"

He adjusts the spectacles on his nose. "I am honored you asked me."

Mr. Yeats exits the kitchen, skipping. I put on clean clothes and rummage through my family's steamer trunk for a couple of hours, scowling when I pick up the translations Nick gave me. Leslie says she'll go through them and create more accurate versions once the semester ends. I throw the binder in the trunk and drive to Ronnie's. When I enter her house, Derek wraps me in his burly arms. The beachy décor of her house has a calming effect—the perfect place to rest right now.

"It's so great to see you, Gwyn," he says. "Ronnie told me what you went through, but you're a strong woman."

We stroll into the kitchen where Ronnie is preparing our meal. I relax in a chair while she places lunch on the table and sits.

"How are you today? You look better than I thought you would."

"I'll leave you two alone," Derek says, kissing Ronnie. "Bye, babe."

"Bye, handsome." She blows him a kiss and waits for him to exit the house. "Now tell me the truth. How are you handling all this?"

"I woke up, went into the bathroom to pee, washed my face, brushed my teeth, combed my hair, put on my clothes from last night, and ate breakfast." I take a bite of my hummus wrap. "And now I'm eating lunch with my best friend. The world didn't end."

"See...I told ya." She bites into her sandwich. "Keep a routine, and you'll get back to normal lickety-split."

"You realize no matter how normal my life becomes going forward, it will never change the fact I killed Nick."

I take another bite, chew deliberately, and swallow. But Ronnie stops mid-bite.

"Well, the alternative sucked. Are you and Archie going to survive? That's the question?"

"What happened wasn't either of our faults, and we love each other. We'll find a way. But the path may have bumps and ruts."

"Whose life doesn't have potholes? I've certainly had my share." Ronnie gets out of her chair and hugs me. "I wouldn't be here if you hadn't impaled the Sluagh. You can depend on me to help you through everything. That's what best friends do."

A week has passed since Ostara, and every day I put one foot in front of the other. I chatted with Aunt Gorawen via video chat after a divination conference with Mom and Dad. They were elated at the news but understood why my actions haunted me. I returned to work at the insurance agency and Mystic Sage, but now I've got a break from classes because of Spring Break. Many of my classmates are taking trips to Florida or Mexico. Not me. I have to stay home and perform an incantation with the coven. The city council approved a "special celebration" request, so we can close the portal for good.

Trinity sends the Fellowship a group text telling us to gather in the Celestial Gardens at midnight. Other than Leslie, Tyler, Zoe, Ronnie, and Shane, I haven't seen the others since that terrible night. When Archie and I arrive, the coven is clearing the debris in preparation. They place a wooden bowl containing the prepared spell mixture next to the mound. The gardens are barely lit under the waxing crescent moon, but the stars sparkle in the clear, indigo skies. Tyler and Zoe wave as Spence and Skye dart to me.

"You look great, sis," Spence says as he hugs me. "After tonight, all your worries will be gone."

Skye wraps me in a tight squeeze. "We'll get this done, Gwyn. And we'll get back to stressing over research papers and presentations."

"Whoever thought that would sound so enticing," I say, chuckling.

Archie points to the coven. "We should join the others. They're forming a circle."

We rush over to them, eager to get started, but wait for Tanner, Shane, Elijah, and Ronnie to carry the collected piles of debris to the far side of the gardens. Trinity, Leslie, and Agnes approach me.

"Gwyn, are you ready to shut this fucker down?" Agnes asks, a confident grin beaming.

"Absolutely," I reply. "I want to move on with my life."

Trinity nods. "The rest of us couldn't agree with you more. Closing this portal will remove stress from the entire coven and our allies on the council will sleep better."

"Let us proceed, my friends," Leslie says with a tap of her staff.

After a brief welcome from Elijah and Tanner, we form a tight circle facing the mound. When the portal lights up. Shailagh and Aonghas skip to me.

"Aunt Gwyn," the children shout. "Did you bring all these friends to play with us?"

"Oh, shit. We forgot about the kids," Ronnie says.

Archie's brow wrinkles. "Gwyn, we don't have much time. Tell them quickly."

"I'd hoped to avoid this." As I squat to talk to the children, I hold their tiny hands. "We aren't here to play. To keep me safe from the other evil fairies, the ones who wanted to take me to the Otherworld, we need to close the door on them."

Shailagh and Aonghas's eyes tear up. "But we won't be able to come and play here ever again. Don't you like us, Aunt Gwyn?"

"Yes. I like you very much, but I'm not meant to live in the Otherworld. So, we must remove the passageway. You don't belong in our world either. Find a new family on your side, because I'm sure there are parents there for you. Opening this portal all those years ago was a mistake. And we have to fix it." I squeeze their teensy hands. "Goodbye Shailagh and Aonghas."

Mint-green tears fall from the eyes of the Seelie Fae, and they dash back to the portal. They wave goodbye with their diminutive hands and disappear into the mound.

"OK. Let's get started," Agnes says as she wipes her eyes. "Set up again as we did the last time to create a balance in our combined energies."

Once we form our circle, Leslie and Agnes chant, repeating the same phrase over and over. They signal to summon our witch energy, and our amber glows combine to form a halo within the circle, lighting the Celestial Gardens in a blaze of orangey yellow. Ominous, billowy clouds invade clear skies, darkening the gardens except for our amber halo.

The winds pick up, and the remaining debris blows all around us, resembling impromptu mini tornadoes. Claps of thunder spark in the clouds, flashing light on the area below, and the ground rumbles. The pitter-patter of rain falls on the roof of the mansion and increases every minute until a deluge of water dumps on us.

"This doesn't seem right," Tanner yells over the pelting rainfall. "Maybe we should stop?"

Shane nods. "I'm inclined to agree with Tanner. This weather is more severe than the last time we cast a spell in here."

Agnes shakes her head. "No need to worry, friends. This happened before. We'll be fine...I think."

"You don't sound confident, Agnes," Spence says. "Are you sure you have the correct words for the chant?"

Leslie shouts through the roar of the wind and the rain. "I translated the old Welsh well. The incantation will be successful. We must press through this."

"I trust Leslie's work," Archie says. "Keep your energy flowing."

A tingling sensation seizes my body, and a second later, lightning strikes near the hawthorn tree. The smell of sulfur and burning electrical wires pervades the gardens. My heart skips a few beats.

"I trust her, too, but we can't finish the spell if we're burned to a crisp," I yell.

"We'll be fine, Gwyn," Trinity shouts through the pelting rain. "Agnes, I pray to the gods you know what you're doing."

The mini tornadoes swirl outside our circle, bombarding us with chips of ice as they drop from the clouds. Leslie and Agnes continue chanting while we struggle to contain our circle. A tiny swirl of air catches Zoe in a spin and hurls her inside the circle. Tyler and Elijah run in after her.

"Zoe, are you hurt?" Tyler asks in an elevated voice.

"I'm OK!" she shouts. "Let's keep going!"

Elijah bellows in his cavernous voice, "Stand between me and Tyler, Zoe. We'll catch you if it happens again."

They rejoin the circle, and we increase the intensity of our combined energy. Claps of thunder increase while lightning bolts strike to the left and right of us, illuminating the gardens in a spray of white streaks. We're trembling from the cold, and the rain has soaked our clothes through to our skin. Rain drips from our hair onto our faces. My entire body aches from flexing my muscles, and I'm sure I've torn some tendons.

"Only a bit longer now, witches," Agnes shouts in her gravelly voice. "Direct your magic toward the portal."

We shift our witch energy to the mound, and the aperture lights up with swirls of yellow and black. On the final clap of thunder, our amber glow recedes abruptly, and we're left in the pitch black of the night. The rain dissipates, and the overlapping clouds drift apart, allowing the crescent moon to spotlight the left corner of the gardens.

"Oh, shit." I move closer, trembling in my wet clothes. "Shit, shit, shit."

"Well, fuck me," Agnes says as she hobbles toward me.

Ronnie darts next to me to get a better view. "Oh, no!"

Spence steps toward the mound, still protruding from the ground and unaffected by the incantation. "What the fuck, Agnes? The damn pile of dirt is still here. What did you do wrong?"

Agnes growls at Spence. "How the fuck would I know? It was a spell from Gwyn's family grimoire?"

"Don't fret over this, Gwyn," Archie says. "We'll search for another spell. We'll not stop until we find one that succeeds."

"Indeed, we shall." Leslie pats my hand.

Trinity chimes in. "The city council allies are gonna blow their stacks. We promised to shut the thing down."

"But maybe the portal is closed," Elijah says. "Just because the mound remains doesn't mean the passageway is still viable."

Tyler steps forward. "This is terrible. Mom, should you call on the fae children to test the spell's success?"

"OK." I lean toward the entrance, wringing my hands. "Shailagh? Aonghas? You can come out."

My fellow witches and I stand back, staring at our phones to monitor the time. A spring breeze plays with our hair while we stand in silence. After several tense minutes, our shoulders relax, and we puff our worry into the cool night air. As we turn to exit, a faint glow emerges from the aperture in the mound. And the mischievous fae cross over.

"Yay!" Shailagh and Aonghas jump up and down. "We can still come out to play!" They dash off to the opposite side of the gardens, skipping and giggling.

Shane speaks in a somber tone. "We will have to begin that search after all, my friends. I'm so sorry, Gwyn."

"Why don't we go home, everyone," Archie says. "We've done all we can tonight."

"But what about the Tuatha Dé Danann?" I ask. "They will come searching for Nuada. What did you do with the..."

"Carcass?" Spence crosses his arms and frowns. "It's in a body bag in our garage."

Tanner elaborates. "We didn't mind hiding the grotesque thing while we closed the portal, but we've got to get rid of it now. It's beginning to emit a peculiar odor."

Trinity rocks her head back and forth. "We should contact coven leaders across the country. Get the body as far away from Gwyn as possible. I say ship it to the West Coast and leave a trail to scatter Nuada's scent."

"To California?" Spence says in a high-pitched voice. "Hell if I'm gonna take part in sending that thing to my home state. My parents and brother still live there."

Agnes chuckles. "I think it's a magnificent plan. A coven out there could take the carcass to the desert and burn it."

"Archie, Mom will be OK, won't she?" my son asks. "To be safe, should she carry the dirk in her purse again?"

I grimace. "Screw that. I just put my hobo bag away and transferred my stuff to a spring floral mini purse. I'm done lugging that old weapon around."

Archie chuckles. "Good luck changing her mind, Tyler. We all know your mum is a..."

"Stubborn woman," the witches say in unison.

I scowl and give them the bird.

Archie winks. "I think your mum is getting better."

They say looks can be deceiving. The vision of an entire fae kingdom invading Bearsden plays in my mind like a silent film. They're coming for me, sporting enormous black and pale-gray wings, flowing platinum blond hair, and piercing green eyes. Except this time, they will want me dead. Where did the spell go wrong?

# Acknowledgments

Many thanks to my entire family for their support through my author journey. You are my rock!

Special thanks go to my editor Christopher Barnes at Cissell Ink. Your expertise is outstanding.

To my book cover designer Charles Clark, I am so lucky to have you on my team.

Extra special thanks to my ARC Reader Team! You all are fabulous! Thank you for your continued support in my author journey!

# ABOUT THE AUTHOR

J.C. YEAMANS is an author of PWF Urban Fantasy and other paranormal fiction. A former public school teacher based in Lewes, Delaware, she writes about all things witchy to find the inherent magic in life's journey of discovery and love—all while making blunders along the way. As the owner of Reed Shore Press, she also publishes fiction and nonfiction works for others. Her prior career revolved around the performing arts. She is married and has two adult children. When she's not putting pen to paper (or more aptly, fingertips to keys), she spends time biking, hiking, and weightlifting.

Sign up for J.C. Yeamans's newsletter at jcyeamans.com to download a free backstory and stay in the loop!

# OTHER BOOKS

**The Bearsden Witch Series**

Secrets of a Midlife Witch

Schooling of a Midlife Witch

Stalking of a Midlife Witch

Trials of a Midlife Witch
(December 2023)

www.ingramcontent.com/pod-product-compliance
Lightning Source LLC
Chambersburg PA
CBHW030149310726
48970CB00005B/1656